UNDER AN ONYX SKY

ELEMENTAL ENCHANTERS SERIES

4

CARRIGAN RICHARDS

also by carrigan richards

Standalone Novels
Pieces of Me
Black Dove

Elemental Enchanters Series
Under a Blood Moon (#1)
Under the Burning Stars (#2)
When Darkness Fell (#2.5)
Under the Winter Sun (#3)
Under an Onyx Sky (#4)

January Dreams Series
January Dreams
Silent Dreams
Shattered Dreams

UNDER AN ONYX SKY

ELEMENTAL ENCHANTERS SERIES

4

CARRIGAN RICHARDS

Carrigan Richards Publishing, LLC

PO Box 3782

Suwanee, GA 30024

First published in the United States 2015

This paperback edition published 2024

Cover Art by Jake @ J Caleb Design

ISBN: PB: 979-8-99051-47-0-6; ASIN: eBook: B00VRTETXC

Printed and bound in the USA

To Paige, my biggest fan, for sticking with me by my side.

Deep into that darkness peering, long I stood
there wondering, fearing,
Doubting, dreaming dreams no mortal ever
dared to dream before;
—Edgar Allan Poe, The Raven

PROLOGUE

Lucinda Hannigan stared at her reflection in the cracked mirror, her trembling fingers tracing the edge of her pentagram necklace. Her face was pale, her auburn hair disheveled, and her eyes—once filled with fire and purpose—were now shadowed with doubt. She barely recognized herself anymore.

Her gaze dropped to the dagger in her hand. The blade felt heavier than it should. *I have to do this. For Connor. For our child.*

Her free hand moved to her stomach, where the faintest curve was showing. *Ava.* She had already chosen the name, though she hadn't told Connor yet. A fleeting smile tugged at her lips. *Ava means "life." That's what she'll have—a life free from Havok's shadow.*

But her smile faded as the Seer's words resurfaced, cutting through her resolve. The vision had been as clear as water: Ava, strong and unyielding, wielding the element of water with unmatched power. She wouldn't be alone—she would stand alongside five others, a coven of Elementals destined to change the world. Or destroy it.

Lucinda swallowed hard, gripping the dagger tighter. *That future will never come to pass if Havok succeeds.* His influence over Colden was growing. The fleeting moments when he surfaced were becoming more frequent, the darkness in Colden's eyes lingering a bit longer each time. She had seen it—heard it in his voice. Havok was taking over.

Killing Colden was the only way to stop him before it was too late. It was cruel, merciless—but necessary.

Lucinda drew a shaky breath, tearing her eyes from the mirror. *This ends tonight.*

The cabin was dark and quiet, lit only by the single candle on the table. Colden sat in a chair by the fireplace, his head bowed, dark hair falling loose around his shoulders. For a moment, he looked peaceful, almost serene.

Hesitating in the doorway, her heart hammered against her ribs. The dagger remained hidden beneath her cloak as she stepped inside and closed the door behind her.

"Lucinda," Colden said without looking up. His voice was warm, familiar. It was him—not Havok. Not yet.

Her grip tightened on the dagger. "Colden."

He lifted his head, meeting her gaze. "Are you all right? You look—" He paused, his brow furrowing. "Different."

Lucinda's chest ached. *This isn't just about Havok. This is Colden. He didn't ask for this. He's been fighting Havok every step of the way.* She thought of his kindness, his quiet humor in rare moments of peace. Killing him wouldn't destroy Havok—it would destroy someone who had fought so hard to stay himself. He didn't deserve this. But neither did her child.

She moved closer. *Just do it. One quick strike. End it before Havok has the chance to take over.*

But as she raised the dagger, Colden's expression shifted. His warm eyes darkened, the color draining into a black abyss. His lips twisted into a cold, cruel smile.

"You hesitated," Havok said, his voice slipping from Colden's lips like a hiss.

Lucinda froze, the dagger trembling in her hand.

"Did you really think I wouldn't notice?" He stood slowly, his movements deliberate, predatory. "Did you think you could kill me, Lucinda? Pathetic."

Her breath caught as she stumbled back. "I—I was trying to—"

"To save him?" Havok sneered. "Don't lie to me. Colden isn't here right now." He stepped closer, his grin widening. "But you already knew that didn't you?"

Lucinda's legs felt like lead. *End his life. Destroy Havok before it's too late.* But standing in front of him now, her resolve crumbled to dust.

"Go on," Havok taunted. "Strike me down. Or are you afraid? Afraid of what your precious Elders would say if they found out what you've done? Afraid of losing that little Ephemeral you've grown so fond of?" His gaze fell to her stomach, and his smile turned wicked. "Afraid of losing her?"

Her hand flew protectively to her stomach, the dagger slipping from her grasp and clattering to the floor. "Leave them alone."

Havok's laugh was low and cold, reverberating through the cabin. "You're in no position to make demands, Lucinda. You've failed your little mission, and now, you'll have to pay the price."

"Please," she choked out. "Don't hurt them. Don't hurt my family."

Havok narrowed his eyes, studying her. "Why should I waste my time on promises and pacts? Your child means nothing to me."

Lucinda swallowed hard, the Seer's vision burning in her mind. "You're wrong. She will mean everything. A Seer saw her future—a Water Enchanter stronger than any who came before her. She'll be part of a coven of Elementals, each one powerful enough to change the balance of this world."

Havok tilted his head. "A coven of Elementals? How convenient."

"You know prophecies don't lie. The Seer was right about you. Everything they saw has come to pass. You can't stop the Elementals—but you could control them."

His thin lips curled into a slow, wicked grin. "Control them," he repeated, almost to himself. "Yes. That would do nicely. A coven, loyal to me. Your daughter will make a fine start. Swear her soul to me, Lucinda. Bind her life to me. I'll even let you live long enough to see her grow. Refuse, and I'll ensure neither of you see another sunrise."

Tears welled in Lucinda's eyes as her knees buckled. "But binding her life to yours—"

"I know what it will do. You can save her now or you both die."

She had no choice. If she fought, she'd lose. If she refused, she'd lose everything. "I swear," she choked out. "I swear her soul to you."

Havok's grin widened, his eyes gleaming with triumph. "Excellent."

A door behind them creaked open, and Gamel, Havok's Spellcaster, shuffled into the room. His scarred, scaly hands reached out as he bound their deal with a glowing green spell.

Lucinda felt the magic sink into her womb, a searing pain that brought fresh tears to her eyes.

"It is done," Gamel rasped.

Havok leaned in close, his voice a whisper in her ear. "Now run along, Lucinda. Play the dutiful mother. But remember—if you betray me, I'll be watching."

Lucinda stumbled out of the cabin. She ran until the cabin was out of sight, collapsing against a tree as a sob tore from her throat. She pressed her hands to her stomach. *Did I save her tonight or doom her? I'll find a way to stop him,* she promised herself, clutching her stomach. *Even if it costs me everything, I'll make sure Ava is safe. I have to.*

When she reached Blackhart Manor, she wiped her tears and forced a smile. She couldn't tell Savina. She couldn't tell anyone. If they knew Havok was inside Colden, they'd turn on her. She'd lose Connor. She'd lose everything.

For now, her secret would stay buried.

CHAPTER ONE

THE RUSE

The cold, rough surface of the wall supported Ava Hannigan as she pressed her shaking body against it. Soft yellow lights lined the ceiling, swaying and leaving distorted trails in her vision. Her legs felt weak, like they might give out at any moment. Her heartbeat was sluggish, the drugs still prickling through her veins like static.

She shook her arms, trying to dispel the tingling sensation. It didn't stop. Her thoughts swirled in fragments, her focus slipping between reality and memory. *Gabriel.* She needed to find him. If anyone could help her make sense of this nightmare, it was him.

He always knew what to do. He had taught her how to shield her thoughts, how to mask her emotions behind the heart of stone. And she'd betrayed him by joining Havok. But she hadn't anticipated getting her mind erased. Except that hadn't happened.

Ava swallowed hard, her chest aching. She had to find him. She had to fix this.

The hallway stretched ahead of her, endless and silent. Dragging her feet, she walked with a slow, unsteady gait, as if wading through mud.

Finally, she saw a faint light spilling from a cracked door. Her heart skipped with a flare of hope. *Gabriel? Could it be him?* Her vision swam, and as she blinked, a hunched man at a desk came into focus.

Leaning against the wall, Ava caught her breath as the door opened.

The man turned, his green eyes meeting hers. "Ava?" he asked, his British accent calm and articulate. "What are you doing out of bed?"

Not Gabriel. Her chest sank with bitter disappointment, the flicker of hope extinguished. She wasn't even sure why she'd expected it to be him, but the ache in her heart deepened all the same.

The man sounded like the one who was supposed to have taken her memory. His name hovered at the edges of her mind but wouldn't solidify.

He crossed the hall and took her by the shoulders. "You shouldn't be here." He glanced both ways down the corridor and pulled her inside.

She stumbled after him, her limbs heavy and uncooperative. The door clicked shut behind her.

"We don't have much time." He fidgeted. "You cannot be seen here."

"What … what did you give me?" she slurred.

"It's a sleep agent. I give it to everyone whose memories I erase. It helps with the transition."

"But you didn't erase mine."

"No, I didn't, and you know why."

"How did you know I was faking my allegiance to Havok?"

"I saw you watching Gabriel."

Her breath hitched. "Did Havok notice?"

"No. You're very good at the heart of stone."

Ava shut her eyes, hoping it would help clear the haze, but the fuzziness remained. "I don't like this feeling."

"I know. It will wear off."

"Can't you give me something to make it go away?"

"I'm not a doctor," he said, his tone clipped. "If you rest, we can speak tomorrow."

He touched her arm, but she jerked away. "No! You said we're supposed to take Havok down. How do we do that?"

"I will tell you more once you're able to hear it."

She slumped against the door and trembled as she slid to the ground. "What am I supposed to know?"

"You need to act like your memories are gone. That's the only way you'll survive here. Havok believes you've been stripped down to a blank slate, ready to be molded into his perfect soldier."

"How do I do that? What do I say?"

"You focus on the version of yourself he expects. You're an Enchanter. A Cimmerian. You grew up here, trained here, and have unwavering loyalty to Havok. That's the story he believes."

Her stomach churned. "And what about everything else? My real memories? What if something slips?"

"You can't let that happen. If Havok even suspects your mind hasn't been erased, it's over—for you and the others."

"The others ... where are they? Are they okay?"

"The Elementals are here. And like you, they're pretending."

"Gabriel?"

"You can't think about him."

Tears burned at the back of her eyes. "No. I need him."

"If Havok sees a blink of hesitation when you're around Gabriel—or any of the other prisoners—it will destroy everything. You bury your real memories so deep Havok can't sense them. You live the lie, Ava. Every second of it."

Her chest ached as Gabriel's face flashed in her mind: his unwavering belief in her, even when she doubted herself; him teaching her the heart of stone. And now she couldn't even think of him? "And how long am I supposed to keep this up?"

"Until the time is right. You're not just pretending for the sake of survival. You're gathering information, learning their weaknesses, finding potential allies. Not all Cimmerians are loyal to Havok. Some can be turned."

"An army," she murmured. "You want us to build an army."

"Yes. When the time comes, you and the other Elementals will lead the fight against Havok. But until then, you have to stay alive. That means playing the part perfectly. I know it's hard, Ava. But you're strong. You've already proven that. Just hold on a little longer."

She nodded weakly. "What if I can't do it?"

"You can. Because you have to. It's not just about you—it's about all of us. If you fail, Havok wins. And you know what that means."

He helped her to her feet. "I'll take you back to your room."

"What's your name?"

"Klaus."

As they moved into the hallway, Ava's drugged mind flashed to another time: Ilya acting as Gabriel, dragging her through a snowy forest, just as drugged and disoriented as she was now. *What if this is a trick?*

She yanked her arm free. "Don't touch me."

Klaus's lips pressed into a hard line. "We don't have time for this." He gripped her arm again.

The walls blurred as they traveled too fast—were they running? She couldn't tell.

A dark figure rounded the corner ahead. "What are you two doing?"

Klaus stiffened, pulling Ava closer. "Sleepwalker."

The man's eyes narrowed, his dark hair framing his angular face. "Is that one of the Elementals?"

"Yes."

He scoffed, crossing his tattooed arms. "We don't need them. Havok's wasting his time."

"They're powerful," Klaus countered. "More than you realize."

"Powerful? They're pathetic. Drugged, memory-wiped—nothing but empty shells. I've fought this war without them." As he stared at her, his disdain cut through her disorientation. "She doesn't even know what's going on, does she?" He stepped closer. "It's sick, what Havok's done. Spent years chasing these Elementals, only to break them into nothing. And for what? Another failed experiment?"

"She's stronger than you think," Klaus said.

The man laughed. "We'll see." He raised his fist, and a searing pain shot through Ava, plunging her into darkness.

CHAPTER TWO

PRISONER

Still groggy from the drugs, Ava stared out the window of her room. Spring had transformed Caprington into a world of vibrant greens and shimmering blues. The fjord below reflected the jagged mountains like a flawless mirror, and the castle perched high on its plateau overlooked the idyllic village nestled beneath it. Dutch-inspired houses in hues of brick red, mustard yellow, and powder blue lined the streets, connected to a sprawling modern city by a long, arching bridge.

The contrast was striking: medieval stone walls clashing with sleek skyscrapers that seemed to touch the clouds. The ocean stretched beyond the city, the water so still it looked like glass.

Ava couldn't deny it—Caprington was beautiful. At least if she was going to be a prisoner, it was in a breathtaking place. *Too bad I might have to destroy it.*

She touched her still-tender cheek, where the tattooed man had punched her. She hadn't healed it. She didn't deserve to—not after everything. The sting reminded her where she was, and what she'd done. Gabriel's face flashed in her mind, his pained expression and hollow eyes. Her stomach twisted. She had wanted to see him last night, to make sure he was okay, but it was impossible. Klaus's words rang in her ears: *Havok can't suspect a thing.*

Her thoughts shifted to the potion she had learned to make from Savina—the one that would keep Havok from prying into her mind. Maybe she could ask Klaus to help gather the ingredients. Without it, her thoughts could betray her, and everything would fall apart.

Focus, Ava. You can't break.

A sharp knock at the door pulled her from her thoughts. She turned, bracing herself against the window as the door creaked open.

"Good morning. Did you sleep well?"

Xavier Holstone.

His voice was casual, even polite, but the sight of him leaning against the doorframe made her skin crawl. He wore a sleek black uniform that fit him like a second skin. The material was fine and tailored, its clean lines and sharp edges lending him an air of quiet authority. Silver accents ran along the seams and buttons, catching the dim light—an understated nod to his rank among the Cimmerians.

His cropped ash-blonde hair, tousled but polished, framed his face, softening the sharp cut of his jaw. Yet his dark eyes gave him away, cold and calculating, a predator's gaze hidden behind a calm veneer. He moved further inside.

He looked every bit the heir to Havok's empire, a man born and molded to stand on the precipice between power and cruelty.

But for all the menace his uniform exuded, Ava noticed something else. His smirk, sharp as a dagger, faltered for a second, and in his dark gaze, she thought she saw something else—something bitter, something human.

Ava clenched her fists at her sides, fighting the urge to glare. He had tormented her for months. Kidnapped Link, Nicole, and others and turned them into Enchanters. He'd kidnapped Peter. Burned her house. Tortured her when she was in a coma. But now, she had to pretend he was a stranger. "Who are you?"

"You don't recognize me? That's a shame. We have history, you and I. But I suppose I'm not supposed to say anything."

"What kind of history?"

"Oh, forget I said that." He moved closer, the dim light illuminating his jawline and the faint scar by his temple. His smile vanished, replaced by anger as his eyes flicked to her cheek. "That's quite the bruise. What happened?"

"Someone hit me."

"Donovan." His tone turned icy, his expression tightening. "That idiot doesn't know when to stop. I'll make sure he doesn't touch you again."

"Should I know who that is?"

He lifted his hand as if to touch her cheek.

Ava recoiled, swatting his hand away. "Don't touch me."

Frowning, he lowered his hand. "You didn't heal it."

"No."

"Why not?"

"Maybe I deserved it."

His jaw clenched, and a flash of something—guilt?—crossed his features. "You didn't."

"You sound so sure. Why do you care?"

"I don't," he said quickly, stepping back. But the tension in his shoulders and the way his smirk didn't quite reach his eyes betrayed him. "Havok won't like seeing you bruised. Heal it."

Ava hesitated, then forced the water within her to smooth the wound. The sting faded as her skin knitted itself back together, but her throat tightened at Xavier's lingering gaze.

"That's so fascinating," he murmured, his tone a mix of awe and something darker.

"Haven't you seen me do that before?"

"It doesn't get old." He shoved his hands into his pockets and leaned against the wall, his casual posture clashing with the intensity of his stare. "What do you remember, Ava?"

"What do you mean?"

"Klaus altered your mind." Xavier watched her closely.

"Altered my mind how?" She furrowed her brow. "Why would he do that?"

"You had some … memories he had to delete. Nothing important. Bad memories you don't need."

"Why are you telling me this?"

"Maybe I'm testing you."

"Testing me?"

"I want to make sure Klaus did his job."

Ava shifted her weight, forcing herself to look uncertain. "I'm confused. I was born here. But there's a huge chunk of memories missing. Did something happen to me?"

"You don't remember anything?"

"Not a lot."

Xavier lingered, his expression conflicted. Then he straightened, his smirk sliding back into place. "Get dressed. I want to show you around. See if something will jog your memory."

Ava blinked. Of all the things he could've said, that wasn't what she'd expected. A tour of Caprington? Was this his attempt at manipulation, or was there something else he wasn't saying? She forced her voice to stay even. "Oh. Okay."

"I'll be right outside." He closed the door behind him, the soft thud leaving Ava in a silence that felt heavier than it should have. Suffocating, almost.

She turned back toward the room, taking it in with a new wariness. It was a stark blend of elegance and constraint, with the kind of carefully curated luxury that didn't invite comfort. The high, arched window poured streams of light over stone walls, softened only by thick velvet drapes in deep emerald. A four-poster bed sat against one wall, the dark wood carved with intricate, almost hypnotic designs. Nearby, a small writing desk and wardrobe completed the sparse furnishings. There were no personal touches, no signs of life—a space designed to impress and contain.

Pulling open the wardrobe, she rifled through the neatly folded clothes, and settled on a black shirt and matching pants. The shirt's rough fabric scratched against her skin, and the pants hung loose on her frame, a stark reminder of how much weight she'd lost.

She paused in front of the mirror, her stomach tightening as she caught her reflection. Angry, scared gray eyes stared back at her. Dark circles sat heavy beneath them, and despite her efforts with the brush, her copper hair remained a tangled mess. Her cheeks were hollow, her skin pale and stretched thin over sharp angles. She hardly recognized the person staring back.

A lump rose in her throat, and she pressed her fingers against the wardrobe to steady herself. Months of fighting for survival had etched themselves into her bones, but this was something else. She wasn't just physically changed; she felt brittle, like one wrong move would shatter her entirely.

She studied her reflection, but it shifted before her eyes. It wasn't her anymore—it was her mother.

The room blurred, replaced by the glow of countless candles. Ava stood frozen, unable to move or speak, as Lucinda appeared before her. Her mother looked confident, poised, and terrifying. Her eyes, cold and unfeeling, locked onto Ava's.

"Is this a vision?" Ava whispered, but her voice didn't sound like her own. It was deeper, commanding, chilling.

She wasn't herself anymore. She was Havok.

"You wanted to see me?" Lucinda asked.

Ava felt the answer form, not from her, but from Havok within her. "I need you to become a spy." Havok's voice was calm and calculating.

Pride surged within her—no, within Havok. She could feel his satisfaction, his dominance, every twisted thought that ran through his mind. It paralyzed her and she couldn't break free.

"I have found the Elders," Havok continued. "I am going to need you to show up, pretending you've been attacked and abandoned. You will live among them. Get to know each and every one of them and their abilities. If they mention anything about attacking us, report back to me."

"Yes, sir," Lucinda replied with a respectful nod. "But couldn't we attack them since you know where they are?"

Ava—Havok—felt rage flare at the suggestion. "I do not want to kill my son and daughter. And do not ever suggest such a thing."

"Absolutely. I am sorry. Will anyone be accompanying me?"

"No. You are strong enough to handle yourself. It will look too suspicious if there are two of you."

"I won't let you down."

"Good."

The candles flickered and dimmed, her mother's form fading into the shadows. In an instant, Ava was back in her room, staring into the mirror.

Her chest heaved as she gripped the edges of the dresser, struggling to steady herself. *What was that?*

Her mother's face lingered in her mind—the icy resolve in her eyes, the cruel edge to her voice. She had barely recognized her.

Was that a warning? Ava's thoughts raced. Had her mother shown her that memory? Or had someone else—Havok, perhaps—forced it into her mind? The experience felt too vivid, too real, to be a hallucination.

Her hands trembled. *Am I like her? Could I become her?*

She closed her eyes, forcing herself to breathe. *No. I'm not a Cimmerian. I'll never be one.*

The thought did nothing to quell her anxiety. Visions and dreams of her mother had haunted her before. Had this been another manipulation? Or a cruel glimpse of what her future could hold if she failed to fight back?

Her heart ached at the memory of her father. Of Gabriel. She longed for their strength, their warmth, but they felt impossibly far away. *You're alone now,* a voice whispered in her mind. *This is your home. Havok is your family.*

She shook the thought away, swallowing hard. *No. This is temporary. I'll get everyone out of this, no matter what it takes.*

Steeling herself, she took a deep breath and turned toward the door. She shut off her emotions as she opened it, stepping forward to meet her fate.

The corridors of the castle loomed around Ava, their vaulted ceilings soaring above her. Long, shifting shadows from the torchlight fell on walls lined with faded tapestries, each a testament to a history she didn't know but felt bound to. The air was thick with the faint tang of wax and damp stone, and the soft echoes of her and Xavier's footsteps reverberated in the heavy silence.

Xavier walked beside her, his posture relaxed, hands tucked into his pockets. Yet his every movement had a calculated care, his dark eyes flicking to her with an unsettling mixture of curiosity and assessment. He moved with the effortless grace of a predator in its domain, each step in the castle deliberate and precise, as if the castle were an extension of himself.

"Caprington isn't just a castle," he said. "It's a fortress. A stronghold. A labyrinth designed to confuse and contain." He glanced at her, his smirk laced with something that might have been pride—or warning. "You'll learn that soon enough."

Ava forced herself to stay neutral. "I grew up here, but I don't remember anything. Were my memories completely erased?"

He slowed his pace. "You've been through a lot of trauma. It's understandable your mind is a little ... out of whack."

"What kind of trauma?"

"Bad things. You were taken, Ava. Stolen from us."

"Taken? By who?" she asked, injecting fear into her voice. She watched him carefully, noting the way his hand clenched at his side before he tucked it back into his pocket.

"The Elders. They tried to kill Havok. They wanted to destroy everything we've built. And they took all of you Elementals with them."

"Why? What did we have to do with it?"

"Because you're powerful," he said quietly, almost bitterly. "Too powerful to leave in their hands. Havok saved you. Saved all of us."

His words were practiced, too smooth. He believed some of it—but not all. "If that's true, why can't I remember anything?"

Xavier stopped and faced her. His smile softened into something almost genuine. "You had memories you didn't need. Painful ones. Klaus ... he erased them for your sake."

Ava tilted her head, letting doubt creep into her expression. "But I recognize this place. It feels familiar. I feel like I should remember more."

He studied her for a long moment, and for a fleeting second, the arrogance in his eyes gave way to something gentler. Vulnerable. But just as quickly, the smirk was back. "Give it time. The memories that matter will come back."

She swallowed hard, forcing herself to nod. "Thanks. I guess."

They continued walking, and Xavier pointed out landmarks—a watchtower overlooking the cliffs, the armory, the stables—but Ava's mind was elsewhere. She filed away every detail, every twist, and turn, each exit. If she ever needed to escape, she would need to know this place better than anyone.

The courtyard took her breath away. A salty coolness from the sea hung in the air. Vibrant green hedges framed stone paths, and a fountain sparkled under the sunlight. The beauty of it all made her chest ache.

"It's beautiful," Ava whispered, her voice tinged with genuine awe.

His rare, genuine smile only heightened her unease. "It is."

They moved on, descending deeper into the castle. A chill filled the air, the stone walls seeming rougher and more imposing. The training pits were stark and utilitarian, filled with the rhythmic clash of steel and the grunts of sparring soldiers. The air smelled of sweat and metal, and Ava braced herself.

"This is where the real work happens." A spark of pride ignited in his eyes. "Welcome to your new home."

As her gaze swept over the pits, her stomach twisted. This wasn't training. It was preparation for war. "It's ... a lot."

"It is. But you'll adapt."

The tension followed them to the Great Hall, which was steeped in memories she couldn't afford to dwell on, and the Throne Room—each space overwhelming in its grandeur, a constant reminder of Havok's ominous presence.

The kitchen bustled with activity as servants and drolls ran around preparing a feast.

"It's for the Initiation tonight," Xavier said.

"For us?"

He let out a soft laugh. "Yes."

"Didn't we already do that?"

"It's different now. You were forced to Initiate with the Elders. So, now you'll be returning to us."

Ava remembered the Initiation with Savina and Colden. She had been so angry with them for keeping so many secrets from them. The thought of them was painful.

Finally, Xavier led her to the library, pushing open the heavy double doors with an almost reverent air. Shelves stretched to the high ceilings, filled with leather-bound tomes and scrolls that smelled of parchment and time. The room was bathed in a warm golden light, and Ava's breath hitched.

"I saved the best for last," he said. "I know you like to read."

The memories of late nights with Gabriel, of whispered conversations in dimly lit libraries, rushed to the surface. She forced herself to smile, nodding faintly. "It's ... incredible."

Xavier lingered, watching her with an intensity that made her skin prickle. "Books hold power. You should spend some time here. You might find something that sparks your memory."

Was he trying to drop her hints?

"Thank you."

When they reached her room, Xavier hesitated. "Your Initiation dress should be delivered. Dinner is at seven sharp. Shall I pick you up?"

She shifted. "Sure."

He nodded, his smirk returning. "Word of advice, Ava: Caprington has secrets. Pay attention, or they'll swallow you whole."

As he walked away, Ava leaned against the doorframe, her gaze drifting to the window. The view was beautiful, the castle a masterpiece of elegance and power. But all she could feel was the cage closing in around her.

CHAPTER THREE

INITIATION

The dress shimmered like liquid light. The fabric was an ethereal blend of blue, white, and green—swirling together like the colors of the sea, catching the light with a subtle, almost otherworldly sheen. It clung to Ava's form in all the right places, the bodice fitted and elegant, while the skirt flowed like cascading waves around her legs. The high slit revealed her left leg with each step, a bold flash of skin that contrasted with the dress's soft, almost dreamlike quality.

Thin, translucent straps rested delicately on her shoulders, and the neckline dipped low enough to be alluring without losing its elegance. The hem of the dress brushed against the floor with each movement, the fabric swaying like water in motion. It felt weightless against her skin, as though it were a part of her—a reminder of the power she carried within.

She left her copper hair down, framing her face in loose waves. She had considered pinning it up but left it as it was, hoping it might distract from the unease simmering beneath her surface. If only Gabriel could see her like this. The thought brought both a pang of longing and a surge of anger.

Taking a deep breath, she left her room. Her heels clicked against the stone floor as she made her way toward the Great Hall, the sound a reminder of how out of place she felt. Memories of Gabriel's wry smile, the warmth of his hand in hers, and whispered reassurances flashed in her mind. Each step felt heavier, as though she were carrying the weight of those lost moments.

When she entered the foyer of the Great Hall, her eyes found Xavier. He stood near the edge of the room, draped in shadow, wearing a tailored black suit. The faint glint of silver cufflinks caught her eye, a small contrast to his otherwise dark and commanding presence. His ash-blond hair was slicked back, highlighting his sharp jawline and the unsettling intensity of his dark eyes as they followed her every movement.

Xavier looked like a predator—poised, calculated, and dangerously confident. His gaze traveled over her dress, lingering for a moment too long before meeting her eyes. A crooked smile curled his lips, one that sent a ripple of discomfort down her spine. "You look stunning," he said, his voice smooth and edged with something she couldn't quite place. "Fitting for a queen of water."

Ava forced a small smile, tilting her chin up. "And you? Dressed for a king of shadows?"

"Always." He offered his arm. "Ready?"

Not remotely. "Yes." She hooked her arm through his.

Together, they entered the Great Hall. The chatter died down briefly, eyes turning toward them before the noise resumed. Ava was acutely aware of every gaze—some curious, some appraising, others cold and hostile. The air was thick with judgment.

The hall itself was transformed. Massive chandeliers hung low, their candles casting light over the polished stone floors and long tables draped in crimson cloth. The scent of roasted meats, freshly baked bread, and spiced ale filled the air. Despite its grandeur, the room felt suffocating, like a gilded cage disguised as celebration.

It had been only days since their arrival at Caprington, yet it felt like weeks. Days since Savina died in that very room. Days since Gabriel was taken as a prisoner. But tonight, she couldn't think about that. Tonight, she had to play the part.

"Impressive, isn't it?" Xavier whispered as they approached a table near the head of the room. "Havok likes to make a spectacle of loyalty."

"It's ... a lot," Ava muttered.

"Get used to it." He gestured to the table and pulled out the chair for her. "You're with me tonight."

She lowered herself into the chair as Xavier settled beside her.

The doors to the Great Hall opened again, drawing Ava's gaze. Melissa entered first, radiant in an emerald dress that hugged her figure, its fabric shimmering under the candlelight. Her blonde hair cascaded in perfect waves, her every movement poised, controlled—too controlled. Lance walked beside her, his eyes soft but fixed on her, admiration thinly veiled beneath his usual stoicism.

Gillian followed, wearing a sleek silver gown that caught the light like spun moonlight. Her curls bounced with each step, but her face remained carefully composed, betraying nothing. Jeremy and Thomas brought up the rear, both dressed to perfection. Thomas's red shirt clashed against his black suit, a small act of rebellion, perhaps. On his arm was a brunette woman with Gustav's sharp features.

Peter entered next wearing a perfectly tailored crisp black suit. Katarina walked beside him in an ice-blue dress that glimmered like frost. Their expressions were blank. Then Eric, Link, and Nicole walked behind them.

A wave of longing washed over Ava, making her chest ache. For a moment, she was back at the pool with Melissa, gossiping late into the night, back before life had fractured and reshaped them. Her friends sat within arm's reach, but a wall—silent and invisible—kept them distant.

And then Eve appeared.

Ava's stomach turned. Eve's navy gown clung to her, her long black hair swept to the side. She smiled, a smug curve of her lips that sent a chill prickling down Ava's spine.

The murmurs in the room died as Havok entered.

Everyone stood, then bowed.

Xavier pulled Ava to her feet. Following his lead, Ava lowered herself to her knees. Her body obeyed, but every fiber of her being rebelled against the gesture. Kneeling for this man felt like kneeling for death itself.

Havok moved like a storm—silent and unstoppable. He wore a flawlessly tailored dark suit. The air shifted around him, heavy and oppressive, as if the very walls leaned closer to listen. Maggie, Kira, and Sorcha flanked him, their presence just as deadly, though diminished in the shadow of his effortless authority. Sorcha walked with predatory ease in a black dress that revealed more than it concealed. Her sharp eyes scanned the room with a hawk-like intensity that made Ava's blood run cold.

Havok's gaze swept the room, lingering on Ava. Just a second longer. Just enough for her to feel the invisible chains tighten around her throat.

A sharp pain struck her temple, and her vision blurred.

Suddenly, she wasn't Ava anymore.

She was Havok.

Across the room where Ava had just been, her mother stood—rigid, defiant. The air crackled with tension, the edges of the vision twisting like smoke.

The image shattered as quickly as it came, leaving Ava gasping, her pulse racing. Her palms were slick, her breaths shallow.

"You okay?" Xavier murmured.

"Yeah." She blinked rapidly, forcing herself back into the moment as Havok stepped forward.

With a flick of his wrist, everyone stood and returned to their seats. "Tonight," Havok began, his voice smooth, "we celebrate loyalty. We welcome back those who were taken from us, and we reaffirm our strength as one united force."

The applause that followed sounded hollow, like echoes in a graveyard.

Her gaze drifted to Melissa, Jeremy, Lance, Gillian, and Thomas. Her friends—her family—sat around the table, but they felt like strangers.

Melissa met her eyes and lifted her wine. "It's so good to be home," she said, her voice warm but laced with something unsettling.

The chandeliers reflected in the dark red liquid, and Ava forced herself to steady her trembling hand as she reached for her own glass. As she raised her glass alongside the others, the metallic clink of crystal filled the air. She brought the rim to her lips, letting the bitter tang of the wine flood her senses. It burned on the way down, drowning the stress, the fear, the pain.

Jeremy leaned in toward Melissa, whispering something that made her smirk—a cruel imitation of the smiles they used to share. His topaz eyes, once filled with earnest kindness, now glinted with something steely and unrecognizable.

Is it all an act? Or have they been corrupted?

Ava's stomach turned as the soft hum of conversation filled the room, blending with the clink of silverware and the faint pop of corks being pulled from bottles. The rich aroma of roasted meats and spiced vegetables should have made her mouth water, but it nauseated her. Her thoughts returned to Gabriel. Moira. Natalia. Joss. Gustav. Konstantin. They were still prisoners, and there she was—playing dress-up and eating fancy food.

Gillian sat across the table, her fingers gripping the stem of her wineglass. Lance stared at his plate, his dark eyes darting to Havok's table every few seconds, his jaw clenched tight enough to crack. Thomas held still, tension radiating from his stiff posture.

"Has Xavier taken you to see the grounds?" Melissa asked.

"Yes," Ava said, her voice steady despite the lump forming in her throat. "I was hoping it would jog my memory."

"It will." Melissa's smile widened, but there was something detached about it, as though it didn't quite reach her eyes. "It's beautiful, though."

"It is." The words were hollow and fragile.

"Your memory will return gradually," Jeremy reassured her, as if reciting a memorized mantra. "Once you find your rhythm, everything else falls into place."

Ava forced herself to nod, but her thoughts churned. Was this the real Jeremy speaking, or the version Havok had created? All of it gave her a headache.

"Let's not dwell on the bad times," Xavier interjected. "Let's eat."

Ava's stomach twisted as the conversation shifted, the others falling into a rhythm she couldn't match. Melissa's laughter rang too loud, Jeremy's smiles too easy. Lance, Gillian, and Thomas stayed quiet, their silence saying more than any words could.

Ava picked at her plate, the food tasteless. Around her, the din of the hall grew louder, the laughter and clinking glasses a stark contrast to the turmoil in her chest. She kept her head down, forcing herself to play the part, all the while feeling like a stranger in her own life.

The murmur of voices hushed as Havok stood at the front of the room, commanding silence without so much as a word.

Xavier nudged Ava. "You need to stand at the front."

Her heart skipped. "What? For what?"

"You'll see." He stood and held out his hand for her. "Don't worry—I'll be right there."

She had no choice but to comply. Her stomach churned as she took his hand and moved to the front of the room. A spotlight illuminated her. She forced herself to remain steady, even as her cheeks burned under so many stares. The rest of her friends stood beside her.

"Tonight," Havok said, "is more than a celebration. It is a reckoning. A reclamation." He paced slowly, his dark eyes sweeping the room, pausing long enough to let his words settle. "For too long, we have lived in the shadows, forced to hide from the Ephemerals who dare to think themselves our equals. Forced to hide from Hunters. Forced to hide from enemy Enchanters. No more."

Ava's stomach churned as the room erupted into applause, the sound echoing off the vaulted ceilings like a storm of thunderclaps. The lights dimmed, plunging the Hall into an eerie semi-darkness. A soft, otherworldly glow emanated from the floor, revealing a pentagram etched in stark, glowing lines that seemed to pulse with an unnatural rhythm.

As if he could sense her fear, Xavier gripped her hand.

"With the Elementals among us, we are unstoppable," Havok continued. "They were stolen from us, their memories twisted by those who sought to destroy us. But now, they are finally where they belong. Home."

The word struck her again, a bitter echo of Melissa's earlier toast.

"And now, we seal their place among us. The Aureole demands loyalty, and loyalty is paid in blood. But we also have others who are returning."

Havok stopped in front of Peter, his eyes narrowing. "You, for example. A protector. Loyal. Fierce. You have proven yourself, time and again. It is only fitting that you stand among us now, where you were always meant to be."

Peter didn't flinch. "Thank you, sir."

Havok's smile deepened, as though Peter's stoicism amused him. "And you." He turned to Link and Nicole. "You were a gamble. Turning Ephemerals into Enchanters doesn't always yield results. But you proved me wrong. You are valuable beyond measure."

Link met his gaze with quiet defiance, his jaw tight, his shoulders squared. Nicole stood beside him, keeping her eyes straight.

His presence was suffocating, the room shrinking with each step he took.

"And you." His black eyes locked onto hers. "My prize. My Water Healer." He leaned in and she couldn't breathe. "You are everything I hoped for."

She held his gaze, though her throat tightened, and her palms grew clammy. "Thank you, sir."

His smile widened as he addressed the room once more. "With you at my side, we will usher in a new era. No longer will we live in fear of the Ephemerals. No longer will we hide in the shadows. We will rule this world, as we were always meant to."

Sorcha stepped forward, the chalice in her hands gleaming like blackened silver, and Maggie followed, holding an ornate dagger.

He took the dagger from Maggie and drew it across his palm without flinching, the blood pooling dark and thick against his pale skin. The nauseating metallic scent permeated the air. He turned to Ava, extending his arm with a faint smile. "Would you do me the honor of healing this, my Water Healer?"

Her heart thundered in her chest as she approached him with a hollow grace. With trembling hands, she summoned the water within her, letting it flow over his wound. The cold, cleansing power rippled through her fingertips, knitting the torn flesh together with ease.

"Perfect." He handed her the blade.

The dagger felt heavy in her hands, its hilt cold. Ava's breath hitched as she pressed the blade to her arm, the sharp sting of the cut making her wince. Blood welled and dripped into the chalice, mingling with Havok's in a swirl of crimson and black. Despite feeling queasy, she maintained a neutral expression.

One by one, the others followed—Melissa, Peter, Link, and the rest of the Elementals—each cut a silent scream of defiance buried beneath their blank faces. Ava's eyes darted to each of them, searching for cracks in their masks, but their composure held. They were all in this together.

They gathered in a circle, and Ava's gaze flicked to Melissa and Jeremy. They were calm, composed—too calm. Lance, Gillian, and Thomas lacked composure. Though their faces were blank, Ava caught the flicker of fear in their eyes, the slight tremble in their hands. Link and Nicole appeared apathetic, but they had been there before. And Eric. He never showed a single emotion.

When the ritual was complete, Havok raised the chalice high. "With this blood, you swear your allegiance to me, to my Aureole, to our cause. Together, we will rise, and the world will tremble at our feet."

The crowd roared its approval as Havok handed the chalice to Ava. The weight of it felt like a noose tightening around her throat. She brought it to her lips, and the metallic tang of blood burned her tongue as she swallowed. She passed the chalice to Peter, and each one drank.

Once the ritual concluded, applause rose around her.

She hated herself for what she had done, hated the lies she was forced to tell. Even if it was all an act, it felt real.

Because it *was* real.

All of the Elementals were Cimmerians now, bound by blood and oath.

Ava barely made it back to her room before the nausea overwhelmed her. Slamming the door shut, she stumbled toward the bathroom, her breath hitching as her stomach lurched. She fell to her knees in front of the toilet, clutching the cool porcelain.

The room tilted around her as her body rebelled, and the contents of the evening came rushing back up. Wine. Rich, oily food. And—most horrifying—the sharp, iron taste of blood. It burned her throat as she heaved as tears spilled down her cheeks. Each retch felt like her body was trying to purge not just the meal but the ritual, the oath, the violation she had endured.

When the heaving finally subsided, she leaned against the tiled wall, her chest heaving as she fought to catch her breath. The coolness of the stone helped settle her nerves. Grabbing a towel from the counter, she wiped her mouth. Her heart raced, and a desperate thought clawed its way to the surface: *What if the blood didn't take?*

The idea was absurd, but it burned in her mind with the intensity of a prayer. If the blood hadn't stayed, if it hadn't seeped into her veins, maybe ... maybe she wasn't truly bound to Havok. Maybe there was still a sliver of herself untouched by his darkness.

Yet deep down, she knew the truth. The initiation wasn't merely physical. The bond Havok forged with her was something more—something deeper, heavier, inescapable. She was bound to him now, her blood mingled with his.

Her stomach churned again, and she pressed her forehead against her knees, curling into herself. She felt hollow, as though the initiation had carved out a piece of her soul and left a raw, gaping wound behind. Her breaths came in shallow gasps, and the room felt too small, too tight.

Stay strong, Ava. Don't give up.

Gabriel's voice whispered in her mind, a faint echo that steadied her trembling hands. She closed her eyes, clinging to the memory of him. But then the image of his face the last time she'd seen him—his disappointment, the hurt shadowing his blue eyes—flashed before her. Her stomach lurched again, but there was nothing left to expel. Just the hollow ache of shame and guilt.

With great effort, she dragged herself to her feet, her legs unsteady as she staggered to the sink. She rinsed her mouth, the cool water washing away the taste of bile but not the memory of blood. She splashed her face, the coldness biting against her skin, but it wasn't enough to numb the burning guilt.

Her reflection stared back at her from the mirror, pale and haunted. The shimmer of her sea-colored dress mocked her, vividly reminding her of the role she had to play. The dark circles under her eyes looked almost bruise-like, and her lips were cracked from the violent retching. She barely recognized herself.

It's all an act. She gripped the sink until her knuckles turned white. *You're still you. You have to be.*

But the thought rang hollow, a mantra spoken to fill the silence.

The bed creaked as she collapsed onto its edge, her body folding under exhaustion. The dress clung to her, soft and flowing, yet suffocating. Her fingers toyed with the hem, the fabric gliding between her fingertips like water. For a fleeting moment, she wanted to rip it off, to shred the symbol of everything Havok had forced her to endure. But she didn't. The dress was part of the charade, and she couldn't afford to abandon her mask now.

Pulling the blanket around herself, she curled into a ball, her head resting against the pillow. The faint scent of lavender clung to the fabric, an unearned comfort that only deepened her unease. She was drowning. Sinking deeper. Deeper into an ocean of lies and pain and charades. And her limbs refused to cooperate.

Her gaze shot up to the ceiling as she tried to calm her racing thoughts. Havok could already get inside her head—she couldn't let him see this moment of weakness. She had to build her walls higher, thicker, stronger. But no matter how hard she tried, the thought wouldn't leave her.

Had the blood taken?

Had she rejected the darkness, or was it simply wishful thinking? The questions grew louder with every heartbeat.

Pressing her hands to her temples, she squeezed her eyes shut. She was bound to Havok, and nothing could change that now. But if there was even the faintest sliver of hope—she would find it, and she would hold on to it with everything she had.

CHAPTER FOUR

COMFORTABLE LIAR

Xavier entered the room with his usual air of practiced indifference, his sharp suit immaculate and his steps measured. His dark eyes scanned the group—Ava, the Elementals, Peter, Katarina, Link, Nicole, and Eric—with a detached curiosity, as if calculating their usefulness or potential failure.

"Well," he drawled, gesturing for them to follow. "Shall we?"

The temperature dropped as they descended the winding stone staircase. The air carried the faint metallic tang of blood and the distant echoes of shouts and cheers. Each step seemed to drag them further into a dark underworld. The narrow walls of smooth, cold stone loomed closer, as if eager to swallow them whole.

Ava's stomach twisted as the noise grew louder, transforming into a deafening roar that reverberated through the corridor. Her pulse quickened. The sound of the crowd, jeering and cheering with feral energy, filled her with unease.

When they reached the end of the corridor, Xavier pushed open a heavy iron door with ease, its hinges groaning in protest. He stood aside and urged them in.

The fighting pit lay before them, a sunken arena of packed dirt encircled by towering stone walls. Torches mounted on the walls cast long, jagged shadows across the pit. Above, a raucous crowd leaned over the railings, their faces wild with bloodlust and excitement.

Ava's breath caught in her throat as her gaze fell to the center of the pit. An unconscious man lay crumpled on the ground, his limbs twisted at unnatural angles. She scanned for any sign of life, but his stillness spoke volumes.

A figure stood nearby, his imposing silhouette framed by the torchlight. His muscled arms were crossed over his broad chest, tattoos snaking up his forearms in intricate patterns. His dark eyes gleamed under a curtain of thick black hair, and his bearded face remained expressionless, save for a faint sneer that tugged at the corner of his lips.

"Did you do this?" Xavier approached the man.

The man shrugged. "He was too weak."

A muscle in Xavier's jaw twitched. "How do you expect us to have an army when you keep killing them?"

The words sent a chill through Ava's spine.

The man smirked, gesturing lazily toward Ava and the others. "What do we need an army for now that *they're* here? Aren't they supposed to be the greatest fighters in history?"

The hostility in his voice was unmistakable, and Ava felt every eye in the room turn to her and her coven.

"They're here to train," Xavier snapped.

A girl—the one Thomas escorted at the Initiation—perched on the railing scoffed, jumping down into the pit. "Train? Don't they already know how to fight?"

"Yes, Anais."

"But I thought they willingly joined us," the tattooed man said.

"Are you talking about us?" Gillian twirled a dark curl lazily around her finger as she leaned against the railing.

Xavier let out a long, exasperated sigh. "They were kidnapped from us at a young age."

"Oh, is that the story?" Anais crossed her arms. "They're pawns. Their minds have been wiped, and now they're just Havok's puppets. Isn't that right?"

"Minds altered?" Melissa bit her lip. "Is she talking about us?"

"It's nothing." Xavier glared at Anais.

"Was I not supposed to say that? Oops." Anais smirked.

Melissa shrugged. "Well, they probably brainwashed us into believing whatever they wanted. I'm okay with forgetting."

Ava stayed silent, her gaze flicking between Anais and Xavier. *What's her angle? Does she want us to fight back, or is this another game to test us?*

Xavier's shoulders slumped, and the tension in his jaw eased as he sighed. "The Elders were masters of manipulation. Havok couldn't risk leaving that poison in your minds. He erased what you didn't need. Besides, we *all* need to practice for the Selection."

Selection? What is that?

"This should be fun," Anais said. "I bet we can easily take them. Again."

Ava's eyes narrowed at the word. *Again?* Her fists clenched at her sides, her nails biting into her palms. *If only you knew what we're capable of,* she wanted to say.

"We are not fighting to the death, Donovan." Xavier raised his voice, cutting through the rising murmurs.

The tattooed man—Donovan—rolled his eyes, leaning against the railing. "We'll see."

"Melissa let's see what you can do," Xavier said. "Donovan, you'll be her opponent."

Melissa moved to the center, her gaze sharp and unflinching as she faced Donovan. He was shorter than her, but his broad arms and the sneer etched across his face exuded confidence. Melissa, however, looked at him like he was nothing more than an annoying insect.

Donovan smirked and flicked his fingers. The surrounding air shimmered, and small orbs of heat formed, glowing orange-red like embers pulled from a fire. With a quick motion, he sent them hurtling toward Melissa. They slammed into her stomach, bursts of heat scorching her clothing and drawing a sharp cry from her lips as she doubled over—but only for a moment.

Her body shifted, the smoothness of her skin replaced by jagged, rocky textures. Every inch of her transformed into living stone, her surface gleaming like molten rock cooled to solid form.

Donovan swung his fist into her face. Chunks of rock chipped away, but they reformed almost instantly.

Ava gripped the railing, her stomach twisting with unease. *Do they have to fight like this? Why can't they see this isn't survival—it's chaos?*

The match intensified. Melissa's punches landed with thunderous cracks, the sound echoing through the fighting pit like distant explosions. Donovan retaliated by extending his arms, the shimmering air around him rippling with a wave of intense heat. The wave struck Melissa head-on, sending shards of stone flying, destabilizing her form. Yet she remained unshaken, her rocky body reforming as she lunged forward, her arm swinging in a devastating arc.

Her punch connected with Donovan's face, the force snapping his head back. He stumbled, cursing as blood poured from his nose. His expression hardened, his cocky sneer transforming into something far more dangerous.

"Never let them see you be weak," Jeremy murmured from beside Ava. His voice was low and firm, meant only for her ears. "Never let them win. They'll use your weakness to break you. Relentlessly. It's how they keep control."

Ava's chest ached at his words. She wanted to cry out, to reach for him, to pull him away from the madness. Jeremy was still himself.

Donovan steadied himself, his glare venomous. He stretched his arms wide, and the heat intensified as though the entire space were about to ignite. Sweat dripped from Melissa's brow, her rocky form hissing as the heat pressed against her.

Melissa dodged as Donovan sent a concentrated blast of heat toward her, the ground beneath her feet scorching black. Despite the weight of her stone form, her movements were fluid, calculated. She was stronger than Donovan, and it was written all over his face.

His frustration soared, and his glare darkened. Donovan's sneer was gone, replaced by a twisted, dangerous expression that sent a chill down Ava's spine.

"Okay, stop," Xavier said. "Next."

Anais sauntered forward, her lips curling into a smug grin. "I think I'll take Thomas."

Xavier motioned for him to join her in the pit.

Thomas rolled his shoulders, his muscles rippling under his fitted black shirt. His wavy, strawberry-blond hair brushed his collar as he stepped into the center of the pit. A cocky smirk tugged at his lips, but Ava could see the tension behind his calm demeanor.

Anais's eyes gleamed with amusement. "It's going to be so hard not to damage that pretty face of yours," she purred, circling him like a predator.

Thomas raised an eyebrow, playing along. "I'd appreciate that."

Anais's fingers grazed Thomas's shirt, her movements slow and deliberate. Electric blue ropes, glowing and crackling with energy, bound him, pinning his arms to his sides. His muscles strained against the restraints. Sparks of electricity shot through him every time he tried to move, the ropes cutting into his skin until blood seeped through his shirt.

"Stop moving," Ava called out.

Everyone turned to her, booing.

Jeremy nudged her. "Never help anyone."

Thomas stilled, though his jaw clenched.

Anais watched him with a gleeful glint in her eyes, her arms crossed in triumph.

The ropes continued to hum and spark, slicing through his clothes and leaving jagged cuts in their wake. But Thomas tilted his hands ever so slightly toward Anais as fire sparked to life.

The flames devoured the ropes, reducing them to ash.

Anais's eyes widened as Thomas freed himself. Fire danced in his palms, and he hurled a flaming ball toward her.

She dodged the first, but the second struck her shoulder, igniting her clothes. She screamed as flames licked up her arms and torso.

Ava drew water from within and flung it toward Anais, extinguishing the fire.

Again, everyone booed her.

Stumbling, Anais coughed as steam rose from her burned skin. "I didn't need your help."

"Didn't look like it." Ava crossed her arms. Pain seared through her body as the electric ropes materialized around her, pinning her to the ground. The charge sent a sharp, stabbing ache through her muscles, but she gritted her teeth and refused to cry out. Ava's vision blurred with rage. She imagined Anais drowning in an unrelenting ocean, the turbulent waves pulling her beneath the surface.

Anais's grip faltered, and she dropped to her knees, choking and gasping for air. The ropes fell from Ava's body. Water spilled from her mouth as she struggled to breathe.

The room fell silent.

Ava released the vision, her chest heaving.

Anais collapsed to the ground, coughing. She glared at Ava with red-rimmed eyes. "This isn't over."

Power still simmered beneath Ava's skin. "Anytime you're ready."

Xavier released a long, exaggerated sigh. "We are all on the same team, okay?"

"Are you sure?" Anais challenged. "Are they really one of us?"

"Yes. Do not question me again."

Anais's grin widened, her defiance sparking again. "Or what? You'll run to your daddy?"

In an instant, Xavier moved. He was a blur of speed as he grabbed Anais by the throat, slamming her against the wall. The impact echoed through the training room, and the air seemed to freeze.

"You think you can test me?" Xavier hissed, inches from her face. His fingers tightened, but not enough to cut off her air. "Let me remind you, Anais, that Havok put *me* in charge. Not you. If you want to challenge that, I'll make sure your next training session leaves you unable to stand."

Anais clawed at his hand with fear in her eyes. "I—"

"You what?"

"I understand."

Xavier held her a second longer as his black eyes bore into hers. He released her with a sharp shove.

Anais stumbled but regained her footing, rubbing her neck. She didn't meet his gaze again.

He turned to the rest of the room. "Anyone else care to question me?" His eyes swept over the Cimmerians, who averted their gazes and said nothing. Satisfied, Xavier straightened his jacket and gestured to the group. "Good. Let's continue. Ava, you're up next."

She took a steadying breath and stepped into the pit, scanning for her opponent.

As Eve descended the steps into the training pit, Ava's stomach churned. The first time Ava had seen her, it had been in a coma dream. Eve had pretended to be Melissa, taunting her with cruel lies about Gabriel. The second time, Eve had kissed Gabriel, holding onto him like he was a lifeline, as though he were hers.

Eve moved with her signature confidence, her dark hair pulled into a sleek ponytail that trailed behind her like a whip.

She wore a fitted black combat suit that accentuated her lean, cat-like frame. The sharp gleam in her dark brown eyes was dangerous, as though she'd already decided the outcome of the match. Her manicured nails, painted jet black, glinted as she played with the silver crescent moon pendant at her throat, an air of ownership radiating from her every move. "Oh, this will be fun." Her lips curving into a smirk that sent a ripple of murmurs through the spectators. Everyone knew Eve wasn't one for physical combat, even though she twirled a dagger in her hand, but her dream-manipulating powers made her a terrifying opponent in other ways.

"Strange, isn't it?" Eve said, her voice smooth and venomous. "How the mind clings to fragments, even when it's been erased."

"Eve," Xavier barked. "Don't push it."

She skimmed him a glance, her grin unyielding. "Relax, Xavier. I'm not about to compromise anything. I know where the line is." She waved a hand dismissively. "Besides, I have everything under control."

Xavier's jaw tightened, but he didn't argue further. His eyes lingered on her for a moment longer and returned to the railing.

Eve crept closer, her boots silent on the packed dirt floor. "Well, Ava," she purred. "Ready to see what a real Cimmerian can do?"

Shadows crept in from the edges, swallowing the arena in darkness. Ava blinked, disoriented, as the world around her dissolved into black. A chill crept up her spine as a low, mocking laugh echoed in her mind.

"You're not afraid of a little darkness, are you?" Eve's voice slithered into her consciousness, close yet impossible to pinpoint. "You've faced worse, haven't you?"

Ava spun in place, her fists clenched, her breath coming in shallow bursts. The shadows shifted and coalesced into a scene—a prison cell. Gabriel was there, his body battered and broken. His head hung low, his breath ragged, and the sight of him made Ava's stomach twist.

This isn't real. She forced herself to breathe, her chest tightening as she tried to push the image away.

But Eve's voice came again, circling her like a predator. "Do you recognize him? Havok was very specific about what you were to forget. But sometimes ... sometimes the heart remembers. Even when the mind cannot."

Ava swallowed hard. "I don't know what you're talking about."

Eve stepped into the light inside the vision. "Oh, I think you do. They say memories are like threads. Pull one, and everything unravels." She gestured toward Gabriel, his pained eyes lifting to meet Ava's. "So, tell me, does this man mean anything to you?"

He's just a prisoner. He's no one special. She let her emotions fall away, pushing them into the cold, empty space within her. Heart of stone. Keeping her face blank, she turned her gaze to Eve. "Should he?"

Eve's smirk wavered, then returned sharper than before. "Maybe not. Maybe he's just another prisoner to you. But to me, he's everything. And I'll do whatever it takes to keep him alive."

Ava forced a laugh, her tone mocking. "You're showing me a prisoner you're in love with? That's your big move? Didn't he betray us? Isn't that why he's being punished?"

"How dare you," Eve hissed. "Your people stole him, twisted him—"

"Eve!" Xavier's voice cut through the illusion like a blade.

Ava seized the moment, letting her water surge around her hands. She concentrated, forcing the illusion to shatter. The shadows dissolved into mist, and Ava found herself back in the pit. She hurled a spiraling torrent of water at Eve, knocking her to the ground.

The crowd erupted in cheers and jeers.

Eve scrambled to her feet, her face a mask of fury. "I know what you did to him."

Xavier let out an annoyed sigh, stepping between them. "Could your obsession with him be any more obvious? If you keep losing focus, Havok will not Select you again."

Eve's gaze snapped to Xavier, the fire in her eyes flaming with a moment of realization. She straightened, brushing off the dirt as though trying to compose herself. But Ava didn't miss the venom in her glare as she turned back to Ava.

Throughout the rest of the day, Ava witnessed an array of brutal abilities. One Cimmerian could redirect attacks back to the attacker, while another amplified Gillian's fears until she cried out in pain. Gillian fought back by manipulating the girl's mind, leaving both of them clutching their heads in agony.

Link faced an opponent who applied crushing pressure to his skull. It was agonizing to watch, but Link eventually prevailed, creating small, explosive bombs that disrupted the attack. The damage to the room was minimal, and Ava wondered if someone would repair it before they returned.

Nicole struggled against her opponent, missing with a blast of ice that shattered the railing. The shards scattered across the floor, reflecting the blood, sweat, and water smeared everywhere.

Ava hated that type of training. It was relentless, unforgiving, and designed to break them. The Cimmerians fought with raw power and endurance, their stamina endless. If Ava and the others wanted to survive, they'd have to adapt to the brutal way of fighting.

What if Xavier pits us against each other? The thought made her stomach churn. They would have no choice but to fight if it meant maintaining their charade. They couldn't afford to break.

We'll play along for now, she thought, her jaw tightening. *But when the time comes, we'll show them what we're really capable of.*

CHAPTER FIVE

THE CIMMERIAN LIFE

Bruised and battered, Ava teetered on the edge of exhaustion. Every muscle ached, her body screaming for rest, but she knew that wasn't a luxury she could afford. Not here. Not now.

What she really wanted—what she *needed*—was a moment to drop the charade. To speak with her friends honestly, to reassure herself that she wasn't completely alone in this nightmare. But most of all, she wanted Gabriel.

Her chest ached at the thought of him. She hadn't seen him since joining Havok's side, and the memory of him being dragged to a cell, battered and defeated, haunted her. The look in his eyes—raw betrayal and heartbreak—played over and over in her mind, a loop of guilt she couldn't escape.

The image Eve had planted—the vision of Gabriel in a cell, broken and battered—resurfaced with merciless clarity. The raw pain in his hollow eyes, his bruised and bloodied body, the way he sagged against the wall as if he'd given up clawed at her heart.

Was that real?

She bit her lip, trying to shake the thought. Eve was a manipulator, a master of deception. That vision could've been a fabrication—a ploy to test her, to see if she remembered anything about Gabriel. But what if it wasn't? What if Eve had amplified the truth, showing her exactly what he looked like, what he was enduring?

Ava clenched her fists against the rough stone, her nails digging into her palms as tears burned her eyes. *If that's what he looks like ... if that's what they've done to him ... how could I have stayed silent?*

A wave of nausea washed over her. *I should've been stronger. I should've fought for him, told him everything.* Instead, she'd allowed the nightmare to unfold. She'd allowed Havok to drag them into the darkness, where Gabriel was suffering, and she was powerless to stop it.

She closed her eyes, trying to banish the vision, but it only grew sharper in her mind.

Is he even alive?

She gasped, breath caught, hit by the force of the thought. Pressing her hands to her temples, she tried to push the fear away. She couldn't let herself spiral—not now. Not when she needed to stay focused.

But the fear lingered, eating at her resolve. *I have to see him. I have to know if he's okay.*

No matter how much she wanted to convince herself that Eve's vision was a lie, a seed of doubt had been planted. And it was growing, twisting, strangling her with worry.

Please, Gabriel. Just hold on.

She vowed to herself that she would find him. She had to. Even if it meant risking everything.

She drew a shaky breath as she fought to steady herself. Falling apart wouldn't help. She had to keep it together. She had to keep turning it off.

Xavier had instructed them to clean up for dinner, so she had trudged back to her room. The mirror in her small bathroom reflected a stranger. Bruises painted her pale skin in violent shades of purple and yellow. Welts stretched across her arms, and shallow cuts adorned her knuckles like grim trophies from the day's training. Her copper hair hung in tangled, blood-matted strands, and her hollow cheeks made her gray eyes appear sunken and lifeless.

She wanted to smash the mirror—shatter the image of herself that she couldn't bear to see. Instead, she pushed away from the sink and turned on the shower.

Hot water scalded her skin as it cascaded over her wounds, each sting like a reprimand she welcomed. She tilted her head back, letting the stream drench her hair and run down her back, carrying with it the blood, dirt, and grime from the day. The pain was sharp, almost cleansing, as though it might wash away more than the physical remnants of her suffering.

But the weight in her heart stayed unmoving.

She grazed her fingers along her cuts, bruises, and sore muscles. She could heal herself. One wave of energy, one simple act, and she could erase it all.

But she didn't.

She couldn't.

I don't deserve it.

Stepping out of the shower, she grabbed a towel, the rough fabric scraping against her raw skin. The hollow ache in her chest intensified as her thoughts drifted back to Gabriel. When they were at Lighthollow, he kissed her, reminding her it was him, not Ilya.

And now, he was enduring far worse than she was. She couldn't allow herself the comfort of healing—not when he had none.

She dressed in the only pair of jeans in the dresser and a long-sleeved top. Havok wasn't as generous as Savina when it came to wardrobe options. She almost laughed at the absurdity of it—of all the things to miss, she missed having a decent closet.

How do I even get clothes here? The thought struck her as ridiculous, but practical. Would she need to get a job? The idea was strangely appealing. Anything to distract her from the charade.

As she moved to grab the door handle, the room shifted. She was cradling a baby girl in her arms, her tiny fingers curling around her thumb, her laugh like sunlight breaking through storm clouds. Except ... it wasn't Ava's hands or arms. It was Havok's.

The scene shifted, and something ripped away the warmth, replacing it with unbearable pain. Her lifeless form, so small and fragile, lay cold in his trembling hands.

Ava felt the scream building in his throat, raw and primal, the kind of pain that could shatter a soul. The grief pressed against her ribs, suffocating her, until it felt as though her own heart had been torn apart. Havok's agony wasn't just something she saw; it was something she *felt*, seeping into every corner of her being.

Gasping, she clutched her chest. *What was that?* Was she actually seeing Havok's memories? Was he dreaming of holding Savina?

A buzz of conversation and the clinking of silverware filled the dining hall. The space was massive, with five elongated wooden tables lined with Cimmerians. Simple chandeliers hung from the high glass ceiling, their light muted by wooden beams. The setting reminded Ava of a private school, but without the plaid uniforms.

Her friends gathered at a table, laughing and chatting as if they didn't have a care in the world. Ava stood frozen in the doorway, watching them. They looked ... happy.

She joined them, sliding into the seat next to Link and across from Melissa.

"Try this." Melissa scooped some kind of cheesy casserole onto Ava's plate.

"Oh, the bread is amazing too." Gillian broke off a piece and handed it to her. "I've missed it so much."

Ava glanced around the table as her friends dug into their meals with enthusiastic moans and groans. They talked about how much they had missed this place—how good it was to be home.

Home. The word rang hollow in Ava's mind. Was she the only one whose memories hadn't been altered? Her friends spoke as if this was where they belonged. She studied their faces, searching for cracks in their performances, but found none. *Is it all an act, or am I the delusional one?*

Ava forced a smile as she looked down at her plate, now piled high with turkey, casserole, green beans, and a pastry. "Looks delicious," she said, her voice steady despite the turmoil inside her.

Link leaned over, nudging her. "The pastry is like a shepherd's pie. Trust me, you'll love it."

She gave him a warm smile and took a bite. The flavors were rich and comforting, a stark contrast to the chaos of her thoughts. It had been so long since she'd felt hungry that she almost let herself enjoy it. But her nerves prevented her from indulging.

But the moment shattered when Xavier plopped down in the chair beside her. "Everyone's heading to the tavern tonight and getting blitzed. You wanna come?"

Ava turned to him, her mind racing. *Stay in character.* She plastered on the most genuine smile she could muster. "That's so sweet of you to ask. I'd love to go."

If she had to play the part of a Cimmerian, she would commit. It seemed her friends already had.

"Great." Xavier glanced at the rest of the group. "You all in?"

"Absolutely," Thomas said.

The tavern was a strange mix of old and new, a modern homage to medieval aesthetics. Wooden beams crisscrossed the ceiling, and an antique chandelier cast a dim, golden glow. Wild, chaotic patterns painted the walls in vivid, yet disorienting colors. A live band thrashed on stage, their lead singer—a striking woman in leather—commanding the room with raspy screams and powerful guitar riffs.

Ava hesitated in the doorway, overwhelmed. The scene reminded her too much of Lighthollow. She could almost hear the laughter of the village children, see the bright stalls at the marketplace, and feel the warmth of Gabriel's hand in hers. The memory came unbidden—Gabriel lying next to her in bed, where they'd stolen a rare moment of peace in the chaos of their war-torn world.

Her breath hitched. *Lighthollow is gone now. Just like everything else.*

She clenched her fists as another memory surfaced—Gabriel confessing how much he cared for her. Ava shook her head. *No more thoughts of the past.*

"Like it?" Xavier asked.

"It's ... lively."

"Would you like a drink?"

Her stomach churned. Was he testing her? "Sure. Um, I'm not sure what, though."

"Oh, I've got this." He winked and headed for the bar, leaving her alone with her thoughts.

As soon as he was out of earshot, Melissa leaned closer. "You know you've got him eating out of the palm of your hand, right?"

"Yep."

Jeremy slid into the seat beside her, flashing a small vial with a sly grin. "If he gets too cozy, I can fix that."

"What is that?" Gillian frowned.

"Something to make him pass out. He'll think he's just drunk." Jeremy tucked the vial back into his pocket.

"Can we talk?" Her blue eyes pleaded.

Melissa gave a sharp shake of her head. "It's not safe to talk here."

"Where?" Gillian asked.

"Klaus's. Later."

Ava's heart skipped a beat. *It's all an act.* They could talk in Klaus's room.

They found a table near the edge of the room, cluttered with half-full glasses and dirty plates. A server swept by, clearing the mess without a word. The singer's wild energy electrified the room, and Ava let herself get lost in the music.

Xavier returned with a pitcher of dark ale, its cream-colored foam frothing over the top. "This is the best ale." He poured them each a glass.

Ava hesitated until he took a sip, then followed suit. The ale was bitter, the flavor sharp and unpleasant, but she forced a smile. "It's really good."

"I'm glad you like it." Xavier's grin widened as he leaned back in his chair.

"What day is it?" Ava asked, genuinely unsure.

"Friday."

"Is this what happens every Friday?"

"If there's a band, sure."

"What happened for us to have been taken from here?"

Xavier hesitated, the smile slipping from his face. He stared at his drink, taking a long sip before answering. "They came into Caprington and stole you." He didn't meet her eyes.

Classic signs of a lie. Ava tilted her head, watching him squirm.

"Wanna dance?" he asked.

Ava glanced at Melissa, who gave her a subtle nod. She forced a grin and got to her feet. "Sure."

The music pounded through the tavern, a relentless rhythm that set Ava's nerves on edge. The crowd around her swayed and stomped, laughing and shouting over the band's raspy screams. Ava followed Xavier onto the crowded dance floor, forcing her feet to move even though every instinct screamed at her to turn back.

Xavier spun her toward him, his hands resting intimately on her waist. "Relax," he shouted over the music, grinning. "It's just a dance."

"I'm relaxed."

She wasn't.

Her heart raced, not from the music or the movement, but from the storm brewing inside her. She couldn't stop thinking about Gabriel. His face hovered in her mind, his blue eyes searching hers with that familiar intensity, his voice low and comforting as he whispered promises.

I'll always protect you, Ava.

But he couldn't protect her now. He was hurting, and she was there, dancing with a man who had tormented her. Her stomach twisted with guilt. *What if Gabriel thinks I've given up on him?*

"You're tense," Xavier said. "Let me guess—you're still adjusting to being back."

"Something like that."

"You'll get used to it." He twirled her again. His fluid, confident movements surprised her. "You belong here. You'll see that soon enough."

Ava's jaw tightened. She hated how easily he acted as though he cared, as though he hadn't spent years making her life miserable. She thought of the time he'd burned her house down, how he'd left her lying unconscious in the school hallway after forcing her to pass out. And now he was spinning her across the floor like they were old friends.

No matter how he acted now, she knew who he really was.

"They brainwashed you into thinking we were evil," Xavier said.

Ava stopped mid-step, staring at him. "They did? Where are they now?"

"Savina and Colden are dead. The rest are being tortured." His words sent a chill through her, and her throat tightened.

"Tortured how?" she managed.

Xavier leaned closer, his breath warm against her ear. "You'll find out," he whispered, his tone almost gleeful.

Ava's stomach twisted, but she forced herself to keep dancing. "Were we a couple?"

"No. But I've always liked you."

His sincerity was unnerving, but Ava felt nothing. *Maybe I can use this.* "Why weren't we a couple?"

"You were taken from us. Gone for over ten years."

Every lie was as obvious as the last, but Ava played along. "Did you miss me?"

"Yes. Very much."

"Then why didn't you come for me?" She wanted to catch him off guard, to make him slip.

He frowned. "I did. Several times. But you were convinced to hate me."

This time, he held her gaze, and Ava couldn't tell if he was lying.

She swallowed her frustration, and let him spin her again, her thoughts drifting back to Gabriel. She remembered the way he'd taught her to focus, to control her emotions. *Heart of stone,* he'd told her. *Don't let them see what you're feeling. Don't let them know what you're thinking.*

She clung to that now, but it was harder than ever. The memory of Gabriel's touch was too fresh, too raw. She could almost feel his hands on hers, guiding her through the steps of a slow dance in the conservatory, the warmth of his body so different from Xavier's cold, clammy grip.

"Why do you keep looking at me like that?" Xavier asked, snapping her back to the present.

"Like what?"

"Like you're somewhere else."

"I just wish I could remember this place. You." She forced a coy smile.

Xavier's eyes darkened, and he leaned closer. "You wouldn't have liked me. But now we get to start over."

"Why?"

"You ask a lot of questions."

"Because I don't remember anything." She frowned. "What were we like before I left?"

"You were stubborn. Always challenging me."

"Sounds familiar." Ava smirked, but her stomach twisted. She didn't want to give him the satisfaction of thinking they'd ever had any sort of bond.

The song ended, and she cleared her throat. "I need something to drink."

They returned to the table, where Xavier chugged his beer and poured himself another. A few minutes later, his eyelids drooped and he struggled to sit upright.

Jeremy caught him before he slumped forward. "Well, let's get this one to bed."

Ava's heart raced as they carried Xavier through the quiet streets.

When they reached his room, Jeremy dropped him onto the bed with little care.

Melissa smirked. "You should give him a goodnight kiss."

Ava rolled her eyes. "I think I'll pass."

Using her invisibility, Melissa led them to Klaus's room, their steps hurried but quiet. When she reached the door, she knocked.

The door opened, and Melissa whispered something.

Klaus opened it wider and stepped aside to let them in. "Quickly."

Once they were inside, he shut the door and motioned for them to follow him through a narrow passage at the back of the room. The stone walls gave way to a hidden staircase, and the air warmed with each step. At the bottom, they entered a small room lit by dozens of candles placed along the mantle and an aged wooden writing table. The light threw soft shadows across the stone walls, and a fire crackled in a corner hearth, casting a cozy but secretive atmosphere. The air whispered of old parchment and burning wood. It felt ... safe.

"What is this place?" Ava asked. "How is it safe?"

Klaus paused at the writing table, lighting a few more candles as he spoke. "This room predates Havok's rule. It was part of the original castle, hidden and forgotten by most. Few people know it exists."

"That doesn't answer my question," Ava pressed. "How can you be sure no one will find us?"

"The entrance is masked by a spell. To anyone else, it's a solid wall. And these walls," he gestured around them, "are enchanted. No sound escapes."

Eric raised an eyebrow. "And you're certain Havok doesn't know about it?"

Klaus's mouth twitched, the faintest hint of a smile. "If he did, we wouldn't be standing here."

Ava frowned, her unease subsiding. "Then why didn't you bring us here sooner?"

"Because you needed to establish yourselves first. If I'd brought you here immediately, it would have drawn suspicion. Havok is watching all of you."

Melissa stepped forward. "It's okay, Ava. You can trust Klaus."

Ava held Melissa's gaze for a moment before exhaling, letting herself relax. The tension in her chest eased as Melissa turned to Lance, throwing her arms around him. Tears slipped down her cheeks as the rest of the group followed suit—Gillian clung to Jeremy, Link embraced Nicole, and Katarina and Peter held each other.

Eric smirked. "I guess that's our cue."

Ava didn't hesitate, letting him pull her into a hug. She clung to him, her exhaustion and grief pressing down on her shoulders. "I miss him."

Eric's hand rubbed her back. "Damn. Way to hurt my ego." He chuckled but sighed. "I know you do."

Ava closed her eyes, imagining Gabriel's voice, his steady presence, the way he always knew how to make her feel safe. She drew a shaky breath, wishing more than anything that she could see him, touch him, know he was okay.

"Is Joss ... is she okay?" Eric asked Klaus once they pulled apart.

Jeremy and Melissa exchanged uneasy glances.

Fear seized Ava. "What is it?"

"She tried to attack a couple of Cimmerians," Klaus whispered. "They still think she lost her memory, and they didn't go easy on her. During training, they were relentless. And she fought back."

"Is she okay?" Ava asked, her heart sinking.

"She's in solitary confinement," Klaus said. "That's their punishment for anyone who resists. She's being treated as a prisoner."

Anger flashed in Eric's russet eyes. "And we're supposed to just sit back and take it?"

"You don't have a choice," Klaus said. "If you push back, they'll target you too. She lashed out, tried to electrocute them, and now she's paying for it."

A faint smirk crossed Eric's face. "That's my girl."

"When will she get out?" Ava asked.

Klaus sighed. "I don't know. Days. Maybe longer."

Ava's stomach churned. "This place is a nightmare."

Melissa pulled Ava into a crushing hug. "I missed you so much."

"Me too," Ava replied. She hugged Gillian next, then Jeremy, who held her with a reassuring squeeze.

When the reunions settled, the couples drifted into their own corners of the room, whispering to one another. Ava, Thomas, and Eric lingered near Klaus, forming a smaller circle around the writing table.

Klaus leaned forward, his hands folded. "How was your first week? Did anyone suspect anything?"

"No." Ava leaned back. "Though Xavier's developed quite a crush on me."

"Yes. He'd asked me to tamper with your mind to make you fall for him."

"What? And what did you say?"

"I told him it didn't work like that. Free will and all. He seemed disappointed but didn't press the issue."

Ava shook her head, a bitter laugh escaping her lips. "Figures."

"I'm confused about something," Melissa said. "Why the hell are Peter and Katarina hugging and kissing each other?" Her face twisted with curiosity, her green eyes wide.

A small laugh escaped Ava's lips. She glanced at Peter and Katarina, who looked away, their faces flushed with embarrassment.

"Oh, Ava and Peter broke up," Gillian said.

Melissa's jaw dropped. "What? When? Why?"

Gillian smirked. "You've missed a lot."

"I'll say. Spill!"

Peter shifted. "I think we're going to our rooms." He stood and helped Katarina to her feet. Ava noticed how gently he took her hand, how his gaze lingered on her. It didn't sting anymore—not like it used to—but it still brought an ache to her chest. Because she couldn't have that with Gabriel.

"Be careful when you leave," Klaus said. "If anyone spots you, tell them you got lost. And you two cannot walk together."

Katarina nodded, her blue hair catching in the firelight. "Thank you."

Ava looked away as Peter leaned in to kiss Katarina. She clenched her jaw, forcing herself not to cry. Not because she wanted Peter back—she didn't—but because she missed Gabriel. She missed his soft words, his warm arms, the way he'd sweep her hair aside to kiss her cheek. Peter and Katarina were lucky. They could be together, unafraid.

When the door clicked shut behind them, Melissa turned back to Ava, her arms crossed. "Okay, what the hell happened? You and Peter were like the epic love story of the century."

"We just … grew apart."

Melissa raised an eyebrow. "Which translates to: he started liking someone else."

"It happens. He's better off with Katarina."

"Weirdly enough, I believe you. But you didn't look thrilled just now. What happened?"

Ava hesitated, then told her about the breakup—the fights, the drifting apart, the realization that they weren't right for each other. "It wasn't easy getting over him. And Havok used that to his advantage."

"I can't believe after all that, Peter just left you."

"It's okay."

Melissa narrowed her eyes, scrutinizing her. "You went through a lot, Ava. How are you seriously okay with this?"

"Because I realized … Peter wasn't the one I loved. There's someone else."

Melissa's lips curled into a knowing smile. "Oh, really? Who's the lucky guy?"

Lance laughed as he shook his head.

"Gabriel," Ava said.

"I *knew* it! I told you, you'd fall for a hot Enchanter. And I knew something was up with him. He always acted all mysterious, but I could tell he was into you."

"I told her that, too," Gillian said. "She ignored it."

Rolling her eyes, Ava smiled. For a moment, it felt like they were teenage girls gossiping about boys. But reality settled back in. "I don't think he understands why I joined the Cimmerians. I need to talk to him."

"He understands more than you think," Eric said. "He loves you, Ava. That's something you can rely on."

"You didn't see the way he looked at me when they took him away." She blinked back tears. "I wish I could see him. But I'm so glad to be here with you."

She turned to Melissa and glanced at Jeremy. Jeremy had his arm around Gillian, holding her close. He kissed her temple, and she closed her eyes with a small smile. Relief washed over Ava. They were still the same, still the people she'd grown up with.

"It was so hard being away from you all," Jeremy said. "And being here … we didn't know what to do. They brought us here as prisoners, hoping it would lure you in so they could take you too."

Lance took Melissa's hand, his dark eyes shadowed with pain. "It was tough without you. We spent months powerless, depressed, and heartbroken."

Melissa frowned. "Powerless?"

"Sorcha put a sleep spell on us and left us without powers," Ava said.

"Damn."

"It was hell," Lance said. "They played with our minds every chance they got. I dreamed of you, Melissa. You were convincing me to join Havok." His voice shook. "And Gillian and Ava…" He hesitated. "Ilya morphed into Peter, Jeremy, and Gabriel to mess with them. Ava fell into a coma. We saw what she went through."

Ava shivered, the memories clawing at the edges of her mind—her friends and herself burning at the stake, Eve pretending to be Melissa, Xavier ripping her arm from its socket. She clenched her fists, her teeth grinding together.

"Hey." Melissa took her hand, prying her fingers apart gently. "It's okay now. They can't hurt you anymore. They'll all pay for what they've done."

Ava bit her lip to keep her chin from quivering. "I've missed you so much."

Melissa pulled her into a tight hug. "I've missed you too. It's been hell, Ava. Living this Cimmerian life, hiding the truth, pretending we belong here, acting like the Elders were the ones who kidnapped us." Her voice cracked.

"All we remember is being knocked out during the battle." Jeremy's topaz eyes shadowed with sorrow. "When we woke up, we were in Klaus's lab room. He was supposed to take our memories but told us everything."

"We were shocked when you willingly joined Havok," Melissa said. "I wondered what you were up to, but you all seemed so ... different. No emotions. Just like us. Who taught you to do that? We had Maggie and Kira."

"Gabriel," Ava whispered, her voice tinged with pride and sorrow.

"Wow. I underestimated him."

Eric scratched the back of his neck. "He used to be a Cimmerian."

Melissa gasped. "What?"

"He didn't know any better," Eric said. "It wasn't until he met me that he learned about the Elders and switched sides."

Jeremy frowned. "So, that's what Havok was talking about when he saw Gabriel."

"Were he and Eve ... a thing?" Melissa asked. "Because she was all over him."

Jealousy stirred in Ava's chest, sharp and bitter. "No. But she loved him. And apparently still does."

"What made you and Jeremy join?" Thomas asked. "Or did Havok send you to Klaus against your will?"

"We followed Maggie's lead," Jeremy answered. "We trusted her."

"Is she faking it?" Ava asked. "She's always at Havok's side, like a shadow."

"That's her job now," Melissa said. "She's one of his Nightwardens. A bodyguard."

"Does that mean she's off-limits?" Lance asked. "Can we talk to her?"

"You can't get to her," Jeremy said. "She's constantly with him. And he's looking for more guards. I imagine some of us will become one. And if that happens ... we won't get to talk."

"Is that what the Selection is?" Gillian asked.

Jeremy nodded. "Yes. It's a big event where Havok chooses his most trusted army, bodyguards, and recruiters. All this training we're doing? It's like tryouts."

Ava took a deep breath. "I hate this so much."

"I am so sorry," Klaus said. "If we want to succeed, you'll have to continue doing things you don't want to. I wish it were different. I wish there were another way."

Thomas crossed his arms, his brow furrowed. "Why are you helping us, Klaus? Really. What's in this for you?"

He hesitated, his expression softening. He looked older in the warm light, the faint lines around his eyes and mouth deepened by sorrow. "For my freedom."

"You're a prisoner?" Ava asked.

"In a sense. My home was attacked years ago. Havok found me. He knew what I was—an Enchanter—and he gave me a choice: lifelong servitude in exchange for my family's safety."

"Why didn't he bring them here?" Gillian asked.

Klaus's lips curved into a wistful smile. "They're Ephemerals. They wouldn't have survived. He allowed them to stay in the village where we lived."

"How do you…" Ava paused, her throat tight. "How do you know they're okay?"

"I have my ways." He opened a drawer in the desk and pulled out a gold bowl marbled with intricate veins of white and black. Candlelight glinted off the bowl's polished surface. "It's a Scrying Bowl. With it, I can see anyone I wish—loved ones, alive or dead."

"You use this to watch them?" she asked.

He ran his fingers along its smooth edge. "I've watched my daughters grow into beautiful young women. My wife…" His voice faltered, his gaze distant. "She still grieves for me. I told her to move on, to find happiness without me. But she hasn't."

Ava thought of Gabriel, alone in the darkness of a cell. *Would he look for me if he had something like this? Would he grieve if I never came back?*

Thomas squirmed in his seat, his fingers fidgeting against his knee. "Can anyone use that bowl to see someone?"

"Yes," Klaus said. "Focus on the person you wish to see. The bowl will do the rest." He slid it across the table, its surface rippling as it stopped in front of Thomas.

Thomas hesitated as he stared at the water. Then, with a small nod, he picked it up. The room seemed to hold its breath as he leaned forward, his eyes locking onto the liquid's surface.

The water shifted, faint tendrils of light weaving through it. Thomas's breath hitched, and his shoulders slumped as his eyes shimmered with tears. With a shaky hand, he handed the bowl to Ava.

She froze. Her heart pounded in her chest as she took the bowl from him, its weight heavier than she expected. The cool ceramic felt icy against her hands, but her palms were slick with nervous sweat. She stared at the still water, her reflection trembling on its surface.

She took a deep, shaky breath and closed her eyes, willing herself to concentrate. The first thought that came to her mind was her father. The water rippled, colors swirling to life. When she opened her eyes, the image in the bowl made her breath catch.

Her father sat on the couch, holding a photo of the three of them—Ava, her mom, and him. Grief etched lines on his face, and his shoulders hunched. Her chest tightened as a lump rose in her throat. She blinked, her vision blurring with tears.

She couldn't look at him anymore. Swallowing hard, she steeled herself and shifted her focus. This time, her thoughts zeroed in on Gabriel. The water darkened, swirling until it settled into a hauntingly clear image.

Ava's heart plummeted. Slumped against the stone cell wall, Gabriel bowed his head; his once-bright blue eyes appeared hollow and distant. Fresh lash marks marred his shirtless chest, and grime smeared his skin. He looked shattered in ways she hadn't prepared herself to see.

Her breath hitched, and the room seemed to tilt. The image of him, beaten, matched the vision Eve had placed in her mind. Only this wasn't a trick. It was real.

The bowl trembled in her hands, and she set it down on the table, shoving it toward Klaus as if it had burned her. "Where are they keeping him?"

Klaus stiffened. His green eyes locked onto hers, warning flashing through them. "Ava, you can't go near them. It's too dangerous."

Thomas clenched his fists. "Why not? We have to save them!"

"I understand your urgency. But you must act as though you don't know them. Any sign of recognition will expose you." He hesitated, his gaze flicking toward Ava. "There is something else. Havok may use them as leverage."

"What do you mean?" Eric asked.

Klaus hesitated. "He may make you torture them. To prove your loyalty."

The room fell silent, the air thick with shock and horror.

Her pulse roared in her ears, a panicked drumbeat that quickened with each passing second. "I can't—I can't do that," she said, the words spilling out in a rasp that didn't feel like her own.

Images of Gabriel in that cell flooded her mind, his lost eyes, his broken expression. Her hands flew to her head, desperate to claw the thoughts away, but they only burrowed deeper. Her chest heaved, breaths shallow and useless. The room tilted. The walls seemed closer, darker, until they were all she could see.

She felt arms around her. "Ava," Melissa said. "Ava, look at me. It's going to be okay."

"No," Ava gasped, shaking her head so hard it hurt. "No, I can't. I can't do this." The words tumbled out, raw and broken, each one tearing at her throat.

She was drowning. Sinking further and further into an ocean of darkness.

CHAPTER SIX

CATCHING UP

Breathe, Ava," Eric said, kneeling before her. "Just breathe. You're okay."

Ava wanted to argue, to push him away, to curl into the darkness and let it swallow her whole. But Eric wouldn't let her. He breathed slowly, deliberately, his chest rising and falling in a rhythm Ava couldn't help but notice.

"Breathe with me," Eric said. "Just breathe."

The words were simple, but they cracked something open in Ava. She closed her eyes and tried to match Eric's breaths, though her own came in fits and starts. The images didn't vanish, but they blurred at the edges, dimming enough to let her world widen again.

The room didn't feel as small. The walls didn't seem to pulse anymore.

The tears came then, hot and unrelenting, cutting lines down her cheeks and Ava buried her face in her hands. "I can't keep doing this."

"You can." Melissa pulled her close. "You know how to turn it off. I saw you this week. You were brilliant."

"Brilliant?" The word was bitter on Ava's tongue. Her laugh broke, jagged as glass. "I'm a monster."

"You're not. You're human. And you're stronger than you think."

"Gabriel..."

"He will be okay," Eric said. "He's strong. He knows how to survive this."

"How can you be so sure?"

"Because I know him. He's survived this before. And I know Joss. They're fighters. They'll hold on."

"He thinks I betrayed him. And I ... I did. And now we're supposed to torture them."

Eric clasped her hands, his russet eyes meeting hers. "You didn't betray him. You're doing this to protect him. Once we explain everything, he'll understand. Gabriel loves you, Ava. That hasn't changed."

"What if he hates me?"

"He doesn't. He knows who you are. He knows your heart."

"Ava, listen to me," Klaus said. "You're strong. You have the power to fool Havok. If you want to succeed over Havok, you'll have to do things you don't want to do."

Melissa squeezed her. "I promise we can do this."

"Can't we warn Moira, Gabe, and the others?" Thomas asked. "Or explain to them what's going on?"

"I can't get you access to them," Klaus said. "I know it's a lot to ask of all of you. I'm well aware of that. But I've seen what you can do."

"Why do you think we can take down Havok?" Ava asked.

"Well, as you know, the Elders tried, and you know how that turned out. But it's because you're Elementals. You're not like the others. You can break his hold. I've been waiting for someone like you for a long time."

"We know how to use the heart of stone," Gillian said. "But it's so hard. There are times I feel like I'm going to break."

Jeremy squeezed her hand. "It's not easy. It's a constant battle."

She shook her head, then a revelation flashed in her eyes. "Ava, what about the potion? Couldn't we use that to help all of us keep Havok out of our heads."

"Yeah. I can't believe I didn't think of it."

"What potion?" Melissa asked.

"When I got out of my coma, Savina showed me how to make an elixir. It helped keep Havok out of my head. I could make it again."

Klaus nodded. "If it worked, it could help. It may not block him completely, but it will give you an edge. He'll only see what you want him to see. Just tell me the ingredients and what you need."

Relief washed over her, mingling with a trace of hope. "Thank you," Ava murmured.

"But be careful. Havok is not easily deceived. One slip, and he'll know."

Ava's stomach turned. That was the reason she'd joined the Cimmerians—to save her friends, even if it meant breaking herself. She took a deep, shaky breath and wiped her tears. "We'll be ready." But in her heart, she wasn't sure she could ever be ready for what was to come.

CHAPTER SEVEN

STRANGERS

Thomas's fist connected with Donovan's jaw, sending him sprawling to the floor. The dull thud reverberated in the training pit as Donovan lay motionless, a crumpled heap of bruised defiance. Thomas stepped back into the crowd, his lips curling into a cocky smirk.

The Cimmerians roared their approval, a cacophony of laughter and cheers. A few stomped their boots on the ground, chanting Thomas's name in mock adoration. It was all a game to them—this brutal, ceaseless competition. For two weeks, Ava and her coven had endured sparring and fighting to prove themselves. The bullying had lessened, but the hatred lingered in every snide remark and dismissive glare.

Ava stood rigid, her arms crossed, her mind a storm of doubt and determination. Every day, she analyzed her surroundings, searching for weaknesses, allies, and ways to bring Havok down. Even if they eliminated him, thousands of Cimmerians still posed a threat. And then there was Xavier. Manipulating him felt like the first step, but her heart ached for a simpler solution—one that wouldn't involve tormenting those she loved.

"Havok is impressed by your strength," Xavier announced, nudging Donovan's limp body with his boot. "But strength alone is not enough. He wants to test your allegiance." His smirk widened as the heavy wooden doors creaked open.

Ava's breath hitched as the prisoners shuffled into the hall, their chains clinking against the stone floor like a funeral procession. The rowdy jeers of the crowd faded into a tense hush, replaced by the sound of ragged breaths and shuffling footsteps.

"These prisoners are enemies of the Cimmerians," Xavier continued. "They kidnapped the Elementals, conspired against us, and now you will teach them the price of their defiance."

Ava's stomach churned as the prisoners stepped into the light. Her gaze landed on Natalia first, her black hair matted with sweat and blood. A swollen eye and cuts marred her face, but her hazel eyes burned with unrelenting fury, locking onto Ava like daggers.

Moira followed, her frail frame trembling. Her gaunt face, etched with exhaustion, masked the quiet strength in her trembling jaw.

Ava clenched her fists. The sight of them both made her feel sick, but nothing could have prepared her for what came next.

Gabriel.

Her chest tightened as he stepped forward. His crystal-blue eyes, once a haven of warmth and quiet strength, now brimmed with raw, unrelenting hatred. The scar on his cheek stretched as his jaw clenched, and his overgrown beard and tangled hair framed a face hardened by suffering. His tattered clothes reeked of mildew, sweat, and the faintest hint of juniper—a ghost of a scent that had once been comforting. Now, it was a cruel reminder of everything they'd lost.

His eyes met hers, and she froze, the storm in his gaze striking her like a physical blow. Hatred. Betrayal. Pain. Every emotion radiated from him, sharp and unforgiving.

Their clothes hung in tattered shreds, their faces were gaunt and pale, and their bodies bore fresh cuts and bruises. Natalia walked in first, her hazel eyes sharp and accusing as they locked onto Ava. Moira followed, trembling with each step. Then Joss. Konstantin. Aaron. Gustav.

And then Gabriel.

She bit the inside of her cheek until the metallic taste of blood filled her mouth. Heart of stone. She couldn't let herself feel anything. She walled off her emotions, shoving the guilt and sorrow into a locked corner of her mind. If Havok or the crowd saw her falter, it would all be over.

Gabriel's stare didn't waver. It pinned her, dissected her, demanded answers she couldn't give. *Does he know I'm lying? Can he see the truth beneath the mask?*

"Show us your allegiance." Xavier cut through the heavy silence. "Prove you belong here."

A bloodthirsty roar erupted from the crowd. "Make them suffer!" someone shouted. "Let's see if they can handle it!" The jeers surrounded her, growing louder with every second.

Gabriel stood motionless in the center of the pit, his bare chest marred with fresh welts and bruises. He didn't beg, didn't plead, didn't even flinch. He stared at her daring her to act, his gaze like ice against her skin. "Finally let him take you over, I see," he muttered, his voice taut with restrained anger.

Xavier raised his hand as if to strike him, but Ava stopped him. "That won't be necessary. I can shut him up myself."

She moved toward Gabriel, each movement measured, though her heart thundered in her chest. "I'll go first," she said, her voice colder than she thought possible. The mask stifled her, but it was her only safeguard.

Xavier grinned. "Perfect." He shoved Gabriel forward, yanking the bindings off his wrists with a sharp snap. The crowd roared in approval, the sound rattling in Ava's ears.

Gabriel stumbled but straightened, his shoulders squaring as he faced her. The faint glow of the green band around his ankle—the one suppressing his powers—was the only thing keeping him in this arena. But the fire in his eyes told her he wasn't helpless. He wouldn't make this easy, and she wouldn't expect him to.

On the edge of the crowd, Eve stood with crossed arms, a venomous expression on her face. Hatred contorted her sharp features as her eyes darted between Ava and Gabriel. Her presence burned at Ava's awareness like a brand.

Ava's fingers twitched at her side. She had to act now. If she hesitated, it was over—for all of them. With a flick of her wrist, she summoned water, the shimmering liquid coiling around her like a serpent.

Gabriel's jaw tightened, and for the briefest of moments, something glinted in his eyes—hurt, betrayal, or something even deeper. The sight of it nearly undid her, but she stayed in control. *Heart of stone. This isn't the man you love. He's just some prisoner.*

With a calculated motion, she sent the water surging toward him. Gabriel moved, fast as lightning, his teleportation sharp but limited by the band on his ankle.

The icy torrent struck Eve, soaking her from head to toe. She let out a sharp cry, her cat-like grace faltering for a single, rare moment. "You stupid bitch!"

"Shut up," Xavier snapped, his glare silencing her. "Let her do her job."

But Eve's dark eyes stayed locked on Ava, radiating pure loathing. Her lips curled in a sneer as she muttered loud enough for Ava to hear, "You don't deserve to be here."

Ava ignored her, forcing her focus back to Gabriel. She twitched her hand, summoning another wave of water, but this time she closed her eyes and projected a vision into his mind. The image appeared—an endless, furious ocean. The dark waves crashed over him, dragging him under, pressing against his lungs.

He collapsed to his knees, coughing violently, clawing at the ground as though fighting to stay above water. His breaths came in ragged gasps, and his body trembled under the force of the illusion. He didn't scream, didn't beg, but his pain etched into every line of his face. The betrayal there cut deeper than any blade.

"Again," Xavier ordered.

She forced the water to strike him again. The illusion dragged him deeper into a dark, unrelenting abyss. Gabriel's gasps grew weaker, his body convulsing as he struggled to rise, only to collapse. His hands clawed at the dirt, his fingers trembling, but his eyes—those penetrating blue eyes—never left hers. The unspoken question seared into her mind: *Why?*

A cold emptiness pressed against her heart, causing her chest to tighten. *Heart of stone.*

"Enough," Xavier said, his smirk fading into boredom. He motioned for a Cimmerian to drag Gabriel away.

The crowd erupted, their bloodthirsty cries crashing over Ava like waves, relentless and deafening. She didn't hear the applause, didn't register Xavier's approving nod. Her world had shrunk to one thing: Gabriel, crumpled and broken, dragged across the dirt like a discarded carcass. His hollow eyes burned into her, searing a mark she knew would never fade.

"Well done, Ava," Xavier said. He turned back to the crowd, his grin sharp and predatory. "Who's next?"

Gabriel swayed as two Cimmerians hauled him upright, his knees buckling beneath him. Blood smeared his chin, his shoulders sagged, but he didn't shatter. He found her gaze one last time.

His eyes reflected more than pain. Loathing consumed it. And worse, despair.

Ava's fists curled at her sides, her nails biting into her palms. The crowd roared. Their approval was a storm she ignored. Her eyes followed Gabriel, every faltering step carving deeper into her.

Eve slid up beside her, a shadow that chilled the air. Her lips curled into a cruel smile as she leaned in, her breath hot against Ava's ear. "You think this makes you one of us? You'll never deserve him. You can break him, but he'll never be yours."

The words struck like a dagger, but Ava forced her expression to harden. "Why would I want *him*?" she bit out, cold and precise. "He's nothing but a traitor."

The lie burned her tongue, thick as ash, but she had to say it. For the role. For survival.

Gabriel stiffened, his head tilting just enough to show he'd heard. His gaze darkened, and the flicker of defiance she had clung to extinguished. His face became a mask—emptiness painted over pain. Resignation.

A lump formed in her throat, and she remained still. She couldn't break now. Couldn't let her horror show, even as it clawed up her throat, threatening to choke her.

Eve chuckled. "You'll pay for this, Ava. Mark my words."

Ava stared ahead, her gaze fixed on nothing, her body rigid as stone. *Heart of stone. Heart of stone.* It became her mantra, a fragile tether to hold herself together.

Xavier's voice cut through the din, casual and commanding. "Bring her forward."

A Cimmerian dragged Moira into the center of the pit, his grip on her arm careless, like she was little more than an object. Her legs gave out beneath her, and she hit her knees hard, her arms hanging limp where her bindings bit into her skin.

Ava's stomach twisted, bile rising as she caught the shimmer of tears in Moira's wide brown eyes. Her chin trembled, but she tilted her head up, trying to gather whatever strength she had left.

"Go ahead," Xavier said, gesturing toward Thomas. His tone was almost bored, as if this was nothing more than a chore to him.

Ava bit her cheek hard enough to draw blood. She fought back a reaction. She was stone—unyielding, unmoving. But every moment, every cry from the crowd, felt like another crack forming in her façade.

Stay calm. Don't react.

Thomas hesitated for the briefest moment, his jaw tightening. Then his hands ignited, flames crackling as they engulfed his fingers. With a flick of his wrist, a jet of fire shot toward Moira.

The crowd around the pit stilled, their collective breath held. Then the flames hit.

Moira screamed.

The sound shattered the air, raw and guttural. The fire consumed her, climbing up her body, licking at her clothes, her skin. She writhed, her voice cracking as the agony overwhelmed her. Her cries ricocheted off the stone walls, mingling with the sharp scent of burning flesh.

Clenching her fists, Ava dug her nails into her palms. She forced herself to look bored, her expression cold and detached, even as bile rose in her throat. *This isn't real. None of this is real.*

Moira fell forward, her screams dying into weak, pained moans. The flames devoured her, scorching her garments and searing her flesh.

Ava couldn't take it anymore. She extended her hand, summoning a stream of water that cascaded over Moira's burning form.

The flames hissed and sputtered out, leaving Moira's body smoking and trembling. Charred patches marked her skin, and her singed clothes clung to her in tatters. The water had healed some burns on her neck and shoulders, but the damage was too extensive.

Gasps rippled through the crowd. Xavier's head snapped toward Ava. "What the hell was that?"

Ava shrugged, folding her arms across her chest. "I'm not a fan of the smell of burning flesh."

The air was thick with tension. Then Xavier's lips curved into a thin smile. "Touché." He turned back to Thomas. "This time, just use your mind. Again."

Thomas's expression betrayed nothing, but Ava saw the way his jaw clenched, the subtle twitch in his fingers. He had turned his emotions off, just as Gabriel had taught them.

Moira gasped as if an invisible hand had gripped her chest. Her screams started again, but this time they were different—raw and desperate. Ava knew Thomas was using his projection ability, making her feel as though she were burning alive all over again.

"You coward," Moira spat through her tears. "I can't believe you'd give up so quickly."

Thomas's face remained stoic, but Ava saw the pain in his eyes.

"Again," Xavier ordered.

And again, Thomas obeyed.

Moira collapsed, her body trembling as she gasped for breath. Two Cimmerians dragged her limp form away.

A knot formed in Ava's stomach. *How much more of this can we take?*

Melissa stepped forward next. She didn't hesitate as Joss was brought into the pit, her hands bound. Joss glared at Melissa, defiance burning in her violet eyes.

Melissa conjured a poison in her hand and whispered something under her breath. Joss's body convulsed as the poison spread through her veins, her face twisting in pain. Sweat poured down her face as she doubled over, retching. The crowd groaned in disgust, several turning away.

"Ugh, what did you do?" Anais asked, wrinkling her nose.

Melissa lifted one shoulder. "Atropine poisoning."

Donovan tilted his head. "You can do that?"

"Yeah."

"What's that?" Gillian asked, her voice strained.

A cold smile touched Melissa's lips. "It comes from the belladonna plant. Makes you hallucinate. Lose your memory. Temporary, of course."

Joss's wide eyes darted around the room, panic seeping into her expression. "Where am I?" she whispered. "Who are you people?"

Ava's gaze flicked to Eric, who stood like a statue, his face blank. But she saw the tension in his posture, the way his hands twitched at his sides. He was holding it together—but barely.

"Someone clean this up and take her back," Xavier said.

One of the Cimmerians carried Joss away and one cleaned up the mess.

"Let's continue." Xavier crossed his arms, impatiently waiting.

Gillian faced Natalia next. Ava hated the sight of Natalia's bruised and bloodied face. A knife appeared in Natalia's hand, and Ava suppressed a shudder as Gillian's manipulation forced her to turn the blade on herself.

Natalia cried out as the knife slashed into her stomach, again and again. Blood pooled around her, staining the stone floor in dark, glistening patches. The crowd watched in silent awe, their expressions a mix of horror and fascination.

Jeremy's turn was no less brutal. His winds tore at Konstantin's flesh, peeling it away in ragged sheets.

Ava willed herself to remain composed, even as her friends' suffering pressed down on her.

The hours dragged on, each punishment more grotesque than the last. They were forced to torture the prisoners over and over again. The Cimmerians cheered and jeered, their bloodlust insatiable. But Ava couldn't stop thinking about the prisoners—her friends, her family. They bore the torment without fighting back, showing no sign of resistance.

Why? she wondered. *Why won't they fight back? Do they think they're proving something? Or are they waiting for us to slip up?*

When Xavier finally called an end to the session, Ava felt hollow. Guards dragged the prisoners away, their bodies broken and bleeding.

How much longer can we keep this up? How many more people will we destroy before we destroy ourselves?

"Do you all want to refresh and regroup tonight?" Lance asked, his voice steady but laced with an unspoken urgency.

"Sure," Thomas said. "Sounds great."

The code was clear—Klaus's secret room. But all she wanted was to get away. Away from the others, away from the training pit, away from her thoughts. She hurried toward her room, her breathing shallow and quick, her pulse thundering in her ears. Her thoughts were a chaotic storm, fragments of Gabriel's broken expression flashing behind her eyes. She needed to remove the mask, if only for a little while. To feel the emotions she'd buried deep. To face what she had done.

When she reached her door, her fingers trembled as they gripped the knob. The metal was cool against her clammy palm. Her chest squeezed, desperate for the silence and solitude that waited inside. She needed to hold it together a little longer.

"Ava!"

The voice stopped her cold, slicing through her haze. Her heart plummeted as she turned, her face carefully neutral.

Xavier stood at the end of the hallway, arms crossed, his infuriatingly smug smirk etched across his face. His eyes, sharp and calculating, bore into her with an intensity that made her skin crawl. "Are you in a rush?"

She forced a small, tight smile. "No. I just need a shower. I'm disgusting."

Xavier chuckled, taking a step closer. "I get it. Today was … intense. You were brutal out there." He cocked an eyebrow, his expression almost admiring. "Not bad for someone who's only just come back home."

Her anger flared, and she clenched the knob tighter to keep herself steady. "They deserved it." Her voice came out low, almost a growl, and for once she wasn't pretending. A hot, relentless anger churned inside her, causing her chest to rise and fall in short, shallow breaths. But it wasn't directed at Gabriel—it never could be. No, the fury burning in her veins was for the Cimmerians, for what they'd done to him, to her friends, to all of them.

"You were just … unrelenting. It was impressive, don't get me wrong, but it seemed personal."

"They took us from our home. They must have caused serious damage for Klaus to erase that part of us. I hate them for it. I hate what they've done to me." The words tasted like poison on her tongue. She had to sell the lie, had to let him believe her fury was real. Tears burned behind her eyes, but she blinked them back, refusing to let them fall.

Xavier's expression softened enough to unsettle her. He closed the distance between them and, before she could protest, pulled her into an embrace. His arms wrapped around her with a strange, unsettling warmth, and the smell of his cologne—something sharp and woody—invaded her senses. "It's okay. You don't have to explain yourself to me. I get it."

Panic seized Ava, her pulse pounding, and her body tensed. She didn't want his comfort. She wanted Gabriel—his arms, his strength, his love—but that was gone now, because she had destroyed it.

"You're stronger than I gave you credit for. You're going to do great things here. I can feel it."

She pulled away, taking a step back as her skin prickled with unease. "Thanks. But I really need to shower."

"See you at the tavern later?"

"Yeah, sure."

The moment Ava stepped inside her room, she slammed the door shut and collapsed against it, her chest heaving as the mask shattered. Tears spilled down her face, hot and relentless, as she stumbled to the bathroom. She dropped to her knees in front of the toilet, her stomach convulsing as guilt and anguish forced their way out.

Clinging to the porcelain edge, she trembled, sobs wracking her body. The image of Gabriel—his gasping breaths, the water she'd forced into his lungs, his broken body crumpled like a marionette—played on an endless, merciless loop. His eyes, full of hate and disbelief, pierced her like daggers, leaving wounds too deep to heal.

She clutched her stomach as if she could hold herself together. Clinging to the bathmat's edge, she huddled on the cold tile floor. The unrelenting agony in her chest was unbearable.

She thought of her father—his warm voice, his steady hands brushing her hair back when she was sick, the way he'd promised that everything would be okay. But he wasn't there. No one was. Just her. Alone.

Ava's fist slammed into the floor with a crack of bone against the tile. Pain cut through the chaos, silencing the storm inside her. Blood welled from her knuckles where the skin had split, vivid and crimson against the white tile.

She clenched her injured hand, smearing the blood across her palm. Healing would be too easy, too merciful. She didn't deserve mercy. The pain was hers to bear. A fitting punishment.

Good. She deserved it.

She struck the floor again, harder, her vision blurring with tears as the pain bloomed. Still, she didn't summon the water to heal it. She wouldn't. The ache in her hand tethered her to something tangible, something other than the hollow echo of Gabriel's gasps or the despair in his eyes.

He'll never forgive me. The thought pierced through her, cruel and absolute. *And I don't deserve it.*

Her breath hitched as the tears came faster. *You're doing this for them,* she told herself, but the words rang hollow. No justification could silence Gabriel's broken voice, or the betrayal etched into his face.

Her emotions surged, sharp and overwhelming, threatening to pull her under. But she stayed on the floor, refusing to reach for the water she could feel thrumming beneath her skin. The pain in her hand throbbed in time with her heartbeat, a constant reminder of what she'd done—and what she'd have to do again.

CHAPTER EIGHT
LINKED

Shadows flickered along the stone walls, cast by the fire in Klaus's room. They stretched toward Ava like grasping hands, clawing for her soul, eager to drag her into the depths of darkness.

Thomas paced in front of the fireplace. His strained muscles looked ready to burst through his skin. "I can't do that again."

"Why didn't he fight back?" Ava whispered, her voice cracking as tears spilled over. "He just took it. All of them did." She shook her head, burying her face in her hands as the sobs wracked her body. "He just took it."

Eric leaned against the wall, his arms crossed over his chest. Tension filled his usually calm, russet eyes. "Gabriel won't fight back, Ava. Not against you. He couldn't."

"Why not? He should hate me. He does hate me."

Eric knelt beside her, his expression unwavering. "No, he doesn't. He's angry, sure—angry at the situation, angry at everything—but he doesn't hate you. He's holding on to something—his belief in you. He's hoping you're still in there. That's why he didn't fight back. He knows you, even if he can't see it right now."

His words cut through her like a blade. She wanted to believe him, but the memory of Gabriel's betrayal-filled stare felt too vivid, too raw. "He doesn't believe in me anymore, Eric. He can't. Not after what I did."

"You're wrong, Ava. That man *loves* you. He always has, even when he's angry or hurt. And deep down, he knows you're doing this for a reason, even if he can't understand it right now."

"Then why does it feel like I've already lost him?"

"You haven't. You think he'll let go of someone who's just as stubborn as he is? He'll hold on. He's not giving up on you, even if it feels like he has."

"Is that why you joined? Because you're looking out for me?"

Eric hesitated. "Partially. But once I realized what you all were doing, I knew I had to as well. Because I knew Gabriel would. And because I believe in you, too."

The group sat in tense silence, scattered across the small room like broken pieces of a puzzle. The only sounds were Ava's muffled sobs and the restless creak of Thomas's boots against the stone floor.

"You'll have to do it again," Klaus said gently. He stood near the writing table, his hands folded in front of him. "Havok will want to see it for himself."

Thomas spun on his heel, his eyes blazing. "You think we don't know that? We know what we have to do! But what happens to us if we keep doing this? What if we become monsters like them?" His voice broke on the last word, and he turned away, raking a hand through his hair.

Gillian hugged her knees to her chest, her blue eyes rimmed with tears. "The whole time, all I wanted to do was kill the Cimmerians. I wanted to burn them to the ground. Why can't we attack now?"

Klaus's frown deepened. "None of us are ready to attack. I know it's hard. This mission cannot be easy for anyone. But you all are our only hope. You're the only ones who can stop him."

"We know that!" Melissa snapped. "We've known that since the beginning. That doesn't make it easier."

Ava's head shot up at Melissa's tone. They locked eyes, and an unspoken understanding passed between them.

"This is what they made us do when they turned us into Enchanters," Link said. "We tortured each other, bullied everyone. It's how they broke us."

Nicole nodded. "We learned how to survive by becoming like them. It wasn't easy then, and it's not easy now."

"You remember your life here?" Ava asked.

"Bits and pieces." Nicole glanced at Link.

"Flashes," Link said. "They come and go."

Klaus cleared his throat. "I promise I'll help as much as I can. There's something else we need to discuss." He moved to the table and retrieved a small box, which he handed to Ava. Inside were bundles of lavender, valerian root, and rosemary, along with a mortar and pestle.

She furrowed her brows. "This isn't enough for everyone."

"It's only for you."

"What? Why only me? Everyone needs it."

"Because of your connection to Havok."

"I already know about my soul," Ava said. "My mother promised it to him."

Klaus met her gaze, his own tinged with sorrow. "Do you understand what that truly means?"

"What are you saying?"

"It means your soul is linked to Havok's. Whatever happens to him, happens to you." Klaus frowned. "I'm sorry. I truly am. But this link—it's why Havok can get inside your head so easily."

"What exactly does this mean?" Thomas demanded.

"If Havok dies, so does Ava."

The silence that followed was deafening. Ava stared at him, her mind reeling. She felt like the ground had been ripped out from under her.

"No." Gillian trembled. "There has to be another way."

The words hit her like a physical blow. She staggered back as the walls seemed to close in around her. A high-pitched tone rang in her ears as she gasped for breath. Spots swam before her eyes as her chest constricted, and the world around her spun. Panic rose, coiling around her neck like invisible hands, strangling her.

"Breathe, Ava." Melissa crouched in front of her, her hands firm on Ava's shoulders. "In through your nose, out through your mouth."

Ava's body shook as she forced herself to follow Melissa's instructions. Her breaths came in short, shallow bursts at first, but they slowed. The ringing in her ears faded, and the room came back into focus. The fire, the stone walls, the concerned faces of her friends—they all came rushing back at once.

"I ... I can't..." Ava gasped, her knees buckling. She collapsed into a chair, gripping the edges as her body trembled.

"I can't be tied to him. I can't—if he dies, I die? What does that even mean?"

"It means we need to find another way," Eric said firmly.

"So, wait." Thomas stopped pacing. "You knew about this link when you told us to take down Havok? You knew Ava would die?"

"Yes, but I have been researching ways to break the spell. It's very ancient. Powerful."

"How is this possible?" Ava whispered.

"When your mother promised your soul to Havok, a spell was placed," Klaus explained. "The link was meant to activate as you grew into your powers, but because Havok was weak, it remained dormant. When you sought the Necromancer, it strengthened the bond."

Rage bubbled up inside her. "My mother..." She spat the words. "How could she do this? How could she give me to him like I was nothing?"

"Ava, turn off the water," Melissa whispered.

She blinked and looked down at the water streaming down her arms, dripping onto the floor in chaotic rivulets. She forced it to stop. "She was supposed to protect me. She didn't even try."

"Okay, so the spell is ancient," Link said. "What else have you learned?"

"Only an Elder can break it."

"There are only four left," Jeremy said. "Maggie, Gustav, Aaron, and Havok. Maggie is probably a lost cause given that we can't separate her from Havok. Gustav and Aaron are prisoners."

"How am I supposed to fight him if I know I'm going to die too? How can I save anyone if I can't even save myself?"

"You're not dying," Eric said. "We *will* figure this out."

"In the meantime, you can still keep Havok out of your mind," Klaus said. "And this potion will help. He doesn't feel the need to torture you, but if you ever feel him trying to read your mind, make him see what he wants. You've done a great job of strengthening your mind. Whoever taught you that is incredibly powerful."

Gabriel. His name echoed in her mind, bringing a wave of guilt and longing. He'd taught her everything about controlling her emotions. She needed him. She needed to tell him everything. He was the only person who could calm her, even if he hated her. Without him, the walls were closing in. And maybe Gustav and Aaron could help figure out the spell. "Where are the prisoners?"

Klaus sighed. "In the South Hall. The prison chambers are the only thing there."

"Can I manipulate the guards?" Gillian asked.

"No," Klaus said firmly. "It will be very hard to manipulate a Cimmerian guard. They're protected by a charm."

"Of course." Gillian crossed her arms. "How can we bypass them?"

"It's too dangerous. You can't be seen there."

"Why?" Water dripped from Ava's fingertips as her anger boiled over. "What's stopping me?"

Thomas cracked his knuckles. "We'll figure out a way whether you help us or not."

Klaus let out a defeated sigh. "I will make an elixir to use on the guard. You will need to give it to him without him suspecting. It will momentarily put him in a trance, and he won't remember. Havok will be gone from the castle tomorrow night. Then you can go."

"Where is he going?" Lance asked.

"He and a group are going to massacre a town."

The words hit like a punch to the gut. Ava's knees nearly buckled, and her breath came out in a shaky gasp. She closed her eyes and forced herself to take deep, even breaths. Slowly, the water trickling from her hands evaporated, but the ache in her chest only deepened. Gabriel, the town, the spell—it was too much. She couldn't hold it all.

She opened her eyes and glanced at the small table where the box of ingredients for the potion sat. Lavender, valerian root, rosemary. The mortar and pestle sat beside a few vials of clear liquid. A distraction. She needed it.

She moved to the table and sat down, her hands trembling as she opened the box. The lavender's soft scent wafted up, its familiarity both calming and infuriating. She crushed the dried flowers in the mortar, the rhythmic grinding calmed her.

"What are you doing?" Jeremy asked.

"Starting the potion," Ava replied. "If Havok gets inside my head again, I need to be ready."

The valerian root was harder to crush, its woody texture splintering under the pestle. The sharp smell mixed with the lavender, creating a strange, almost bitter aroma. As she worked, she focused on the task, the methodical movements dulling the sharp edges of her thoughts.

Her friends watched in silence. It was the only thing she could control right now.

As she added a few drops of liquid to the crushed herbs, a faint steam rose, carrying a scent that was both familiar and foreign. Her mind flashed back to Savina teaching her and Gabriel's patient instructions on focus and clarity. Each memory felt like a dagger to her heart, but she welcomed the pain. It was better than the numbness.

"I need to see him," Ava said again.

"You will," Klaus said gently. "Tomorrow night. But tonight, focus on this."

Ava clenched her jaw, grinding the pestle harder than necessary. As she continued to work, the room seemed to exhale with her, the tension easing. For now, there was something to do, a step forward in a sea of uncertainty.

CHAPTER NINE

NOT AN ANGEL

Today, we're going to continue the torture on the prisoners." Xavier twirled a sleek police baton between his fingers as he paced the room. His voice sounded bored.

Ava was going to puke.

The room was smaller and darker than the training pit. The stone walls were cold and damp, with iron shackles embedded deep into the cement. Nearby, cruel tools gleamed in the fluorescent lighting—hooks, whips, and blades, each designed for pain. The air reeked of iron and mildew, sharp enough to sting Ava's nose. It was the Torture Chamber. She didn't need the name to know what it was.

Her stomach coiled as images of what could happen flashed in her mind—blood, screams, the terrible emptiness of silence that followed. She clenched her fists to keep from trembling, forcing her mind blank. *You can't think about it. Not here. Not now.*

"Only today is different." Xavier halted his pacing. He tossed the baton into the air and caught it with a smirk. "Havok will be watching."

A ripple of unease moved through the room.

"Great," Eve muttered. "He makes me nervous."

Ava shot her a sideways glance. "Why does he watch?"

Anais rolled her eyes, shifting her weight. "Who knows? He's sadistic. Maybe he likes to see us sweat."

"Were we friends before?" Ava pressed, testing her.

Eve barked a laugh.

Anais arched a brow. "No."

"Enemies?"

"Stop asking so many questions."

Ava shrugged. "Just trying to figure things out. My memory's fuzzy."

"Doesn't matter." Anais sighed. "We're here to do what Havok says. Nothing else matters."

"He'd better not make me hurt Gabriel," Eve said.

Ava's heart flipped at his name. "Doesn't he deserve it?"

Eve clenched her teeth. "How dare you. If you even lay a hand—"

"Shut up," Anais said. "You know he deserves it. He deserted us."

"No. The Elders stole him and warped his mind."

Anais shook her head. "You're so delusional."

The heavy door creaked open, and Havok entered, flanked by Maggie, Kira, and Sorcha as usual. The room dropped into a chilling stillness.

Havok moved with unhurried arrogance. He squared his shoulders, each step a proclamation of power.

Everyone dropped to their knees.

Bile rose in her throat as he swept his stony gaze over the room. When he flicked his wrist, everyone rose.

Ava swallowed hard, keeping her face neutral. She was nothing to him—none of them were. Just tools, puppets for his amusement.

Xavier opened another door, and a familiar sound filled the chamber—the clinking of chains. Ava's stomach clenched. Her pulse roared in her ears as Natalia, Moira, Gabriel, Joss, Konstantin, Aaron, and Gustav walked inside. They looked even worse than before.

Two guards placed Gabriel in shackles that were connected to the wall.

"Stand here," Xavier ordered, motioning for Ava to join him.

Every step was a struggle, her legs heavy with dread. She stopped behind Gabriel, her breath hitching when her eyes landed on his back. The sight of his bare skin made her chest tighten. She remembered tracing those contours with her fingertips in moments filled with whispered promises and stolen warmth. Now, jagged scars and raw wounds marred the surface—testaments to his suffering, to what she was about to add.

"You're going to create a whip with your water," Xavier said. "And strike his back."

Her heart stopped as she stared at Xavier. "I've never done that before."

He narrowed his eyes, and his smirk vanished. "You're going to do it. Now. Ten lashes will do."

With a stiff nod, she turned her attention to Gabriel, who had bowed his head.

The atmosphere differed vastly from the pit. It was quiet. Too quiet.

She hesitated, summoning water to her hands. It coiled around her fingers like liquid silver, cool and pliant. Her mind raced. She didn't know how to wield a whip, didn't want to, but Xavier's gaze burned into her like a brand. She raised the water, shaping it into a long, fluid strand.

The first crack split the air like thunder, the whip snapping against Gabriel's back. He grunted, his muscles twitching, but he didn't cry out. Blood welled at the thin, jagged line carved into his skin, glistening like crimson ribbons in the harsh light.

Ava's heart clenched, but she locked her expression into a mask of cold indifference. *One down. Nine to go.*

Each lash felt heavier than the last. The water whip sang through the air, each crack reverberating through the chamber. Gabriel's breathing grew ragged, his shoulders trembling, but he stayed upright, defiant in his silence. His fists clenched, knuckles white, blood dripping from where his nails pierced his palms.

By the seventh lash, Ava's vision blurred. The room tilted and spun, and she felt herself slipping. Suddenly, she wasn't in control anymore. She was watching herself from a distance—or someone else entirely. Her mother stood in her place, her face alight with cruel satisfaction. The whip lashed with precision, her movements fluid, practiced. Havok's voice echoed in her mind, sharp and taunting. *She's finally becoming what I always knew she could be. Just like me.*

"Are you just going to stand there?" Xavier barked, his voice slicing through her haze. "Three more. Finish it."

Ava blinked hard, and the vision shattered. She was back in her body, her hands trembling, the water whip still coiled in her grasp. She raised the whip again, her arms aching, the water heavy and unyielding. Three more. Just three more. Each strike sent pain radiating through her chest, as if she were the one being punished.

Gabriel sagged in his chains, his head lolling forward. His silence was deafening, louder than any scream.

When the last lash fell, Xavier clapped his hands together, his grin wolfish. "Not bad for your first time."

Ava dropped the whip, the water splattering against the stone floor. Her knees felt weak, her stomach roiling, but she forced herself to stand tall. She couldn't falter, couldn't show weakness.

"Take him away," Xavier ordered. Two burly Cimmerians unshackled Gabriel and dragged him out of the chamber. He didn't resist, his body limp, but his eyes—icy and burning all at once—met hers for a fleeting moment. The hatred in his gaze was a knife twisting in her chest.

As Gabriel disappeared through the door, Ava stood frozen, the echoes of the whip still ringing in her ears. She clenched her fists at her sides, trying to bury the ache that was seconds from consuming her.

Xavier chuckled, breaking her thoughts. "You might just be a natural, Ava."

Her lips pressed into a thin line as she turned away. She hated him. She hated Havok. But most of all, she hated herself.

Each of the prisoners endured painful torture. The room felt suffocating. The stale air clung to Ava's skin, and the faint metallic tang of blood refused to dissipate. Even when the prisoners left, the Torture Chamber felt alive—thrumming with a sinister energy that made her want to claw her way out.

When Havok moved to the center of the room, the oppressive silence deepened. His steps echoed like a drumbeat of inevitability. His angular face was a study in shadows, the sharp lines of his jaw and cheekbones made sharper by the unforgiving light. The way he carried himself—commanding, untouchable—made her stomach churn. He didn't just dominate the room. He *owned* it.

"I am pleased with what I have seen," Havok announced. His gaze swept over the remaining Cimmerians, but when his eyes landed on Ava, they lingered for a beat too long. "Tonight, the army prepares for the massacre of Tokyo. I will personally oversee it, but soon ... soon I hope that I will no longer need to lead." His thin smile curled upward, mocking and triumphant. "For now, rest. I have big plans for you."

Havok dismissed the crowd with a wave of his hand, and the Cimmerians surged toward the exits like eager children racing home from school.

Ava lingered, her limbs heavy and reluctant. *Tokyo.* The word rattled in her mind like a death knell. An entire city. Gone.

Was that what she had trained for? To stand by while innocents were slaughtered? She tried to smother the emotions tearing their way to the surface. *Heart of stone, Ava. Heart of stone.*

"Ava. A word." Havok's voice broke through the silence, smooth and cold.

Her heart hammered against her ribs as she turned to face him. "Yes?"

"You have impressed me." He tilted his head, studying her like a chess piece he was about to move. "You're adapting well. Better than I expected."

She forced a slight nod, swallowing against the bile rising in her throat. "Thank you."

His smile widened, thin and sharp. "Conviction is what separates the strong from the weak. You've learned to wield your power with conviction. That is good." His gaze hardened, and the air between them thickened. "But don't let me see hesitation again."

"You won't."

"Good." He turned as if to leave, but paused, glancing over his shoulder. His tone softened, almost mockingly gentle. "You remind me of your mother sometimes, Ava. I hope you don't make her same mistakes."

Her breath caught in her throat, and the world seemed to tilt. His footsteps echoed as he exited the room, but his words clung to her like a curse. *The same mistakes.*

A stiff hand gripped her arm, snapping her back to the present. She flinched, looking up to find Xavier standing before her. His dark eyes studied her with a mixture of curiosity and concern. "You okay?"

"I'm fine."

"You sure? You kinda hesitated back there." His grip tightened a little.

Did he suspect her? Did he think she hesitated because she couldn't bear to whip Gabriel? "I just … thought I saw something."

"Like what?"

"Nothing important. Just the lights or something."

"I get it. Sometimes your mind plays games with you in this place." His tone was almost understanding. Almost.

"Yeah. Exactly. And producing that whip … it took a lot out of me."

He tilted his head, his smirk creeping back. "I know. I only pushed because Havok was watching. You need a break. Come out tonight after the massacre. Help us celebrate."

Her stomach clenched at the mention of the massacre. "Getting ahead of yourself, aren't you?"

His grin widened. "You don't think we can annihilate Tokyo?"

"I don't know. You don't have the Elementals."

"Is that so? Care to make it interesting?"

"What are the terms?"

"If we wipe out Tokyo tonight, you go on a date with me." He stepped closer, and the heat of his presence made her skin crawl.

"And if you don't?"

He chuckled. "Then I'll give you anything you want."

"Anything?"

"Anything."

She forced a playful smirk, even as her mind screamed at her to walk away. "I'll think about it."

His grin broadened, confident and maddening. "I'll see you tomorrow then. Have a good night, Ava."

"Good luck tonight." A surge of nausea overcame her.

Xavier winked and sauntered away, his swagger grating on her nerves. As soon as he disappeared down the corridor, Ava leaned against the wall, her head spinning. *Tokyo.* The word echoed in her mind, each syllable a dagger in her resolve.

What kind of monster had she agreed to become?

Dinner at the castle felt heavier than usual. A heavy sense of dread settled over Ava. Every clatter of silverware against plates was louder than it should have been. No one spoke much, and when the meal ended, they left the dining hall without their usual detour to the tavern. Havok had taken his army to prepare for the massacre, and in his absence, Ava and the others retreated to the relative safety of Klaus's hidden room.

The moment the door closed behind them, Ava's mask cracked. She leaned against the cool stone wall, her breathing shallow and uneven. The familiar warmth of Melissa's arms wrapped around her, and she clung to her friend like a lifeline. The tears she had been holding back surged forward, spilling over her cheeks as her body shook with quiet sobs.

"I don't even know what to tell him," she whispered. "But he has to know. How will he ever forgive me?"

Melissa pulled back enough to meet her gaze, her green eyes filled with quiet determination. "He will, Ava. You have to believe that. Just tell him the truth. He'll understand."

Ava wanted to believe her, but the memory of Gabriel's tortured eyes haunted her. The way he had looked at her, filled with hatred and pain, cut deeper than any whip she could summon. "What if he doesn't? What if it's too much?"

Eric moved forward. His russet eyes met hers, steady and reassuring. "He'll listen. Gabriel is stubborn as hell, but he's not stupid. He knows you, Ava. Deep down, he knows why you're doing this."

"He hates me. He looked at me like—like I'm the enemy."

"That's because he's hurt. But hate? No. He doesn't have it in him to hate you, not really. He's probably blaming himself for this whole mess, knowing him. He's been through hell before. He'll get through this. You need to remind him that you're still in there. That this isn't who you really are."

"What about Moira?" Thomas asked. "She'll never look at me the same."

"Everything will be fine," Eric tried to reason.

"Go at midnight," Klaus instructed. He reached into a drawer and pulled out a small vial of dark liquid, handing it to Melissa. "Persuade the guard to drink this."

Gillian frowned. "I thought you said they couldn't be manipulated."

"They can't," Klaus admitted. "But there are other ways to persuade people. Trust me, when Havok is gone, they're lax. You'll have exactly one hour. No more." He surveyed them with a sharp and commanding gaze. "Let Melissa go first. Don't rush in and draw attention. And Peter and Katarina must be with you. I imagine emotions will be running high." He turned to Ava. "You drank your potion?"

She nodded.

"Good. Now, only Ava, Melissa, Thomas, Eric, and the Protectors are allowed to go. We can't risk too many people. It's already a big group."

Ava's heart raced. "What time is it?"

"9:26," Klaus said.

Her shoulders slumped as the tension in her chest threatened to choke her. Two and a half hours. The wait felt unbearable, a cruel stretch of time between her and the chance to see Gabriel. To explain. To apologize. She sank into one of the plush chairs, clutching the armrests until her knuckles turned white.

Eric sat beside her, leaning forward with his elbows on his knees. "You need to stop overthinking it. You're going to drive yourself crazy."

"How can I not overthink it?" Ava shot back. "I tortured him, Eric. I hurt him, and I can't take that back."

"You're right, you can't. But you can make him understand why. And knowing Gabriel, he'll forgive you. He's too damn loyal not to. Think of all the times he stood by you before. He loves you. You have to trust that."

Ava let out a shaky laugh, her tears still glistening on her cheeks. "He's stubborn. Just like you."

Eric smirked. "Takes one to know one."

Melissa sat beside her, rubbing her back in soothing circles. "You'll get through this. We all will."

Time crawled. The minutes felt like hours, each tick of the clock drawing her closer to the confrontation she both craved and dreaded. By 11:30, Ava was pacing the room, her arms crossed over her chest. The others sat in tense silence, their faces pale and drawn. The gravity of what they were about to do hung heavy in the air.

Finally, the clock struck midnight.

Klaus stood. "It's time. Remember—one hour. Be careful. And don't get caught."

Eric took Ava's hand as they followed Melissa out the door. "We've got this. And if Gabe tries to give you the silent treatment, remind him who dragged his sorry ass out of this castle last time."

Ava gave a weak smile. "Thanks."

"Anytime."

A sharp coolness from the castle corridor struck her face. Ava squared her shoulders, each step bringing her closer to the prisoners—and to Gabriel.

CHAPTER TEN

BROKEN

The cold, damp air of the castle corridors wrapped around Ava like a shroud, each step echoing off the stone walls. They masked their tension with a drunken charade. Plastic cups filled with beer sloshed in their hands, and they stumbled and swayed in exaggerated movements. The pretense wasn't hard; their nerves had them so on edge it was easy to appear unsteady.

Ava struggled to focus on the others. Her heart thundered in her chest as her mind raced ahead to Gabriel. The thought of seeing him again, of trying to explain herself, sent a wave of nausea rolling through her. Would he even listen? Would he believe her?

The group stopped at the heavy iron door leading to the cells. The dim light from the overhead torches illuminated the prison guard, Jared. His bored expression barely shifted as they approached. He rolled his brown eyes.

Melissa took the lead, a practiced, mischievous smile plastered across her face as she staggered up to him. "Jared," she slurred with mock drunkenness, twirling a lock of her blonde hair around her finger. "You coming to party, or what?"

Jared rolled his eyes but couldn't suppress a smirk. "You're funny when you're drunk, Melissa."

She leaned in, her fingers trailing through his blond hair before gripping the back of his neck in a flirtatious hold. Her confidence oozed with every movement. "Come on," she purred. "Drinks are on me." She held up a shot glass with the spiked drink Gillian had prepared, tipping it to catch the light.

Jared's eyes narrowed.

Melissa timed her pout perfectly. "Just one," she coaxed, her lips curving into a sultry smile. "For me?"

Ava's pulse quickened, her grip tightening on her cup. If this failed, their entire plan would unravel before it even began.

But Jared sighed, his resistance crumbling under Melissa's practiced charm. "Just one drink." He reached for the shot glass and downed the liquid, his Adam's apple bobbing. He coughed once, his face screwing up at the strength of the alcohol. "Damn, that's strong."

"Just the way I like it." Melissa winked, flashing a grin that melted him on the spot.

"You're trouble." He shook his head.

"Wanna come have some fun with the prisoners?" Melissa teased, tilting her head.

"You know I can't," Jared replied, though his voice was laced with regret.

"Suit yourself." Melissa patted his cheek, the gesture flirtatious enough to keep him captivated. She glanced over her shoulder as he fumbled with the keys, unlocking the heavy door. "You'll be back?"

Melissa chuckled, her tone light and carefree. "Of course." She tapped the tip of his nose, and he glowed under her attention. As soon as the door clicked shut behind them, her demeanor shifted. The smile dropped from her face as she turned back to the group, pulling a ring of keys from her pocket.

Melissa shrugged. "Let's hurry."

The group moved in a single file down the narrow corridor, their steps careful and measured. Icy needles pierced their clothes as the air grew colder. She couldn't warm herself and hated knowing Gabriel lived in such an environment. The musty scent of damp stone and decay filled Ava's nostrils, making her stomach churn. The dim torchlight cast jagged shadows on the walls, and every creak and groan of the old structure set her teeth on edge.

Cold stone formed the walls, and a small window in each door offered the only view inside. Cells stretched along both sides of the shadowy hallway. This was going to take forever.

A muffled cough broke the silence, drawing her back to the oppressive atmosphere. It reminded her of the Cruciari, where pain and despair clung to the air like an unshakable curse. The memory twisted her stomach and tightened her throat. Cold. Hopeless. The faces of those who had suffered there flashed through her mind.

Gabriel.

Her heart ached at the thought of him in a place like this. Would he even be able to look at her after everything she'd done? She swallowed hard, forcing the thought away.

Eric nudged her with his elbow. "Breathe."

She gave him a fleeting nod, though her pulse refused to settle. The group pressed forward, their footsteps echoing as they approached their destination. Fear brewed inside her.

After what felt like an eternity, Thomas froze mid-step. "Moira?"

Melissa unlocked the door and pushed it open. She and Eric moved farther down the hall, leaving Thomas and Ava to enter the cell.

A shadowed figure slumped in the corner. Slowly, she lifted her head. Dark hair, matted with dirt and dried blood, hung in clumps around a gaunt face, etched with exhaustion. Her brown eyes, blazing with fury, locked onto Thomas.

"Came back for more?"

"Moira, no. I never wanted to hurt you. Please believe me."

Her laugh was hollow, cutting through the thick, stale air of the prison. "Never wanted to hurt me? Then why did you?"

"We're all faking this." Ava moved beside him.

Moira struggled to a standing position. Her piercing gaze shifted from Thomas to Ava, her expression hardening. "You." She tilted her head, studying Ava with something between disdain and heartbreak. "You're standing next to Havok, just like I saw in my vision. How could you betray us? How could any of you do this to us?"

Ava swallowed hard, the lump in her throat suffocating. "We have a plan."

"I had another vision of you." Her voice dropped, chilling and final. "You're going to die."

The words struck Ava hard, reverberating in her chest. She'd known it. She'd felt it. But hearing it aloud made it real, a truth she couldn't escape. Her breath hitched. "I know."

"We're trying to find a way, so she doesn't," Thomas said. "We're going to fix this. All of it."

Moira shook her head. "Why would you side with the Cimmerians? Do you see what they do? Do you see what you've done? You're going to die because of it. Because you chose their side. I can't believe I ever thought you were a friend."

Ava's knees weakened.

"You're all cowards. You all let Aidan, Ronan, Sean die … for nothing."

"Please, Moira, let me explain everything," Thomas pleaded. The pain in his eyes was unmistakable, raw and exposed. Ava could see it—the anguish, the guilt, and something deeper. Love.

Moira's hardened expression faltered. The fire in her eyes dimmed, replaced by something softer. But it was gone as quickly as it appeared. She raised her hand and slapped Thomas hard across the face, the sharp crack echoing in the quiet hall.

Thomas didn't move. He didn't flinch. He stood there, head bowed, his cheek reddening as Moira glared at him, her chest heaving. But her hand trembled, and in her eyes, beneath the fury, was a flicker of pain—of love she couldn't quell.

Moira moved back, her fists clenched at her sides. "Start talking."

Walking out, she saw Melissa motioning to her she'd found Gabriel's cell. With a deep breath, Ava approached the cell with hesitant steps, her heart pounding against her ribs, certain it echoed off the cold stone walls. She hadn't seen Gabriel outside the torture chamber for weeks, and every moment without him had weighed on her like a stone. Her breath hitched as she peered through the small, barred window in the cell door. He lay on the floor, his bare, whip-marked back illuminated by the pale glow of moonlight streaming through the window high above. Every lash mark was a testament to her betrayal, every bruise an echo of her failure.

Her trembling hand pressed against the cold metal of the door. Part of her wanted to turn and run—to avoid the confrontation she knew was inevitable. But she couldn't. She owed him this. She owed him everything.

Melissa unlocked the door, her face unreadable as she gestured for Ava to step inside. Ava hesitated, her legs frozen in place until she forced herself to move forward, her guilt dragging behind her like chains.

Gabriel's head snapped up, his piercing blue eyes locking onto hers. Even dulled with exhaustion and pain, his gaze still burned with an intensity that made her stomach twist. He pushed himself upright, his muscles coiled, his movements sharp and defensive. "Get out," he growled.

Ava flinched at the raw anger in his tone. "Gabriel, it's me."

"I know exactly who you are," he spat. "What do you want? To finish what you started? Go ahead." He spread his arms wide, the gesture both a challenge and a resignation. "I'm already broken, Ava."

A stabbing pain shot through her chest. "I came to apologize. To explain."

He rose to his feet in one swift motion, his bare chest illuminated by the faint moonlight. His torn pants and dirt- and blood-streaked skin were almost too much for her to bear; seeing the man she loved reduced to this state was almost unbearable. He closed the distance with slow, deliberate steps, and she stumbled back, her breath catching as her spine collided with the cold wall. He towered over her—inescapable, overwhelming, a storm she couldn't outrun.

"You couldn't tell me?" he demanded, his voice cracking, raw with disbelief. "You couldn't trust me enough to let me in on your little plan?"

"It wasn't about trust—"

"Don't lie to me, Ava!" His palm slapped the wall beside her head. She flinched, but he didn't back away. "You didn't care enough to tell me. You didn't want us to face this together. Admit it. You think you're the only one who can fix this. You think you can save the world on your own."

"No. I care about you more than anything. I couldn't tell you because—"

"Because you didn't want me to stop you. You didn't trust me to stand by you, did you? You just decided for both of us. You always decide for everyone. You think you know best."

Tears blurred her vision. His closeness was a torment—a reminder of everything she'd shattered. The faint scent of juniper clung to him beneath the grime, igniting a longing so fierce it left her breathless.

Her trembling hands rose toward his face, but he seized her wrists in a vice-like grip, his touch rough and unyielding. "Don't fucking touch me."

"Please, I just want to heal you."

He released her wrists with a forceful shove, stepping back as if her very presence disgusted him. "You can't heal me. If you do, they'll know you were here. And you wouldn't want to disappoint *them*, would you?"

The bitterness in his voice sliced through her, but his words—despite the anger—still carried a thread of protection. Even now, he was shielding her. Tears slipped down her cheeks as she forced herself to speak. "I thought I was doing the right thing. I thought I was protecting you."

"You didn't protect me, Ava. You left me in the dark. Do you have any idea what this has done to me? To think you'd abandoned me, too? You used what I taught you against me. You—You didn't just betray me. You *used* me. The heart of stone, the mental defenses ... you twisted it all to hurt me."

"No! That's not true! I didn't use you. I would never—"

"No? Then what was it all for? Did you even care? Or was it a game to you? Were you just trying to learn how to shut me out? To manipulate me? Hell, was sleeping with me part of your strategy too?"

"No!" she gasped. "I loved you. I still love you. Everything we shared, every moment—it was real. It still is. I swear to you, Gabriel." His words devastated her. She hadn't prepared for this—for the idea that he'd think she had abandoned him. Of course, he would think that. How could he not? The realization crashed over her like a wave, leaving her breathless and trembling.

He let out a harsh breath, his jaw clenching as he turned away. His shoulders rose and fell with each labored breath. "But you didn't trust me," he whispered.

"Because I was afraid. I was afraid of losing you, of you getting hurt. And I thought if I carried the burden alone, it would keep you safe."

Gabriel's shoulders sagged, the fire in his eyes dimming to a smoldering ache. "You don't get it, do you? I was already yours to lose, Ava. All you had to do was trust me. I would've stood by you, no matter what. But you pushed me away."

The raw vulnerability in his voice shattered her composure. Tears streamed down her face as she tried to find the words to make him understand. "I never wanted you to think I abandoned you."

The silence between them was suffocating, filled only by the faint hum of the night air through the window.

"I don't know if I can ever trust you again."

Desperate to close the distance, she inched closer to him. "Gabriel, I'm here now, trying to make this right. Please, tell me how to fix it."

He looked away, his jaw tightening, his throat working as though swallowing words he wasn't sure he could say. "I don't know if you can." He turned back to her, his blue eyes burning with an anguish that made her chest ache.

"No, please—"

"You should go."

"Gabriel..."

"Go."

The finality in his tone cut deeper than any blade. Ava hesitated, her trembling hands falling to her sides as her vision blurred. She forced herself to turn, each step away from him feeling like a betrayal all over again. She paused at the door, gripping the cold metal frame for support, her breaths shallow and uneven.

"I never abandoned you," she whispered. She wasn't sure if he heard her or if it even mattered anymore.

As the door closed behind her with a hollow clang, she lingered in the corridor, her back pressed against the stone wall. Inside, she could hear the faint rustle of Gabriel shifting on the floor. His anguish pressed down on her like a vise. She squeezed her eyes shut, willing herself not to break down.

I'll fix this. I'll make it right. I don't care how long it takes.

The cold stone of the corridor seeped through her skin as she pushed off the wall and walked away, hating herself even more.

CHAPTER ELEVEN

APRIL IS THE CRUELEST MONTH

Sitting on the edge of her bed, Ava hugged her knees to her chest. She focused on her breathing. In. Out. Slow and deliberate. Yet, no matter how hard she tried, she couldn't silence the echoes of Gabriel's voice in her mind—the venom, the fury, the heartbreak. Every word he'd spoken replayed like a broken record, each one cutting deeper than the last.

I broke him.

She trembled, unable to make it stop. Her chest felt tight, her breath shallow and uneven. Nerves churned in her stomach, growing and twisting. She squeezed her knees tighter against her chest, as if the pressure could keep the wave of guilt at bay.

But the memory wouldn't fade. Gabriel, lying on the cold, unforgiving floor of his cell. His bare back marred with lash marks—marks she'd put there. But it was his eyes that haunted her the most. Hollow. Exhausted. Void of the light she used to find comfort in.

A sob clawed its way up her throat, and she bit down hard on her lip to stifle it. The metallic tang of blood grounded her.

Her gaze shifted to the candle on her nightstand. The tiny flame danced and swayed, mocking her with its warmth. She reached for it, gripping the cold brass holder as her fingers trembled. Bringing it close to her, she stared into the flickering light until her vision blurred, and the room seemed to fade.

Her mind betrayed her again. She saw the water whip in her hands, the crack of it striking Gabriel's back, the way his body jerked under the force. The image was too much.

Lowering her arm, she hovered it over the flame. The heat kissed her skin first, then seared. She gritted her teeth, refusing to move as pain lanced through her. Her breath came in brief gasps, her arm trembling as the flame licked her flesh. She removed it only when the burn became unbearable.

Ten lashes. Ten burns. She'd earned every single one.

Setting the candle down, she glanced at her bed, its soft blankets and inviting comfort feeling foreign—wrong. Gabriel was lying on stone, cold and in pain, and there she was, surrounded by ease. Her chest constricted, shame binding her heart.

Sliding off the bed, she knelt on the floor, the chill of the stone biting into her knees. Slowly, she stretched out, pressing her cheek against the rough surface. The cold seeped into her skin, wrapping around her like an unfeeling embrace. She closed her eyes, curling into herself.

If Gabriel has to endure it, so will I.

She ran her fingers along the uneven grooves of the stone, feeling every crack, every imperfection. It was a cruel contrast to the warmth of the mattress she had abandoned, but it felt right. Her body ached already, the cold digging deep into her bones, but she welcomed it. She deserved this penance.

Turning onto her side, Ava hugged her arms around herself. Her nails dug into her skin, sharp and punishing, as if the physical pain could drown out the ache in her chest.

You broke me.

Her breathing hitched, and she groped for the small vial on the nightstand. Tipping it to her lips, she let the bitter potion slide down her throat, its acrid taste clinging to her tongue. The potion wouldn't dull her emotions. It couldn't. But it would keep Havok out of her mind, protect her thoughts from his intrusion. Her connection to him still loomed—a chain she couldn't sever—but this small defense was all she had. She wiped her mouth with the back of her hand, setting the empty vial down as she lay back on the floor.

Her mind raced as the potion took hold. Could Havok still feel her guilt? Her pain? Could he see these moments of weakness, of grief, and use them against her? Would he know she had seen Gabriel, spoken to him, broken down in front of him?

The thought made her stomach churn.

She squeezed her eyes shut, but Gabriel's face was there again, his exhaustion, his anger, his misery. She hated herself more with every passing second.

Her mind raced. Could she see Gabriel again? Could she risk it? Klaus had said she only had an hour before. Maybe she could pretend to check on the prisoners, but Havok was too calculated for that excuse to work. He would see through it.

The weight of the decision crushed her, leaving her paralyzed on the cold stone floor. As the potion dulled the sharp edges of her emotions, she vowed one thing:

She would see Gabriel again. No matter the risk.

The cold stone walls of the hallway pressed in around Ava as she trudged back from training, her body aching from the day's brutal drills. The sting of bruises and the dull throb of exhaustion latched onto her, but her mind was elsewhere—still trapped in that cell with Gabriel. His hoarse accusations and the raw despair in his eyes replayed, a torment she couldn't escape.

I was already yours to lose.

The words echoed in her mind, cutting deeper with every step. She kept her pace even, her expression composed, but inside, her thoughts raged like a storm. Gabriel had been right. She'd made decisions without him, thinking it was for his sake.

She rounded a corner, her room just ahead, when the measured sound of boots behind her on stone made her pulse quicken.

"Ava," Xavier's smooth and confident voice came from behind her.

She turned slowly, schooling her face into a neutral expression. "What is it?"

His hands tucked into his pockets, but his dark eyes were searching. His casual stance belied the deliberate hunt of a predator circling its prey.

Careful, Ava thought, keeping her mask in place.

"You've been distant lately. Even for someone with no memories."

She shrugged, crossing her arms. "Maybe that's the problem. I don't remember who I am."

He tilted his head, a small smirk tugging at his lips. "Or maybe you're afraid to let anyone get close."

Is that what you think? Or what you want me to admit? "Is there a point to this?"

"Are you sleeping at all? Don't take this the wrong way, but ... you look..." He glanced down, almost sheepishly. "Kinda rough."

The concern in his tone almost caught her off guard. Almost. She allowed her shoulders to relax a little, letting her voice falter enough to keep the act believable. "I ... I have nightmares."

"What kind of nightmares?" He leaned in, his brow furrowed, his easy demeanor slipping into something more genuine—or at least, that's what he wanted her to think.

She bit her lip, hesitating as if unsure whether to share. "It's hard to explain. I see things ... memories that don't feel like mine. Sometimes I wake up forgetting where I am." She paused, studying his reaction. *Do you know what's happening to me, Xavier? Will you slip up if I keep pushing?*

He frowned, his jaw tightening for a fraction of a second before he looked away. "That's ... unusual." His voice was careful, measured. "I'm sorry you're going through that."

Liar. Ava tilted her head, her tone softening as she tried to coax more from him. "Do you know what it means? Could it be part of ... whatever they did to us?"

His gaze flicked back to her. His hand lifted as if to reach for her shoulder, but he dropped it before the gesture was complete. "I wish I could say."

"Don't tell me she's got you wrapped around her little finger." Eve narrowed her dark eyes as she approached. Her sleek ponytail swayed like a pendulum behind her.

Xavier muttered a curse under his breath, straightening as if preparing for battle. "Eve," he said dryly. "Always a pleasure."

Her lips curled into a feline smirk as her gaze flicked between them. "I can't believe you're into her. After everything she's done."

Ava stiffened, but forced her expression to remain neutral. "What are you talking about?"

"Nothing," Xavier said. "Eve's just—"

"Eve's just reminding you not to lose focus," she interrupted, her smirk widening. She turned her attention to Ava. "It's funny, isn't it? How some people can just forget everything they've done. Move on so easily. But then, I suppose forgetting is easier for some than others."

Ava's chest tightened, but she didn't rise to the bait. She couldn't. Instead, she forced a slight tilt of her head, feigning curiosity. "Are you always this cryptic or is today special?"

"Just a friendly warning," she purred. "Be careful whose trust you try to earn. Some of us don't forget so easily."

"Eve," Xavier snapped. "That's enough."

She turned to him, her eyes gleaming with challenge. "What? Afraid I'll say too much?" She leaned closer to Xavier. "Don't worry, I know the rules. I won't ruin your little crush."

The muscle in his jaw twitched. "Walk away. Now."

Eve held his glare for a moment longer and turned on her heel. As she passed Ava, she muttered loud enough for her to hear, "You'll never be good enough for him." Eve disappeared down the corridor, her sharp words lingering like a shadow.

"She's jealous," Xavier said after a beat, his tone light but strained. He turned back to Ava, his expression softening. "Don't let her get to you."

"Jealous of what?"

His smirk returned. "Of how much time I've been spending with you. Let me take you to dinner tonight. You look like you could use some fun."

Ava forced a small smile, keeping her tone light. "Rain check?"

"Just one dinner? You're really going to turn me down?"

Her heart pounded, but she shrugged. "Sure, but ... not tonight. I'm just not up for company."

Xavier hesitated. His gaze lingered, searching her face for something she wasn't willing to give. Finally, he nodded, though his expression tightened ever so slightly. "Fine. But don't keep me waiting too long." He turned, his movements casual, though she noticed the slight tension in his shoulders as he walked away.

As soon as he was out of sight, Ava let her mask slip. She exhaled, her shoulders sagging. *He's hiding something.* His charm, his concern—it all felt too deliberate, too staged. There was something bigger beneath the surface, something he didn't want her to see.

Eve is never going to let this go. Eve's spiteful words haunted her thoughts, a painful reminder of her loss.

Eve could love Gabriel freely, could be with him without the weight of impossible risks. But Ava couldn't. *Gabriel will never truly be mine.* The thought sliced through her, sharper than she wanted to admit. What if Gabriel went back to Eve?

She shook her head, forcing the fear aside. *No. I won't believe that.*

She had to see him again, had to fix what was broken between them. The uncertainty was unbearable. Every step down the dimly lit corridor felt heavier, her resolve pulling her forward.

Klaus. She needed him. Now.

Reaching his room, Ava rapped her knuckles against the wooden door.

The door creaked open, and Klaus's face appeared in the narrow gap, his sharp eyes narrowing with suspicion. "Ava, come in."

"I need your help." She walked inside smelling herbs and smoke and candlelight. Rows of vials, jars, and books cluttered every available surface. "What are you doing?"

Leaning against the doorframe, Klaus crossed his arms. "Experimenting. A book mentioned an elixir that could bring someone back to life."

"You found something?"

"I don't know. I'm still experimenting. What do you need help with? And why do I get the feeling I'm not going to like this?"

"I need to see Gabriel."

"Ava, no. You saw him last night. You can't risk it again."

"I have to. I have to try to make things right."

Klaus's long, calculating stare made her squirm. "You're not thinking clearly. You're letting your emotions take over, and that's a mistake. He won't be a prisoner forever."

"Don't talk to me about mistakes. I know what I'm risking. I know what I've already done. But I can't—I won't—just leave him like that. I can't go another day under this charade knowing he thinks I abandoned him."

He rubbed the bridge of his nose. "If you get caught—"

"I won't. I'll be careful. I'll go when the guards change shifts or when Havok and Xavier are distracted."

"And what happens if you're wrong? If they see you? If they figure out what you're doing? This isn't just about you, Ava. It's risking everyone."

"I know. But I have to try. Please, Klaus."

He studied her for a long moment. Finally, he let out a resigned sigh. "You're stubborn, you know that?"

She managed a faint smile. "Is that a yes?"

Klaus shook his head but walked over to his desk, pulling out a folded piece of parchment. He scribbled something and handed it to her. "This is the schedule for the guard shifts in the lower cells. The best window is after midnight. You'll have fifteen minutes, tops. Get in, get out, and for the love of everything, don't draw attention to yourself."

Ava gripped the parchment in her trembling hands. "Thank you, Klaus."

"Don't thank me. If you get caught, I will not back you. I cannot risk everyone else."

Nodding, she tucked the parchment into her pocket. As she turned to leave, Klaus's voice stopped her.

"Ava, be careful."

She glanced back at him. "I will."

And with that, she slipped out of his room and into the shadows, her heart pounding with anticipation—and fear.

CHAPTER TWELVE

ALIVE AND AWAKE

Hurrying toward Gabriel's cell, Ava's breath came in shallow bursts, her heart pounding like a drumbeat in her chest. The key Melissa had procured from a guard felt heavy in her hand, its cold metal biting into her palm.

Reaching the cell door, she paused, her trembling hand hovering over the lock. The corridor was silent, the kind of quiet that amplified her racing heartbeat. Her other hand pressed against the door, steadying herself. *Fifteen minutes. That's all I have.*

The key turned with a soft click, and she slipped inside. The dim moonlight filtering through the narrow window painted silver streaks across Gabriel's bare back. He lay on the floor, his breaths slow and shallow, the scars from her water whip stark against his skin.

"Gabriel," she whispered.

He stirred, his muscles tensing as he turned his head toward her. His crystal-blue eyes, hollow and rimmed with exhaustion, locked onto hers. "What are you doing here?" His voice was low, quiet, but carried a sharp edge.

"I had to see you again. I couldn't leave it like that."

Gabriel got to his feet, his expression guarded. "Ava ... this isn't safe."

Her throat tightened, but she forced herself to hold his gaze. "I know I can't undo what I've done. I know I've hurt you in ways I can't take back. But I couldn't let you think that I abandoned you. I never stopped loving you. Every lash, every time I drowned you—it was like cutting pieces of my soul. I thought if I could shoulder this alone, you wouldn't have to suffer more."

"You really think I wouldn't have chosen to suffer with you?" he asked, his tone softening. "You think I'd want you to carry all of this alone?"

"It's because I love you so much, and I didn't want you to get caught up in this. I thought ... I thought if we surrendered Havok would've let the rest of you go. I know how stupid and naïve it was to think that. But I had to try." She took a deep breath.

"You already had me, Ava."

"Let me finish. They think our memories were erased. They think we don't remember anything."

Gabriel stilled, his brows furrowed in confusion. "What are you talking about?"

"The day they took you away. Havok ordered Klaus to erase our minds. But Klaus didn't do it. He said we're the only ones who can stop Havok. He told us we had to pretend—to live like we'd forgotten everything, like the Elders kidnapped us. That's why we've been doing everything Havok asks. To gain his trust."

"Klaus didn't erase your memories?"

"No." She shifted closer. "We're still ourselves. We're trying to get close enough to Havok to take him down. We have to turn the Cimmerians against him. We have to make them see that they're fighting for nothing. But until then, we have to play our parts."

He rested his head against the wall. "Including torturing us."

"Yes. I turn off my emotions only so I can't break. Havok ... can't know. I didn't have a choice. I couldn't just walk away. Havok ... he's tied to me in ways I can't explain." Her voice cracked, her words spilling out in a frantic rush. "This isn't just about saving everyone else—I'm trapped, too."

"I know your mother promised your soul to him, but you aren't trapped, Ava. You don't have to do this alone. I've been telling you that over and over again. Why don't you believe me?"

Ava's breath hitched, her chest tightening as she hesitated. She couldn't tell him the truth of that promise. Not yet.

Biting her lip, she reached for him, and he let her touch his hand, but his hesitation made her heart fracture. "I'm so sorry, Gabriel. For all of it. I never wanted to hurt you. I love you. I wanted so much to stop and run to you, to tell you everything. I couldn't think of any of these things. I know you can't forgive me, but please don't hate me. I know I don't deserve you. But I need you."

His eyes, so often a calm sea of blue, were now a storm—waves of hurt, anger, and longing crashing against each other. "I'm pissed that you joined the Cimmerians because I don't want this place to take any more of you. Watching you become this ... this version of yourself?" He shook his head. "You've changed, Ava. And I don't want you to lose any more of yourself to this hell."

"I know I'm not as experienced as you are. But I'm trying." She covered her face with trembling hands, the tears falling harder as her body shook. "I hate what I've become. I hate this. But I'm doing everything I can to save us. I'm trying to do what's right."

She felt him draw closer, his warmth cutting through the cold of the cell. Gently, he took her hands from her face, his thumbs wiping away the tears tracing her cheeks. His touch was tentative, as though uncertain he had the right, yet it was enough to break the fragile dam holding her emotions in check.

His hands cradled her face, and their eyes locked. Even through the anger and betrayal, she saw the love that lingered.

"I never wanted to lose you," she whispered. "But I need you to trust me. Please."

Gabriel's breath hitched as his eyes softened. "I don't fully understand, but I trust you."

Ava's trembling hands hesitated above his face, her breath hitching as she debated whether she should even touch him. She could still feel the pain that had passed between them. But the way his shoulders slumped now, the way his jaw had stopped clenching, made her heart ache. Slowly, she let her fingers brush against his beard, coarse and familiar beneath her touch.

"I love you," she whispered. "I'm so sorry."

For a moment, he didn't move. The silence stretched between them, dense and unbearable, a thousand unanswered questions hanging in the air. *I've already lost him. My words will never be enough.*

But then he exhaled, a shuddering breath that seemed to tear through the tension. His gaze dropped to her lips, and her heart stumbled, skipping and stalling as if unsure how to keep beating.

His expression shifted—hesitation and longing colliding in his eyes. He raised his trembling hand and brushed his fingers against her cheek with a gentleness that unraveled her completely. She leaned into his touch, desperate, clinging to the fragile thread of connection she feared had already snapped.

Unspoken truths and hope and regret hung heavy in the air between them, causing a shimmer. He leaned in, a whispered question hanging between them. His lips grazed hers, soft and searching, and her breath caught, a sharp intake that left her dizzy. The second kiss was slower, deliberate, as though he were tracing every curve, committing her to memory.

Her chest cracked open, the tenderness in his touch spilling into the hollow spaces inside her. She couldn't hold it in anymore, couldn't stop the flood of emotions crashing through her. Her hands slid up his chest, her fingers clutching at him as though he were the only thing keeping her tethered to the ground.

And then his lips claimed hers with a new intensity, his kiss no longer a question but a declaration. Heat surged through her veins, electrifying every inch of her. Ava's hands flew to his face, her fingers tangling in his hair as his lips moved against hers with an urgency that stole the breath from her lungs.

The rough scrape of his beard sent shivers cascading down her spine, a delicious contrast to the softness of his mouth. She moaned, the sound swallowed by his kiss as his hands gripped her hips, firm and possessive, pulling her closer. The wall pressed into her back, but she barely felt it, too consumed by the searing heat of him.

"I love you, Ava." His voice was rough, sending warmth coursing through her.

His lips left a trail of fire along her jawline, down the curve of her neck, his breath hot against her skin. Each kiss sparked a jolt of electricity that left her gasping, her pulse racing beneath his touch. His hands slid lower, gripping her thighs with a surety that made her breath hitch. In one swift motion, he lifted her, and she wrapped her legs around his waist, their bodies aligning as though they'd been made for this—made for each other.

His touch grew urgent, almost frantic, his fingers digging into her hips, his body pressing against hers with a heat that obliterated the cold around them. Her hands roamed his shoulders, his chest, memorizing the hard lines of him as his lips found hers again.

She lost herself in him, in the storm of his touch and his kiss and the way he made her feel as though nothing else existed. She didn't want to think, didn't want to breathe anything that wasn't him. A desperation consumed her, and she wanted him—all of him.

"I missed you," he murmured. "I can't stop thinking about you."

Her hands tightened around him, her voice trembling as she choked out, "Me too. I hate this. I hate being apart from you." His hands slipped under her shirt, his touch warm against her skin, sending a rush of heat through her.

She gasped softly, leaning into him, craving the connection, the way he made everything else fall away. She allowed herself to believe this was real—that he still loved her, that he could forgive her.

But then he paused, his fingers brushing over the uneven texture on her arm. Panic shot through her as he stilled, his thumb tracing the rough marks with hesitant curiosity.

She tensed, her pulse pounding in her ears. *Please don't notice. Please don't ask.*

His hand shifted, pushing back the sleeve of her shirt. Her stomach dropped as the bruises and burns came into view. The dim light exposed the dark smudges and angry scars.

She froze, her breath catching as the warmth of the moment shattered. She didn't dare look at him, couldn't bear to see his expression.

He eased her to her feet. "Ava…" His voice was low, cautious, each word laced with quiet disbelief. "What is this?"

Shame and fear warred within her, twisting in her chest. She swallowed hard, wishing she could disappear, wishing he hadn't seen. She tugged the fabric down, but his eyes remained fixed on her arm. "It's nothing."

"It's not nothing." He caught her wrist before she could retreat, his grip firm but gentle. His blue eyes darkened with worry. "You're covered in burns."

"It's from training. It's normal."

Gabriel's jaw tensed as his eyes flicked to a faint bruise peeking out beneath her collar. His fingers grazed it, sending a shiver through her. "These aren't from training," he whispered. "Why aren't you healing yourself? You're not … eating either."

His intense stare made her want to crumble. She pulled her wrist free, hugging herself. "I—I forgot."

"Bullshit. Why are you punishing yourself?"

"Because I deserve it. After everything I've done—after what I've done to you—how can I not?"

He tilted her chin up with a gentle but firm touch, forcing her to meet his gaze. The intensity in his eyes made it impossible to look away. "Listen to me. Hurting yourself isn't going to make this better. It's not going to undo anything."

Tears blurred her vision as she shook her head. "You don't understand. I feel like I'm drowning, Gabriel. Every time I look at myself, I see what I've done. I can't make it stop."

His expression softened, the anger in his gaze giving way to raw pain. "You're not alone. You have me. Even after everything, you still have me. Even if I'm locked up."

Her tears spilled now, and she sagged against him, her head resting on his chest. The steady rhythm of his heartbeat was a small comfort, a reminder that he was still here, still alive. He embraced her as sobs wracked her body.

"I'll never stop loving you," he murmured into her hair. His hand moved in slow, soothing strokes along her back. "But you have to let me in. You have to let me help you."

"I'm trying. But it's so hard. It's so damn hard."

Gabriel pressed a kiss to the crown of her head as his hand lingered on her back. "We'll get through this. Together. Do you hear me?"

She nodded against him, her throat too tight to form words.

"Good." He pulled back slightly, his hands resting on her arms as he looked her in the eyes. "Now, heal yourself."

She shook her head, the tears still falling. "No. Not when you're like this."

"Ava…" Frustration crept into his words. "You can't keep doing this to yourself."

"*No.* We're in this together, which means I share your pain. I won't stand here healed while you're left like this."

"This isn't sharing pain. This is punishing yourself."

Her hands fisted against his chest. "I deserve it. Maybe I need to feel it, so I don't forget."

Gabriel let out a slow, measured breath, his grip on her arms softening. He leaned in, his forehead pressing against hers. "I won't let you destroy yourself. I can't. You can't save us if you don't save yourself. Heal yourself, Ava. Not for me—for you."

"I can't. I can't just make it go away."

He brushed her hair back from her face. "It's not about making it go away. It's about surviving this. And you're a fighter. Trust me, I've seen it."

"How much longer are you in here?"

"I don't know. But you shouldn't have come. You can't keep risking yourself like this."

"I know the risk. But you're worth it. I had to see you. I needed you to know that I love you and I'm so so sorry for betraying you. For torturing you. I hate myself for it."

Gabriel sighed, his hand sliding from her face to rest on her shoulder. "You made choices you thought you had to make. You hurt me, and I'm not talking about the torture. But the way you shut me out. If we're going to be together, we have to do this *together*. You and me. That's what love is, Ava. Standing together. Fighting together. Not shutting each other out."

"I know. I know I should have trusted you. I was afraid, Gabriel. Afraid of losing you. Afraid of what Havok would do if he knew how much you meant to me."

"Do you think I don't have the same fears? Ava, I love you. I will stand by you—if you let me. That won't change." He paused. "But I can't say I forgive the way you went about it. You didn't give me a choice. You didn't let me decide what risks I was willing to take."

Her chest constricted. "I'll make it right. I don't know how yet, but I will. I'll prove to you that you can trust me again."

He cupped her face in his hands. "It's not about proving anything, Ava. I trust you. I just don't trust the way you think you have to carry everything alone. I know your heart. And I know you're doing all this because you think it's the only way."

The lump in her throat grew, and fresh tears spilled down her cheeks. "I don't deserve you."

"You've got me anyway." His lips quirked into the faintest of smiles, though his eyes shone with unshed tears. "And you always will. We're together."

His kiss was both a soothing balm and a tender promise to her. She clung to him like he was her only tether to the world.

When the kiss broke, he rested his forehead against hers, his breath warm against her lips. "You can't come back here, Ava. It's too dangerous."

She hugged him, burying her face in his neck. "I love you."

"I love you too. Always."

Their lips met one last time, the kiss lingering, full of promises unspoken. "Go." His eyes betrayed his reluctance. "And heal yourself."

She nodded, and with a heavy heart, she rushed out of the cell, her vision blurred by tears. Even as she turned off her emotions, the feel of his kiss lingered on her lips, a reminder of what she was fighting for—and what she might never have again.

CHAPTER THIRTEEN

TYRANT

Two months had passed since Ava swore her allegiance to Havok. Two months of grueling training, endless torture, and sheer survival. The days blurred together in a haze of brutality and numbing exhaustion. It had been more than a week since she'd visited Gabriel in his cell, though she saw him during every torture session. Each glance, every fleeting moment their eyes met, twisted the knife of her guilt deeper, but she forced herself to bury it, to keep her emotions locked away. She had to. It was the only way to endure.

Every muscle in her body ached, and the air in the training pit was thick, as though it had absorbed every drop of blood, sweat, and despair spilled over the years. Thankfully, today's session didn't involve torture, just endless combat drills designed to push them to the edge of exhaustion.

Before dismissing them, Xavier moved to the center with his signature smug grin. "Listen up. The big Selection dinner is this Saturday. Attendance is mandatory. Dress your best—this isn't just dinner, it's your chance to prove you belong in his ranks."

Ava bit the inside of her cheek, resisting the urge to roll her eyes. *Dress your best? Really?* They were supposed to act like this was some glamorous awards banquet? A celebration of the noble feat of … what? Proving their worth through violence and cruelty? Perfecting the art of torment as if it were a sport?

Her stomach churned as she thought of the other trainees—how they puffed their chests with pride, eager to serve Havok. Couldn't they see what they were really doing? Couldn't they feel how wrong this all was? But if they grew up only knowing this life, she guessed they couldn't.

"Good job today, Ava." Xavier cut through her spiraling thoughts. His voice was closer than she expected, and she flinched.

"Thanks," she muttered, keeping her tone even. The last thing she needed was anyone noticing Xavier's attention. Her skin prickled with unease as she glanced at the few people remaining nearby.

He leaned closer. "So … I know we've been busy with training, but we haven't had a chance to go out on that date."

She stopped breathing. Had anyone heard that? She glanced around, her pulse quickening. She'd completely forgotten he ever mentioned it. "It's okay."

"I'd love to accompany you to the dinner. Although I have to assist Havok during the event, after that, I'm all yours."

She arched an eyebrow. "Is that your idea of asking me out?"

He laughed, rubbing the back of his neck. "Fair point. That was bad. Let me try again." He cleared his throat, his smile turning sheepish. "How about we spend some time together? I'll make it worth your while."

"Why don't we hang out after dinner?" she suggested. She refused to let him think she was flattered.

"Sounds good," he agreed, his grin returning. "But that won't count as our date."

Lucky me. Ava forced a polite smile, eager to steer the conversation elsewhere. "Where are we supposed to find clothes for this thing?"

"In the village. Or the city. If you'd like, I could take you shopping."

A chill ran through her, though she kept her face impassive. "How about I surprise you?"

His eyes lit up, and a slow, almost predatory smile spread across his face. "A surprise from you? Now that's something I'll look forward to." His gaze lingered on her longer than she was comfortable with. "I'm sure it'll be unforgettable."

Ava felt a pang of nausea, but hid it behind a strained smile. "Well, you'll just have to wait and see."

"I like surprises, Ava. Especially ones from someone like you."

Her pulse quickened, but not from flattery. His intensity was suffocating, and she fought the urge to step back. "Good to know."

"Just let whichever shop you choose know to put it on my tab. They won't ask questions."

His generosity, his charm—it all grated on her nerves. Where was this kindness when they first met? He'd been so cruel, manipulative, and condescending. Why had he suddenly changed when her mind was supposedly erased? Did he suspect something?

"Thanks," she said curtly, eager to escape. "I've got to go. I'll see you later."

He nodded, his gaze lingering as she turned and walked away. Ava's pulse raced, not from nerves but from the quiet fury simmering beneath her skin.

The Selection dinner loomed, a charade she had no choice but to participate in. And Xavier's persistence… She shoved the thought aside. There were bigger things to worry about—like how to keep the whole ruse from crumbling under her lies and growing guilt.

The cold stone hallway felt like it was closing in on Ava as someone called her name.

She stopped and turned around.

Eve approached, her movements precise and feline. Her sleek black ponytail swayed behind her, and her lips pressed into a thin, disapproving line. There was no friendliness in her sharp brown eyes, just an irritation that seemed as deeply rooted as her arrogance.

"What?" Ava asked.

Eve hesitated, rolling her eyes with a theatrical sigh before speaking. "I need your help." She spoke in a clipped voice, each word laced with reluctant admission.

Ava raised an eyebrow, the faintest smirk tugging at her lips. "Help? From me? That must've been hard to say. What's the favor?"

"Come with me."

"Sure. Not like I've got anything else on my agenda." Ava followed her.

The silence that stretched between them was suffocating, each step echoing against the stone walls. Ava's thoughts churned as they walked, her unease growing with every passing second. Every interaction with Eve felt like stepping into a den of vipers—dangerous and unpredictable. Memories of Eve flooded her mind—kissing Gabriel, spewing venomous words. Whatever this was, it wasn't going to end well.

Eve finally stopped at a door and hesitated, her fingers hovering over the handle. For a moment, her confident mask slipped. She bit her lip. "I came to you because you're the only one who can make his pain go away."

A knot formed in Ava's stomach. She knew, even before Eve opened the door. "Who?"

Eve pushed the door open and stepped inside. The room was warm, too warm, the air heavy with clove and something sickly sweet. Vanilla.

Ava's eyes landed on the couch, and her breath caught. Gabriel.

He lay sprawled on the velvet cushions, his shirtless body marred by angry lash marks, his skin streaked with dirt and grime. His bare feet hung limp over the edge of the couch. Even in the dim light, Ava could see the toll the punishment had taken on him—the way his shoulders sagged, the faint tremor in his hands. The sight of him sent a sharp ache through her chest, but she forced herself to appear indifferent.

"Fix him." Ava's blood boiled at the possessive way Eve knelt beside Gabriel. She wanted to tackle Eve as she combed through his hair, her touch tender and intimate. "He needs to heal."

Gabriel stirred under her touch, his jaw tightening. His eyes flicked to Ava, and for a fleeting moment, his mask slipped. In the depths of his crystal-blue gaze, she saw it—the love that still burned, buried under layers of pain and exhaustion.

But the moment passed, and his features hardened as he turned his gaze back to the ceiling, shutting her out.

"How did he even get here?" Ava's tone was icy. "He's a prisoner. I thought they weren't allowed in cozy little rooms like this."

Eve's eyes snapped to hers, her glare sharp enough to cut glass. "He's not a prisoner anymore. Havok released him this morning. He's one of us now. He's paid for what you all made him do."

"What?"

"Nothing," Eve said. She brushed her hand along Gabriel's jaw. "Havok gave me permission to bring him here. He's one of his best soldiers. And I outrank you, so if I say heal him, you heal him."

Ava crossed her arms. "If Havok wants me to heal him, he can ask me himself."

Eve shot to her feet, her fists clenched at her sides. "You're such a selfish bitch, keeping your gift to yourself. I love him, and he needs healing. Are you really so heartless?"

"Maybe I'm just not stupid enough to walk into an obvious trap. I'm not going to risk defying Havok because you're obsessed with him."

"You think you're clever, don't you? Acting like you belong here, like you're one of us. But you're not. And you never will be."

"That hurts so much," she said dryly.

"You think you can waltz in here and take everything you want. But I see through you. Gabriel might've been yours once, but not anymore. He's mine now."

The words struck a nerve. "If you're so sure, why are you so threatened by me?"

Gabriel shifted, and for a moment, his gaze locked with Ava's again. The faintest bit of amusement flashed in his eyes, as though he found Eve's jealousy ridiculous. But he schooled his expression, feigning indifference once more.

"You won't survive this," Eve hissed. "I'll make sure of it. I can get into your head, Ava. Make you dream things that will shatter your mind."

"I dare you. Just remember, I can attack without lifting a finger."

"Get out of my room," Eve spat.

With a slow, deliberate smile, Ava turned and strode to the door. "Pleasure as always." She left without looking back, but her heart was about to explode.

As she stepped into the hallway, Ava cast a final glance through the crack in the door. Gabriel's eyes were closed again, his body still, but his hand rested over the lash marks on his chest—the ones she'd put there. The sight made her stomach twist, and the guilt clawed at her insides. She wanted to push the door open, to rush back in and heal him. To shove Eve aside and hold him herself, where she knew he belonged.

But she couldn't. Not now. Not with Eve watching his every breath like a hawk, staking her claim on him as though he were a prize. The thought sent a ripple of fury through Ava's chest, but she buried it deep.

Her footsteps echoed in the corridor as she turned away. Yet, beneath the suffocating guilt, a small trace of relief broke through—Gabriel was no longer in that cell. The cold stone floor, the suffocating silence, the walls that seemed to close in on him with every passing second. He was free from that, even if only by degrees. The knowledge settled in her chest, a bittersweet balm to the ache she carried.

Still, the questions gnawed at her. How did Eve get him here? Had she used her influence, her rank, to pull strings? Had Havok really granted permission or was this another one of Eve's manipulations? Either way, it was calculated. And the way Eve had touched him, claimed him—it made Ava's blood simmer with anger she couldn't express.

As she neared her room, her hands curled into fists at her sides. *How am I supposed to keep this up?* The charade was suffocating her, each lie heavier than the last. It was like navigating a minefield, one wrong step away from disaster. And now, seeing Gabriel like that—broken, vulnerable, in the hands of someone else—it threatened to unravel her.

Once inside her room, she leaned against the door, squeezing her eyes shut, willing the tears to stay buried. *You can't break now. Not yet.*

Her gaze fell to the burn marks on her arm, the faint outlines of wounds she hadn't healed as a penance. Her fingers brushed over them, the sting keeping her emotions from boiling over.

A sharp knock on her door startled her. Ava wiped her face, forcing her expression into something neutral. She opened the door to see Melissa and Gillian standing there, their faces bright with excitement. But it wasn't their presence that stopped her breath—it was the figure lingering behind them.

Anais.

The sight of her, with her cold, assessing gaze and ever-present smirk, was like a bucket of ice water over Ava's spiraling emotions. Her heart lurched, the tears she'd been holding back freezing in their tracks. If Anais suspected anything, she would use it against her.

"Hey." Melissa gave her a curious look. "We're going dress shopping for the Selection. Come on."

"Dress shopping?" Ava hadn't set foot outside the castle since she arrived, and now they wanted to shop for dresses like everything was normal? Still, she nodded, her thoughts clouded. "Sure."

Melissa grabbed her arm, tugging her into the hallway. Leaving her room felt strange, like stepping out of a cage into unfamiliar freedom. The suffocating halls, so well-known yet oppressive, stretched toward the outside world. Ava glanced at Melissa, trying to decipher if her excitement was real or just another mask. She couldn't tell.

The castle gates emerged ahead, their dark iron twisted into menacing shapes. Beyond them lay freedom—or its cruel illusion. Ava's breath hitched as the gates creaked open, and the cool, salty air hit her face. She froze, overwhelmed by the rush of sensation: wind brushing her skin, the distant cries of seagulls, and the mingling scents of sea spray and damp earth. It was too much after two months of stone walls and stale air.

Melissa squeezed her arm. "You okay?"

"Fine," Ava lied, forcing herself forward. Her boots clicked against the cobblestone path as they stepped into the sunlight. She tilted her head back, letting its warmth soak into her skin. It felt foreign, like a dream she was barely holding onto. Her chest tightened as the bustling village came into view—the vibrant shopfronts, waves crashing in the distance.

But the beauty felt wrong. How could a place so picturesque exist in a place ruled by darkness?

"How do we pay for dresses?" Ava asked as they descended the winding path toward the village. "It's not like we have jobs."

Anais let out a sharp laugh, the sound cutting through the air like a blade. "Pay? We don't need to. Havok takes care of us—or at least, he makes sure we're fed, clothed, and armed. Everything else? That's up to us."

Anais smirked. "It means if you want something extra, you barter, you take, or you let the villagers grovel at your feet. They'll give you anything if they think it'll keep them safe."

Ava's stomach turned. "So … they're scared of us?"

"Of course they are." Anais shrugged as if it were the most obvious thing in the world. "We're Havok's chosen. They bow, scrape, and hand over whatever we want because they know the alternative isn't pretty. Enjoy it while it lasts. Once you fall out of favor, it's a different story."

"Then why aren't they in the army?" Ava gestured toward the villagers bustling about their day.

"Some flunked out of training. Some refused to fight. Havok doesn't waste resources on the weak. He wants the best. And apparently, he thinks that's you."

Ava didn't miss her bitterness. She swallowed hard and flicked her gaze toward the village. The cheerful shopfronts and colorful wares seemed to mock her, their brightness a stark contrast to the shadow she and the other Sentinels cast. *They're afraid of us.* The thought sat heavy in her chest, like a stone sinking deeper with each step.

She imagined the villagers handing over goods with trembling hands, their eyes wide with fear, praying they wouldn't be deemed "useless" by Havok's twisted standards. Was that why they barely looked at her? Why they seemed to avoid even glancing at the path where they walked?

This isn't respect—it's survival.

Her hands balled into fists. The weight of Havok's system was suffocating, but what stung most was her complicity in it. Even if she didn't demand tributes or revel in their fear, she still walked this path, wore this title, lived under the privilege Havok gave her.

How much of myself have I already lost to this place?

The wind carried the scent of salt and baked bread, but it only twisted her stomach further. Ava glanced at Anais, whose smirk seemed more bitter than cruel. How much of her sharpness was armor, forged by a system designed to pit them against each other? How much was survival?

Ava's gaze drifted to the distant docks, where boats danced with the tide. She wondered what it would feel like to step onto one of those boats and disappear—far, far away from there.

"How long have you been in Havok's army?" she asked Anais.

"Since I was thirteen."

"Your powers manifested that early?"

She shrugged. "Yeah. Guess you can call me a prodigy."

Damn. Ava couldn't imagine being in this role since she was thirteen. It was all the Sentinels knew. The villagers. Everyone in Caprington. Would they be able to convince any of them to rebel against Havok?

They walked inside a small store crammed with elegant gowns, their rich fabrics shimmering under the soft lighting. The smell of perfume and freshly pressed fabric, and the sheer volume of dresses overwhelmed Ava. She didn't belong there—not in this shop, not in this world.

"Look at this one!" Gillian squealed, holding up a violet ball gown that sparkled faintly. "It's perfect!"

Melissa clapped her hands. "You'll look amazing! I can already see it—you, with your hair up, maybe some gloves…"

Gillian's eyes lit up. "I've always wanted to wear fancy gloves. Like, really elegant ones."

Ava smiled faintly at Gillian's excitement, but it made her chest ache. Would this be the last time any of them got to feel normal? The last time they got to dress up, laugh, and pretend they were just regular girls? The thought sickened her. *For me, it's definitely the last time.*

Melissa held up a silky green dress, her face glowing with happiness. "What do you think?"

"It's perfect," Ava said.

"Ugh, I hate wearing dresses." Anais flipped through the rack, dismissing one dress after another with a frown.

"Me, too," Ava said. "How come you didn't go with Eve?"

Her eyebrows shot up. "We are not friends."

"Oh."

"Besides, now that Gabriel's back, she's obsessed. He's all she cares about."

"How long were they together before he deserted her?"

She shrugged. "I don't think they were ever *together* in the traditional sense. Maybe in the beginning. He doesn't love her, though. She's just ridiculously obsessive. Believes everything he says—like how the Elders kidnapped him and brainwashed him. Please. I don't buy it for a second."

"Why not? What do you think happened?"

"Because he was in love with—" Anais stopped abruptly, her gaze snapping to Ava's. The realization flickered in her eyes, like she'd said too much. "Nothing," she muttered, turning back to the rack. "I need to find a dress."

Ava's heart hammered against her ribs, every beat echoing the question she couldn't bring herself to ask. *Was Anais about to say me?*

She shook her head, forcing herself to focus on finding a dress. Grateful as she was for a sliver of normalcy, *dress shopping* wasn't exactly her idea of fun. She'd always hated shopping with Melissa and Gillian—couldn't she just wear jeans and a sweater?

The last time she'd worn a dress was that ridiculous Queen of Hearts outfit Melissa insisted on. She'd been mortified, certain everyone was laughing at her. But Gabriel ... Gabriel had convinced her she needed a night of fun.

It was the first time he'd ever called her beautiful.

Taking a deep breath, she pushed the memory deep down. She scanned the racks half-heartedly, her fingers brushing against soft silks and shimmering satins that all seemed wrong. Then, out of the corner of her eye, she saw it—a light blue gown, its delicate fabric almost the exact color of Gabriel's eyes. Her breath caught as she lifted it off the rack. It was strapless, form-fitting, and impossibly elegant.

Back in her room, Ava hung the dress outside her closet door. Candlelight glinted on the shimmering fabric, a beauty that only intensified her sorrow. She stared at it for a long moment, her mind drifting.

She closed her eyes and let herself imagine—wearing the dress, Gabriel by her side in a crisp suit, his hand on hers as they danced under the stars. A normal life. A normal night. A future they could never have.

A tear slipped down her cheek, and she buried her face in the pillow, clinging to the fantasy even as reality loomed like a storm cloud.

And then a knock came.

CHAPTER FOURTEEN

FRACTURE

Ava froze, her pulse quickening. She thought of ignoring it, but the knock came again—firmer, more insistent.

"Open up, Ava." Xavier's voice, calm yet commanding, sent a ripple of unease through her.

She exhaled and crossed the room, opening the door.

Xavier's dark eyes scanned her with a blink of something she couldn't quite place. Concern? Caution? "Havok wants to see you," he said flatly.

"What for?"

He shrugged, but the gesture was too casual, too practiced. "He didn't say." Moving aside, he gestured for her to follow.

A feeling of dread overcame her as she stepped into the shadowed hallway. Every step dragged her closer to some inevitable reckoning.

This has to be about Eve. The thought tightened like a noose around her mind. What had Eve told him? Would Havok even care if the truth was twisted? He was the kind of man who enforced loyalty with precision, and she'd crossed a line.

When they reached Havok's chamber, Xavier pushed open the heavy door, his expression neutral but his eyes lingering on her as she passed. "Good luck," he murmured, so softly she almost missed it.

The door shut behind her, cutting off her escape.

Havok's chambers were expansive, the glass walls allowing light to pour in and offering an unbroken view of the surrounding landscape. The openness was startling, a stark contrast to the cold, enclosed spaces Ava had grown used to. Heavy, velvet drapes hung in the corners, their rich colors adding to the room's ambiance, while a crackling brazier cast a warm glow. Havok sat in a high-backed chair at the far end, his posture relaxed, as though he belonged in this serene space. His fingers drummed against the armrest, his face calm, almost inviting.

That calm terrified her more than rage ever could.

"Ava," Havok said. "Come closer."

Her legs felt heavy, but she forced them to move, stopping a few paces from him. She stood straight with a neutral face, though her heart thundered like a drumbeat in her ears.

"I understand there was some confusion earlier. He watched her, his dark, unblinking eyes sharp and dissecting. "Eve seemed ... upset. Said you refused to heal someone very important to me."

She chose her words carefully. "I didn't realize it was an order."

Havok chuckled, a low sound that sent a shiver down her spine. "Eve is a trusted lieutenant. When she gives an instruction, it is not a suggestion. Do you understand?"

"Yes."

"Good. Because Gabriel is one of my finest soldiers, and I expect him to remain useful. You will heal him. Immediately."

Ava's breath caught at Havok's words. For a fleeting moment, relief washed over her—Gabriel would be healed. She could ease his suffering. But just as quickly, she forced the feeling down, burying it deep beneath the mask she wore. She couldn't let Havok see or feel her.

"Of course." She kept her eyes fixed just below his, not daring to meet his sharp gaze.

Havok leaned back, his expression softening into a faint smile. "And Ava," he added, his voice dropping to a silken whisper, "the next time a lieutenant asks something of you, you will do it without question. I do not tolerate insubordination. Are we clear?"

"Yes, Havok."

"Excellent." He waved a dismissive hand, as if her presence no longer mattered. "You're dismissed."

Ava turned to leave, but before she could reach the door, her vision blurred.

The world shifted, the firelight of Havok's chamber dimming to a cold, pale glow. A sudden chill permeated the air around her. When her vision cleared, she wasn't in the hallway anymore.

She was in a different room—a memory, vivid and overbearing.

Lucinda.

Her mother stood before Havok, younger but unmistakable. Her auburn hair framed her face, loose and untamed, her eyes blazing with defiance.

"I won't do it," Lucinda said. "This is cruel, even for you."

Havok circled her like a predator sizing up its prey. His dark eyes gleamed with amusement, his lips curling into a mocking smile. "Cruelty is subjective, Lucinda. I asked for loyalty, not morality."

She crossed her arms. "I'm not your pawn. And I won't be part of this."

Ava's heart pounded as she watched the memory unfold. She wanted to scream at her mother, to tell her to stop, to beg her to comply. But the image played on.

Havok's calm facade cracked, his smile sharpening into something dangerous. "You think you're above consequences, Lucinda? Above me?"

The vision blurred again, and Ava found herself back in the hallway, her heart racing.

"Ava?" Xavier's voice snapped her back, and he touched her arm lightly. "You okay? You look like you've seen a ghost."

She blinked several times, struggling to steady her breathing. "I'm fine. I just ... I'm fine."

Xavier studied her for a moment longer, his brow furrowing. "If you say so. Eve's room is this way."

She nodded, and her legs moved on autopilot. Her mother's defiance, and Havok's malice filled her thoughts. She couldn't shake the feeling that history was repeating itself.

Xavier left her at Eve's door, and Ava hesitated, her hand hovering over the handle. With a shaky breath, she braced herself.

Don't break. It's just another task. Nothing personal.

But it *was* personal. And she hated that Eve knew it.

The door creaked open before Ava even knocked. Eve leaned against the frame, her smirk as sharp as the edge of a blade. Her dark ponytail gleamed in the dim light. "Took you long enough."

Ava glared at her. "I came as soon as Havok ordered."

"Of course you did. After all, it's not like you had much of a choice."

Ava stepped into the room, the warmth hitting her like a wall. Vanilla and clove clung to the air, its cloying scent at odds with the sight that met her eyes.

Gabriel still lay on the couch, his breathing shallow but steady. His blue eyes fluttered open at the sound of their voices, locking onto hers for the briefest moment. The look he gave her was fleeting, but it was enough—enough to make her heart clench and her stomach twist. Recognition, relief, love. And yet, it was gone too soon, masked behind a guarded expression.

Eve crossed to Gabriel and brushed his hair. "Sweetheart, the Healer is here."

"Let's get this over with." Ava forced her voice to stay cold as she walked closer.

Eve lingered nearby, crossing her arms. "Careful. He's delicate right now. Wouldn't want you to break him any more than you already have."

Ava knelt beside Gabriel, her jaw tightening at Eve's words. Her breath caught as Gabriel's eyes met hers, softer now, speaking words he couldn't say aloud.

I'm here, his gaze told her. *I'm okay.*

She summoned her water, the cool, shimmering liquid curling around her fingers. It spread across Gabriel's chest, cascading over the angry bruises and raw lash marks. The tension in his body eased under her touch, his breathing evening out, but her pulse raced with every second her hands remained on his skin.

Eve's voice shattered the moment like glass. "Don't tell me you're struggling. Surely the great Ava can manage something as simple as this."

She snapped her head toward Eve. "If you want this done properly, stop hovering. Either leave or stand quietly in the corner."

"Oh, I think I'll stay right here. It's fascinating, watching you work. You're so ... invested."

Gabriel's fingers twitched beneath Ava's hand, a subtle squeeze that steadied her fraying nerves. *Ignore her. Just focus.*

Ava drew in a breath and turned her attention back to him. The water glided over his ribs, and the lash marks faded. Her hand drifted lower, brushing against the faint bruising along his hip. The heat from his body seeped through her, igniting memories she couldn't afford to indulge.

Gabriel stiffened, his gaze meeting hers, and for a heartbeat, the air between them crackled. She couldn't look away, couldn't ignore the magnetic pull that threatened to shatter her focus. Her fingers faltered for just a second, and the memory surged forward unbidden—the feel of his skin beneath her hands, his breath against her cheek, the moment when—

"You're taking your sweet time. Is there some reason you're being so ... thorough?"

"Do you want him healed or not?"

"Just don't take all day."

Ava pressed her lips together, forcing the anger into submission. "Turn over," she said softly to Gabriel. "I need to see your back."

He moved, his muscles flexing as he pushed himself up and flipped onto his stomach. His hand, dangling off the couch, skimming her knee, the contact brief but searing, leaving her skin tingling where it touched.

Her hands hovered over his back as the water swirled to life once more, erasing the deep gashes she had inflicted. Every movement was deliberate, her fingers grazing his shoulder blades as she worked, her touch betraying a tenderness she couldn't suppress.

His arm shifted again, grazing her thigh. Her breath hitched. The sensation burned through her like fire, and she bit the inside of her cheek, struggling to stay focused.

The last of the wounds closed under her hand, the scars disappearing as if they had never existed. Gabriel's body finally relaxed. For the first time in weeks, he looked at peace.

Ava pulled back, the water in her hand fading as exhaustion tugged at her edges. She stood, her legs unsteady beneath her. "There. He's healed."

Eve wasted no time. She moved to Gabriel's side, her fingers brushing through his hair with infuriating familiarity. "Do you feel better?"

Gabriel nodded, and as Eve hugged him, his gaze flicked to Ava one last time, filled with gratitude, longing, and something deeper—something that made Ava's chest tighten.

"I'm so glad you're okay." Eve leaned down and pressed a kiss to his forehead.

Ava's breath snagged in her throat, and she tore her gaze away. She moved toward the door, each step slow, deliberate, as if something was trying to drag her back. *Don't turn around.*

The door closed behind her with a thud, and she let out a shaky breath, her hands trembling at her sides. Gabriel was healed. He was safe.

Pulling the water from within her, she let it glide over her skin, erasing the bruises, burns, and cuts she had carried for weeks—marks left by training, and by her own hand.

Not until he's healed. That had been her promise. And now, with every wound she closed, a quiet resolve settled in her chest.

As the last mark faded, Ava exhaled a ragged breath, the weight of it all pressing down on her. Gabriel was safe, but the battle wasn't over—not for either of them.

CHAPTER FIFTEEN

THE SELECTION

After a week of staring at the blue dress, Ava finally slipped it on. The silky fabric skimmed her skin, cool and weightless, as though it didn't exist. She caught her reflection in the mirror and stilled. For a moment, she didn't recognize the woman looking back at her. The light blue dress molded her figure, the color reminding her of Gabriel's eyes. She had pulled her copper hair up, except for a single curled strand framing her face. She almost looked ... beautiful.

The fantasy came rushing in: Gabriel beside her, dressed to match, his hand on her waist as they danced at prom—or some other event where love wasn't a secret, where she didn't have to pretend he didn't exist. The ache in her chest deepened, sharp and insistent. She shook the thought away, tearing her gaze from the woman in the mirror.

She turned for the door but froze mid-step. A strange sensation rippled through her, like the world was slipping out from under her feet. Her body felt distant, disconnected, and then it wasn't hers anymore. Her hand wasn't hers—it was larger, calloused, and strong. The room dissolved in a flash of golden light, and panic bloomed in her chest.

What's happening to me? Ava thought, her heart racing as the unfamiliar sensation intensified. She stumbled, clutching at the doorframe, but there was nothing solid left to hold on to. The floor seemed to vanish beneath her, and her mind was no longer her own. She wasn't Ava.

She was Havok.

He stared into the mirror, adjusting his tie. He was ready for the Selection, but his mind went back to that day. The day he married his beloved.

His heart raced as he looked into Lenorah's eyes—clear, bright, and filled with a love so pure it stole his breath. The sunlight filtering through the trees cast a golden glow over her, making her appear almost otherworldly. Her hand in his felt steady, even as emotion swelled in his chest, thick and unrelenting. Ava could feel it all: his awe, his joy, the way the moment stretched, perfect and whole.

Lenorah spoke her vows in a soft but unwavering voice, her words resonating through him as though etched into his soul. When it was his turn, his voice trembled, raw and exposed, every syllable a declaration of his devotion. The faint scent of pear from her hair mixed with the aroma of fresh blossoms carried by the breeze. There was only her, his sweet Lenorah, and the promise that she was his, and he was hers, forever.

The intensity of Corbin's emotions—*her* emotions—made Ava's chest tighten as the memory consumed her. She wasn't just seeing it; she *was* him. The overwhelming love, the fragile hope, and impending loss tore her apart. *What is this? Am I seeing Havok's memories?*

The vision faded, leaving her breathless and trembling in the center of her room, clutching at her chest as if to keep her heart from shattering.

Taking a deep breath, Ava opened the door and stepped into the hallway, feeling off. The soft click of her heels against the stone floors felt foreign, too delicate for a place like Caprington. All she saw was Lenorah's face. Who was she? Had Havok been in love?

As she neared the Great Hall, voices echoed through the corridor. She squared her shoulders, her fingers brushing against the smooth fabric of her dress for reassurance. When she stepped through the arched entrance, the room's grandeur hit her all at once.

Crystal chandeliers hung above, casting a soft golden light over the crowd. The clinking of glasses and bursts of laughter filled the air. The hall was alive with movement and color—dresses of every shade swirling around as people found their seats. Ava hesitated, suddenly feeling too exposed.

"You look beautiful," came a voice behind her.

Thomas had pulled his strawberry blond hair into a neat ponytail, and he wore a black suit that made him look far more polished than she was used to.

"Thanks." She offered a small smile. "You don't look bad yourself, handsome."

"Appreciate it." His smile faded as he added, "Wish Moira was here."

"I know."

They walked together toward a table, but Thomas hesitated mid-step. "Did you see him?"

"Who?"

Thomas gave her a knowing look.

He's here?

Her heart raced as she scanned the room. She spotted Gabriel, and the sight knocked the breath out of her.

He looked breathtaking. His tailored black suit showed off his broad shoulders and lean frame, exuding quiet strength. He transformed his usually rugged appearance: his clean-shaved face revealing sharp jaw angles, and combed his dark hair, although one lock fell rebelliously across his forehead. He looked almost regal, but the raw intensity in his blue eyes reminded her he was anything but tame.

And then, as though sensing her presence, his head lifted. Their eyes met.

The hum of conversation dulled to a faint buzz, and the candlelight softened, casting everything in a hazy glow. For a heartbeat, the world was only him and her. She felt the weight of his gaze as it roamed over her—slowly, deliberately—taking in every detail. Heat crept up her neck as his eyes lingered, and she became acutely aware of the curve of her shoulders in the delicate blue fabric, the way the dress clung to her figure, and the fiery strand of hair curling against her cheek.

His eyes burned with something that sent a shiver racing down her spine. It wasn't just admiration—it was hunger, longing, and an unspoken claim that made her knees unstable. For a moment, his jaw tightened, and his lips parted, as if he might speak, but he didn't. The heat in his gaze was undeniable, searing into her, making her pulse quicken.

She couldn't look away, couldn't move. Her heart hammered against her ribs, and she felt exposed in a way that wasn't unwelcome. Although his expression gave nothing away, his eyes revealed his true feelings. Beneath the restraint was the man she knew—the one who loved her with a depth that both thrilled and terrified her.

Then, as if the spell broke, Gabriel blinked and turned his attention to the woman next to him. Eve.

She was saying something, her hand resting on his arm. The corner of his mouth lifted in a faint, practiced smile.

A sharp pain stabbed Ava's chest. The noise of the hall returned in a rush, the laughter and clinking of glasses cutting through the moment like a blade.

Thomas grabbed her elbow, steadying her as he guided her to a seat. "Keep walking," he whispered. "You're staring."

Ava tore her gaze away, her cheeks burning. Thomas pulled out her chair, and she sat down, positioning herself so her back was to Gabriel. Her hands trembled as she rested them in her lap.

"It'll be okay," Thomas whispered again. "He's not a prisoner anymore."

That was one thing she could be happy about. Yet, the sight of Eve's hand trailing down Gabriel's back as she leaned close to him overshadowed everything else. Ava swallowed hard, forcing herself to focus on Thomas. "Thanks."

"I thought for so long we'd get to dress up like this for prom." Thomas rested his elbows on the table.

"I know."

"Remember sophomore year? Homecoming dance?"

Ava smiled faintly. "Yeah. You were the homecoming king, and Nicole was queen. You wore that stupid crown all night."

"That crown was awesome. It was like a real king's crown."

"Sure, it was," she teased. "I always hated those dances."

"Maybe, but we still had fun."

"Yeah. We did."

Melissa, Lance, Link, and Nicole joined them at the table, each dressed to perfection. Melissa's shamrock-green dress complemented her golden waves, while Nicole's white satin gown glowed under the warm light. Lance and Link looked dashing. Gillian walked in her violet ball gown with Jeremy escorting her. Eric entered wearing a black tux.

Lance smiled at Ava. "You look beautiful."

"Thanks."

Nicole leaned over. "That dress is stunning on you."

Ava returned the compliment, but her thoughts drifted again to Gabriel. She caught another glimpse of him over her shoulder—his easy smile, the way Eve leaned in as if she owned him. It made her sick to her stomach.

"Stop staring," Thomas mumbled under his breath, his elbow nudging hers.

Sighing, Ava turned back and stared at her empty plate. Wanting to sit beside Gabriel, to touch him, to kiss him, was a dangerous fantasy she couldn't afford.

The chatter in the hall quieted as Havok entered, flanked by Xavier, Sorcha, Kira, and Maggie. Havok's presence dominated the room as he scanned the crowd. Beside him, Sorcha strutted in a short black dress, while Maggie's crimson gown was equally eye-catching. Xavier, dressed in a black suit, looked every bit the smug commander, his expression sharp as his gaze swept over the tables.

Ava kept her head down, her hands gripping her lap beneath the table. The dinner had begun, and the night stretched out before her—an orchestrated game she couldn't escape.

The tantalizing aroma of roasted meats and herbs wafted through the air as servers in crisp white uniforms began placing plates before them. Ava barely tasted the first bite, her thoughts consumed by the man sitting only a few tables away. A man she couldn't look at, couldn't touch, couldn't claim.

She forced herself to take another bite, ignoring the lump in her throat as the sound of Gabriel's laughter reached her ears.

After the last plates had been cleared and the wine glasses refilled, Havok stood from his place at the head of the table. The room fell silent almost instantly, all eyes on him as he surveyed the hall with an expression of quiet triumph. "Congratulations," he said, his smile sharp as a blade. The smile repulsed Ava. "You've all passed your training, and I'm pleased to announce your assignments."

Ava's fingers curled into her lap, her knuckles white against her dress. *Was he serious?* She swallowed hard. Who in their right mind would celebrate passing that *training*? But the crowd erupted into applause, and she forced herself to join in, clapping with enough enthusiasm to blend in. The sound reverberated around her like a dull roar, every cheer another nail in her resolve to maintain the charade.

Havok raised a hand to quiet the room, his gaze sweeping across the sea of eager faces. "First, let me say I am eager to see how well you all perform in your new roles. As I call your names, please come forward."

Ava's breath hitched as she straightened in her seat. The knot in her stomach twisted tighter with every passing second.

"For the Onyx Order, my primary army," Havok announced with pride. "Melissa Rollins."

Melissa scooted her chair back with practiced ease, standing tall as though she'd been born for this moment. Her emerald dress shimmered in the candlelight as she strode to the front.

"Jeremy Stahl," Havok continued.

Jeremy moved to the front with measured steps, his broad shoulders straight, his topaz eyes scanning the crowd like a soldier taking stock of his battlefield.

"Ava Hannigan."

Her heart leapt into her throat, and the applause dimmed to a dull hum. *You knew this was coming. Act normal. Breathe.* Forcing her legs to move, she stood and made her way to the front. Her heels clicked against the polished stone floor. She kept her chin up, her gaze skimming over the faces in the crowd—until it landed on Gabriel.

Her pulse quickened. His gaze was fixed on her; the intensity in his eyes sent a flush through her. She looked away, focusing on the floor, the chandeliers, the back of a chair.

Havok continued calling names. "Gillian Madison. Thomas Arrington. Lance Reid." Polite applause greeted each name, but Ava couldn't help noticing the murmurs rippling through the crowd. She caught snippets of their whispers—the skepticism, the resentment. "Two months of training? Are they serious?" "Ridiculous. They're not ready."

The words made her blood simmer. Didn't they see how powerful the Elementals were? Didn't they realize what they were capable of? But she buried her anger, keeping her expression calm and neutral.

"Link Harris. Nicole Eckrich." When Havok called out the final names, Eve Samaris and Anais Kovalevsky, the applause swelled. Both women rose with practiced grace. Eve cast a smug glance in Ava's direction and took her place near the center. Anais, as stoic and unreadable as ever, moved without a word.

"And, of course," Havok said, "you will all be led by Xavier."

Xavier stood, his all-black suit absorbing the light like a void. He inclined his head, his smirk faint but unmistakable.

Havok clapped his hands once, and the sound echoed like a gavel striking wood. "Your job will be to annihilate the Ephemerals and recruit new members to our cause. Show the world what true power looks like."

A chill ran down Ava's spine at his words, but she kept her gaze steady, her mask in place.

Havok shifted his attention to the next group. "As for the Nighwardens, my bodyguards. Maggie Zhang. Sorcha Draycott. Peter McNabb. Katarina Obolensky. Eric Cadogan. Benjamin Kessler. And Kira Wei." Each name drew scattered applause as they stood, their expressions guarded.

Ava's heart sank. *Not Eric.* Peter. Katarina. Eric. People she trusted, people she relied on. Now relegated to roles that would keep them out of her reach. *How am I supposed to do this without them?* She glanced at Eric, his face stoic, but his eyes carried a defiance that gave her a sliver of hope.

"And for the Blood Vanguard, my recruiters," Havok continued, his smile sharpening, "Donovan Hargrove. Zeke Lockwood. Mallory Winslow. And, of course, their leader— Gabriel DaCosta."

The room erupted into applause as Gabriel rose from his seat, his proud smile a carefully constructed facade. Ava's heart twisted as he approached the front, his every movement measured and precise. He looked every inch the commander Havok wanted him to be, but she knew better. She saw the way his hand clenched at his side, the tightness in his jaw.

When the applause subsided, Havok raised his hand. "And now, I would like to invite you all next door to continue the celebration."

The tall doors swung open, revealing a grand ballroom bathed in golden light. A live orchestra began playing, the melody light and airy, as though this were a simple celebration and not a gathering of war-bound soldiers.

Ava followed the others into the ballroom, her dress brushing against her legs with every step. The grandeur of the room was overwhelming—the gilded walls, the sparkling chandeliers, the polished marble floor. But all Ava could feel was Havok's words, the heaviness of the forced roles they had to accept.

She cast a glance at Gabriel, his face half-hidden in the shadows of the room. Their eyes met, and in that moment, she saw the truth behind his mask. They were both playing a dangerous game.

As the orchestra swelled, Havok's voice echoed in her mind. *"You are mine now."*

And for the first time, Ava wondered if she would ever escape.

The clink of crystal glasses and the lilting strains of the orchestra were distant echoes in Ava's ears as she drifted toward the shadowed edges of the Great Hall. The light of the chandeliers above cast golden halos over the swirling couples on the dance floor. She tried to melt into the backdrop, desperate to avoid attention, but the sight of Xavier weaving through the crowd toward her shattered that hope.

Her stomach coiled with frustration. *Of course, he had to find her.* She forced a smile, slipping on her mask of naivety. *Play the part. Be convincing.*

Xavier's smirk was slight, but his dark eyes gleamed with amusement as he stopped before her. "Congratulations," he said smoothly, as if the evening were some grand achievement.

She tilted her head, returning his polite smile. "Thank you."

"You look stunning tonight."

Ava glanced at the blue fabric clinging to her figure and shrugged. "Thanks. You clean up pretty well yourself."

He gave a nonchalant shrug. "I'm ready to get out of these clothes."

His hand brushed hers, a light, almost accidental touch, but it sent a jolt through her like she'd touched a live wire. She yanked her hand back, the revulsion sharp and immediate. He raised an eyebrow at her reaction, and Ava, gritting her teeth, forced herself to lower her hand back to her side. When his fingers slid between hers, she wanted to scream. His grip was cold, clammy, and yet oddly soft—an infuriating contradiction.

Ava's gaze darted upward, landing on the balcony where Havok loomed like a shadow, his sharp eyes surveying the room. She saw his bodyguards leave his side and join the crowd below, their movements deliberate and watchful. The sight made her shoulders tighten.

"What else is there to do here besides drinking and pretending this is normal?" she asked, her voice laced with feigned innocence. Her mind raced, hoping to keep Xavier's attention focused on conversation and away from the growing heat in her chest every time she saw Gabriel.

"This is our life," Xavier replied simply. "The army is our privilege. Protecting Caprington is our purpose."

"Protect it from what? Aren't the bad guys locked up?"

Xavier frowned, glancing away. "From the Ephemerals."

Ava had to bite back a laugh. The thought of these savage, powerful Cimmerians fearing Ephemerals was almost comical. "Do they attack us often?"

"They've taken enough from us."

"Your parents?"

"Yes," he said stiffly. "And yours too."

Her blood ran cold, fury flashing through her veins. *How dare he say that?* Her father had been an Ephemeral. But she smothered the anger, pulling her mask tighter. "Why don't I remember?"

"Your mind has been through a lot." Xavier frowned. "Some things ... had to be erased." The orchestra struck up a waltz, and his smile returned. "Would you like to dance?"

"I don't know this dance," she said flatly, hoping her irritation wasn't too obvious.

"It's easy." He offered his hand. "Just follow my lead."

Reluctantly, she allowed him to guide her to the dance floor. His hand pressed against the small of her back, pulling her closer than she wanted. Ava hated how his gaze lingered on her face, his movements precise and confident as he led her across the polished floor. Around them, couples twirled and laughed, oblivious to the icy battle waging inside her.

His smirk returned. "You look distracted. Not enjoying yourself?"

She forced a polite laugh. "I am."

Her gaze flicked past Xavier's shoulder, and her breath caught. *Gabriel.* But it wasn't just his appearance—it was the way he moved with Eve in his arms, spinning her effortlessly.

"What's up with him?" Ava asked, trying to sound casual.

"Who, Gabriel?"

"Yeah. He was a prisoner, right? How does he end up in Havok's army?"

Xavier's hand tensed a little against hers. "He's finished his punishment."

"So now he gets promoted? Seems unfair."

"He's earned it. He's one of our best recruiters. It's good to have him back. The Elders took him too and brainwashed him. But Klaus altered his mem—" Xavier's words cut off, his throat bobbing as he swallowed. He cleared his throat and looked away.

"What?"

"Nothing."

Her heart raced. *Had Klaus really erased Gabriel's memories?* The idea burrowed deep, cold and cruel, twisting in her gut. Was that why he seemed to fit in so easily now? But then she remembered the way he had looked at her in Eve's room— not the indifferent gaze of a man who had forgotten, but one filled with emotion, raw and unspoken. Could it have been her imagination?

"Did they erase his mind?" she whispered in his ear.

"I can't talk about it. And you shouldn't ask questions."

"What makes him so privileged?"

"I wasn't born when he was at his peak. But I've heard nothing but good things. They say he recruited some of our best soldiers."

"Eve seems happy."

He shrugged, rolling his eyes. "Yeah, they're like a thing or something. She's obsessed with him."

"Oh." Ava feigned indifference, but the word sat heavy on her tongue, leaving a bitter aftertaste.

"We're about to switch partners, okay?"

"What do I do?" she asked, trying to mask the nerves fluttering in her chest.

He smiled. "Just follow along. You'll be fine."

Dancers swirled, the room spinning as couples exchanged partners in a choreographed move. Ava turned—and found herself face-to-face with Gabriel. Her breath caught, her chest tightening as his hands found hers, pulling her close. The heat of his palm against hers sparked a shiver, and the air thrummed with a tension that no amount of pretense could mask.

His hand settled at her lower back, firm but careful, and her cheeks warmed under his intense gaze. Her heart pounded, a frantic rhythm that matched the music but felt far too personal. She looked everywhere but at him, her eyes darting to the chandeliers, the sweeping dresses of the other dancers, but the pull of his presence was impossible to resist.

Gabriel spun them, guiding her through the crowd as though they were the only two people in the room. He moved with such fluid confidence, drawing Ava into his orbit, unable to pull away even if she'd wanted to. The scent of juniper and fresh water clung to him, familiar and intoxicating, stirring memories she couldn't afford to relive. Ava's fingers curled against his shoulder, her grip tightening as though holding on would keep her from falling apart.

"You look..." Gabriel's voice was low, rough, the words slipping past his restraint. His gaze swept over her. "You look breathtaking."

The raw emotion in his tone cracked something in her. He hadn't forgotten. Not even a little.

Heat flushed through her. She struggled to keep her composure steady, as though her heart wasn't threatening to break free from her chest. "I see you're done with your punishment," she said, her tone clipped, her words deliberate.

"Yes." His hand flexed at her back, his thumb brushing against her dress, sending an involuntary shiver up her spine. "You know he can't hear us."

"He can read thoughts."

"You'll know when he's trying." His gaze burned through her.

From the corner of her eye, she caught Peter's steady, knowing gaze across the room. He gave her the faintest nod, a subtle reassurance that loosened something in her chest. For a fleeting moment, she allowed herself to drop the mask.

"I love you," she whispered, her voice so soft it was almost drowned out by the music. She didn't dare look at him as the words slipped.

Gabriel's hand tightened over hers, his thumb brushing her knuckles in response. "I love you. This is absolute agony."

"What? Did I not heal you properly?"

His lips quirked into the faintest smile as he leaned in, his breath brushing against her ear. "That isn't what's agonizing me, and you know it." His rough tone sent a rush of warmth through her that she couldn't contain. "I hate this. Watching you pretend not to know me. Pretending I don't want to—" He stopped himself, as though holding back a tidal wave of emotion.

"Pretending you don't want to what?"

His hand slid lower on her back, his fingers caressing the curve of her waist. "I want to rip that dress off you."

Her cheeks flushed, her body betraying her as a warmth spread through her. Her fingers gripped his shoulder, and she leaned into his chest, as though being closer might quiet the storm building between them. "You can't say things like that."

"I can't stop thinking it," he murmured, his lips brushing her ear. "You're driving me insane."

The music shifted, signaling the next partner switch, and Gabriel's hold lingered for a moment longer than it should have. Then she was swept back into Xavier's arms, the warmth of Gabriel's touch replaced by Xavier's cold, detached grip. It was like plunging into icy water after standing in the sun, and the contrast stole her breath in the worst way.

"Are you okay?" Xavier's dark eyes searched hers. "Did he say anything to you?"

"No. He just said my dress was pretty."

Xavier studied her for a moment, then nodded, his grip softening. "If you want, we can stop dancing."

Ava forced a small smile. "No, it's fine. I don't want to dance with anyone else."

The words made his expression brighten. He smiled back, boyish and sincere. "If you dance with me, I promise we won't switch partners again."

She wanted to escape, to flee to the solitude of her room and let herself crumble, but she couldn't falter. Not yet. "Okay," she whispered, letting him take her hand once more.

The music swelled, and they moved together, but Ava's mind drifted back to Gabriel. His warmth, his words, the way his eyes had burned with something she didn't dare name. It was all a cruel reminder of what she couldn't have—and what she was willing to fight to protect.

CHAPTER SIXTEEN

STOLEN KISSES

The Selection had left Ava feeling hollow. She'd endured the laughter, the dancing, and the forced smiles, but they had only deepened the void inside her. The quiet of her room was both a solace and a stark reminder of her solitude. As she closed the door, her eyes caught a small piece of parchment lying inside the threshold.

Her heart skipped a beat as she bent to pick it up, her fingers trembling. The paper felt rough and crumpled, and the ink was dark, rushed, yet unmistakable.

Grasshopper, meet me at the cove near the eastern cliffs. Midnight.

The breath caught in her throat. *Gabriel.* Only he called her that. But was it really him? Could she trust this? Her mind raced, doubts warring with the aching hope blooming in her chest. The handwriting was his, but asking her to meet outside the castle—so risky, so reckless—was unlike him. Yet the thought of seeing him, of being near him, pushed her doubts aside.

With a racing heart, she draped a black cloak over her dress. The fabric of the cloak felt heavy, like the weight of the choices she'd made. She glided through the castle corridors like a shadow. As she went outside, the cool night air and the scent of the ocean greeted her.

The path to the cove was narrow and winding, illuminated only by the pale silver of the moon. Waves crashed against the rocks below, their rhythm steady yet powerful. The climb down to the beach was treacherous, the jagged rocks slick with mist.

When she reached the sand, the sound of the ocean engulfed her. The moonlight painted the cove in an ethereal glow, the white-capped waves sparkling like shards of glass. She spotted him—a lone figure near the water's edge, his dark cloak rippling in the wind. His back was to her, but she knew it was him. She could feel it in her bones.

"Gabriel," she whispered.

He turned, and her heart clenched at the sight of his face. The moonlight caught his features—his crystal-blue eyes, the sharp lines of his jaw, the way his hair curled in the damp air. His expression softened as he saw her, his shoulders relaxing.

For a moment, they stood there, the space between them charged with unspoken words.

"You're here," he whispered. "You're really here."

"How ... how do I know it's really you?"

"The Cliffs of Dover. Lighthollow. The first time..." His voice broke, and he closed the distance between them in three quick strides, his arms wrapping around her.

Ava clung to him, her fingers gripping his cloak as though he might disappear if she let go. She pulled back enough to look into his eyes. "Why did you ask me to meet you here? It's dangerous."

"Because I needed to see you. Away from them. Away from all of it. I needed to remind myself that this isn't all a lie. That we're still us."

"Gabriel, I——"

"No apologies. I told you, I forgave you. But this..." He gestured around them. "This moment is all I wanted. Just us."

"I hate this place. I hate what it's doing to us."

"So do I." He brushed a stray curl from her face. "But for now, we survive. Together." His fingers lingered against her cheek. She closed her eyes, leaning into his touch. When she opened them, he was studying her, his gaze intense and unwavering.

"You're still the most beautiful thing I've ever seen."

Her breath hitched. "I don't deserve you."

His hand cupped her face, his thumb tracing the curve of her cheekbone. "You deserve everything, Ava. Don't let anyone make you think otherwise."

The world seemed to hold its breath as he leaned in, his lips brushing hers. Ocean salt permeated the air, mixing with the warmth of his breath. The moment ignited something deep within her, a fire that had been smoldering under everything they'd endured.

His hands slid from her waist to the curve of her back, pulling her closer, as if proximity alone could shield her from the world. The crashing waves faded into a distant murmur, eclipsed by the wild, uneven rhythm of their breaths. His lips met hers with a desperation that tore through her. It wasn't just a kiss. It was every unspoken word, every stolen glance, every aching second they'd spent apart. His kiss carried a longing so raw, and she clutched his shirt as if afraid he might vanish again.

The smooth stone wall pressed against her back as Gabriel's gaze burned into hers, stripped bare of pretense. "Ava," he whispered, her name trembling on his lips like a prayer, reverent and broken. "You undo me."

Her fingers grazed over the stubble on his jawline. "You have no idea what you do to me."

His eyes searched hers, and for a fleeting moment, hesitation wavered there, so fragile it made her chest tighten. "We don't have much time," he murmured, his voice rough but soft at the edges. "But I need this. I need you."

Her pulse thundered a frantic rhythm against her ribs as her hands slid up his chest, her palms pressing against the heat of his taut muscles. "I'm yours."

The kiss deepened, slower now, like they were trying to piece themselves back together after months of being torn apart. His hands traced her back, her sides, her stomach. Her cloak slipped from her shoulders, pooling at her feet, but the cool night air couldn't reach her—not when his touch burned like fire against her skin.

Lifting the hem of her dress, he brushed the bare skin of her thigh, trailing upward with an aching tenderness that left her breathless.

"Gabriel," she whispered. "I want you."

He kissed her again; the intensity reigniting like a flame catching in the wind. His touch grew bolder, his hands mapping every curve as though she were something sacred. In his arms, she felt more than wanted—she felt seen, whole, as though she was not a pawn in someone else's game, but the only thing that mattered in his world.

"Wait," he murmured, stepping back just enough to pull off his cloak. He spread it over the sand as though creating a space that belonged only to them.

Her heart thundered as she sank onto the makeshift bed, her breaths uneven, anticipation threading through her veins.

Gabriel slipped off his pants, his gaze never leaving hers, and when he lowered himself above her, his tenderness stole what little breath she had left.

The cove wrapped them in its shadows, creating a world that felt separate from the chaos outside.

The press of his lips was slower now, as if each kiss held a thousand words he couldn't say. His fingers tangled in her hair, his touch soft and steady, even as the heat between them grew, threatening to burn everything else away.

She tasted the briny mist on his skin. A deep groan escaped his lips, making her shiver. His hands roamed her body with a tenderness that ignited something raw and uncontainable within her. She arched into him, her body responding to his with an urgency she couldn't suppress, and for the first time in months, she felt whole—as if every fractured piece of her was finally falling into place.

Time dissolved, the world narrowing to them, to the quiet exchange of gasps and whispers, to the ache and solace they found in each other's arms. It wasn't just desire—it was desperation, love, and something deeper, something defiant against the chaos that threatened to pull them apart.

Gabriel's breath came in ragged bursts as he pressed his forehead to hers. "I love you, Ava."

"I love you."

They lay twisted together, his cloak beneath them, the cool air brushing against her flushed skin. His arms stayed around her, his hand smoothing over her hair as their breaths slowed in unison.

"I thought I'd forgotten what this felt like," she whispered. "To be safe."

"You are." His eyes burned with intensity. "You're safe with me. Always. You're the only thing holding me together."

"I am?"

He tilted his head, skimming his nose against hers. "You know you are. Why do you act surprised?"

"Because you're you. And I'm..." She hesitated, searching for the words. "I'm just me."

Frustration crossed his eyes before it softened into something more tender. "And that's supposed to mean what?"

"I don't know. I can't believe I'm the one you've chosen to love."

A shadow of vulnerability passed over his features, replaced by a lust that made her pulse race. His blue eyes darkened, his voice dropping to a husky murmur. "Believe it. You're the only one for me, Ava. I've always wanted someone like you, but I never found it. Don't ever doubt my love for you. I mean it—every word. You are my soul mate."

As he leaned in, her breath caught, their lips meeting in a tender kiss that felt like a vow. She could taste the salt of the sea mingled with his warmth, a combination as intoxicating as it was comforting.

"I didn't get to rip your dress off," he murmured.

She laughed, a genuine, unguarded sound that surprised even her. When was the last time she had laughed like this? "One day." But reality reminded her of the truth she could no longer keep from him. No more secrets. They were in this together.

Untangling herself from his arms, she sat up and leaned against the cool, jagged surface of the cove wall. "Gabriel..."

He furrowed his brow, concern shadowing his face as he moved to sit beside her, his hand seeking hers. "What is it?" His thumb brushed over her knuckles.

She squeezed his hand. "You said we're in this together. And I believe that. But I have to tell you something ... something I should have told you sooner."

The concern in his eyes deepened as he leaned closer. "Ava, whatever it is, just tell me."

Taking a shaky breath, she closed her eyes for a moment to steady herself. "My mom didn't just promise my soul to Havok. She linked our souls."

Gabriel froze, his eyes widening as the words sank in. "What? What does that mean?"

"It means..." She swallowed hard. "It means that whatever happens to Havok happens to me. If he dies, I die."

The air stilled around them, the rhythmic crashing of the waves becoming distant and muffled. Gabriel's face darkened, his features tightening as fury and fear battled for dominance. "How is that possible?"

"When she promised my soul to him, a spell was put in place. It linked us. When I went to the Necromancer, I set the curse in motion. And when I initiated into his coven, binding myself to him, it strengthened the connection." She hesitated, the words sticking in her throat. "Lately ... lately I've been seeing things. His memories."

"His memories? What kind of memories?"

"At least I think that's what they are. I keep seeing my mom, but through his eyes. It's like I'm watching her ... the way he watched her."

He swore under his breath, his hand raking through his hair. "Have you told anyone else?"

"Klaus told me the truth after we arrived. Everyone knows," she admitted. "Link said he'd try to find a way to break it, but Klaus was clear: only an Elder with immense power can undo it. And the Elders who might be able to—Aaron, Gustav—they're locked up. Maggie..." She trailed off. "Maggie's a Nighwarden."

He cursed again, his face pale as he met her gaze. "Ava, we will fix this. You will not die because of him."

Tears spilled down her cheeks as she shook her head. "It's my fault. I went to the Necromancer ... I started this."

"No. This isn't your fault. Havok and your mother did this—not you. And I promise you, Ava, we'll figure it out. I'm not losing you."

A small, hiccupped sob escaped her lips as his words broke through her defenses. "I have to act like I hate you."

"I know."

"If I don't—if I slip, even for a second—they'll know. Havok will know. I can't risk them seeing what's between us."

Gabriel's hand slid to cradle her face, his touch gentle but firm. "Ava, I don't care what they see. I don't care what they think. I care about you. And I'll endure whatever it takes as long as it means keeping you safe."

Her shoulders shook as she clutched his shirt, her fingers twisting in the fabric. "I hate this," she choked out. "Pretending. Watching you with Eve. Acting like I don't feel anything for you. It's killing me."

His hand tilted her chin up, forcing her to meet his gaze. "I know. It's killing me, too. But we survive this—together.

Even if we have to lie to everyone else, we don't lie to each other."

Ava nodded, the knot in her chest loosening slightly under his unwavering gaze. "I'll survive this if I know you're with me. But ... how many moments like this do we get?"

His forehead rested against hers. "Not enough. But I'll steal every single one I can."

The thought of Gabriel slipping back into Havok's world sent a shiver of dread through her. "How did you even get away from Eve tonight?"

"I took her to her room, acted like I was heading to mine, then left the note at your door. She thinks I went out for a drink."

Ava hesitated, her emotions bubbling to the surface. "How far would she take things with you?"

He froze for a moment, his grip tightening around her. "Ava..."

"I need to know." Pulling back, she met his gaze. "She's always hovering around you, touching you, looking at you like..." Her voice faltered before she forced it steady. "Like she's waiting for something. She loves you. Everyone sees it."

"Eve is possessive, and she's dangerous. But I'm not hers. I never have been."

Her heart ached at his words, even as they brought relief. "But would she try? I mean ... has she ever?"

He sighed, regret flickering in his eyes. "A long time ago. But it meant nothing, Ava. Not then, and definitely not now. Whatever Eve thinks she had, it was never real."

"She still thinks she owns you."

"She doesn't." He grazed her chin with his fingers, lifting her face to his. "She never did. And I'll make sure she knows that. But I can't risk exposing you and me. I have to let her believe what she wants, as long as it keeps her from suspecting the truth. If she thinks for a second, I love you, she could hurt you."

"What if she tries? If you turn her down, what would she do?"

"I'll handle Eve. Whatever it takes, I'll protect you. Always." He pulled her back into his arms, cradling her.

Ava closed her eyes, allowing herself this one stolen moment. For now, there was no Havok, no Eve, no soul-binding curse. Just Gabriel—his warmth, his scent of juniper and clean water, and the quiet promise that tethered them to each other despite everything.

"We should go," he whispered, his reluctance heavy in the still air. The words hung between them like a lingering shadow neither wanted to acknowledge. "You leave first." His thumb brushed against her cheek as he cupped her face. "I'll wait a few minutes before heading back. I need to see you safe."

He helped her to her feet, his hands lingering at her sides as if reluctant to let go. He wrapped her cloak around her shoulders, his fingers brushing her skin like a memory he was afraid to lose. Then he kissed her again, soft, deliberate, as though trying to seal the moment in his mind. "No matter what it looks like out there," he murmured against her lips. "I'm yours, Ava. Always."

"I know." She hesitated at the edge of the cove, turning to look back at him one last time, memorizing every detail of his silhouette against the moonlit waves.

As she stepped onto the rocky path, the night's chill seeped through her cloak, and a mix of hope and dread weighed on her chest. How many more stolen moments like this could they have before the world they lived in tore them apart? She tightened the fabric around her, as though it could protect her from the cold reality waiting beyond the cove.

CHAPTER SEVENTEEN
WICKED GAME

Ava woke before the sun, the faint light of dawn filtering through the heavy drapes of her room. The quiet hum of the castle was unsettling, the stillness too fragile, like the calm before a storm. Her fingers brushed the edge of her cloak, still damp from the midnight air, and her thoughts drifted back to Gabriel.

The memory of his gentle touch, his whispered promises still warm on her skin, lingered like a soothing balm against the storm of chaos, but it wasn't enough to quell the icy dread coiling in her stomach. They had shared something real, something sacred, but the world beyond that cove remained unchanged—dark, relentless, and heartless.

She got up and pulled on a black shirt, leggings, and boots. Taking a deep breath, she drank a potion for the day.

The merciless sun cast sharp shadows across the rocky path toward the training grounds. It was different, and at least they would be outside instead of in that oppressive pit. All she could think about was Gabriel. And the fact that they still had made zero progress in creating an army or getting any Cimmerians on their side. But how could they convince them? The Cimmerians lived this life. They were born into it. It was all they knew. She didn't know how long it would take for them to trust her enough, or any of the Elementals, for them to switch sides.

She buried her feelings and put on her mask. She hated the emptiness of it. Hated how exhausted it made her.

Training took place on the outside grounds instead of the pit. Melissa, Lance, Thomas, and Anais were already there.

"Morning, Sunshine." Thomas smiled.

She forced a small smirk. "Don't call me that."

"Why not? You look like you're glowing." His lips twitched with a hint of a smile. His eyes, however, carried a weight that only she could catch.

"Sure. Radiant as ever."

"Congrats on being part of the Onyx Order," Anais told Ava.

"Thanks."

"Xavier's giving us our first mission today," Anais said.

"Do you know what it is?" Melissa asked.

She shook her head. "I'm just as much in the dark as you."

More soldiers trickled in, including Gabriel and Eve. Ava forced her gaze away, her heart tightening in her chest. She could feel his eyes on her, but she didn't dare look back. Not with Eve trailing so close to him, her laughter grating like nails on glass.

The grounds buzzed with a low hum of conversation, the scrape of boots on dirt, and the clash of steel from a nearby sparring match. Ava adjusted her gloves, trying to ground herself in the motions, but her thoughts betrayed her, spiraling back to last night and the way Gabriel had held her.

Xavier's commanding voice echoed, snapping their attention forward. "Pair up." He seemed angry about something. Or stressed. Ava couldn't tell. "Today's focus is precision. No hesitation. No mercy. I want to see how far you've come."

The tension in the pit thickened as soldiers and Elementals alike fell into line. Ava joined them, her expression unreadable. As she took her place, her gaze drifted once more to Gabriel, standing across the pit beside Eve. She quickly looked away, masking the storm brewing within her.

"Ava, you're with Gabriel." Xavier's smirk was sharp, his eyes gleaming with a sadistic satisfaction.

Her heart skipped a beat.

Gabriel faced her, his posture calm and collected. To anyone watching, he was just another soldier obeying orders, his face a mask of indifference. But Ava knew him too well. The faint clench of his jaw, the flicker of something unreadable in his eyes—he was every bit as aware of their situation as she was.

She met his gaze, her eyes narrowing with feigned disdain. *You have to believe he's your enemy, she told herself. Hate him. Sell the performance.*

Gabriel's lips curved into the faintest smirk, one only she would notice. "Try not to embarrass yourself."

"Don't worry. I won't."

"Begin!" Xavier barked, and the training grounds erupted into chaos.

The air between them crackled as they circled each other. Gabriel moved like a predator, his steps deliberate, his gaze locked onto hers. Every nerve in Ava's body was alight, every muscle tense, but not from fear. His closeness made her feel raw, exposed in a way she couldn't afford to show.

She struck first, a sharp arc of water slicing toward him, but Gabriel teleported in an instant, her attack hitting empty space. He reappeared behind her, his shoulder slamming into her back with controlled force. She stumbled forward, catching herself spinning just in time to send another jet of water at him.

He dodged, closing the distance between them in a flash. His arm snaked around her neck in a mock chokehold, his breath warm against her ear. "You'll have to do better than that," he murmured, his voice low, teasing.

Heat surged through her, sharp and unwelcome, but undeniable. For a moment, she could feel the strength of him, the way his body molded against hers. Her breath hitched, but she forced herself to twist out of his grasp, grabbing his arm and freezing it with water.

"Not bad," Gabriel said, smirking as the ice crept up his wrist. He yanked free, the ice shattering like glass. He teleported again, his leg sweeping out and knocking her down.

She hit the dirt hard, pain shooting through her ribs. But she didn't stay down. She rolled, her water lashing out that struck his face. Gabriel froze for a heartbeat, droplets of icy water dripping from his hair. His expression glimmered— amusement, surprise, and something else, something darker.

"That all you've got?" he taunted, his voice loud enough for the onlookers to hear, though the smirk tugging at his lips was meant for her alone.

"Not even close," she snapped, her chest heaving.

The fight escalated, every clash a mix of precision and raw emotion. His hand brushed her shoulder as he teleported behind her, the touch brief but scorching, and when he spun her to face him, his grip was firm but almost gentle.

"Come on, Grasshopper," he murmured so low only she could hear. "You can do better."

Her cheeks burned, her chest tightening with emotions she couldn't name. The nickname hit her like a spark, igniting a dangerous fire within her. She shoved him back with a burst of water, her limbs trembling with the effort to keep her composure.

To the others, it looked like hatred. But for her, every strike, every touch was a confession—a silent reminder of everything they couldn't say.

The crowd murmured, the intensity of their battle drawing attention. Her heart pounded, her limbs burning as they fought on, a deadly, intricate dance. She caught glimpses of Xavier watching with a twisted approval, his arms crossed, his gaze sharp.

Finally, Xavier's sharp voice rang out. "Enough!"

Both of them froze, their breaths coming in ragged gasps. Gabriel's hand dropped to his side, but not before his fingers brushed hers—a fleeting, forbidden touch that sent her pulse racing. He stepped back, his face blank.

Xavier strode forward, his expression one of approval. "Impressive. Both of you." His gaze lingered on Ava, his smirk deepening. "Maybe you're not as soft as I thought."

"Guess not."

Gabriel walked away, his shoulders stiff, his posture perfect. To everyone else, he looked detached. But Ava knew the truth. She had felt it in every touch, every move.

"Good," Xavier said. "You'll need every ounce of that skill for your next mission."

The murmurs grew louder, uncertainty spreading through the group.

Xavier's smile didn't falter. "Tomorrow, we're taking the fight not to the Ephemerals, but to our own deserters." He paused, letting his words settle over the group. "A village to the east. There are those who once called themselves loyal to Havok but chose cowardice instead. Our task is simple: bring them back—or eliminate them. Completely."

Ava's stomach dropped. Her blood felt like ice coursing through her veins. She fought to keep her expression neutral, but Xavier's words threatened to crack her mask.

"They are not just deserters," Xavier continued, his gaze sweeping over them. "They're traitors. Betrayers of everything we stand for. And their families have harbored them, fed their rebellion. If these deserters refuse to return, then you will deal with them and their families accordingly."

Melissa stood beside Ava, her stoic mask slipping enough for Ava to catch the flicker of fear in her green eyes. Thomas clenched his fists so tightly that his knuckles turned white.

Eve stepped forward, her lips curling into an intimidating smile. "Finally, we get to show them what we're made of."

Xavier pulled out a folded piece of parchment and held it up. "The deserters' names are here. Memorize them. Simon Calder. Moriah Vasquez. Elias Lorne. Gabriel will escort any who willingly submits back to Caprington. But if they resist, they die—and so do their families."

Ava's throat tightened, a lump forming that she couldn't swallow. Her mind reeled as she tried to process the cruelty of the mission. Killing deserters was one thing, but wiping out entire families? It was more than monstrous—it was calculated annihilation.

"I'll be going, along with the Elementals, and I'll need Anais, Eve, and..." Xavier's gaze roamed lazily over the crowd.

Hands shot into the air, as if he were picking a dodgeball team instead of a death squad.

Ava suppressed a shiver at their eagerness, the hollowness in their eyes chilling her.

"Link." His lips twisted into a satisfied smile. "That should do it." His sharp gaze landed on Ava. "I trust you won't disappoint. I expect to see you prove your worth tomorrow."

Xavier's eyes narrowed, then flicked to the rest of the group. "We leave at tomorrow at dusk. Prepare yourselves. This is your first true test of loyalty, and there's no room for weakness." He strode past them and made his way back to the castle.

Ava's gaze darted to Gabriel. His shoulders were tense, his jaw tight, but his eyes—when they met hers—were heavy with understanding. He knew. He always knew.

Melissa exhaled beside her. "How can we do this?"

Thomas's fists remained clenched. "We don't have much of a choice."

A crushing sense of their impossible mission bore down on Ava and the others. For now, they had to pretend. They had to endure.

As the group dispersed, Ava lingered, her thoughts a storm of doubt and dread. Tomorrow, they would be expected to commit atrocities. And somehow, she had to survive it— without losing the last fragments of herself.

Ava tossed and turned in her bed, Havok's orders for tomorrow's mission replaying in her mind. Sleep refused to come. The expected mission clawed at her chest, leaving her breathless and restless.

Unable to stay confined in her room, she threw on clothes and slipped out into the darkened corridors. The stone walls felt colder at night, the air heavy with an eerie stillness broken only by the faint drip of water somewhere deep in the castle's bowels.

Her feet carried her to the training pits. She didn't expect anyone to be there; it was well past midnight. Yet, as she approached the open space, the faint sound of movement—precise, deliberate—stopped her in her tracks.

Gabriel.

He stood shirtless in the center of the pit, his body illuminated by the dim torchlight. His fists moved with lethal precision, punching and striking the air in a blur of controlled power. Each strike was purposeful, as though he were trying to dismantle something invisible—or keep something darker at bay. The muscles in his back rippled with each movement, his skin slick with sweat that glinted in the light. His breath was steady, controlled, a stark contrast to the storm she felt brewing inside her.

"Can't sleep either?" she asked, stepping into the pit.

Gabriel froze mid-punch, his head snapping toward her. For a moment, his guarded expression faltered, replaced by something raw, unspoken. Then he straightened, his fists lowering as he met her gaze. "Ava, what are you doing here?"

"Same as you. Trying to clear my head."

He nodded once, his shoulders relaxing. "It's not going to get any easier. Tomorrow ... it's going to test you."

She moved closer. "It's already testing me. I don't know if I can do it. What Havok's asking—it's not who I am."

"You have to be someone else, Ava. For now. Play the part, survive, and we'll figure out the rest."

"How do you do it? How do you live with it?"

He took a step closer, close enough that she could feel the heat radiating off him. "I focus on what I'm fighting for. Who I'm fighting for. You don't lose yourself, Ava. Not as long as you hold onto what matters."

"What if I already feel lost?"

Gabriel reached out, brushing a stray strand of hair from her face. His hand lingered, his thumb grazing her cheek. "Then I'll find you."

Ava leaned into his touch. Every part of her wanted to collapse into him, to let the storm raging inside her melt away in the warmth of his arms.

Her gaze fell to his lips, and the urge to close the distance, to lose herself in him even for a fleeting moment, burned fiercely. It would be so easy—so dangerous—but so utterly worth it.

Gabriel's hand lingered for a heartbeat longer, his fingers trembling as if he felt the same pull. His gaze softened, longing breaking through his composed exterior. But then, as though some invisible force yanked him back to reality, he stepped away, his hand falling to his side.

The fragile moment shattered, leaving an ache in its wake. The absence of his touch felt like a sharp, cold wind. She straightened, forcing herself to breathe, to mask the disappointment threatening to spill from her eyes.

"We can't," he murmured. The words sounded as though they pained him as much as they did her.

"I know." Every fiber of her being screamed for her to defy those words.

Gabriel let out a sharp exhale, as if steadying himself. "Come on. Let's wear ourselves out training."

As they moved into position, the tension in her chest eased a little. For now, she had this—this connection, this fleeting moment of clarity with Gabriel. And somehow, that was enough to keep her going.

His movements were swift, precise, a perfect blend of power and control. He lunged, his arm sweeping toward her in a feigned strike. She blocked it, twisting her body to dodge his follow-up blow, but he was relentless. His hand grazed her side enough to unbalance her before she twisted free.

"You're holding back." He teased.

"You'd know if I wasn't."

He smirked, stepping closer to her. "Prove it."

Ava surged forward, her fists moving in a flurry of precise strikes. He deflected each one with ease, his smirk growing as their sparring intensified.

She feinted to the left, sending a sharp blast of water toward his side.

Gabriel dodged, hooking his arm around hers, spinning her toward him until their faces were inches apart. His breath mingled with hers, his grip firm but not cruel. "Better."

She yanked free, her water surging again, catching him square in the chest and knocking him off balance.

He stumbled, his grin faltering as he regained his footing.

"What are you doing?" Eve screamed.

Ava froze for half a second, and Eve lunged at her.

She raised her hand, summoning a sharp stream of water. The blast struck Eve in the chest, sending her stumbling back a few paces. Water dripped from Eve's hair and clothes as she steadied herself, her face twisted with fury.

"Why are you attacking him?" Eve snarled. Her dark eyes flicked between Gabriel and Ava, her suspicion sharp as a blade.

Ava's heart thundered, her mind racing. If Eve believed Ava was attacking Gabriel, she could run straight to Havok. But if Ava claimed it was just training, Eve might doubt her loyalty—or worse, report her as faking everything.

Eve lunged again.

Gabriel was quicker, stepping between them and grabbing Eve's arm. "Enough!" he barked. "We're all on the same team."

Eve wrenched her arm free from his grasp, her glare burning. "She's trying to kill you! I saw her earlier—she wasn't holding back. She's—"

"I can take care of myself," Gabriel interrupted, his tone calm but edged with steel.

"Can you? You're not as strong as you used to be, Gabriel. I've seen it. You hesitate. You're distracted. You're not the fighter you were before the Elders got their claws into you."

Gabriel's jaw tightened. "I don't need you to fight my battles."

"You're defending her? Why? Because you still love her?"

Ava's heart slammed against her ribs, her throat tightening as the air thickened.

"Eve, this isn't about her—or you. It's about tomorrow."

"You're weak, and it's because of *her*."

"You're imagining things."

"Am I? You think I haven't noticed how you refuse to touch me or come to my room at night or you holding back?"

"That's enough," Gabriel growled.

Ava seized the moment, forcing her mask into place. "I don't have time for your lover's quarrel. Figure it out. Just make sure you're ready for tomorrow." She turned on her heel and strode out of the pit. A dagger twisted in her ribs as Eve's gaze prickled at her back.

She didn't want to leave Gabriel—not like this—but she had no choice.

As the pit faded into the distance, Ava clenched her fists. A smoldering anger joined the icy dread in her chest—not at Gabriel, or even Eve, but at the cruel game they were all forced to play.

CHAPTER EIGHTEEN

SHADOWS IN THE MOONLIGHT

Ava stared at her reflection, her gray eyes narrowed, though they betrayed doubt she couldn't quite suppress. With every strand neatly in place, she had pulled her fiery red hair back into a tight ponytail. Not a single hair dared to rebel. Her usual black ensemble—long-sleeved shirt, spandex pants tucked into knee-high boots. The fabric, though flexible, felt heavier tonight.

Her muscles were lean and strong, shaped by years of training, yet her posture sagged slightly under the mental toll of weeks spent in Caprington. Ten weeks in the heart of the enemy, and she was still trying to hold on to the person she used to be. Tonight, though, would test everything. Kidnap deserters or kill them—and their families.

You can do this.

Her voice in her mind sounded hollow. She gripped the door handle, her knuckles whitening, and closed her eyes, drawing in a deep, shuddering breath. Then, with a practiced precision she'd honed over weeks, she turned off her emotions. The icy calm settled over her like armor as she opened the door and stepped into the corridor.

The Great Hall felt colder than usual, the air heavy with unspoken tension. Ava's boots echoed against the stone floor as she joined the others, all clad in identical black attire. The somber atmosphere clung to the group like a storm cloud, muting even the smallest sound. She had expected bloodlust, excitement, perhaps even a cruel eagerness among the Cimmerians—but there was an ominous quiet.

The others had already assembled. Melissa stood to her left, her usually vibrant green eyes dull with dread. Thomas's bulging muscles strained, and he stared straight ahead. Lance avoided everyone's gaze, his dark hair falling into his eyes as though shielding him. Gillian and Jeremy stood stoic. Link looked bored. Gabriel lingered at the edge of the group, his expression neutral. His eyes flicked to Ava for the briefest second.

Then there were the others—the true Cimmerians. Eve's smirk twisted her face into something monstrous as she twirled her knife. Anais stood beside her, her posture relaxed, her sharp eyes calculating.

Xavier strode into the room and paused in front of them, his cold smile making her stomach churn. "Tonight, we remind the deserters of their place. There's no room for weakness in Havok's Aureole. You have your assignments. Carry them out with precision. And remember—hesitation will not be tolerated. We'll split into teams. Melissa, Thomas, Lance—you'll serve as lookouts. Watch the perimeter and make sure no one escapes. Link, Eve, Anais, Ava—you're the interrogators. Use any means necessary to extract information about other deserters or Ephemeral sympathizers."

Ava's heart thudded against her ribs, but she nodded.

"Jeremy, Gillian, Gabriel—you'll contain the prisoners. Bring them back to Caprington. If they resist, eliminate them and anyone who gets in your way."

His words hung in the air, sinking into her like stones. They echoed in her mind, leaving an icy chill in its wake.

"Remember, this is more than a mission. This is a statement. Failure is not an option. Let's go."

The village lay quiet under the blanket of night, its cobblestone streets lit only by the faint glow of lanterns swaying in the cool breeze.

Ava crouched behind a crumbling wall, her breath catching in her throat. The air was sharp with the scent of damp earth and wood smoke, but it couldn't mask the cold dread that tightened her chest. The mission's goal played over and over in her mind like a twisted mantra: Find the deserters. Bring them back or kill them. If they resist, kill their families.

Xavier's voice crackled through the comms device tucked in her ear. "Team two, move into position."

Ava exchanged a brief look with Anais, who nodded.

Eve moved ahead, blending into the shadows.

Ava's pulse raced as she followed, every step plunging her deeper into the nightmare she couldn't escape.

The first house was easy to find. The name *Calder* was etched into the wooden plaque by the door—one of the deserters Xavier had listed. Ava's hand clenched into a fist as they approached. *It's just a mission. Play the part. Survive.*

Eve reached the door first. She knocked, but there was no answer.

Anais tilted her head, her lips twitching with amusement. "Let's not waste time knocking." She stared at Link.

He stepped toward the door as they retreated, his hands igniting with intense heat. With a swift motion, he hurled an explosive blast at the door, the force splintering the wood into jagged shards. The sound ripped through the stillness, echoing like a gunshot in the quiet.

The four of them crossed the threshold into a room shrouded in shadow, smelling of stale bread and wood smoke.

Water swirled at Ava's fingertips, ready to strike—or protect.

A man stood at the center of the room, his wide brown eyes darting between them. His broad shoulders hunched, like a man ready to fight despite knowing he couldn't win. Behind him, his wife clutched a small, wailing child to her chest, her face pale and tear streaked.

"Well, hello, Simon." Eve spun her knife. "You've been quite the disappointment to Havok."

Simon raised his hands. "Please, you don't have to do this. We—my family—they're innocent."

"Innocent?" Anais's sharp laugh cut through the room like a blade. Sparks of electricity danced along her fingertips. "Were you innocent when you sent an army to fight us? When you killed our drolls?"

Simon's face hardened, but he said nothing.

Tilting her head, Eve's lips curled into a wicked smile. "Are you coming back willingly, or are we making an example of you?"

His jaw clenched and positioned himself between the intruders and his family. "I won't go back. Do what you want to me but leave my wife and child out of this."

Eve let out a harsh, humorless laugh. "You know that's not how this works."

Simon's desperate eyes landed on Ava, pleading.

Her stomach flipped. She had to say something, anything, to delay the inevitable. "Don't make this harder than it has to be. If you cooperate, we can spare them."

Come on, Simon. Don't make us kill all of you.

Simon's gaze lingered on her, hope flashing for a brief, fragile moment. But his eyes narrowed, catching the hesitation she couldn't fully hide. His shoulders squared, his fists clenching. "No." With a guttural yell, he lunged at her, his eyes wide with rage. His movements were quick, desperate. Water surged at her fingertips, snapping into a sharp blade that sliced across his arm. He staggered back with a cry of pain, clutching the wound.

It wasn't enough to stop him.

But Eve was faster. Her knife struck without hesitation, plunging into his chest. Simon gasped, his body jerking as his knees buckled beneath him. His wife's scream tore through the room as he crumpled to the floor, lifeless.

"No!" the woman cried, holding her baby tighter.

Eve turned toward her, her blade still dripping with blood, her smile twisted with dark satisfaction. "Your turn."

The woman dropped to her knees, sobbing. "Please, spare my baby. Let him grow into a soldier." Her trembling hands extended the child toward Eve.

Eve hesitated. Her brows furrowed, but she sighed, taking the squirming infant into her arms. "Fine," she said. "He can live. For now."

Anais shot electric ropes from her hands, wrapping around the woman. Her body convulsed, her screams silenced as her heart gave out. She collapsed beside her husband, lifeless and still.

"One down," Eve muttered, wiping her blade on Simon's shirt. She held up the crying infant, her nose wrinkling in distaste. "What am I supposed to do with this?"

Anais snorted. "You took him. Give him to Gabriel so he can bring him to Caprington."

They stepped outside, the cold air biting against Ava's skin. She fought back a rising tide of nausea, bile burning in her throat.

Xavier, Gabriel, Gillian, and Jeremy approached them in the middle of the street, their faces shadowed by torchlight.

Eve thrust the crying baby into Gabriel's arms.

"What the hell do you want me to do with this?" he asked, his voice flat, but Ava didn't miss the unease in his eyes.

"What the hell happened?" Xavier demanded.

"Well," Eve drawled. "Simon said no, so he died. His wife said we could raise this boy as a soldier."

Xavier rolled his eyes, muttering a curse under his breath. "Take him to Caprington. We don't have time for this."

The baby's wails pierced the air, louder than seemed possible, echoing through the silent street like a ghostly lament. Ava's stomach twisted as the cries burrowed into her, a haunting reminder of what they'd done—and what they were about to do again. This boy would never know how his parents had fought, how they'd died to defy a ruthless man.

Gabriel's jaw tightened as he vanished into the night, the baby's cries ceasing. The silence that followed was more suffocating than the noise had been.

The second house stood quiet, its windows dark and lifeless. But as they entered, Ava's heart sank. The faint warmth of the stove and the lingering scent of freshly extinguished candles told her the occupants were close.

"They're hiding," Anais chirped. "Search the house."

Ava crept upstairs, water winding at her fingertips. The hall was dark, but faint whispers reached her ears. She hesitated, her pulse quickening. What would happen if she told them no one was there? Could she buy these people more time?

A door burst open behind her. A figure lunged, their hands gripping her shoulders as a jolt of power surged through her body. She collapsed to the floor, paralyzed.

Another figure appeared, this one holding a gun. The shot rang out, white-hot pain exploding in her shoulder. Ava cried out, her vision blurring.

Kill them. Kill them now.

A sharp and commanding voice surged in her mind. Water coiled around her wrists, and she unleashed it. The jet struck the gunman first, slamming him into the wall. The second attacker didn't have time to react before a torrent of water engulfed both attackers, crushing the life from their bodies.

As their lifeless forms slumped to the floor, Ava's chest heaved. She pressed a hand to her bleeding shoulder.

"Find something?" Eve called from the stairs.

Ava wiped her face and stood. "Not anymore." Pressing her back against the wall, she steadied her breath as the sound of footsteps thundered from downstairs. More of them. She gritted her teeth, forcing herself to move despite the searing pain in her shoulder. Blood seeped between her fingers as she clutched the wound, but there was no time to heal herself now.

Kill them. All of them must die.

Two figures rushed out of a bedroom, their faces grim and determined. One—a man with a makeshift weapon— charged first, swinging a heavy iron bar toward her. Ava ducked, the edge of the bar grazing her injured shoulder and sending fresh pain radiating through her body.

She stumbled back, summoning water in a desperate arc. The torrent hit the man square in the chest, knocking him off balance. He fell backward, tumbling down the stairs with a sickening crash.

The second figure—a woman, her dark eyes wild with fury—hurled a burst of fire in Ava's direction. Ava barely managed to deflect it with a wall of water. The opposing elements hissed and steamed as they collided. Her vision swam, but she stood her ground, her water swirling around her like a protective shield.

"Get out!" the woman screamed. "You've done enough!"

Ava wanted to scream back, to say she hadn't wanted this. The woman lunged, her flames roaring brighter.

Anais appeared at the top of the stairs. Her electric ropes wrapped around the woman, cutting her off mid-attack. The fire sputtered out, and the woman collapsed to the floor, unconscious. Ava's water splashed against the floor in a sharp, resounding wave.

"Let's finish clearing the house," Anais said.

Ava swayed a little, the blood loss making her lightheaded. She leaned against the wall for support, her water splattering to the floor. Her shoulder throbbed, each pulse of pain a reminder of how close she'd come to losing control. The voice. What or whose was it?

Eve glanced at her, her lips curling into a smirk. "You look like hell."

Ava didn't have the energy to muster a retort.

They regrouped with everyone else outside. The pain had spread, a dull, relentless ache that made every movement excruciating. She kept her head down, unwilling to meet anyone's gaze.

Xavier was the first to notice. His sharp eyes scanned her bloodied clothes, his brow furrowing. "What happened?"

"Ran into resistance," Ava said. "It's handled."

"You should've healed yourself. You're no use to me if you're half-dead."

"I'll take care of it." She glanced at Gabriel. His expression remained aloof, but there—a flicker of something in his blue eyes. Worry. She felt it like a spark, brief but unmistakable, before he turned away.

Ava gasped, her hand trembling as she pressed it over the wound. Her water surged forth, cool and soothing as it pushed the bullet free. She cried out, the sharp pain stealing her breath, but she held firm. The water flowed over the torn flesh, knitting it back together with an almost tender precision. The pain ebbed, replaced by a dull ache and the creeping stiffness of exhaustion.

Xavier watched her. "Good. You'll need to be at full strength for the next one."

The last house appeared ahead, its modest structure casting long shadows in the moonlight. Unlike the others, the door stood ajar, a single lantern on the porch. Ava's pulse quickened as they approached.

Xavier motioned for silence as they surrounded the house. He pushed the door open.

Inside, Elias Lorne stood waiting, his hands raised in surrender. He was a wiry man with sharp features, his dark hair streaked with silver. His eyes, though cautious, held no fear. Behind him, several people huddled together—his family, Ava realized, their faces pale and tense.

"I knew you'd come," he said calmly. "I won't fight you."

Xavier's lips curved into a bitter smile. "Smart. Saves us the trouble."

"I'll go willingly. But my family stays here."

Xavier's smile faltered, his eyes narrowing. "You're in no position to make demands."

"They have nothing to do with this. They're innocent. Take me and leave them alone."

For a moment, the room fell into heavy silence. Xavier studied him, his gaze sharp and calculating. Finally, he gave a single nod. "Fine. But if I find out you lied to me—if they cause any trouble—I'll make sure they pay for your mistakes."

Elias didn't flinch, his shoulders squaring as he stepped forward. "Understood."

As he passed his family, a small voice broke the quiet. "Papa?"

A little girl with dark curls darted from behind her mother, her tiny hands reaching for Elias. "Don't go!"

Elias froze, his composure cracking as he crouched down to meet her. "Lila, sweetheart. You have to be brave for me now, okay? Stay with Mama. Take care of her."

Tears streamed down the girl's face as she clung to his arm. "But I don't want you to go! I'll be good, I promise! Please, Papa!"

Ava's heart tore in half as she watched the scene unfold. She could feel the raw, quiet agony in Elias's movements as he gently pried his daughter's fingers from his arm. He stood, his gaze lingering on her for a moment.

But Lila wasn't done. She took a step forward, her tiny fists balled up in defiance. "Papa!"

Ava acted on instinct, kneeling down and catching the girl by the shoulders. "No, Lila," she said gently but firmly. "You have to stay here. It's what your papa wants."

The little girl looked up at her with wide, tear-filled eyes, her small frame trembling. "Why can't I go with him?"

Ava bit her lip. "Because he's doing this to keep you safe."

The girl sobbed uncontrollably as her mother pulled her close, holding her tight. Ava stood, her hands shaking, as Gabriel took Elias's arm. The older man cast one last glance over his shoulder at his family, his expression fractured with love and sorrow.

Then they vanished, leaving behind a silence that felt heavier than the world.

Ava stared at the space where they'd been, her heart a knot of anguish. *How long will he be a prisoner? Will she ever see her father again?* The weight of what they'd done—what she'd been a part of—settled over her like a shroud.

CHAPTER NINETEEN

BREAKING POINT

Simon's lifeless eyes, the desperate cries of his wife, his baby's cries, Lila clutching to Elias—all of it played on a cruel loop, stealing her breath and gripping her chest like iron chains.

As soon as she entered her bathroom, she fell to her knees. The cool porcelain felt sharp and unyielding under her trembling fingers as she heaved. The sound echoed in the small space. Her body shook, her throat burning, and cold sweat clung to her brow. Weak and hollow, she sagged against the wall, pressing her forehead to the cold tiles.

A sudden intense vision tore through her mind.

A younger Havok appeared, not the cold, menacing figure she knew, but someone almost unrecognizable. His black eyes held warmth, his laughter soft and genuine as he leaned toward a woman with shimmering dark hair. They were in a sun-dappled garden, surrounded by vibrant blossoms swaying in a gentle breeze. Havok's armor was gone, replaced by simple robes. His hand lay on the woman's cheek, his whispered words inaudible but filled with a love so deep that Ava felt it like a physical ache.

The vision ceased, yanking her back to the stark reality of her bathroom. She gasped for air, clutching her chest as if the memory were a living thing trying to claw its way out of her.

Why was she having visions of Havok's memories? Was it the link? Did that mean he could see her memories?

After cleaning herself up, Ava grabbed her cloak and slipped out of her room. By the time she reached Klaus's quarters, her fingers felt numb from gripping her cloak. She hesitated for a moment before pushing the heavy wooden door open. Warmth greeted her, along with the low hum of voices.

The dim light of lanterns revealed Klaus's workspace, a chaotic labyrinth of books, scrolls, and discarded parchment. The scent of old ink and musty paper hung thick in the air. Ava had expected solitude but found the room alive with quiet intensity.

Melissa sat with her arms crossed, her face taut and her gaze distant. Lance was leaning over a book, his brows furrowed in concentration, while Link, Nicole, and Eric whispered in hurried tones. The collective exhaustion etched onto their faces mirrored her own.

"You look like hell," Lance said.

"Thanks." Ava dropped into an empty chair. "So, is this some kind of secret meeting I wasn't invited to?"

"We've been trying to figure out a way to break your connection to Havok," Link explained softly. "Klaus thinks there might be something in the older texts."

"Might being the key word," Klaus grumbled without looking up, his face shadowed as he pored over a faded scroll. "Curses like this are ancient and complicated. They don't come with instruction manuals."

Ava sighed. "I can't take this much longer. Tonight was…"

"Too much," Melissa finished quietly.

"It's only going to get worse," Link said.

"What do you mean?" Ava asked. "What's worse than having to kill innocent people?"

Link hesitated. "This was a test. To see how far you'd go. Next … next, you're going to massacre villages. Cities. The scale will be unimaginable."

Her fingers curled into fists in her lap. She couldn't suppress the shudder that rippled through her.

Lance stood, stretching. "I'll be back in a bit." He left without another word, the door clicking shut behind him.

Ava glanced at Melissa. "What's his deal?"

Melissa shrugged. "Probably needed air. We all do." She slid a cup of water toward her. "Drink. You need your strength. I saw you struggling to heal yourself tonight."

Ava wrapped her fingers around the cool ceramic and sipped, the water soothing her parched throat, but did little to calm her.

The door creaked open. Ava turned, her breath catching as Gabriel stepped in behind Lance.

The moment Ava saw him, everything else faded. She shot to her feet and ran to him, throwing her arms around his neck.

He caught her, his arms locking around her waist, his warmth seeping into her. She clung to him, burying her face against his shoulder. "I can't do this," she whispered. "I want to leave."

"I know." His lips brushed her temple. "Me, too. But we can't. Not yet."

She shook her head against him, tears threatening to spill. "I'm falling apart, Gabriel. I can't keep doing this. Tonight—" Her voice broke. "I saw another vision. It was him. Havok. Laughing. He was with someone he loved. And then everything turned to darkness."

Gabriel cursed under his breath.

"The link is deepening," Klaus said. "His emotions, his past—they're bleeding into you. Is the potion not helping?"

Ava gripped Gabriel's arms as if letting go would send her spiraling. "It keeps him out of my head, but it doesn't stop me from slipping into his. How do I stop it?"

Klaus hesitated, his fingers drumming on the table. "You might not be able to," he said finally. "The bond isn't just magic—it's a soul tether. His essence is entwined with yours now. The longer this goes on, the harder it will be to separate. And the more of him you'll absorb."

The words knocked the breath out of her. She glanced around the room. Melissa sat stiff, her lips pressed into a thin line. Lance clenched his fists. Link stared at the floor, his silence heavier than words.

"Maggie's an Elder," Melissa said. "Could she do it?"

Klaus sighed, dragging a hand over his face. The shadows under his eyes seemed darker in the dim light. "Maybe. But she's more than an Elder—she's Havok's confidant. Reaching her would be nearly impossible."

"So, what then?" Lance snapped. "We just wait for an opportunity that might never come?"

"There's another possibility," Klaus said slowly. "But it's dangerous."

"What is it?" Melissa asked.

"The bond could theoretically be transferred," Klaus explained. "But it would require someone willing to take it on. Someone strong enough to handle the darkness."

The room seemed to hold its breath.

Gabriel's hand tightened around Ava's. His face remained blank, but she sensed the tension radiating from him. She knew what he was thinking.

"No." Ava shook her head. "Absolutely not. How is that any better? No one's taking my place. I won't allow it."

"It's not a solution," Klaus said, "just a theory. Until we find something definitive, you all need to keep up the charade."

Ava's frustration boiled over. "How long? How much more of this do I have to endure before we figure this out?"

Klaus frowned. "It will take time, Ava."

"That's all anyone ever says!" she snapped, her voice breaking. "Time to gather an army. Time to defeat Havok. Time to heal. What if I don't have time?"

Gabriel spoke, his tone low and sharp. "Then we make the time. But we have to break the bond first—before we even think about killing Havok."

"What if I lose myself?" Ava whispered. "What if his darkness consumes me?"

"You won't." With a gentle touch, Gabriel caressed her cheek, his thumb grazing her skin. "I won't let you fall."

Klaus cut in, his voice grim. "There is one thing that might help—cutting off his supply."

Ava's brow furrowed. "What are you saying?"

"Havok's bond to you is fueled by your emotions. Fear, anger, guilt—they strengthen the link. If you suppress them, it might weaken his influence."

A heavy silence fell.

"You're asking her to turn off her emotions completely?" Gabriel narrowed his eyes. "Do you have any idea what that would do to her?"

"It's temporary," Klaus said, his patience fraying. "If it gives her a chance to regain control, it's worth considering."

"I don't know if I can," Ava said. "I'm already pretending every second of every day. If I shut everything out ... what's left of me?"

Klaus met her gaze. "A version of you that can survive."

Gabriel's grip on her hand tightened. "She doesn't need to lose her humanity to survive. That's exactly what Havok wants."

"Do you have a better idea?" Klaus snapped. "I'm not saying it's perfect. But it's an option. And right now, Ava needs every advantage she can get. I'll keep researching. In the meantime, you need to build an army."

Lance crossed his arms. "How do we even convince the Cimmerians to switch sides?"

"They've been conditioned for centuries to see themselves as superior, their cause righteous," Klaus said. "But that kind of loyalty is fragile. Fear is a powerful motivator, but it can be turned against them. Exploit the cracks in their faith."

"What about the villagers?" Melissa asked. "If we can turn the Cimmerians' own people against them, maybe it'll weaken their hold."

"The villagers are a starting point," he said.

All of them had begun discussing the army and strategies, voices overlapping in a steady hum of plans and possibilities. But Ava barely heard them. The words blurred together, distant and meaningless, as her thoughts spiraled deeper into the terrifying unknown. Could she do it? Could she really become completely emotionless?

Her chest tightened, the weight of the question pressing down on her. What would happen to her if she did? Would she still be Ava? Or just a hollow version of herself, something unrecognizable, something *broken*?

"We're leaving. Now."

Gabriel's voice broke through her spiraling thoughts.

Ava blinked, startled by the intensity in his tone. "Gabriel, we can't—"

"Not permanently," he clarified. His eyes burned with a fierce determination, one that both steadied and unsettled her. "Just for a little while. You need air. I need..." He glanced at Klaus, then back at her. "I need to get you out of here."

"Wait," Melissa said. "Let me help you out of the castle without being seen."

Gabriel nodded, and he tightened his grip on Ava's hand.

Melissa reached out, covering the three of them with her cloak of invisibility. She led them through the castle grounds, each step echoing faintly in the eerie stillness of the night.

When they reached the edge of the grounds, Melissa dropped the projection and squeezed Ava's shoulder. "Be careful," she murmured and retreated into the shadows.

He took Ava's hand. "Hold on."

The world blurred around her, the familiar pull of teleportation tightening her chest and stomach. When the spinning sensation stopped, Ava stumbled, clutching Gabriel's arm as her surroundings came into focus.

They were standing in a small, secluded grove. The air here felt cleaner, freer, untouched by the suffocating weight of Caprington. Moonlight streamed through the canopy of trees, painting the mossy ground in a patchwork of silver and shadow. A soft breeze carried the scent of wildflowers and pine, mingling with the faint trickle of a nearby stream.

Ava blinked, her breath hitching. "Where are we?"

"Somewhere safe," Gabriel said. "I found this place a while ago. No one comes here. We can talk here without worrying about being overheard."

She looked around, her heart constricting as the peacefulness of the grove clashed with the chaos inside her. Gabriel hadn't let go of her hand, and his steady grip was the only thing keeping her from unraveling.

"I couldn't take another minute in that place," he said. "Somehow, we will figure this out, Ava. I will not lose you."

Tears stung her eyes. "Promise me you won't take my place."

"Ava..."

"No, Gabriel. Promise me. I can't survive this without you. I need you here."

"How do you think I feel?"

"Promise me," she pressed.

After a moment, he nodded. "I promise. But you have to promise me something, too."

She frowned, her chest tightening. "What?"

"You won't sacrifice yourself," he said. "I know you, Ava. I know it's crossed your mind. Don't do it."

She took a shuddering breath. "I promise." Her gaze drifted to the stream, the gentle murmur of water barely soothing the ache in her chest. "I can't stop seeing their faces—Simon's family, Elias's... The way they begged. And I just—" She pressed her hand against her mouth to stifle a sob.

Gabriel drew her into his arms. "You're not like them. And you never will be."

"How do you know that? How can you be so sure? I keep doing these horrible things. What if I can't come back from this?"

"You will." His hands slid down to her arms.

"I have Cimmerian blood in me, Gabriel. What if—"

"That doesn't make you evil. I know it's hard. And I'm trying everything I can to help you."

"You can't do everything."

"No. But I can try. I'll find a way to speak to Maggie or visit Aaron in the prison. Whatever it takes, Ava."

His words cracked the wall she'd built around her emotions. Leaning into him, she wrapped her arms around his waist. For a long moment, neither of them spoke. He stroked her hair, the repetitive motion calming her.

She pulled back, her gaze meeting his. In the moonlight, his face was raw and open, the sharp lines softened by the silvery glow. "You're all I have left that feels real," she whispered. "Don't let me lose that."

"You won't. You never will."

"I need ... distract me, Gabriel."

Their lips met, slow and tentative at first, but the kiss deepened, a desperate attempt to cling to something solid in the chaos. His hands tightened on her waist, pulling her closer, while her fingers tangled in his hair.

The world blurred, the cool night air mingling with the heat radiating between them. She became aware of the damp earth beneath her as she lay on her back. He pressed his body against hers. His hands ventured beneath her shirt, their warmth contrasting against the coolness of her skin. Slowly, he slid his fingers inside the waistband of her pants, the gentle friction causing her heart to race. A flush of heat spread across her body, causing her skin to tingle.

As Gabriel's lips traveled down her neck, a sudden, searing vision crashed into Ava's mind like a tidal wave.

The grove dissolved in an instant. She was no longer lying in the grove, no longer feeling Gabriel's warmth against her. She was in a sunlit field, vibrant and alive, surrounded by wildflowers swaying in the breeze. A woman's melodic laughter echoed through the scene, light and carefree.

Ava blinked, but her vision was no longer her own. She was *him*—Corbin.

The overwhelming sensation of love flooded her chest, raw and all-encompassing. It wasn't her heart beating this way—it was his. Every movement, every thought, was no longer hers but his. She could feel his longing, his determination.

The woman, Lenorah, spun toward him, her dark eyes sparkling as she grinned. Her dark hair shimmered in the sunlight, and she exuded a warmth that made Ava's heart—no, Corbin's heart—ache with the depth of his affection for her.

He reached for her, his hands firm yet reverent as they circled her waist. "Lenorah," he said, his voice rough but tender, the sound of it unfamiliar to Ava's ears yet so intimately tied to the emotions coursing through her.

Lenorah tilted her head, her expression softening. "What is it?"

"I will tell my family of our marriage plans," Corbin—Ava—said.

Her smile faltered. "Corbin, you cannot risk such a thing. They expect you to follow the path laid before you—to serve in their army. And you know they would never accept a peasant like me."

His jaw tightened. "It should not matter. None of it should matter."

She reached up, her hands featherlight against his face, her touch both soothing and heart-wrenching. "But it does."

Ava felt the battle within him—the anger, the frustration, and the love that refused to be smothered by duty or expectation.

"I will marry you," Corbin vowed.

Tears welled in Lenorah's eyes as she hugged him. "I love you."

The vision shifted, the warmth fading into a cold, suffocating emptiness as the field dissolved into shadow.

Ava gasped, jerking away from Gabriel as though his touch had burned her. Her breath came in sharp, uneven bursts, her body trembling as she struggled to anchor herself in the present.

Gabriel's chest heaved, his face pale with concern as he knelt before her. "It happened again, didn't it?"

She nodded, her trembling hands rising to clutch her head as tears spilled down her cheeks. The feelings—the love, the anguish—still clung to her. "It's getting stronger," she whispered. "I could feel everything—his love, his anger. It's like I was him."

Frustration flashed across his face. He pulled her into his lap, wrapping his arms around her, as if his embrace could shield her from the darkness invading her mind. "We'll find a way," he murmured. "We'll find a way."

Ava buried her face in his shoulder, her tears soaking into his shirt. "What if I become him?"

"You won't. Not if I have anything to do with it."

For a long moment, they stayed there, the grove silent except for the soft rustle of leaves and the faint murmur of the stream. Slowly, the storm inside her began to quiet, not gone but distant, as if Gabriel's presence was the eye of the hurricane.

When she finally pulled away, her cheeks still damp, he brushed a thumb across her skin, his touch warm. "We'll take it one step at a time."

Ava nodded. Sitting in silence, the night held them in its embrace, as if the grove itself had paused to give them this fleeting moment of peace before the world crashed back in.

CHAPTER TWENTY

ALL THE LIGHTS WENT OUT

Tonight, we're to massacre Ephemerals," Xavier announced. "Unfortunately, not all of you will be coming."

A ripple of confusion swept through the group, punctuated by murmurs of frustration and barely concealed relief. Unspoken tension filled the air, a mixture of anticipation and dread in every glance and whisper.

Ava's stomach churned as she caught Melissa's eye. The furrow in her brows mirrored Ava's own unease. What did Xavier mean by *not everyone*? Wasn't the whole point of the Selection to prove they were ready for missions like this?

"We're testing the Elementals tonight." Xavier's grin was sharp enough to draw blood. "Only the Elementals and Link will be going."

The crowd erupted into whispers, a chaotic blend of disappointment and palpable relief.

Then Havok entered.

The murmurs ceased, snuffed out like a flame under a boot. His presence swallowed the room whole, suffocating and inescapable, an oppressive force that seemed to pull the oxygen from the air. Flanked by his Nightwardens—Maggie, Kira, Katarina, Eric, Peter, Sorcha, and Benjamin—he drained the air from the room, as his dark gaze raked over the crowd, dissecting them as if cataloging their worth.

"I cannot wait to hear of the results. You will all make me proud." Without another glance, he turned on his heel and strode out of the room, leaving a gaping void in his wake.

Ava's gaze lingered on him as he left, her thoughts swirling in chaos. Havok, the architect of endless bloodshed, never dirtied his hands with the violence he orchestrated. Did the killing bore him now, or did he indulge in darker amusements behind closed doors? Did he mourn the ghosts of his past, or mock them in solitude? The mystery of him only deepened her unease.

Her attention flicked to Gabriel, but Eve broke the connection when she slid her hand into his and murmured something Ava couldn't hear. The sight made Ava sick to her stomach, and she looked away.

"Such a small group of people," a voice muttered from the back.

Heads turned toward Donovan, who stood with his arms crossed over his broad, tattooed chest. He glared at Xavier. "Is this your rule?" he demanded, his tone dripping with disdain.

"You're a Blood Vanguard, Donovan," Xavier shot back. "I don't need any lip from you. This was Havok's request, and you know that."

Donovan shrugged, his deliberate steps forward, daring Xavier to react. "Why? Because of his precious Elementals now? What makes them so damn special? They're just

Enchanters like the rest of us. But we've been training for this for a year. They haven't. I bet they'll fail."

The insult landed like a slap. Ava bristled, even though anger ignited inside her. Hadn't they proven themselves time and time again? She clenched her fists at her sides, water swirling at her fingertips.

As Donovan passed her, her hand shot out, gripping his throat. His eyes widened in shock, his hands clawing at hers.

"You don't think we're strong enough?" she hissed. The water slithered like a serpent around Donovan's neck. A red flush crept across his face as he gasped for air. "Is that your problem?"

Donovan's lips curled into a mocking smile, but it didn't reach his eyes. She felt a faint, sharp prickle in her chest—his attempt to counter—but she drowned it in her own power. His eyes bulged as the air in his lungs dwindled, his defiance flickering like a dying flame.

"Aww, I'm sorry," Ava taunted. "Were you trying to hurt me?"

The room seemed to hold its breath, tension crackling like a live wire. Whispers rippled through the crowd—some amused, others wary.

"Really, Ava?" Gabriel sneered. "Getting worked up over *him*?"

Ava's head snapped toward him, but she didn't release Donovan. "Stay out of this."

"Oh, I'm sorry," he drawled, his voice dripping with mockery. "Am I interrupting your grand performance? Or are you just desperate to prove something?"

Water tightened around Donovan's throat as her anger flared. The crowd murmured, watching the exchange with wide-eyed fascination.

"Okay, enough," Xavier's laughter rang out. He placed his hand on her arm, his grin dark and laced with approval. "You've made your point. Don't ruin the fun by killing him. We still need him."

Ava's water unraveled with a sharp hiss, and Donovan crumpled to the ground, gasping for air. She turned her back on Gabriel, her jaw clenched so tightly it ached, while he stood motionless, his expression still cold, detached—nothing like the storm raging beneath the surface.

"Let's go," Xavier said.

Falling into step with the group, Ava's heartbeat still pounded in her ears. She couldn't believe she lashed out like that—even if Donovan deserved it.

"Glad someone else stands up to Donovan," Xavier said, beside her.

"He annoys me."

"Yeah." He chuckled. "His arrogance is testing. But don't let him get under your skin too much. He's all bark until you put him in his place."

Ava didn't respond. The cool air brushed against her skin, but it did little to temper the heat of her frustration or the dread curling in her stomach. Tonight would test them all in ways she wasn't sure she could endure—and she wasn't certain who she'd be when the night was over.

They descended into the smothering depths of the prison cells. Ava followed in silence, her emotions locked away, her heart encased in ice. It was the only way she could do this.

Each step whispered off the cold stone walls, a sound that seemed to reverberate inside her hollow chest.

Xavier stopped, his hand pressing against what appeared to be an unremarkable stone in the wall. A mechanical click broke the silence, and the entire room quaked as dust and gravel rained down from above. The stone wall parted, revealing a yawning void of darkness. "Thomas, light us up."

Thomas moved to the front, his fists igniting in a blaze of fire. The flames revealed a narrow tunnel stretching ahead. She hated tunnels—the ominous feeling of being enclosed, of the world pressing in on all sides—but she forced the unease down, shoving it into the void where her emotions now resided.

Xavier moved with confidence, his steps echoing in the confined space as he led the way through the labyrinthine passage. Left, right, another right, straight, left again. The twists and turns seemed endless. Ava focused on the rhythmic sound of her boots on the stone floor, using it as an anchor against the disorientation of the maze.

Finally, they came to a simple wooden door. Xavier keyed in a code, and opened it, revealing not another tunnel but the warm, humid embrace of the outside world.

Walking over the threshold, a flood of sensations hit Ava. She inhaled the sweet and heady aroma of magnolias and jasmine, underscored by the faint tang of mown grass. Stars pin-pricked the deep navy sky above.

Ahead of them stretched a vast field overlooking a city, its vibrant lights twinkling like a galaxy fallen to earth. The distant strains of jazz music floated on the breeze, blending with the rhythmic hum of life from Bourbon Street. The Mississippi River gleamed like liquid silver under the moonlight, its tranquil surface broken only by the soft chug of a passing steamboat horn.

Ava's chest tightened as recognition struck. New Orleans.

Her mind flashed back to her last visit to this city with Gabriel, Joss, and Eric. The beignets, the bustling streets filled with music and laughter, the warmth of friendship. She remembered meeting Caroline, Sophia, Rene, and Marcel— and learning the dark truth about her mother's Cimmerian heritage. The memory dissolved into the harsh reality of the present. Were they still in New Orleans? Would they be killed?

The vibrant city below was alive with joy and light, and soon, it would be nothing but ash and water.

She hardened herself, turning away from the beauty of it all. The past was gone. And soon, so would New Orleans be.

"So," Ava asked, "how do you want to start this?"

Xavier smirked, his eyes gleaming with a sadistic edge. "Why don't we begin with a tornado?"

Jeremy advanced, and within seconds, the air shifted, the breeze becoming a feral wind. A funnel formed, small at first but quickly growing into a monstrous vortex. The roar of the tornado was deafening, a freight train of destruction. The cyclone sucked vehicles, hurling them like toys into buildings that crumbled under the impact. Glass shattered, raining shards onto the streets below.

Melissa added her power, sending boulders hurtling into homes. The chaos escalated as sirens wailed in the distance, their cries swallowed by the cacophony of destruction.

The tornado carved a path of ruin through the city, leaving behind a scar of mangled debris and broken lives. Bombs detonated, their fiery blasts illuminating the apocalyptic scene. The acrid scent of sulfur and charred flesh hung heavy in the air, mingling with the metallic tang of blood. Flames roared to life, surging outward in a fiery cascade. Buildings buckled under the inferno's wrath, their wooden frames crackling and splintering. The fire consumed everything, painting the streets in a hellish glow.

Gillian raised her hands, her fingers curling as if pulling an invisible tide. The air grew dense, as if the weight of the moon itself pressed down on them. Gravity around the city intensified, and bodies collapsed to the ground, pinned under the crushing force. Their movements became sluggish, desperate, as if trapped in an unyielding current.

Ava stood motionless, her gaze fixed on the devastation, her mind blank. The lively city she'd once wandered was now a hellscape of fire and rubble. The Mississippi reflected the flames, its waters an inferno of orange and red.

"Your turn." Xavier nudged Ava.

Staring down at the remnants of New Orleans, she called upon the river. The water surged, building into a towering wave that grew into a tsunami. It loomed over the city, casting a shadow of dread before crashing down with unrelenting force. The tidal wave swept away everything in its path—buildings, trees, vehicles, people.

Hands clawed above the water's surface, fighting for life before disappearing into the churning depths. Lifeless bodies floated like debris, their faces eerily peaceful in death.

The jazz music was gone. The lights extinguished. The city that had once pulsed with life was now silent, reduced to ruins under an onyx sky. Smoke billowed into the air, a dark flag of surrender rising from the ashes.

Ava felt nothing.

Nothing but the hollow ache of a soul pushed to the brink.

CHAPTER TWENTY-ONE

HEAD RUSH

The group trudged back to Caprington in heavy silence. Ava's limbs ached not just from physical exertion but from the emotional toll of the night. Her mind reeled with questions, doubts, and guilt she couldn't escape, no matter how much she tried to shut it down.

Did it even bother the Cimmerians that they'd wiped a city off the map? That hundreds—thousands—of lives were gone in a single night?

Ahead, Xavier strode with an unsettling calm, his posture rigid.

Ava picked up her pace and fell into step beside him, the quiet between them heavy. "How often do we do this?"

"It depends. We used to do it monthly. But now, with all of you here, I suspect Havok will want to escalate. He'll push harder, faster. He's not one for patience."

"To wipe them all out quicker."

He gave a curt nod, his gaze fixed ahead. "Precisely."

"And no thought to keeping any for slaves?"

"It's been discussed." He shrugged. "But Havok isn't in the mood to preserve right now. He's evaluating all of you. Seeing what you're capable of. Tonight's results will make him happy. We've never completely destroyed a city like that before."

"Not even Tokyo?"

"Not like that. I can't exactly cause too much damage with my shadows."

"Good thing you have us."

Xavier cast her a sidelong glance, and his expression turned distant. He clenched his jaw and looked away.

When they reached the castle doors, Xavier pushed them open, the sound of the heavy wood groaning. The castle's chill seeped into Ava's skin as they passed through the main room and into the twisting corridors. The layout still felt like a labyrinth, every shadowy corner a potential trap if she didn't keep track of her surroundings.

"What now?" she asked.

"We meet with Havok," Xavier said flatly. There was something in his tone—hesitation, maybe even dread. He quickened his pace toward a smaller parlor off the main hall.

Havok sat perched on an ornate chair, the soft glow of the firelight casting long shadows across the room. A book rested in his lap, and a glass of dark red wine dangled loosely in his bony fingers. He looked up as they entered, and a slow, superior smirk spread across his face. "Welcome back." He swirled the liquid in his glass, the deep crimson catching the firelight. Ava's stomach twisted. The wine's color was too much like blood.

The group lined up before him, stiff and silent. Ava's hands itched at her sides, her muscles taut as she fought the urge to scream at him, to shove the glass out of his hand and demand answers. Instead, she kept her face blank, letting the hollow emptiness of her emotions shield her.

Havok finally rose from his chair. His face—Colden's face—twisted into a sinister grin. No matter how many times she reminded herself it wasn't really Colden, the sight of him filled her with a sickening mix of fury and despair.

"What was the outcome?" Havok asked.

"Total annihilation," Xavier said. "The city is gone. Completely leveled."

Havok's grin widened, his jagged teeth gleaming. "Excellent," he purred. "This pleases me greatly. You have exceeded expectations."

Ava's jaw tightened. His satisfaction was nauseating. What happened when there were no more Ephemerals to kill? Would they turn on each other? On Havok himself?

"Your next assignment is New York," he said. "You are free for the weekend. Rest. Celebrate." With a dismissive wave, he turned back to his book as if they were nothing more than tools to him.

They filed out and waited for Xavier's direction.

"Celebratory party tonight at the tavern," Xavier said finally, lacking enthusiasm. "Get cleaned up. We'll start in an hour."

"Thank God." Gillian ran a hand through her curls.

Xavier gave them a brief nod and headed off down the corridor.

"We need to go to Klaus's," Melissa whispered. "We'll go to the party for a bit and then head over."

As if Klaus could fix the horrors of what they'd done.

Ava returned to her room. She stepped into the shower, letting the scalding water wash away the grime and blood. It couldn't touch the guilt. The faces of the people they'd slaughtered flashed in her mind, their screams echoing in the recesses of her mind.

When she emerged from the bathroom, her reflection in the mirror startled her. The face staring back was pale, drained of warmth, and shadowed with exhaustion. Hollow eyes stared back at her, their light dimmed, and her lips pressed into a hard line. She let her hair fall loose; the waves cascading over her shoulders like a dark curtain and applied smoky makeup. The boldness felt like armor, a mask to hide the cracks threatening to split her open.

Her chest tightened as she surveyed herself one last time. The person in the mirror didn't look like Ava—she looked like someone who belonged in Caprington. Someone who could do what was necessary, no matter the cost.

Noise and light of the tavern surged forward in a chaotic symphony—the raucous laughter, the clinking of glasses, the occasional burst of rowdy shouting. Thick scents of ale, sweat, and charred wood wafted in the air. The lanterns sputtered, their feeble light battling the creeping haze.

She forced a smile, slipping into the noise and chaos. Every step felt mechanical, every gesture calculated. She moved through the crowd with a confidence that didn't belong to her, letting the dim light and the press of bodies drown out the guilt clawing at her chest.

Her humanity flickered, a faint ember beneath the cold veneer she had built around herself. She crushed the echoes of those desperate pleas and the hollow sound of her own voice as she delivered the final blow. The emotions she buried—the guilt, the grief, the horror—threatened to claw their way back to the surface.

Not tonight. She shoved them down deeper, locking them away where they couldn't reach her. Tonight, she wouldn't be haunted. She wouldn't feel. She would let herself forget, even if only for a little while.

Her smile stretched wider, hollow and sharp, as she accepted a drink offered by a soldier. The first sip burned her throat, the bitterness coating her tongue, but it was a welcome burn—a distraction from the cold pit that had settled deep inside her chest.

"Damn." Xavier approached her. His eyes roved over her, lingering long enough to make her uncomfortable. "You look hot."

Her lips curved into a faint smile, detached but effortless. "Thanks. You don't look bad yourself." She nodded toward his dark jeans and button-down shirt.

"I do what I can." He led her to an empty table, enough for the others to join. "Drink?" He raised a hand to summon a waitress.

"You choose."

The waitress, wearing black shorts and a too-tight white shirt, appeared moments later. Her brown hair spilled messily over her face, but she didn't seem to care. Xavier barely glanced at her as he ordered. "Two stouts."

Ava leaned back in her chair, watching as the waitress walked away. She felt Xavier's eyes on her before she turned back. When she did, he surprised her by leaning forward and taking her hands.

"How are you doing?" he asked.

The gesture made her skin crawl, though she kept her expression neutral. "I'm fine. Why?"

He released her hand and scratched the back of his neck. He looked nervous, awkward. "It's just ... this was your first."

"Okay." She tilted her head. "Should I feel something else?"

He stared at her for a moment, his jaw tightening as though he wanted to say more but couldn't. "No. Sorry."

The waitress returned, placing two beers in front of them before disappearing back into the crowd. Xavier downed a long sip of his beer, his eyes distant, his posture tense.

"Are you okay?" she asked.

"Fine," he said curtly, though the tightness in his tone suggested otherwise.

She leaned forward, her fingers brushing the rim of her glass. "They were Ephemerals, right? We're supposed to kill them. How did you act your first time?"

Xavier hesitated, the clink of his glass against the table the only sound for a beat. "That wasn't my first time killing Ephemerals. But ... tonight was the first time we completely annihilated a city. There's nothing left."

"How do you feel about it?"

"I'm fine." He glanced at her, his expression hardening. "But I don't know. It's different, isn't it? Wiping out an entire place."

"What's wrong?"

He shook his head. "Nothing."

The conversation fizzled into silence. Was he second-guessing Havok? Could Ava convince him to switch sides?

The rest of the group arrived. Melissa strutted in, her blond hair pulled high into a sleek ponytail. She wore an off-the-shoulder black and white striped blouse tucked into tight black leggings, the silver hoops in her ears catching the light. Nicole, dressed in jeans and a red sequined shirt, trailed Gillian. The boys followed, all in variations of t-shirts and jeans.

Xavier flagged down the waitress again, murmuring something that made her smirk, and she walked off. "The band will start playing in a few minutes. Are you all ready to party all night?"

Ava forced a smile, lifting her glass to clink against his. "Hell yeah."

When the waitress returned, she set down a tray of shot glasses and a bottle of golden liquid. She handed the bottle to Xavier, winking as she said, "On the house."

Xavier poured the liquid into each shot glass with a flourish, raising his high in the air. The others followed, their faces illuminated by the light. "To the Elementals!"

"To the Elementals," Ava echoed, the words bitter on her tongue as she downed the shot. The liquid burned its way down her throat, but she welcomed it, the sting drowning out the ache in her chest—if only for a moment.

The laughter and clinking glasses blurred into a chaotic hum as she reached for another drink. Somewhere in the noise, she began to unravel—not as Ava, the girl with too much blood on her hands, but as someone else. Someone who didn't care. Someone who didn't feel.

Two shots deep, warmth spread through her, loosening the tension that had been her constant companion. Loud music, boisterous laughter, and drunken shouts filled the air. Nearby, a girl lay on her back, strangers leaning over her to do body shots, their laughter cutting through the din.

Normally, the scene would repulse Ava, a glaring reminder of everything she hated about this place. But tonight? She felt nothing. Detached. The haze of alcohol dulled the sharp edges of her guilt, her anger, her despair. For the first time in weeks, she felt almost alive.

Her gaze drifted—unwillingly, inexorably—to Gabriel. He stood at the bar, his broad shoulders set, his usually guarded expression fixed in place.

But he wasn't alone.

Eve leaned against him, her hand resting on his arm as she whispered something in his ear. Gabriel glanced down at her with a blank face.

Then Eve tilted her head up and kissed him.

The world tilted, the air knocked from Ava's lungs. The noise of the tavern became a distant hum. The colors blurred. She should look away. She wanted to—needed to—but her body betrayed her, locking her in place.

Gabriel didn't push Eve away. He didn't kiss her back either, not fully. But he didn't stop her.

Ava's grip tightened on her glass, the edges biting into her palm. She told herself it didn't matter, that it couldn't matter. She had no claim to him. No right to feel the sharp ache in her chest.

She drained the rest of her drink in one defiant gulp. And took another shot.

Her body swayed as she stood, unsteady from the liquor burning through her veins. She stumbled, but caught herself on the edge of the table, and turned toward the thrumming chaos. The world sloped with every step, but she didn't care. She wanted to drown in it—to lose herself in the noise and the lights, to forget everything for one night.

A firm hand gripped her arm, yanking her back.

"Hey!" she snapped, spinning to confront whoever dared to stop her.

Her anger fizzled when she met Melissa's sharp gaze.

She pulled Ava toward the bathroom.

The smell of stale alcohol and cheap perfume mingled with the faint chemical tang of cleaner. Melissa waited until the last few women shuffled out, locking the door behind them with a sharp click. "What is up with you?"

Ava leaned back against the sink, crossing her arms. "What are you talking about?"

"You're drunk."

"Yeah, so? Am I not allowed to have a little fun?"

"This isn't you. Stop hiding behind your wall."

Ava rolled her eyes, pushing off the sink. "Fat chance of that happening. I *am* having fun."

"Don't lose yourself, Ava."

"If you can't beat 'em, join 'em."

Disgust twisted Melissa's features. "Turn them back on."

"Why? I don't want to feel every little thing we've done. You don't get it, Mel. If I don't lose myself, this—" Her voice broke for a fraction of a second. "—this will destroy me."

"We can get through this."

"Easy for you to say. Your mother didn't promise your soul to Havok. You don't have to fear *death*."

"Are you kidding me right now? Of course, I fear death. We all do."

"Honestly, I think we should kill him now. We're stronger than him."

Melissa let out a frustrated sigh. "Do you have a death wish? You know we can't do that—not until we figure out how to break the curse."

"Good luck with that." Ava pushed past her. "Are we done here?"

"Let's go to Klaus's, Ava. It'll help."

"Why? So, we can sit in a circle and wish for things we can't have? No thanks."

Melissa grabbed her arm. "Ava, you need this. You need to let it out."

With a sharp jerk, she freed herself. "I don't need anything. I'm not going to sit around feeling sorry for myself, crying into a pillow every night."

"Keeping your emotions off isn't going to work forever. It's going to catch up to you, and when it does, it'll break you."

"What part of this *isn't* breaking me? Everything is a mess. And I'm sorry I can't be perfect like you, flipping my emotions on and off at will, crying it out, and moving on."

"So, you're just going to be like this until it's over?"

"Klaus said I should. Why not? Might as well make the best of it."

"Don't give up."

Her anger flared. "Stop saying that! Don't talk to me about giving up!"

"That's exactly what you're doing. You think you're in this alone. You always think that, and it drives me crazy. You're not the only one who's killed innocent people. You're not the only one sacrificing themselves for this cause. Yeah, you're linked to Havok, but we're trying to break that curse. Stop acting like it's all on you."

She clenched her teeth. "Stop wasting your time on trying to save me, Mel. I've accepted my fate."

Melissa's face fell, shock giving way to hurt. "Have you now? Does Gabriel know?"

"Gabriel's too busy with Eve," she spat. "And yes, he knows. He's given up on me."

"What? No, he hasn't."

"We should focus on convincing the Cimmerians to switch sides. In the meantime, I'm going to have some fun."

"Ava, please. Let's go to Klaus's. I don't want to fight anymore."

She brushed past her and unlocked the door. "You should stop while you're ahead. We're stuck here, Mel. Until I kill Havok."

The door swung shut behind her. The noise of the crowded room hit Ava like a wave, the pounding music vibrating in her chest. She scanned the room, her eyes finding Xavier leaning against the bar. His grin widened when he spotted her, and he held out a glass.

"There you are." He handed her another shot. "Everything okay?"

Ava downed it in one motion, the burn in her throat a welcome distraction. "All good."

The lights dimmed, and the crowd roared. The band began playing, heavy and raw. Red lights strobed over the writhing crowd, painting everything in shades of fire and shadow.

Xavier extended his hand, and Ava took it, letting him lead her to the dance floor. The alcohol numbed her, and the music vibrated through her body, drowning out her thoughts. She lost herself in the rhythm, her movements fluid and careless.

But as she turned, her breath caught. Gabriel stood at the edge of the crowd, his eyes locked on hers. His gaze was intense, unyielding, slicing through the haze like a blade.

Eve sidled up to him, her hand sliding into his hand. He didn't look at her. His eyes stayed on Ava, piercing through the chaos and the red glow.

Ava turned away, forcing herself to ignore the tightness in her chest. Let him watch. Let him see her like this. It didn't matter anymore.

She closed her eyes, letting the music swallow her whole. For tonight, she would allow it. She would let the rhythm bury her guilt, her pain, her fears. Because if she didn't, all of it would crush her.

CHAPTER TWENTY-TWO

PLAY WITH FIRE

Groaning, Ava rolled onto her side, each movement unleashing a fresh wave of aching protest from her strained muscles. Her head throbbed, sharp and insistent, as if the very act of thinking had become unbearable. A fog blanketed her mind, dragging her deeper into the mire of her guilt and exhaustion. She lay still for a moment, the bed beneath her too soft, too indulgent for the tempest inside her. The quiet of the room felt gloomy, as if the walls themselves were closing in to trap her with the memories of what she'd done.

The faint scent of sweat and stale alcohol clung to her skin, mingling with the coppery tang of lingering blood—hers, theirs—she didn't know anymore. The grotesque tapestry of last night's carnage refused to fade, haunting her with every shallow breath. She squeezed her eyes shut, trying to force it away, but the memories clung like smoke, choking her with their permanence.

And then *that* memory surfaced.

Eve's lips brushing Gabriel's, the fleeting touch Ava couldn't erase no matter how hard she tried. The scene replayed in her mind like a cruel trick.

Why had she looked? Why hadn't she turned away before the image burned into her mind? She told herself it didn't matter—*couldn't* matter. But the sting of it, the bitterness, crawled under her skin, a wound that refused to heal.

Her last words to Melissa rang out in her mind: *"We're stuck here."* Ava's stomach turned. She hadn't needed to lash out, hadn't needed to wound. But the cold detachment was all she had left. If she softened now, if she allowed herself to feel, she would drown in what they'd done, in the knowledge of what they still had to do.

More cities to burn. More lives to extinguish.

A hollowness in her chest spread, deepening with each inhale. Gabriel had been right to question her. The thought of ending it all—to throw herself into the void and deny Havok his pawn—had crossed her mind more times than she cared to admit. But the cowardice of it stung. She wasn't ready to die. Not yet. A small, fragile part of her still clung to the hope of something else—something *normal.*

She craved a life where she could agonize over which coffee to drink, stress over exams, or waste time debating what to wear on a first date. Instead, she was left with the taste of ash on her tongue and the knowledge of entire families who would never see tomorrow. The rebellion was no salvation—it was a machine. And she was just another cog, bound to it by Havok's iron grip.

If Havok died now, she doubted the rebellion would end. It would fracture, turning inward on itself. And what would the Cimmerians do with the Elementals then? There would be no peace, only more war. The growing tension between the two factions already felt like a coiled snake ready to strike. If she wanted to survive, if she wanted them to survive, she had to keep up the act. She had to be one of them.

The thought made her stomach twist. They hated her anyway. They saw her as a threat, and they weren't wrong. The Elementals could end the world in mere seconds. But that was why Havok kept them close—tools for his arsenal, pawns in his endless war. Even if they destroyed the Ephemerals, Havok wouldn't stop. She knew that. He'd find another enemy, another reason to burn the world.

She rolled to her side, staring at the gray light seeping through her curtains. Clouds hung heavy over the mountains, cloaking the peaks in shadow. The grass below the castle stretched out like an emerald carpet, lush and unyielding, mocking her with its serenity. She wanted to open the window, to let the June air cut through her, but it would never feel like home. It wasn't the warmth of New Orleans.

With a sigh, she forced herself to her feet. The cold air of her room prickled her skin as she moved to the bathroom. The shower scalded her at first, but she let the water do what it did best—heal. She called the water from within her, letting it weave through her muscles and over her skin. It soothed her aches and mended her bruises, but it couldn't touch the hollow ache in her chest. Her heart was stone now, and no amount of water could soften it.

After the shower, she refused to meet her reflection in the mirror. She went through the motions, applying light makeup and tying her hair into a ponytail. Dressed in dark jeans, a white top, and her reliable black boots, she turned for the door, pausing as her hand brushed the doorknob. The world shifted.

The vision struck like lightning.

Ava wasn't herself anymore. She was *him* again. Corbin.

The world blurred into motion as he tore through the woods, his feet pounding against the dirt, breath coming in short, frantic gasps. The cool air burned in his lungs, but he didn't stop. He couldn't. The sound of rushing water grew louder, a relentless roar that filled his ears. His heart raced, dread tightening its grip as the river came into view.

A delicate hand floated in the current, pale and still.

"Lenorah!" Corbin stumbled forward and plunged his hands into the icy water. He grasped her body, the cold seeping into his bones as he pulled her from the river's embrace. Her face was porcelain, her eyes closed, lips tinged with blue.

And then his gaze fell on the child. Esmerelda.

The baby's tiny face was a haunting shade of blue, her lips still. Corbin's breath caught, his chest constricting as a wave of despair crashed over him.

The vision shattered.

Ava staggered back from the door, her chest heaving. The icy river clung to her like a phantom, its chill wrapping around her ribs and squeezing. She sank to the floor and gripped her knees as she tried to ground herself. The room felt too small, her breaths too shallow. Tears blurred her vision as she pressed her back against the wall.

Why am I seeing this?

Lenorah. Esmerelda. She didn't know their story, but the pain, the love—it was *his*. And now, somehow, it was hers too.

Ava couldn't take it anymore. Havok's pain and loss weren't just invading her—they were consuming her, seeping into the cracks of her being like water, freezing in stone, threatening to split her apart. His darkness snaked around her, insidious and unrelenting, sinking its fangs into the corners of her mind. And yet, somewhere deep inside, a part of her began to understand him.

His grief pressed down on her chest, a relentless ache that mirrored the rhythm of her own heartbeat. It wasn't just an emotion—it was a presence, heavy and unyielding, pulling at her like an anchor dragging her into the depths. The pain wasn't confined to her mind; it reverberated through her body, a dull, ceaseless throbbing that left her weak and trembling.

The lines between them began to blur, her sense of self unraveling like threads pulled too tight. Havok's anguish became her anguish, his rage her own. Each stolen emotion carved into her like a mark in stone, reshaping her in ways she couldn't control. Her identity slipped further from her grasp, submerged in a tide of grief and fury that wasn't hers yet felt too real to ignore.

For a fleeting, terrifying moment, she couldn't tell where Havok ended, and she began.

She clenched her fists. She had to move. Sitting there, stewing in the chaos of her mind, would only make it worse.

Her eyes flicked toward the door, a surge of longing pulling at her. She thought of visiting Klaus. But others may be there, and she wasn't ready to face anyone. Not after her fight with Melissa.

Ava's stomach twisted, guilt adding another layer. She couldn't face Melissa. Not yet. Not when the last remnants of the fight still clung to her like static. No, Klaus wasn't an option. Not now.

She pushed herself to her feet, legs shaky beneath her, and smoothed her hands over her jeans. Her reflection in the window caught her eye—pale, hollow, and unfamiliar. With a sharp exhale, she turned away and opened the door. The corridors of the castle were mercifully quiet, but the silence felt like it was watching her, waiting for her to crack. She darted down the stairs, her boots clicking against the stone, and exited.

A slap of crisp mountain air revived her, allowing her to breathe again for a moment. The tension in her shoulders eased as she wandered down the cobbled path into the village. Before her, a small cluster of cottages sprawled like a forgotten painting, their warm lights spilling onto the darkened streets. The soft murmur of distant voices carried on the breeze, but no one paid her any mind. It was better that way.

She let her feet guide her, aimless but searching. The village had a rhythm of its own, a quiet defiance against the chaos she carried inside her. But she couldn't shake the sensation of being watched—not by anyone visible, but by something intangible, pressing at the edges of her awareness.

And then, out of nowhere, someone's hand slipped into hers.

Ava froze. The warmth of the touch jolted through her like an electric current, sharp and undeniable, snapping her out of her spiraling thoughts. Her breath hitched as she turned, her pulse hammering in her ears.

Gabriel's blue eyes met hers, their depths filled with an unspoken urgency that cut through the chaos in her chest.

His intense gaze made her want to recoil, to hide the mess she'd become, but her feet stayed rooted.

The tug of teleportation seized her, wrenching her through the suffocating stillness of the village. Her stomach lurched as colors and shapes streaked past her vision. Then, with a jarring snap, her feet hit solid ground.

A grove unfolded around her, bathed in the silvery light of the moon. The air was cooler there, carrying the crisp, earthy scent of damp moss and pine, mingled with the faint sweetness of wildflowers. The whisper of leaves above and the distant murmur of a creek wrapped the space in a fragile serenity.

He let go of her hand, stepping back enough to meet her gaze again. The worry etched into his face made her throat tighten.

"Gabriel," she breathed.

His jaw tensed. "We need to talk."

She lowered her gaze. "I know."

"What happened last night?" he whispered, but there was no mistaking the edge in his voice.

Her heart sank deeper. The tavern's dim lights flashed in her memory—the burn of whiskey down her throat, Eve kissing Gabriel, the hollow laughter that bubbled out of Ava as she tried to drown her feelings and thoughts and actions. But it hadn't worked. Nothing did. The blood, the faces of the innocent she'd killed, the screams that haunted her dreams—they were all still there. "I was trying to forget. For one night, I needed to not feel like I was drowning."

"You kept your emotions off," Gabriel said sharply. "You know how dangerous that is. Do you even realize what could've happened?"

Her head snapped up, anger flaring. "You don't get it! You weren't the one who had to kill innocent people. You didn't hear their screams or see their faces—"

"Don't you dare. Don't think for a second that I don't feel this, too. I see it every time I close my eyes, Ava. The blood, the fear, the lives we've stolen—it's tearing me apart just as much as it's tearing you apart."

His vulnerability hit her like a tidal wave, but it only fueled her anger. "Then why are you lecturing me? Why can't you let me deal with this my way?"

"Because your way is destroying you. And if you keep going like this, there won't be anything left of you to save."

The words cut deep, deflating her fury. She stepped back, shaking her head. "Don't act like you can fix this, Gabriel. You shouldn't have to carry this for me. I don't want to burden you with it."

He gripped her shoulders, holding her in place. "You're not a burden. I'm scared for you. Last night, I saw something in your eyes—something dark. Like you were starting to lose yourself."

Tears burned her eyes, and she broke free from his hold. "I am losing myself," she choked out. "I feel it, Gabriel. Every mission, every order—it's like pieces of me are breaking away, and I can't put them back together." Her voice trembled, her words spilling out in a frantic rush. "Havok is inside me. His memories, his grief, his pain—it's not just his anymore. It's mine. I feel it every second, and it's eating me alive. Sometimes I think about turning it all off. For good. If I did, maybe I wouldn't feel this way anymore. Maybe I wouldn't feel anything."

Gabriel's breath caught, and his hands found her shoulders again, this time gentler, as if she might shatter beneath his touch. "Is that what you want?" he asked quietly. "To shut it all out? To lose everything that makes you *you*?"

Her knees buckled, and tears streamed down her cheeks as she shook her head. "I don't want to feel Havok's grief, his rage, his … love. I don't want to see his dead wife and baby every time I close my eyes. I don't want to remember New Orleans. The bodies. The faces. And we just left them." She buried her face in her hands. "I'm scared. Scared of what I'm becoming. Scared of what I might do."

He pulled her into his arms, wrapping her in a protective embrace. She stiffened at first, but as his hand pressed against her back, she crumbled, her sobs shaking both of them. "I'm so sorry." He kissed the top of her head, his breath warm against her hair. "I wish I knew how to help you. I'm trying, Ava. I'm trying so hard. But please … please don't turn it off. Don't lose yourself. I can't lose you."

Her tears soaked into his shirt as she clung to him. "It hurts. It's too much. Havok is so much stronger than me."

He held her tighter. "Whatever it takes, we'll figure this out."

But Ava was losing hope.

When they reappeared in a quiet alley of the village, Gabriel's gaze lingered on Ava. The dim glow of a nearby lantern reflected in his blue eyes, and for a moment, neither of them spoke.

"I hate this part," he whispered.

She nodded. "Me, too."

He hesitated, like he wanted to say more, but the moment passed. With a deep breath, he vanished, the faint rush of air from his teleportation stirring the stillness around her.

Even amidst the village lights and sounds, she felt imprisoned. The world seemed too big and too small all at once, her emotions swirling. Wrapping her arms around herself, she walked down the uneven cobblestone path, the sound of her boots crunching against the gravel.

As she passed by the tavern, the pungent scent of spilled ale and stale sweat hit her nose. A retching sound caught her attention, sharp and guttural, cutting through the quiet.

Her eyes landed on a man hunched over near the tavern wall, his shoulders shaking with each heave. "Xavier?"

He wiped his mouth with the back of his hand and turned toward her, swaying on his feet. "Ava," he slurred, a crooked smile spreading across his face. His hair fell into his eyes, disheveled and damp with sweat.

"Are you okay?" she asked.

"Couldn't be better. I may have drunk too much."

"I can see that."

"You're out late." As he straightened, he winced, holding his head like the movement had cost him. "I missed you tonight. Thought for sure you'd want to hang out after last night."

Ava stiffened. The memory of the tavern and her reckless laughter cutting through her like a shard of glass. "I didn't feel like it."

He tilted his head, his bleary eyes narrowing as he studied her. His gaze pierced despite his drunken state, like he could see past her walls. "Why do you look like you've been crying?"

Her hand flew to her cheek, but she stopped herself, scowling instead. "What do you want, Xavier?"

He stumbled toward her as a faint smile tugged at his lips. "You came up to me. Checking on me."

"Right. My bad." She turned away. "I'll see you later."

As she moved to walk past him, his hand shot out and caught hers. His grip was firm but not aggressive, and the unexpected warmth of his touch stopped her in her tracks.

"Wait. I'm sorry. I had fun last night with you. But there was something ... I saw."

Her stomach twisted. Had he seen Gabriel watching her? Worse—had he noticed the way she'd looked at Gabriel? She froze, her voice strained. "What did you see?"

He hesitated, his brow furrowing as if he were trying to piece together a puzzle. "It could be my imagination. But your eyes ... I don't know."

"Tell me."

"There was a darkness." His grip on her hand tightened, then loosened, as if he were second-guessing himself. "And only one other person I know has that same look."

"What are you saying?"

"I don't know. I'm drunk. Don't listen to me."

Ava pulled her hand from his grasp. "I need to go."

"Ava—" he started, but she was already walking away, her boots striking the ground with more force than necessary. Her breath came in shallow bursts as she put distance between them, Xavier's words echoing in her mind: *There was a darkness.*

Her hands clenched into fists as she walked, the night air sharp and cold against her flushed skin. Her thoughts churned, tangled with Havok's lingering presence. She couldn't shake the way Xavier had looked at her, like he'd seen something she couldn't hide. Something she didn't want to admit to herself. Did Xavier know about their link?

Staring at the ceiling, Ava's eyes begged to close. But every time her lids fluttered shut, they flew open again, haunted by the horrors she might see in Havok's mind. Exhaustion wore on her, but the terror of another vision kept her rigid and alert. She turned her head toward the window, watching the world slowly wake up. The sun's orange glow melted into the purple and white hues of the fading night, spilling over the horizon like a brushstroke wiping away darkness.

Darkness.

The word lodged itself in her mind like a splinter. Gabriel saw it. Xavier saw it. Melissa saw it. They all looked at her with worry or fear, as if waiting for her to break. Gabriel would do anything to help her, she knew that, but it had been months. Months without a solution, without hope. The darkness was still there, growing, feeding off her failures.

She closed her eyes, bracing herself as her body went still.

The memory struck, yanking her from herself.

Corbin sighed, heavy with dread, as he finished gathering his belongings for the trip to Caprington with his sister, Veronica. His hands trembled, his nerves betraying him. It had been years since he'd set foot in that vile castle, and even the thought of returning made his skin crawl. But Veronica needed him. She'd killed her husband, Edward—a Hunter who had married her only to infiltrate the Havok family and destroy them from within.

Corbin's stomach churned. Edward's betrayal wasn't surprising, not after what the Hunters had done to his own family. Yet he couldn't help but feel torn. He'd abandoned Caprington years ago, renouncing his family and their bloodlust. He'd chosen Lenorah, his sweet, gentle Lenorah, and their baby girl over them. But his family had taken that from him, slaughtering Lenorah and Esmerelda. They had always hated her—hated her lower status, her quiet strength, her refusal to join their wars. They'd seen her as a distraction, a weakness, someone who had stolen Corbin from them.

And yet … he'd never avenged them.

The thought was a bitter pill he couldn't swallow. His family was stronger, more ruthless. To challenge them would have meant his death. And part of him, deep down, was afraid. They were still his family, after all.

As he and Veronica arrived at Caprington, dread coiled in his gut. The castle appeared above them, its dark spires piercing the sky like jagged teeth. The heavy, frigid air stifled him the moment they passed through the massive doors. His instincts screamed he should turn back.

He should not have come.

"Corbin," his father's deep voice boomed across the entry hall. The man stood tall, broad-shouldered, his eyes as hard as the stone walls around them. They stared at each other, tension crackling in the air like a storm about to break.

Veronica hesitated, then hugged her father. "I brought him home, Father."

"Thank you, child. We have much to discuss."

Corbin bristled at the ease with which his father dismissed his years of absence. "I cannot believe you have the nerve to speak to me."

"Please, do not fight," Veronica pleaded, her eyes darting between them.

His father grunted, turning his back on Corbin and gesturing for them to follow. They entered a dark chamber where their mother and the rest of the family waited, their expressions cold and expectant.

His mother, always so stern and obstinate, glared at him. "It is good to see you, my son. I have missed you. I am sorry about Lenorah and Esmerelda." Her tone held no sincerity, only a calculated coldness.

The names hit him hard. Corbin's hands curled into fists as rage surged in his veins. "How dare you speak their names, you vile creature," he snarled. "All of you. How could you have done that?"

His mother tilted her head. "What are you talking about?"

"You murdered them," he growled. "You killed my wife and child!"

"Corbin," his father interrupted, "you abandoned us, and now you come here with accusations? We had nothing to do with their deaths. The Ephemerals are to blame."

"No." Corbin shook his head. "You hated Lenorah. You all did."

His father smirked. "Disliking her does not mean we killed her. But if you truly seek answers, ask the Ephemeral prisoners in our dungeons. They are responsible."

Corbin's heart pounded as the truth he had clung to wavered. Could it be? Could the Ephemerals have betrayed him? He didn't want to believe it, but the seed of doubt took root. His legs moved before his mind could catch up, carrying him to the prison chamber below.

He gripped the iron bars of a cell where a young man with dirty blond hair sat glaring at him. The man's defiance sent a chill through Corbin.

"Did you kill my wife and child?" Corbin demanded.

The man smirked. "Lenorah, was it? Long black hair, green eyes?"

Corbin froze, his blood turning to ice.

"She begged," the man continued. "But we don't spare abominations like you. I strapped the baby to her chest and sent them both over the edge. She screamed the whole way down."

The rage inside Corbin ignited like wildfire, surging through his veins with a ferocity he'd never known. The cell bars splintered under his desperate strength, his fingers closing like a vise around the man's throat. A deadly energy coursed through him, and within seconds, the man's skin erupted in bloody sores. His screams echoed off the stone walls, but Corbin didn't stop. When the man's body went limp, Corbin snapped his neck and let him fall.

The silence that followed was deafening, but the rage remained, boiling beneath his skin. Killing one man wasn't enough. It would never be enough. He now understood his father's war, his hatred. The Ephemerals were merciless killers, and Corbin would have his revenge.

Ava gasped as the vision shattered. Her chest heaved, her lungs burning as if she'd been underwater too long. Tremors wracked her body as she clutched the sheets. Havok's memory pulsed in her mind, a throbbing, insistent thing, like a trapped bird beating its wings. The rage, the pain, the all-consuming thirst for vengeance—it wasn't just something she'd witnessed. She had *felt* it. It had lived in her, coursed through her veins, as if it were her own.

Her stomach churned, bile rising as the faces of Lenorah and Esmerelda swam before her eyes. The warmth of Lenorah's hand in Corbin's, the sweet innocence of Esmerelda's tiny form—they were ghosts now, shadows snuffed out in the cruelest way. And yet, the fury that followed was sharper, louder, drowning out the sorrow. It clawed at her insides, raw and unrelenting, demanding retribution.

Was this the truth? She wondered, the question slicing through the fog in her mind. *Was this why the war began?* If the Ephemerals killed Havok's family, then everything she thought she knew—the alliances, the cause, the sacrifices—felt fragile, paper-thin.

The questions swirled, a storm of uncertainty and guilt. But the rage—Havok's rage—was louder. It filled every corner of her being, burning away the doubt and demanding action. For the first time, she didn't fight it. For the first time, she understood Havok, felt the pull of his hatred, and let it consume her. And for the first time, she didn't want to resist.

She squeezed her eyes shut, inhaling a shaky breath. *I can't handle this. I have to let go.* The pain, the sadness, the endless weight of the questions—they were too much. One by one, she forced them down, burying each emotion deep inside her until they were no longer hers to carry. Chains of sorrow melted away from her, replaced by a cold, numbing emptiness.

When she opened her eyes, the world felt different. Still. Quiet. Inside her mind, there was nothing but the void.

Much better, she thought, her lips curving into a faint, detached smile. No feelings. No pain. No thoughts. Just silence.

CHAPTER TWENTY-THREE

NIGHT OF HUNTERS

A fine mist hung in the air, soft and cool against Ava's skin, blurring the edges of the cobblestone streets and the distant outline of the docks. The muted sunlight filtered through the haze, casting the village in a pale, silvery glow that seemed to quiet the world around her. The rhythmic lap of water against the docks and the creak of boats swaying in the current broke the silence, their sounds soothing, almost hypnotic.

The air carried the scent of brine and weathered wood, mingled with the faint aroma of baking bread from a nearby stall. Ava hadn't been on a boat since her journey to the Cruciari—a rough trip filled with storms and seasickness that had left her vowing never to board one again.

And yet, as she stood there now, surrounded by the crisp salt air and the hum of village life, a strange sense of peace settled over her. The atmosphere was grounding, like she belonged there in a way she had felt nowhere else.

The energy simmering beneath her skin demanded release, prickling at her nerves like an itch she couldn't scratch. She wanted destruction—craved it. Her powers begged to be unleashed, to tear something apart, but she forced herself to ignore the urge for now. *Soon,* she promised herself, the thought oddly soothing.

As she neared the tavern, the familiar hum of voices and clinking glass spilled into the street. She pushed open the heavy wooden door, the scent of spilled beer and fried food washing over her. Her eyes scanned the room and landed on Anais, Xavier, and Donovan at a corner table. They were laughing—well, Anais and Xavier were—while Donovan looked as sour as ever.

"Come join us," Xavier called out, lifting his drink in greeting.

Donovan sighed, his disdain palpable, and rolled his eyes as if it tortured him to see her.

He's such a child. He should get over it. We're not going anywhere.

She crossed the room to them and dropped into the seat next to Xavier. "Hey."

He studied her face, his expression shifting from cheer to concern. "Are you okay?"

"I'm great. How are *you* feeling?"

He shook his head and let out a half-laugh. "Glued to my bed for most of the morning. But I'm used to it."

"That's something to be proud of," Ava replied dryly, smirking as she sipped from the water glass in front of her.

"Maybe you shouldn't drink so much." Anais rolled her eyes and took a bite of her sandwich.

Xavier sighed. "Are you still pissed about the other night?"

"He chose *all* of us to be in the army," she said. "That means all of us go. Not just your favorites."

"Amen." Donovan saluted his beer toward her.

Xavier's smile vanished, replaced by a glare as cold as ice. "You do realize that even though I'm in charge of the army, Havok still makes decisions. This is what he wanted. Get over it." He turned to Ava. "Good job, by the way."

"Yeah, congratulations," Anais said. "I heard you guys completely wiped out New Orleans."

"Yeah, it's all gone," Ava said. She felt nothing as she said it—no regret, no pride. Just the cold satisfaction of a mission completed. *Havok wanted this. I wanted this.*

Donovan drained his beer. "Good riddance."

Anais glanced at Xavier, her expression hard. "You think Havok will let us go anymore now that they're here?" She nodded toward Ava.

Xavier leaned back in his chair and shrugged. "Probably. He still wants the Blood Vanguard to find more Ephemerals for the army."

Ava tilted her head. "Why Ephemerals?"

He sipped his drink. "They can cause damage, same as us. You've seen what Link and Nicole can do."

"True," Ava said. "How does that work exactly? I mean, we're born this way." She knew the answer, but her expression remained innocent, her tone curious.

"We give them some of our power. Then they get an ability."

The waitress arrived with their drinks. Her smile was too bright, and she smacked her gum far too loudly. Ava resisted the urge to glare, though her fingers itched to shove the sound down her throat.

"How do you choose the Ephemerals?" Ava asked after ordering a panini. "Don't they all pretty much deserve to die?"

Anais let out a dry laugh. "You have no idea. I hate finding them. I want to kill them all. It's hard figuring out who's worth keeping."

"Calm down." Xavier chuckled. "We don't have to do it anymore now that Gabriel's here. But we usually go to random places, watch them, and test them. If they pass, they make the cut."

"Or if their spirit doesn't break first," Anais added with a sneer. "How many months did you waste on Peter?"

Xavier's glare darkened. "That wasn't my fault. He was a Paramortal."

Ava's pulse quickened, though she kept her face neutral, her hands encircled her drink. *Peter.* His name was like a faint echo in her mind, distant and hollow. They'd kidnapped and tortured him, tried breaking him in ways no one should endure. She'd tried to protect him, to save him. But she'd failed. And in the end, he had broken her heart.

Yet now, with her emotions buried beneath layers of stone, she felt none of the guilt or sorrow that had once haunted her. Only a faint, detached curiosity.

Anais rolled her eyes and shrugged. "Whatever."

"What are you talking about?" Ava asked.

"Nothing," Xavier said.

"You say that a lot."

Anais choked on her drink, coughing as she struggled to regain composure. "Get used to it."

Xavier scowled, the muscle in his jaw twitching as his eyes flicked toward her. "Maybe tonight we can go find some Ephemerals."

"Ugh, no," Anais groaned. "I want a night off."

"*You* do? From what, exactly? We were the ones who went out the other night."

"Thanks for reminding me," Anais shot back.

The door creaked open, and she looked up.

Link, Nicole, Gabriel, and Eve walked into the tavern.

Ava's heart should have leapt at the sight of them, but there was nothing—just a hollow stillness that had taken its place. Her eyes zeroed in on Gabriel. He didn't look at her—not even a trace of acknowledgment. His gaze stayed forward, his expression a mask of ease, but there was something in the tightness of his jaw, the restrained way he moved, that didn't sit right.

Beside him, Eve clung to his arm, her black hair shining in the dim light as she leaned in close, her grip possessive. Gabriel didn't shrug her off. He didn't even seem to notice. When Xavier called them over, Gabriel followed, his steps measured, his gaze unfaltering. He let Eve lead him to the table, sitting wherever she pulled him, like it didn't matter. Like he didn't care.

Ava's stomach twisted. He acted like he was Eve's puppet.

Anais raised an eyebrow. "Trying to make new friends?"

"You don't have to be enemies with everyone, you know." Xavier smirked.

Anais pressed her lips into a hard line. "Go hang out with your new friends. See if I care." She shoved her chair back, the scrape of wood against stone and stormed out of the tavern. The door slammed behind her, the sound reverberating through the space.

Eve wasted no time running out after her.

Gabriel slid into the seat across from Ava. He still didn't look at her.

Link and Nicole followed, filling the chairs to Ava's left, their expressions open and unbothered.

Gabriel sat, his hands resting on the table as if anchoring himself, his knuckles pale from tension Ava wasn't supposed to notice.

Ava turned to Xavier. "What was that about?"

"Anais?" Xavier rolled his eyes and sighed. "She's jealous."

"Of what?"

He pointed his beer at her and took a sip. "You."

"Me?" Ava raised an eyebrow, leaning back in her chair.

"All of you," Xavier clarified. "She feels like she's got no purpose now that Havok wants you guys for the massacres."

Ava's lips curved into a faint, humorless smile. "She's still in the army. She'll still be used for the massacres. What's there to be jealous about? She's just as powerful and useful as any of us."

Xavier cocked an eyebrow, the corner of his mouth twitching. "You really don't get it, do you? You have no idea how powerful you are."

"I do. But you all have been training since you could remember."

"True. But Havok likes to change things up. He'll probably swap the group out each time we go out. That's how it's always been."

Eve reappeared, slipping into the seat beside Gabriel and scooting so close their knees brushed. She reached for his hand, intertwining her fingers with his. Ava turned away, her gaze fixed on the table, the hollow sensation in her chest deepening. Gabriel didn't pull away.

Let me deal with Eve, he'd told her. A lie, clearly. If this was how he "dealt" with her, Ava wanted no part of it.

"Glad to have you back, Gabriel." Xavier raised his drink.

"Good to be back," Gabriel replied with an easy smile that didn't reach his eyes. His voice was steady, casual—too casual. Ava noticed the way his fingers tightened around his mug, the tension in his jaw when he thought no one was looking. He still didn't look at her. Not once.

Donovan rose from his chair and stretched. "Let me know when we're going tonight. I'm gonna head out. See ya." He strolled out of the tavern.

"What's tonight?" Link asked.

"We're going to find some Ephemerals," Ava said.

"You and Nicole should come." Xavier took a sip of his beer. "Would be good experience."

"Why are you going?" Eve asked, flipping her hair over her shoulder. "That's Gabriel's job now."

Xavier shrugged. "Just for fun. Besides, it'd be good for them to learn."

"We could go and show them how it's done." Eve's grin turned predatory.

Ava chuckled, a cold, detached sound. "Shouldn't be too hard. It'll be harder keeping them alive, though."

Her words sliced through the conversation like a knife, leaving an uneasy quiet in their wake. She felt their stares—curious, cautious—but she didn't care. The waitress arrived with her food, and Ava began eating in silence, ignoring Xavier's penetrating stare.

"Why do you keep staring at me?" she asked.

He hesitated, his beer halfway to his mouth. "Nothing."

Ava leaned back in her chair, crossing her arms as her eyes locked on Gabriel. "So, do we get to experience Gabriel's wonderful ability tonight?"

"Probably not," he said.

"What good are you then?" Ava's words were sharp, a knife aimed directly at him.

Eve narrowed her eyes. "Better than you."

"I doubt that." Her gaze pinned Gabriel, cold and unyielding. "He's weak. What's the point of ending his punishment if he isn't even going to use his powers? Didn't he betray us?"

Eve leaned forward. "He's already paid his debt. You don't know what he's been through."

"Has he? He left you. He left all of us. For what?" Her words dripped with venom as her mind spiraled. *He deserves to drown. To suffocate in the waves of his betrayal, just like he left us drowning.*

Gabriel gasped, clutching his chest as his breath hitched. His face contorted in pain, his body jerking as he coughed and sputtered. Water poured from his lips, drenching the table as he struggled for air.

Eve's eyes widened in alarm, her hands flying to Gabriel's shoulders. "Gabriel!" she exclaimed, her voice sharp with panic. "What's wrong? What's happening?"

Ava's focus sharpened on the throbbing vein in his neck, her lips curving into a faint, satisfied smile. She wanted to see it burst. Wanted him to break. A shadow passed over her vision, and darkness crowded her mind.

"Stop!" Xavier's voice broke through, snapping her out of the haze. The darkness receded as quickly as it had come.

When she blinked, the five of them stared at her, their faces pale, their eyes wide with shock. Eve's hand shielded Gabriel's back as he gasped for air. Her gaze shot daggers at Ava.

"What the hell did you do to him?" Eve spat.

Ava shrugged and took a sip of her water. "Just having a little fun, is all."

"Fun?" Eve fumed. "You nearly killed him, you psycho!"

Ava's eyes flicked to Gabriel, who was still struggling for breath as Eve rubbed his back, murmuring to him. The sight was sickening, but if they claimed he'd paid for his betrayal, so be it. Who was she to argue?

Night had fallen, cloaking the training pit in a heavy darkness pierced only by the light of torches. The faint scent of damp earth lingered in the air, mingling with the metallic tang of old blood and sweat. Ava joined Xavier, Gabriel, Eve, Link, and Nicole.

Xavier stood at the center of the group, a mischievous grin stretched across his face. "Okay, some things to pay attention to," he began. "The recruits have to be strong. If they're cautious of you, that's a good thing. If they're too eager to talk to you—not a good candidate. If they appear angry or sad, go for it. Be friendly. Get to know them. Any questions?"

Nicole tilted her head. "What do we do when we've found one?" she asked, her tone uncertain, though her gaze flicked to Link for reassurance.

Ava glanced at them both, wondering how they of all people would manage this task. *Sweet, moral Link and Nicole. Do they even realize what they've signed up for?*

"Get them alone and knock them out," Xavier replied. "Do not kill them. It's best if you pick someone of the opposite sex. Flirting makes it more fun."

"Let's go," Ava urged. She didn't want to waste time listening to Xavier's theatrics.

Xavier smirked and turned, leading the way through the winding tunnels. The passageways were narrow, the air stale and cool.

Ava was very aware of Gabriel's presence behind her. Even with their emotions suppressed, the air crackled with an almost suffocating tension, thick enough to taste. His measured footsteps matched hers, as if he were forcing himself not to look at her. She ignored him. *He's with Eve now.* The thought drifted, detached, like a fact she no longer cared about.

When Xavier opened the heavy iron door at the end of the tunnel, the cool night air hit Ava's face like a slap. The world beyond was alive with noise and movement. Across the street, a university campus sprawled before them, its towering buildings framed by palm trees swaying in the breeze. The air smelled of sage and fried food, a strange mix that made Ava's stomach churn. Oddly shaped houses—some modern, some split-level—lined the street, their clean stucco facades a sharp contrast to the chaotic students milling about. Fraternity and sorority signs with bold and gaudy letters adorned balconies.

"Where are we?" Nicole asked.

Xavier grinned. "Some university. Come on. I'm sure we can find a frat party somewhere."

As they walked down the street, the rhythmic thump of music grew louder, pounding in Ava's ears. She spotted the party before they reached it: a two-story house bathed in neon lights, its front lawn crowded with girls in string bikinis and yellow shirts running through sprinklers. Their high-pitched, incessant laughter grated on Ava's nerves.

Inside, the house was a blur of bodies, the air thick with sweat and alcohol. Ava's sharp gaze darted around the room, her detachment morphing into disdain. The students here were careless, oblivious to the wider world. *Spoiled rich kids. They don't deserve this life. They don't deserve to live.*

Her eyes landed on a boy slouched on the couch, a red cup in his hand. He was tall, a little chubby, his shaved head gleaming under the dim light. His vacant stare suggested he was miles away from the chaos around him.

Ava crossed the room and sat next to him. "How's it going?"

He shrugged and tipped his cup, draining the last of its contents. Without a word, he stood and headed for the kitchen.

Interesting. She followed him, weaving through the crowd until she found him at the fridge, pulling out another beer.

"Are you following me?" he asked.

"Maybe."

"What do you want?"

"Just looking for a friend."

"Well, I really don't feel like talking to you." He moved to walk past her, but she stepped into his path, blocking him.

"Why not?" She tilted her head and gave him the most angelic look she could muster.

He furrowed his brows, suspicion flashing in his eyes. "What the hell is your problem? Don't you know when to leave someone alone?"

She leaned closer, the sharp scent of his cheap cologne stinging her nose. "Yeah, but I don't feel like leaving you alone. You looked like you needed someone to talk to."

"What are you? A self-help guru?"

She laughed. "Hardly. More like the opposite." She moved closer and pressed her hands against his chest. "But I can help make you forget. Forget everything."

His lips twitched into a smirk, but his eyes remained cautious. "How are you gonna do that? Even if you give me the best night of my life, I'm still gonna remember it tomorrow."

She stared into his eyes. "Trust me. I'll make you forget forever."

Something shifted in his gaze—a flicker of uncertainty. *Got him.* She took his hand, leading him out of the kitchen, through the crowded main room, and onto the lawn.

"Where are we going?" he asked.

She turned to him. "You'll make a great soldier."

His face twisted into confusion. "What the hell are you talking about?"

Her fist connected with his face in a swift, brutal motion. His eyes rolled back, and he crumpled to the ground with a thud. The metallic scent of blood mixed with the night air as Ava grabbed his foot, dragging his unconscious body toward the tunnel entrance.

The faint sound of the party faded behind her as she waited, the darkness of the tunnel pressing against her.

Ava didn't have to wait long. Just a couple of hours after finding her recruit, the others arrived with their captives.

"What took you so long?" she asked, leaning against the wall.

Xavier raised a curious eyebrow, his grin cocky as ever. "How long have you been sitting here?"

"For a while. He was easy." She shrugged, motioning to the unconscious Ephemeral slumped in the cell behind her.

He shook his head. "Guess you're good at this. He looks like he'll be useful."

"That's what I said."

Nicole grimaced as she peered at Ava's recruit. "Did you carry him?"

"No, I dragged him."

"That explains the scrapes on his face," Nicole said.

"Let's go." Xavier gestured for them to follow.

Ava hoisted her recruit over her shoulder, his weight unnoticeable, and fell in line behind the others. The sound of their boots on the stone floor echoed through the tunnels as they entered the shadowy prison.

Xavier directed them to deposit their recruits in separate cells.

Ava watched with vague disinterest as the others handled their captives, her mind already elsewhere. Her thoughts flickered to Gabriel, who had remained silent the entire time. She avoided looking at him, though she could feel his presence—steady, deliberate, like he was holding himself together by sheer will.

"That was fun." Eve clutched Gabriel's arm like a trophy.

"Tavern tonight?" Xavier asked.

"Nah." Eve glanced up at Gabriel. "I think we're gonna go back to the room."

Ava's gaze darted to Gabriel, but he didn't react—didn't pull away, didn't protest. He let Eve hold him, his face a careful mask of indifference. *So, this is the game he's playing now.*

It wasn't jealousy that flickered through Ava's mind. It was calculation. Gabriel chose to maintain his role with Eve, letting her cling to him like a lifeline. It was a smart move, tactically speaking. But it also meant he wasn't hers anymore—not in any way that mattered.

The acknowledgment was cold and final in her mind, like a door slamming shut. *He's unreliable now.* The thought settled, solid and unshakable, leaving no room for regret or longing. If Gabriel had chosen his side, then she would choose hers.

"I'm game." Ava brushed past them. She wouldn't sit around watching Eve parade him like some conquest. If Gabriel wanted to play the role of Eve's pet, so be it.

"Let's go." Xavier motioned toward the exit. They left the prison and started up the stairs.

Halfway up, Xavier turned to her. "Would you mind if I changed shirts?"

"Go ahead." She wasn't sure why she didn't have him meet her at the tavern, but something about the prospect of seeing Xavier's space intrigued her. Maybe it was curiosity. Maybe it was boredom.

They climbed another flight of stairs in silence. When they reached his room, Xavier pushed the door open and gestured for her to enter first.

The room was sparse, identical to hers in layout, but utterly devoid of personality. No decorations, no personal touches— just a bed, a desk, and a dresser, all as plain as the walls.

"Either you never spend time in here or you hate decorating," Ava said.

He smirked.

"What?"

"Nothing."

"I hate it when you do that."

"Do what?"

"That thing. Smirking like you know something I don't."

"Maybe I do." He went to his dresser, pulling out a blue shirt. He peeled off his black one, revealing a smooth, muscular back. When he turned around, Ava glimpsed of his chest—light blond hair trailing down to his stomach, toned but not overly built.

She turned her gaze away, uninterested. "You have a lot of secrets."

"I know."

"It's okay." She leaned against the dresser. "Everyone does."

"Mine are ... different."

"There's something I want to know. And I hope you can tell me."

"I can try."

"How did my parents die? I don't remember. You said Ephemerals killed them. How?"

His face darkened, his jaw tightening as he crossed his arms. He stared at the floor. "Your mom ran away and got married. When they didn't come back, they were killed by..." He hesitated, biting his lip.

"Killed by Ephemerals?"

He sighed, meeting her gaze with a knowing look.

"Havok?" she guessed.

"Let's go to the tavern." He took a step toward the door, but Ava seized his arm. "Please tell me what happened." She had to act like she wanted to trust him. They were on the same side.

His face fell. "Sometimes, when someone betrays Havok, he has them killed. Your mom acted as a spy to the Elders but fell in love with an Ephemeral."

The word sent Ava's blood boiling. The rage set in again, and she wanted to find some and kill them. Her powers throbbed beneath her skin. Water trickled down her arms, dripping onto the floor.

"Hey." Xavier grasped her arm. The water ceased. "Calm down."

"She got herself killed, didn't she? She betrayed him."

"She was supposed to come back with you," Xavier said carefully. "But they never returned. The Elders kept you until now."

"How could my mother marry one of them?"

"We think the Elders brainwashed her. It's the only explanation for why anyone would fall in love with *them*."

"It's disgusting," Ava muttered. "Well, good riddance to both of them."

Xavier studied her. "Are you sure you're okay?"

"I'm fine," she snapped. "Why do you keep asking?"

He sighed, frustration flashing in his dark eyes. "Come with me." He took her hand. His grip was firm, his touch warm against her cold skin. He led her out of the room without another word, guiding her through the corridors of the castle. They passed Havok's chambers—its heavy door looming like a sentinel in the torchlight—and crept through another doorway that led to a narrow stairwell.

The air grew cooler as they ascended. The old wooden steps groaned, the sound sharp and hollow, as though the stairs themselves were warning them not to proceed. Ava didn't care. She let Xavier lead, her curiosity muted but still present, simmering beneath the surface of her detachment.

When they finally reached the top, Xavier pushed open a door.

Ava blinked as the crisp night air hit her, carrying the faint, earthy scent of rain that hadn't yet fallen. The darkness beyond was vast, a deep canvas of midnight blue scattered with millions of stars. Wispy clouds drifted across the sky, their edges glowing in the moonlight.

Ava stepped out onto the ledge, her boots crunching against the gravel. She stopped, her gaze drawn to the landscape stretched out before her. The castle's moat shimmered far below, reflecting the stars like a broken mirror. Beyond it, the distant roar of a waterfall echoed through the stillness, its silver cascade glinting in the moonlight. She recognized it—the same waterfall she and the Elders had crossed on their way to Caprington. The memory flashed in her mind, cold and detached. *I thought I would die that day.* Looking back now, she wished she had let the Elders drown. They had been wrong about everything. Havok and the Cimmerians weren't the monsters they had claimed them to be. *The Elders were the true villains.*

"Look," Xavier said. "I know something's wrong with you." His blond strands gleamed under the starlight, and his expression was a mixture of frustration and concern.

She turned to face him, the light breeze tugging at her hair. "Why do you say that?"

"It's just… You've been acting different the last couple of days. Especially today. Something's happened."

Shrugging, she turned her attention back to the waterfall, her arms folded. "I don't know what you're talking about. I'm acting the same. How have I been different?" Was Xavier perceptive enough to notice she'd turned off her emotions? Or that she had finally embraced the truth Havok had shown her? *Or maybe it was the stunt with Gabriel earlier.* That had probably raised a red flag.

"You just seem ... darker or something. I don't know. It feels like there's a cloud hanging over you. Kinda like with Havok. I feel like he's around."

"I feel fine. Great, in fact. I can't remember the last time I felt this amazing, honestly." She could feel Xavier's eyes on her, searching for something she wasn't offering.

After a moment, he sighed, his breath visible in the cool night air.

"What is this place?" She swept her hand across the view.

"It's just a spot to have some quiet time," Xavier said. "Havok sometimes comes here, but mostly it's just me."

"It's beautiful."

They stood in silence for a while, staring out at the stars and the endless dark horizon.

"Are you ready to head back?" he asked.

"Sure."

They made their way down the creaky wooden stairs, the darkness swallowing them once again.

"Can we look for more Ephemerals tomorrow?" she asked.

"We're not really the ones for that though."

"When's our next massacre?"

He stopped in his tracks, turning to face her. "I don't know. A week or so. Why are you so eager?"

"It's exciting. I want to kill them. Is that bad?"

His frown deepened, and he studied her for a long moment. "No. I guess not."

"Good. Can we go to the tavern now?"

Xavier hesitated, his expression shadowed with something she couldn't quite place—concern, maybe? Or frustration? "Sure."

The hate inside her burned, a constant hum beneath her skin, demanding release. The idea of waiting another week before the next massacre felt unbearable. She smirked at the thought of venturing out alone tomorrow, annihilating an entire city on her own. Havok would be proud. Her smile widened at the thought.

She couldn't wait.

The tavern buzzed with life—laughter, clinking glasses, and the tang of spilled ale filling the air. Ava set the empty shot glass down. The warmth of the alcohol spread through her body like a distant memory, a sensation she registered but didn't feel.

Across the table, Xavier's gaze locked onto hers, sharp and assessing. He leaned back in his chair, arms crossed.

"You're staring," she said.

"Just making sure you don't flood this place down."

A faint smile ghosted across her lips, calculated and humorless. She stood, circling the table with deliberate steps until she stopped in front of him, her head tilting.

"You're always so serious, Xavier. Stoic. Controlled. Is that all there is to you? Or is that just the mask you wear?"

"What are you doing, Ava?"

She leaned closer, her hand brushing against his chest. "I want to see what's underneath," she said, her voice low and smooth, her lips hovering near his. It wasn't longing. It wasn't need. It was curiosity—a calculated move to see how far she could push him.

His hand shot up, seizing her wrist, but without malice. "Don't."

Her expression faltered—just for a moment—as if his response had pierced something in her. "Why not?" she asked, her voice quiet, laced with just enough vulnerability to make it believable. "Am I that repulsive to you?"

"You're drunk. And whatever this is, it's not you."

Her lips parted, and she let her hand drop, stepping back as if his words had struck her. Her gaze darted to the floor, her shoulders stiffening. "I'm sorry." She wheeled around, pushing past the crowd and out the tavern door.

"Ava! Wait!"

She had Xavier right where she wanted him.

As Ava walked past an alley, a hand shot out, grabbing her and pressing her into the cold, unforgiving brick wall.

Gabriel.

"Want me to drown you again?" she hissed.

"Ava, stop. Please, turn on your emotions."

Her lips twisted into a mock pout. "Aww, are you sad? Missing your owner, Eve? Is that why you're here? Did she let you off your leash?"

His jaw tightened, anger flashing in his eyes. "Don't do this. Don't go down this path. I know you're scared—"

She barked a laugh. "Scared? Don't insult me, Gabriel. If anyone here is scared, it's you. Tell me, do you tremble when Eve kisses you? When she clings to you like she owns you? Or do you enjoy it? Do you like the way she looks at you, like you're the only thing that matters?"

He froze, the tension in his body coiled tight. "That's not fair."

"Fair? Life isn't fair, Gabriel. Or did you forget that when you let her drape herself all over you? You didn't stop her. You didn't even hesitate."

"You know why I had to. You know it's all a performance."

"Do I? Because from where I'm standing, it looks real enough. And maybe it is. Maybe it's easier to let her think you care. To let her touch you. Kiss you. Pretend she matters to you."

"You think I *wanted* that? You think I had a choice?"

"There's always a choice," she said coolly. "But maybe you've made yours. You chose her. You chose this. So don't come crying to me about what you have to do. You don't even have the decency to admit you like it."

He stepped closer. "And what about you, Ava? What choices have you made? Turning yourself into this—this hollow shell—because you're too afraid to feel anything anymore?"

She laughed softly, a sound devoid of warmth. "Afraid? I've seen what happens when people let themselves feel. It weakens them. It kills them. I'm not afraid—I'm done. I finally realized that caring about you, about anyone, is a waste of time. You're all just distractions. We're all going to end up dead anyway."

"You don't mean that."

She tilted her head. "Maybe I do. Maybe I've finally figured out how to survive. And maybe you're just too weak to accept it."

"Ava." He reached for her arm, gripping it firmly, his touch warm despite the cold wall at her back.

Her eyes flicked to his hand, a dark thought curling in her mind. She imagined him drowning—the panic in his eyes, the water filling his lungs.

He stumbled back, releasing her arm as he bent over, coughing. His hands shot to his chest, his breaths ragged as water spilled from his lips.

She stood there, unflinching, watching him as though he were a stranger.

When he finally caught his breath, he looked up at her, his eyes wide with shock, pain, and something she couldn't name.

Then he was gone.

CHAPTER TWENTY-FOUR

DEVOTED

The bar reeked of desperation, and Ava found she didn't mind.

The smell of stale beer and cigarette smoke clung to the air, mingling with the acrid scent of sweat and regret. Ava pushed the door open, and a screeching guitar riff from the jukebox stabbed through the haze of noise. Dim yellow lights cast everything in a jaundiced glow, their flicker highlighting the ghosts of dust swirling above the pool tables.

Her head pounded—not from exhaustion, but from Havok's voice, slithering through her mind like a serpent. *They don't understand what we're capable of. But I do. Show them, Ava. Show them who you really are.*

The words coiled tighter with every step she took, her fists clenching at her sides. The emptiness she'd cultivated within herself was no longer comforting; it was a gaping void, hungry and restless. Hatred bubbled up to fill it—hatred for the Ephemerals, for the world that had rejected her, for the weakness she had once carried. The need to destroy gnawed at her insides like an itch she couldn't scratch.

Ava slid onto a barstool, ignoring the wary glances cast her way. The bartender, a gaunt woman with a tight braid and a permanent scowl, barely glanced at her as she cracked open a bottle of beer and slid it across the counter. The cold glass steadied Ava's hand, the liquid bitterness offering a fleeting moment of clarity as it slid down her throat.

Scanning the room, she saw a boy sitting alone by the jukebox. He didn't belong there. His clean clothes and bright, innocent eyes marked him as prey in a den of wolves. Too perfect. Too breakable. He looked up, and their eyes met.

A flirtatious smile tugged at her lips, but it was hollow—a weapon, not an invitation.

He grinned back, and within moments, he was beside her.

"Hi, I'm Logan."

Ava finished her beer and set the empty bottle down with a clink. "I'm out."

"I'll buy you another one," he offered quickly, motioning to the bartender. His eagerness grated on her, and yet she let him.

She gave him a nonchalant shrug, watching as he flagged down the bartender. The new beer was cold and crisp. She let Logan talk—about his father's death, about moving to Caprington, about his search for family history. The words washed over her like static, meaningless noise. All she cared about was why he was there.

"No one just comes to Caprington," she said.

Logan shifted, his hand tightening around his beer. "I told you, my dad grew up here."

He's lying, Havok whispered. *They always lie. Prove your worth.*

The rage bubbling beneath her skin surged, and she grabbed Logan's arm. "Let's get out of here."

The rain came down in a relentless drizzle, soaking through Ava's hair and clothes as she pulled Logan into the narrow alley behind the bar.

"My place isn't far," Logan offered nervously.

Ava spun to face him, her eyes narrowing. "Why are you really here, Logan?"

"I already told you—"

He's weak. A waste of breath. Havok's voice curled through her mind, dark and insistent. *Do it, Ava. You know you want to.*

She imagined him drowning. Logan dropped to his knees, coughing and gasping as water filled his lungs. His wide eyes locked on hers, begging for mercy.

"Tell me the truth!" she hissed. "Are you hunting us?"

"I don't know what you're talking about!" he choked out between coughs.

The red haze clouding her vision grew darker. Her hands found their way around his neck. Power surged through her veins, and disease flowed from her fingertips like a living thing. His skin bubbled and split, boils erupting across his face and arms, oozing blood and pus. His scream tore through the rain, raw and piercing.

She felt the shift before she saw it.

The alley faded, replaced by firelight and the acrid stench of charred flesh. Ava gasped, but she wasn't Ava anymore. She was Havok.

His hands were around a man's throat, the flesh beneath his fingers splitting and blistering. The man's screams were a chorus of agony, his body writhing as the disease coursed through his veins. Blood oozed from open sores, pooling at Havok's feet.

"You'll never win," the man rasped. "We will burn you out."

Havok's fury ignited like wildfire, roaring in her chest. His grip tightened, and the man's screams silenced as his body crumbled into a lifeless heap.

Weakling, Havok growled, searing through Ava's thoughts. *That's what they all are. And you're better than them, Ava. You know this.*

The memory shattered, and Ava gasped as reality rushed back in. Rain pelted her face, cold and unrelenting. Logan lay twitching at her feet, his body riddled with boils, his face pale and slick with blood. Her hands trembled, still pulsing with residual power.

Finish it. Prove to me you are worthy of my trust.

She tightened her grip, her body trembling. The disease surged again, and Logan's body arched, his mouth opening in a silent scream.

Her grip tightened, her nails digging into his skin. The rage wasn't hers anymore—it was Havok's. And she welcomed it.

"Ava, stop!"

A pair of muscular arms yanked her backward, the force knocking the air from her lungs. The grip was unrelenting, and she stumbled, her boots slipping on the slick pavement as Xavier spun her around to face him.

His dark eyes bore into hers, wide with a mix of fear and anger, his wet hair plastered to his forehead. "What the hell are you doing?"

Short, ragged breaths escaped Ava's lips, her chest heaving. The cold rainwater trickled down her face, mingling with the heat still radiating from her trembling hands. Her gaze flicked to Logan, his body sprawled on the ground. The boils and blood that covered his skin were no longer there.

"He's one of us!" Xavier snapped. "What is wrong with you?"

Ava blinked, water dripping into her eyes as she shook her head. "I…" Her voice faltered, her throat tightening. She took a step back, the cold rain soaking her through to her skin. *You're stronger than this.*

Xavier's expression shifted, his anger giving way to something softer—something almost like concern. His shoulders dropped. "You'd better watch yourself, Ava, before you fall too deep."

Her eyes snapped to his, narrowing into a glare. A deafening emptiness raged within her, devouring any trace of vulnerability. "I don't care."

She turned on her heel and started walking away. Her boots splashed through puddles that reflected the fractured glow of the streetlights. But then darkness swallowed her. Shadows closed in like a suffocating blanket, blotting out everything around her.

Her teeth clenched as she halted, spinning on her heel. "Lift your damn shadow, Xavier."

He emerged from the darkness, his face hard, his tone sharper now. "You'd better care."

The heat of his presence was too stifling. The rain struck his shoulders and rolled down the curve of his jaw, but he didn't flinch.

"Ava, please." His fingers grazed her cheek. She recoiled. He cradled her head and pressed his lips to hers, his touch firm yet cautious, as though he were afraid she might break.

Water surged inside her, rising like a tidal wave. Her hands moved without thought, wrapping around his neck as the water coursed over them both. The rain seemed to intensify, the droplets bouncing off the pavement as the water she controlled circled his face.

Xavier gasped, his body jerking as the water constricted, cutting off his air. His hands clawed at hers, his strength faltering.

Ava released him, stepping back as she stared at her trembling hands. A cold wave of realization washed over her. Her lips parted, and her breath hitched as she whispered, "I'm so sorry." She let tears fall, forcing her voice to tremble. "What's happening to me?"

Xavier staggered, rubbing his neck as he caught his breath. The hardness in his eyes softened, his expression falling into one of quiet defeat. "I'll clean this up," he said hoarsely. "Just … go back to your room. Rest. We'll talk later."

Ava tilted her head. "Are you okay? I wasn't expecting you to—"

"It's fine." He waved her off with a weary motion. "Go. I'll handle it."

She nodded once and walked away. The rain soaked through her clothes, chilling her to the bone, but she didn't feel it. A faint smile curled her lips as she stepped into the shadow of the castle. Xavier was hers now, tangled in her web, wrapped around her little finger like all the others.

Ava slammed the door to her room shut, the echo reverberating through the empty space. She leaned back against the cold stone, letting out a slow, measured breath.

Her mind buzzed, the remnants of Havok's memory pulsing like an open wound. She could still feel his fury, the weight of his power, and the raw, unrelenting rage that had seared through her veins. The image of boiling flesh, the wet sound of ruptured blisters, and the sickly sweet stench of decay clung to her senses.

You are stronger than this, Havok's voice echoed in her mind. *You are mine, Ava. Don't forget that.*

She crossed the room and collapsed onto her bed. As she shifted, her hand brushed against something tucked beneath her pillow—a folded piece of paper.

Her chest tightened, her pulse quickening as she unfolded it. Gabriel's familiar handwriting scrawled across the page: *Ava, we need to talk. Please.*

Her breath hitched. A flicker of something unrecognizable sparked deep within her. *Don't let them see you falter. They are watching.*

Ava froze, her fingers tightening around the paper. He couldn't know. Not this. His rage still lingered in her chest, but it felt distant now, like the embers of a fire smoldering in the dark.

With a quick, decisive motion, she ripped the note into tiny pieces, the sound of tearing paper sharp in the silence. She let the pieces flutter to the ground like dying leaves, her face cold and unreadable.

Good, Havok purred, his presence retreating slightly. *You're learning.*

The emptiness inside her swelled, swallowing everything else. Gabriel didn't matter. Nothing mattered but the darkness that had become her home.

CHAPTER TWENTY-FIVE

DAUGHTER OF DARKNESS

The tunnels were silent, but Ava's rage was deafening. Xavier led Ava, the Elementals, Eve, and Anais through the dark, winding paths beneath Caprington, their shadows stretching long against the damp stone walls. Ahead of them lay their next target: New York.

It had been a week since Ava had killed Logan in the alley. A week since she let go of restraint—and she hadn't stopped.

Under the pretense of recruiting, she ventured out almost daily, prowling the shadows of Caprington's outskirts. Each time she returned alone, her hands streaked with blood and her smile sharper than before.

"They weren't strong enough," she'd say when Xavier questioned her. "Weaklings don't belong in Havok's army."

He never pushed her, not yet. But the unease in his eyes was unmistakable, and the tension between them simmered like a storm waiting to break.

No one could stop her. They didn't feel the power inside her, thrumming beneath her skin, begging for release.

The air was damp and thick, the distant echoes of dripping water and scuttling rats their only company.

Ava's heart thudded in her chest—not from fear, but anticipation. Above them, the city pulsed with life—Ephemeral life. Soon, it would be gone, swallowed by the tide of destruction screaming for release inside her.

She trailed beside Xavier, her sharp gaze catching the way his eyes flicked toward her now and then. His expression was impassive, but she could feel his scrutiny.

"What?" she asked.

He shrugged. "Nothing. Are you doing okay?"

"Fine. Why?"

"Just curious."

"Don't worry about me, Xavier. I can handle myself."

"I know. That's what worries me."

Ava rolled her eyes and quickened her pace.

The tunnels spat them out into a narrow alley, the sudden shift from darkness to dim daylight jarring. A steady rain slicked the pavement, its gleam reflecting on the crowded streets.

Ava looked up, taking in the towering skyscrapers above. Their peaks disappeared into a thick, gray fog that seemed to press down on the city. People passed by them, heads buried in their phones, umbrellas bobbing in the sea of moving bodies. No one noticed them.

Her lip curled in disdain. They were all so oblivious, so fragile. They had no idea that their lives were about to end.

They're nothing, Ava, Havok murmured in her mind. *Show them what true power looks like. Prove to them you are unstoppable.*

Her fingers twitched, the water beginning to pool at her fingertips, the cool liquid dripping to the ground. The rage inside her surged, pumping through her veins like liquid fire. She didn't want to wait for Xavier's signal. Why should she?

With a flick of her wrist, a jet of water sliced through the air, shattering the windows of the building across the street. Glass exploded outward, raining down on the crowd below.

Screams erupted, shrill and panicked.

"Ava!" Xavier cried.

But she didn't care. The power demanded release. She stepped into the street, ignoring the screech of tires and blaring horns. Another wave of water tore through the vehicles, flipping them like toys. The crash of metal against concrete reverberated through the air, chaos spreading with every step she took.

Ava caught a man by the throat as he tried to flee, lifting him off the ground. "Let's see you drown," she whispered.

Water gushed from his mouth, his body convulsing as she tightened her grip. When his eyes rolled back, she let him fall, his lifeless form crumpling at her feet.

Yes, Havok's voice growled. Drown them. Cleanse this filth from the world.

"Ava, stop!" Xavier yelled.

Sirens wailed in the distance, growing louder with each passing second. Above them, a helicopter appeared, its spotlight cutting through the fog.

The crowd scattered, but not fast enough. Ava sent another wave crashing into a building, shattering windows and sending debris on the fleeing masses.

A bullet whizzed past her ear, close enough to make her pause. She turned, catching sight of Melissa clutching her side, blood seeping through her fingers. Eve staggered against a wall, her face pale, her shirt blooming red. Lance dove behind a cover, dragging Gillian with him as more shots rang out. Jeremy was pulling an injured Thomas back into the alley.

"Damn it, Ava!" Xavier roared, grabbing her arm. Lance appeared at her other side, yanking her back toward the alley.

"Let go of me!" She struggled against their grip as they dragged her out of the open.

Xavier shoved her into the wall, his face inches from hers, fury blazing in his eyes. "You've just brought every goddamn authority in the city down on us!"

"You're welcome," she said, her lips curling into a smirk.

"Fix this," Xavier snapped. He gestured to Melissa, Eve, and Thomas slumped against the wall, their blood pooling beneath them.

Ava crouched beside Melissa, and water swirled over the wound. With a sickening wet sound, she forced the bullets out, and under her touch, the gash sealed shut. She moved to Eve, then to Thomas.

"There," she said coolly as she stood, her gaze flicking to Xavier. "Happy now?"

But his grip didn't loosen. "You're done," he growled. "You're not going back out there. Do you hear me?"

"I don't take orders from you, Xavier." She twisted free, shoving him aside.

"Ava!" Lance shouted.

She emerged back into the chaos, the storm raging above her. Sirens blared, and debris littered the streets. Raising her arms, she called to the bay.

Rising like a monstrous wall of water, the tidal wave's shadow swallowing the city.

The roar of the wave drowned out everything else—the cries of the people, the wail of sirens, even Xavier's distant shouts. Ava's heart thundered as she watched it surge forward, unstoppable and untamed, consuming everything in its path.

Vicious waves smashed into buildings, shaking the ground with their force. The water carried debris—twisted metal, shattered glass, broken bodies—through the streets. Everywhere Ava walked, the water cleared a path for her. She stepped over corpses, their lifeless faces twisted in fear, their skin bloated and blue. Blood swirled in the currents, staining the sea red.

The destruction was absolute, and the power was intoxicating.

Xavier's shadowed figure appeared behind her, but she deflected him with a barrier of water.

In the distance, the Statue of Liberty crumbled into the perilous sea. Triumph swelled inside her as she watched the iconic symbol of freedom sink beneath the waves. She had created all of this, and she loved every second.

"Enough!" Gillian's voice rang out.

Ava turned, her eyes narrowing as Gillian raised trembling hands.

"You think you can control me?"

"Ava, stop. You're not like him." Gillian's energy brushed against Ava's mind.

The connection was tenuous. It crept into her mind, soft but insistent. *Don't let her in. You're stronger than this.*

The darkness roared within her. She pushed back, sending Gillian staggering. Blood dripped from Gillian's nose.

"Hold her!" Xavier shouted.

"I'm trying!"

Xavier's shadow surged, stretching toward Ava and pinning her arms to her sides. The tidal wave behind her faltered, collapsing into the streets below.

"Let me go!" Ava screamed.

"Not until you stand down," Xavier growled, stepping in front of her.

Ava's struggles slowed, but her smirk lingered. She was biding her time, waiting for her chance to strike.

Then everything went black.

CHAPTER TWENTY-SIX

PUNISHMENT

Ava awoke with the coppery taste of blood on her tongue and the sharp sting of rain-soaked air against her face. She was disoriented, and her head throbbed as the world came back into focus. The dim tunnels around her reeked of damp stone and iron, and the muted echoes of hurried footsteps reminded her where she was—dragged back to the depths of Caprington like a disobedient dog.

She recalled losing consciousness, but the fury inside her hadn't dimmed. If anything, it burned brighter now, sharper and more relentlessly. She had leveled New York City. She'd drowned its streets, shattered its skyline, and torn its heart out. And they dared to stop her?

Xavier jerked her upright. "You're lucky I didn't leave you there."

Ava smirked, the taste of defiance sweeter than the pain in her ribs. "Lucky? We finished the mission. I did what needed to be done."

"You almost got us killed!" Xavier dragged her forward. Around them, the rest of the group limped along, soaked and bloodied. Eve shot Ava a venomous glare, pressing her hand to her stomach where her shirt was still damp with blood. Gillian and Melissa leaned on each other for support, their faces pale, and Thomas's arm hung limp at his side.

None of them spoke to her. Not that she cared.

The heavy door creaked open, revealing Havok's chamber.

Xavier threw her forward. She landed hard on her knees, the stone floor scraping her skin. She tilted her head back, meeting Havok's gaze as he rose from his throne-like chair at the center of the room. His silhouette was gaunt and menacing, his pale skin almost glowing in the dim light.

"What is this?" Havok spoke softly, yet his words held the force of a thunderclap.

Xavier stood at attention. "Ava disobeyed orders during the New York mission." His jaw tightened, his words clipped. "She acted before I gave the command, compromised the mission, and—"

"She destroyed the entire city." Eve walked in with her arms crossed. Her eyes flicked between Ava and Havok. "She nearly got us all killed."

Havok's dark eyes narrowed, his lips pressing into a thin line. "Destroyed it?"

"Yes," Xavier said.

Havok's gaze flicked to Ava. "Is this true?"

Ava rose to her feet, brushing dirt from her hands. "You wanted New York destroyed. I made sure it was done right."

"You leveled it," Havok hissed. "The entire city. Do you know how much I needed New York, Ava? It was a base. A foothold for expansion. And now it's nothing but rubble and corpses."

Ava's lips curled into a smirk. "Then I saved you the trouble of dealing with it later. It's clean now. Free of weakness."

Havok sauntered toward her. "Do not mistake recklessness for strength, child. You acted without thought, without strategy. What you did wasn't power—it was waste. You wasted a valuable asset." His breath was icy against her skin, each word sinking into her like shards of glass. "You are like your mother—insolent, arrogant, and foolish."

Ava's smile faltered, her fists clenching. "I am nothing like my mother."

"No. She at least had the good sense to know when she'd crossed the line." He leaned in, his stony gaze boring into hers. "You will not make me do the same to her daughter. Do I make myself clear?"

Ava glared back, refusing to let him see her falter. "Crystal."

Havok straightened, his gaze shifting to Xavier. "Am I to understand this wasn't your first warning to her?"

"No, sir."

A shadow passed over Havok's face. "Then perhaps I should accompany you personally next time."

"That won't be necessary, sir."

"Good. You will deal with her, Xavier. Teach her the consequences of disobedience. If she steps out of line again, I will make an example of her myself."

Xavier nodded. "Yes, sir."

"And you." Havok's gaze snapped to Eve.

"Yes, sir?"

"Do not ever burst into my chambers like some petulant child again. Xavier is the leader of the army. If you have an issue, you bring it to him. Do you understand?"

"Yes, sir," she whispered.

Havok waved them away with a flick of his hand, his eyes lingering on Ava for a moment longer. "Go. And Xavier, ensure she learns her lesson."

"Yes, sir." Xavier seized Ava's arm and dragged her through the dimly lit corridor outside Havok's chamber, his grip firm and unrelenting. The echo of their footsteps on the cold stone floor filled the silence until Eve caught up.

"I was going to tell him," Xavier muttered without turning.

"Yeah? When?" Eve shot back. "She's trouble, Xavier. She's let this whole Elemental thing go straight to her head."

"I'll take care of it."

"Don't let her change you," Eve warned, her eyes narrowing. "I know you've always had your eye on her."

He stopped, spinning on his heel to face her. "What, like Gabriel hasn't changed you?"

Eve's lips pressed into a thin line. "Whatever."

Xavier leaned closer. "I seem to recall you being defeated before, if you've forgotten. She's the one who figured you out when she was in a damn coma. All because of your obsession with Gabriel."

"Take care of her." She spun on her heel and stormed off.

"What was that about?" Ava asked, feigning curiosity even as a smirk tugged at her lips. "What coma?"

She knew exactly what he meant. She remembered the coma Havok had trapped her in, twisting her mind, breaking her down. And Eve? Eve had played her part, morphing into Melissa, taunting her with Gabriel's name until Ava had turned the tables and stabbed her.

Xavier didn't answer, his jaw tightening as he resumed pulling her forward.

"Of course you won't tell me," Ava said with a hollow laugh. "You expect me to have any kind of trust in you when you keep me in the dark. What's my punishment? Picking up trash? Cleaning the village? Or maybe training the new recruits? They're a bit rusty."

Xavier slammed her against the wall, his forearm pinning her there. The cold stone bit into her back, but Ava didn't flinch. If anything, her smile widened.

"Whatever this is, Ava, you need to stop," Xavier growled, his face inches from hers. "I can't help you if you keep going down this path. You have to control yourself."

She laughed. "Why? What does it matter that I didn't follow your precious command? We still obliterated New York. I'm still the killing machine you all want me to be. All those vile creatures are dead."

His gaze softened, as if something had dawned on him. "You've blocked your emotions, haven't you?"

"What if I have?"

"That's not it. This isn't just about turning off your feelings. You wouldn't be this callous if it were. This..." He trailed off, his brow furrowing as he studied her. "This is darker. You're in too deep, Ava."

"And who do you think pulled me under, Xavier? Maybe it's not so bad down here."

He sighed. "You'll want to keep your emotions off for this."

"Is that supposed to scare me?" She cocked her head. "Try harder."

Xavier hauled her through the corridors, his jaw clenched and his silence heavy with tension. The faint torchlight painted shadows across his face, but the glint in his eyes was clear: fear—not of Ava herself, but of what she was becoming.

The pit reeked of blood and sweat. With a firm grip on her arm, Xavier marched Ava forward. She had spent the night in the cell—cold, her body stiff from the unforgiving stone floor—but she felt nothing.

She met the semi-circle of faces waiting for her: Gabriel, Melissa, Jeremy, Thomas, Gillian, Lance, Eve, and Anais. Their faces were pale, their eyes flicking anywhere but at Ava. Behind them, the gathered Cimmerians buzzed with anticipation, their jeers and murmurs rising like a low, hungry growl.

Xavier and Donovan secured her wrists to the wall, the cold iron biting into her skin as the chains clanged against the stone.

Xavier raised a needle, the glint of it catching in the dim light. "This is for your own good," he muttered and plunged it into her arm.

A sharp sting shot through her, followed by a chilling emptiness. The rush of her powers—always humming beneath her skin—was gone, leaving a hollow ache in its place. Ava's breaths quickened as the realization sank in, her strength extinguished like a snuffed-out flame.

"I hope you suffer," Donovan spat.

She straightened her spine, refusing to bow, though her muscles ached from exhaustion. She caught Xavier's eye, but his gaze was distant, shadowed.

"Begin," he said flatly.

The sensation hit like a tidal wave. Cold, crushing water filled Ava's lungs as if someone plunged her into a deep, unforgiving ocean. Her chest burned, every instinct screaming for air as her head swam. She gasped, but no relief came—only the bitter, briny taste of saltwater invading her throat.

Her vision blurred, her muscles spasming as she fought against the phantom drowning. The world around her dimmed, the jeers fading into a dull roar. As the darkness threatened to take her, the sensation released. She coughed and gasped, water spewing from her lips. But she wouldn't make a single sound.

Ava stared at Lance, her vision swimming. He had been there for her once, her anchor when everything fell apart after Peter's betrayal. And now he was drowning her. Again and again.

Lance's dark eyes met hers. His jaw twitched, his hands trembling as he readied the next wave. The drowning began again, sharper, more suffocating this time.

Ava's head throbbed, her lungs screaming as her body convulsed.

When it ended, Lance turned away, his shoulders stiff with tension.

Melissa cradled a handful of white powder. Her lips trembled as she met Ava's eyes. She blew the powder into Ava's face.

The metallic taste clawed at Ava's senses, burning her nostrils and leaving her stomach in a violent churn. She doubled over as nausea tore through her. The world spun in sickening spirals. A fiery pain spread through her veins as though her insides were being twisted and burned. Saliva flooded her mouth, spilling past her lips. Violent convulsions seized her, and she retched. Her body heaved with each gag, bile splattering onto the ground in harsh, acidic bursts.

The Cimmerians' laughter echoed in the pit, sharp and mocking. Ava backed against the wall, slamming her head against the rough stone to quell the dizziness. A sharp, blinding pain burst behind her eyes, and she felt warm blood trickling down her nose and lips. Melissa's watery gaze broke as she stepped away, guilt written across her features.

A faint hum reverberated through the pit, a low, insidious vibration that burrowed into Ava's skull. Gillian's hands shook as she reached out, her powers snaking into Ava's mind like icy tendrils. Ava's body lurched, her head snapping back and slamming into the stone wall with a sickening thud. Once. Twice. The jagged surface bit into her scalp, sharp edges tearing flesh as white-hot pain streaked through her like lightning.

She could see Gillian's face, pale and horrified, as her powers forced Ava to keep smashing her head into the stone.

When the manipulation finally ceased, Ava sagged against the wall. Blood dripped from her hairline down her face, and she trembled with exhaustion.

The air shifted, heavy and oppressive, as a whirlwind formed around Ava. The roar of the tornado drowned out the crowd, the violent wind ripping at her hair and clothes.

Then the pain came. The razor-sharp gusts peeled away strips of her skin, each tearing accompanied by a blinding, electric agony. Blood speckled the air, carried by the merciless gale. Ava bit down hard on her lip, tasting the iron tang of her own blood as the skin around her arms and legs flayed under the storm's fury. Still, she wouldn't scream.

When the tornado dissipated, she hung limp and trembled with aftershocks of pain.

The pit dissolved into golden sunlight that felt too warm, too inviting. Ava stood in a meadow, the sickly sweet scent of wildflowers wafted in the air. The gentle rustling of the breeze through the grass and the melodic chirp of birds created a scene so idyllic it was almost grotesque.

It didn't take long for her to spot them.

Gabriel stood ahead, his posture relaxed, his blue eyes alight with an intense fervor. But his gaze wasn't on her. It was on Eve.

A knot formed in Ava's stomach as something buried too deep surfaced for a second. She forced her fists to relax. The scene was nothing. A trick. A fabrication meant to elicit a reaction she refused to give.

But then he moved closer to Eve, his hand brushing her cheek with a tenderness Ava had never let herself imagine. She swallowed, and the faintest flicker of something stirred in the void she'd crafted within herself.

Gabriel leaned in, his lips meeting Eve's in a kiss so gentle, so maddeningly perfect, that Ava felt her chest tighten—a phantom ache she shouldn't have been capable of feeling.

No.

The thought was sharp, an echo that ricocheted in her mind. She felt the briefest sting of jealousy and rage that threatened to ignite. But she crushed it underfoot, locking it away deep down inside. It wasn't real. It didn't matter.

The meadow melted away, leaving her battered body in the pit. The laughter of the crowd greeted her in return, Eve's smirk a triumphant dagger aimed at Ava's pride.

Xavier glanced at Gabriel. "Your turn."

Gabriel didn't move at first, his fists tightening at his sides, but there was no hesitation in his face—just a blank mask.

Ava drooped in the shackles, her body battered and broken. Her eyes, though, didn't waver. They locked on Gabriel. If she could have summoned her emotions, they would have been fury, but for now, she was hollow.

"Don't hold back," Xavier added.

Gabriel advanced, moving with calm deliberation. His face betrayed nothing—not frustration, not regret, not anger. He was a soldier, following orders without question. The torchlight painted harsh shadows across his features, making him look even more distant, untouchable.

Her lips curled into a faint smirk. "What's wrong, Gabriel? Afraid to hurt me?"

His eyes barely flicked in her direction. He lifted his hand, and she felt the pull.

Ava's stomach gave a violent lurch as the pit blurred. The sharp force of teleportation wrenched her body upward. Dangling high above the abyss, the freezing wind hit her like knives, stinging her torn skin. The iron shackles bit into her wrists.

The crowd below roared with laughter, their jeers rising like a crescendo of cruelty. The height twisted her stomach, the yawning darkness beneath her taunting her with promises of endless pain.

And then, without warning, the pull came again.

The sharp snap of teleportation ripped her downward. Her body slammed into the stone floor with a bone-jarring crash. Pain radiated through her limbs as her knees buckled beneath her. She had little time to suck in a breath before it happened again.

And again.

The wind and sharp impacts blended into one relentless rhythm, each strike of the ground robbing her of air and strength. Her vision swam, the edges of the pit fading in and out with each agonizing shift.

Gabriel remained a shadow in the chaos, his face impassive, his movements precise. He carried out the punishment with the same detachment he always wore, no more affected than if he were practicing an ordinary maneuver.

When he finished, Ava gasped for air.

But Thomas appeared before her with his hands ignited. Flames licked his fingers.

Ava braced herself, her teeth clenching, but nothing could prepare her for the fire's ferocity.

Heat engulfed her, blistering her skin and searing deep into her flesh. A raw, guttural scream tore from her throat as her body writhed against the unyielding chains. The fire consumed her with relentless hunger.

The flames vanished, leaving her gasping, her body trembling in the fleeting reprieve.

The fire roared to life again.

Her scream pierced the air once more, echoing through the pit as the inferno devoured her anew.

The flames extinguished. Drool dripped from her lips, mingling with the blood on her chin. Her vision swam, but she refused to cry. She had asked for this. She had earned it.

The darkness seemed alive, pressing against her skin and choking the breath from her lungs. It whispered in her ears, echoing with Havok's voice: *You are mine, Ava. Always.*

CHAPTER TWENTY-SEVEN

SOLACE

The cell was a void—no windows, no bars, just strangling darkness. Ava lay motionless on the cold stone floor, her body a landscape of raw agony, her soul buried beneath the void she had carved out within herself.

The chill of the stone beneath her felt like knives, its jagged surface biting into her blistered, ruined skin. A faint, pulsating aura clung to her. The spell suppressed her healing and was alive, feeding off her torment. Each heartbeat sent shockwaves of agony rippling through her, a cruel rhythm she couldn't escape.

Curled into herself, Ava wrapped her arms around her knees, the only position that offered the faintest reprieve. She dared not move; even the smallest shift sent molten fire ripping through her body. The synthetic fibers of her clothing had melted into her flesh, their jagged edges embedded like glass, a constant reminder of the inferno that had devoured her.

Fever radiated from her, scorching her veins as if the flames still lingered beneath her skin, while the icy dungeon air gnawed at her exposed wounds. Her stomach churned, nausea threatening to overtake her with every shallow, ragged breath. Each inhale felt like fire scraping through her lungs, the effort of it a torment in itself.

She stared into the void, her mind as silent as her surroundings, willing herself not to break. The darkness offered no comfort, only the reminder that there was no escape—not from this cell, not from the pain, not from the hollow nothingness inside her.

The grating creak of the cell door pulled Ava from the haze of her torment. She didn't stir, her body too broken to react, but her ears caught the rhythm of approaching footsteps—soft, deliberate, hesitant.

Not Havok.

Gabriel.

The faint warmth of the torch reached her before its light did, seeping into the darkness. Her body tensed, and when the fire's glow finally pierced through the void, she flinched. The memory of searing heat flashed through her mind like a phantom pain.

He stepped into view. His blue eyes, usually guarded and distant, were stormy with anguish as they settled on her battered form.

Ava didn't lift her head to meet his gaze. She didn't have the strength—or the will. But the faint scent of juniper clung to him, curling in the air between them. It should have brought comfort, a fragile echo of something familiar. Instead, it passed over her like a ghost, leaving her cold and unresponsive.

"Ava," he whispered, the emotion barely contained in his gruff tone. Kneeling beside her, he clenched his hands tight, as if restraining himself from touching her.

She didn't respond. She couldn't. The pain wrapped around her like a cocoon, a prison from which she had no strength to escape. Her breaths came in shallow bursts, each inhale slicing her throat anew.

"I love you."

Her body remained motionless, but inside, something stirred—faint and fleeting, like a ghost brushing against her consciousness.

Gabriel ran a hand through his hair, his frustration simmering beneath the surface. His words tumbled out, raw and unfiltered. "I hate this. I hate what they've done to you. I hate what you're doing to yourself. I wish I could heal you." He paused, his voice cracking. "I knew this would happen. I knew turning it all off, burying yourself so deep that no one can reach you... It's killing you, Ava. I can see it. You're slipping further away."

Still, Ava didn't move. Her battered body curled tighter, as if to shield herself from his words.

"Please, come back," he whispered. "I need you. We all need you."

A single tear slid down her cheek, the salt searing her tender skin like acid. A faint, broken sound escaped her lips—a noise that could have been a gasp or a sob, though she wasn't sure herself.

Gabriel's jaw clenched as tears welled in his eyes. He lowered himself beside her, his movements cautious, as if afraid even his presence might worsen her pain. Lying next to her, he gazed into her eyes. "Please, Ava. Come back to me. Feel something. Feel *me*."

In the silence that followed, Ava's breaths rasped against the quiet. The faint tremor in her fingers went unnoticed by all but him. His words hung in the air, pressing against the darkness that swirled within her.

But the darkness within her didn't yield.

Blinking awake, Ava's vision wavered, her eyes stinging from the salty tears that clung stubbornly to her lashes. Every muscle screamed in protest, her battered body a prison of pain. She didn't know how long she'd been lying there, unmoving. Time had dissolved into an endless abyss of agony.

Had Gabriel really been there? Or had her fractured mind conjured him in a moment of desperation?

The sharp creak of the cell door cut through the suffocating silence. The sound scraped against her nerves, each echo ricocheting off the unforgiving stone walls. Footsteps followed. The rhythm of each step carried a weight that made the air seem heavier, pressing against her chest.

Ava's heart pounded. Another figure stood behind them—a protector, of course. Katarina, perhaps, or Peter. Always one of them, a shield between Havok and the suffering he inflicted on others.

"Greetings." Havok's velvety whisper slithered into the room. It was a sound both refined and cruel, laced with venom that sent a chill racing down her spine. "I can't imagine what that must have felt like."

His words coiled around her like a predator's snare. She clenched her jaw, forcing back the sob that threatened to escape. He wouldn't see her break. Not this time. But the effort sent fresh waves of pain rippling through her, her blistered skin pulling against the melted fibers fused into her flesh.

As Havok stepped closer, his presence hovered like a smothering shadow. The boots in her line of sight gleamed as they shifted slightly, the polished leather a stark contrast to the filth of the dungeon floor. She dared not lift her head, the fire in her lungs making even breathing an ordeal.

"On your knees," he commanded.

Her muscles protested, but she obeyed, collapsing into the position he demanded. Breathing was a torment—her lungs screamed for relief, and every rasping inhale felt like shards of glass scraping her insides.

"Have you learned your lesson?"

Her lips trembled as she tried to form a response. It took several agonizing attempts. The words clawed their way out, raw and broken. "Yes," she rasped at last, each syllable tearing through her throat like jagged metal.

"Good." His boots shifted closer, his towering form a silhouette of menace. "Let this serve as a reminder of what happens when you disobey. You will follow my orders and respect your leaders. Do you understand?"

"Yes."

Havok leaned down, gripping her chin with cold fingers and forcing her face upward. Her body screamed in protest as his pale, cruel visage filled her vision. He studied her like a collector admiring a broken prize. "You are fortunate that healing is within your grasp. But only when I permit it." His lips curled into a mockery of a smile. "The spell will remain in place for a while longer to ensure there are no ... lapses in judgment."

Her chest heaved. Her skin burned, her muscles trembled, but she refused to meet his gaze.

"I trust we won't need to have this conversation again." His voice was smooth, but the icy undertone promised far worse if she faltered once more.

He rose, his long coat whispering against the stone floor as he turned. The boots retreated, their echoing footsteps punctuated by the heavy cell door groaning shut behind him.

Her strength gave out, and she crumpled to the floor. Pain lanced through every inch of her body, her muscles quivering. Fever and agony blurred the edges of her mind until, at last, the merciful darkness claimed her.

Ava's body screamed in protest as she tried to stir, her limbs stiff and unyielding, as though her muscles had fused into stone. The cold floor pressed against her raw, blistered skin like shards of ice, sending sharp jolts of pain through her with even the slightest movement. Each breath was its own torment, scraping against her lungs like jagged glass.

"The spell has been lifted," Xavier's voice cut through the silence, low and cautious. He stepped into view and dropped a bundle of clothes next to her.

Ava closed her eyes, forcing herself to focus inward. The effort was monumental, her thoughts sluggish under the weight of the drugs and the spell suppressing her power. She willed the water within her to stir, but it resisted, sluggish and unresponsive.

When the familiar warmth finally bloomed, it was faint, fragile—more ember than flame—but she clung to it desperately. The searing pain dulled as her flesh knitted itself back together, each agonizing effort draining what little strength she had left.

Her breathing remained shallow, scraping against her battered lungs. The relief was fleeting, a fragile victory against the forces working to keep her broken.

When she sat up, her limbs trembled, exhaustion crashing over her. The pain lingered, dulled but not gone, a stark reminder of how far she'd fallen.

Xavier stepped outside with his back turned to her. "Are you okay?" he asked, his tone quiet but insistent.

She didn't answer. Instead, she grabbed the clothes, the fabric rough and nondescript in her hands, and pulled the basic black shirt over her head. It clung to her damp skin. The jogging pants hung as she slipped them on, her movements stiff. She forced her feet into the scuffed shoes he'd brought, the worn soles gritty against her toes.

He sighed, leaning against the door. "Why did you do it?"

"I was just doing what we were supposed to do."

"Why did you snap? You said you were okay."

She let out a hollow laugh. "Why do you care so much? You just put me through hell. I don't even know who you are anymore. You were so nice a few weeks ago, and now you're cruel."

"What about you? Why did you turn off your emotions? I knew something wasn't right with you after New Orleans."

Ava met his gaze. "What do you expect, Xavier? I was angry. And I had just killed an entire town of people."

His face softened, the anger in his eyes dimming. "I know it's not easy. Especially now that Havok wants us to do this more often. Maybe I can convince him that we should focus on adding more to the army for a while."

"Don't do it on my account. He wouldn't be happy with you anyway." She leaned back against the wall with her knees drawn to her chest. The chill seeped into her skin.

"Look," he started, running a hand through his hair, "I know all of this is ... traumatic. But just try, Ava. Turn your emotions back on. It's no way to live like this. I know."

"Are you going to let me out of here?"

"I want to, but Havok wants you to stay another night."

She nodded and rested her head against the cool wall. "Well, you'd better go and make sure his highness is okay."

"Don't be like this, Ava. I've seen who you can be. Don't lose yourself."

The silence stretched between them, heavy with unspoken words, until Xavier finally turned and walked away. The echo of his boots faded into the corridor, leaving Ava alone in the suffocating stillness of the cell.

Darkness. It claimed her, wrapped around her like a comforting embrace. Ava thrived in it—the endless silence, the emptiness in her mind. It was easier that way. Safer. It had to be.

The door groaned open, and Ava glanced up.

Long blond hair caught the faint light from the hall as Melissa stepped into the cell. She looked exhausted, the lines around her eyes deeper than Ava remembered. Her clothes were clean, but her face bore the weight of sleepless nights and too many battles. The sight of her sparked something faint, like a whisper in the back of Ava's mind, but she shoved it down.

Ava braced herself for anger, for accusations, for the bitter edge of resentment.

Instead, Melissa knelt beside Ava. "How are you?"

Ava tilted her head back against the wall, letting the rough surface scrape her skin. "Why are you here?"

"Because no one else could come."

"They couldn't come. Or they didn't want to."

"They're afraid, Ava. Afraid of what's happening to you. Afraid of losing you."

The words sliced through her defenses, but Ava clung to the cold indifference she'd built around herself. She turned her head away, staring at the far wall. "I don't care."

But she did. The admission flickered at the edges of her mind, a truth she wasn't ready to face. She clenched her fists tighter, trying to suffocate it.

"Yes, you do. You care so much it's killing you. That's why you turned it off, isn't it? To stop feeling everything."

A tightness constricted Ava's chest, but she stayed quiet. She couldn't. If she spoke, her walls might crack, and she couldn't let that happen. Not now.

"You're letting Havok consume you," Melissa pressed. "I've seen it. The way you act, the things you say—it's not you, Ava. You're better than this."

"You don't know anything about it."

"I know enough," Melissa snapped. "I know the Ava who fought to save people wouldn't let Havok turn her into this."

Her words hit their mark, and the first tremor of doubt rippled through her. She buried her head in her knees.

"You turned your emotions to stone, and his rage took over. Haven't you noticed it? The way his thoughts creep in? The way you've started to sound like him?"

The truth hit like a punch to the gut. She had noticed. The cold satisfaction after every kill, the hatred that didn't feel entirely her own. The thought revolted her, but she forced it down, burying it even further.

"I saw what happened to him, Mel," she said through gritted teeth. "Ephemerals killed his family. That's what they do. They kill."

"Not all of them, and you know that. Your father is one. You love him. He's not evil, and neither are most of them. You fell in love with one. Or have you forgotten?"

"I was brainwashed."

"Turn. Them. On."

"No." She glared at Melissa.

"What about our plan to end this? Are you really going to let him win?"

"I decided I don't really want to end Havok. I'm just not ready to die yet."

"You do care. That's why this hurts so much. You can't shut it out forever. It'll break you."

"I can't handle what we've done. It's too much."

Melissa grabbed her hand. "I know. But we have each other. That's why I'm here, Ava. Because I need you. We all do. And we're here to put an end to this, no matter what it takes. You're one of my best friends, and I can't lose you. Not to him. Not to this."

Ava shook her head, trying to push Melissa's words away. But her chest tightened, and her constructed walls began to crumble.

"I need you," Melissa repeated.

The dam cracked. Ava's shoulders shook as her chest heaved, the first sob ripping from her throat like a wound being torn open. Tears burned hot trails down her cheeks, each one slicing through the fragile remnants of her indifference. Everything—New York, Gabriel, the punishment—crashed into her like a tidal wave.

Her mind screamed against the flood of emotions. *Why did I let it get this far? How did I become this person?*

Her cries filled the tiny cell, raw and unrelenting. She buried her face in her arms, her tears soaking the sleeves of her shirt. The agony of letting it all in again was almost worse than the physical pain.

Melissa didn't move, didn't speak. She stayed beside her.

Ava finally looked up. "What have I done?"

"Don't focus on that. Focus on our plan. On what we're fighting for. Use this ... all of it ... but don't let it be Havok's rage. You're stronger than him."

"I'm sorry ... for everything."

Melissa smiled, her own eyes shining. "It's in the past. We move forward. Together."

"How can you be so quick to forgive?"

"Because. You are my friend. We've all done terrible things, but we've done them together—for a reason. I know you, even if you don't feel like yourself right now."

"It was easier when I turned it all off. I couldn't stand feeling *his* and my pain. I thought I could handle turning it off. I didn't expect to lose myself like that—or to hurt everyone."

"He's twisted, Ava, and he wants us broken. Don't give him that. Just focus on the plan, like I do. It's how we survive. When this is over, I'll have my life with Lance. You'll have yours, too."

Ava bit her lip and stared at the floor. "I don't think that's possible," she murmured, the ache of missing Gabriel clawing at her chest.

"It is," Melissa said firmly. "You'll find your way back. We all will." She offered Ava a faint smile. "Get some rest. We'll need our strength."

Melissa vanished from sight, her hand lingering for a moment before the cell door creaked open and closed. Ava stared at the empty space, the ghost of Melissa's presence a quiet comfort in the suffocating dark.

Time moved with agonizing slowness. She had no idea if it was day or night. What day it was. The guilt and darkness were her only companions. She rested her head against the cold stone wall, trying to clear her mind, but the effort only brought a flicker of something foreign—an unfamiliar memory.

It felt like a dream, surreal yet vivid, the edges too sharp to dismiss. She closed her eyes and let it take over.

Havok paced the room with an agitated rhythm. His boots left wet trails on the wooden floor, the rain from his long journey still clinging to his cloak. The fire crackled in the hearth, casting shadows that danced across his gaunt features. His hands trembled as he clenched them into fists, his mind consumed by a singular image: Lenorah's lifeless face.

Her laughter, her touch, her warmth—they were gone. And Esmerelda—his sweet, innocent daughter. His breath hitched as their deaths flashed through his mind, the vile Ephemerals responsible, burning in his memory like an eternal brand.

A knock jarred him from his torment. He sighed. "Yes?"

The door opened, revealing Veronica, her expression a careful mask of concern. She stepped inside, closing the door with quiet precision. Her long dress swished against the floor as she approached him.

"What troubles you, Corbin?"

He turned to her and clenched his jaw. "I cannot tell Savina and Colden."

"Do you not want them to know the truth? They must understand. Savina is *engaged* to one," she spat, the word dripping with disgust.

His eyes flicked to the fire. "It would mean nothing to them. They grew up with Ephemerals. They were taught to see them as allies. My words would fall on deaf ears. They need to see it for themselves."

"And how do you propose that?"

Corbin never wanted to hurt his children. They had been his only family for years, but he couldn't bring himself to tell them about Lenorah and Esmerelda. He needed to expose the truth in a way that affected them. He needed to let them see the evil. See how quickly Ephemerals turned their backs on them. Then they would gladly join him and his family.

His grip tightened on the edge of the mantel, his knuckles whitening. The firelight danced along the taut lines of his face as a plan solidified in his mind. "I will have my man spread word of Savina's witchcraft to the villagers."

"Why only her?"

"They would never believe it of Colden. He is a powerless fool. But Savina … they will fear her."

"And if they do not side with us?"

His gaze darkened, and for a moment, the firelight seemed to dim. "Then they will feel what I feel. They will know rage. Loss. Vengeance."

The memory shifted, and Ava jolted awake, her chest rising and falling with shallow breaths. The cold of the cell rushed back in, and her heart thudded in her chest.

Anger ignited inside her—both at Havok and herself. He hadn't just let his family's deaths consume him; he had weaponized his grief, inflicting his pain onto Savina and Colden. He had been so twisted by loss that he chose cruelty over honesty, forcing his children to see the world through his hateful lens.

And yet, Ava couldn't deny how easily she had fallen into his footsteps. She had let Havok's rage consume her, clouding her mind and drowning her in his hatred. How many Ephemerals had she killed with that same blind fury? She had been no better than him, no stronger than his darkness.

Fresh shame flooded her. *This isn't who I am*, she thought, a lump rising in her throat. *I've become the monster I vowed to fight.*

But her shame turned inward, finding a familiar target. *And my mother… she's the reason I'm here.* The bitter thought gnawed at her, just as it always did. She hated she couldn't stop fixating on her mother's choices—on how she'd abandoned Ava to this fate. Had it been fear? Cowardice? Indifference? The questions circled, feeding her resentment.

But no matter how much she hated her mother, Ava knew the truth: the responsibility was hers. She had let herself become this. She had buried her emotions to let Havok's rage take root.

Enough. The word echoed through her, a quiet but fierce command. She drew a shaky breath, her raw lungs protesting. *I have to fight back. I have to be better than this.*

Her grip tightened on her knees, and for the first time in weeks, a trace of resolve settled over her. She had the power to control her own destiny. And she would fight—not just against Havok's control, but against the darkness she had let consume her. *I am not him. I will never be him.*

CHAPTER TWENTY-EIGHT

REFLECTION

When Xavier released her, she barely registered his presence, her body too weak and her mind too worn to react. Every movement sent sharp reminders of the punishment she had endured, her muscles protesting as she stood on shaky legs.

"Get cleaned up," Xavier said softly, a hint of regret in his voice. "We'll go have lunch."

Though the idea of food turned her stomach, she nodded. She didn't want to be around anyone. She didn't want to be around anyone. She wanted solitude, silence, and most of all, rest. But her hollow ache demanded sustenance.

Ava stumbled into her room and collapsed against the door until it clicked shut. For a moment, she stood there, staring at the bathroom door. Then, with slow, deliberate movements, she shuffled inside and turned on the shower faucet.

Steam filled the room, fogging the mirror and cloaking her reflection. She peeled the clothes from her body. When she wiped the mirror, she flinched at the stranger staring back at her.

Her copper hair clumped in matted, frizzy tangles, dull from neglect. Puffy gray eyes, bloodshot and rimmed with dark circles. Her skin was pale and hollow, her face gaunt. She didn't look eighteen—she looked like someone who had carried decades of suffering on her shoulders.

What have I become? Her fingers curled against the edge of the sink as a tremor ran through her arms. *I don't even know who I am anymore.*

The water from the shower called to her, its steady rhythm like an old, comforting lullaby. She stepped inside, the scalding heat hitting her skin and coaxing a hiss from her lips. But she didn't turn it down. The pain felt deserved—necessary, even.

As the water cascaded over her, washing away grime and blood, Ava tried to focus on the one thing Melissa had said to her: *Find something good to hold on to.* She let her thoughts drift to Gabriel, but the longing only made her chest tighten. *Would he still want me?* She had tried to drown him. Twice. Pushed him away. And the memory of Eve kissing him, and her illusion of them kissing in the meadow, poisoned her thoughts, a torment she couldn't escape.

The water wasn't enough to drown the ache in her chest, but it numbed her for a time, offering solace in its warmth. She stayed under until the shower ran cold, then dressed in simple clothes—a white button-down, black leggings, and boots.

As she reached for the door, her vision shifted.

It wasn't her room anymore. The walls distorted, and the faint scent of damp stone gave way to the smell of wet wood and burnt embers. Her fingers clutched the doorframe as a man's figure materialized in her mind—a tall, imposing figure with white-blond hair and vibrant green eyes. Devon Maunsell.

"It's done," Devon said. "She's dead."

"Good," Ava—or rather, Havok—replied, the voice low and guttural, not her own. "And the child?"

"Zara left her crying over Luci."

Havok gasped. A twinge of something—grief? Regret?—flickered in his chest. "Ava won't cry for her mother forever. Once she learns the truth, she'll hate her."

Devon's jaw tightened. "Zara could've taken the girl. She could grow up here. It's better than coercing them."

"Are you in charge, Devon?"

"No sir."

"Then know your place. Until I can fully take this body, we cannot bring them here. I am not strong enough to train six Elementals, and neither are you."

Devon hesitated. "Do you think Savina and the Elders are?"

"You underestimate their power," Havok growled. "Do not make the mistake of arrogance, Devon. Or have you forgotten the men we lost when they attacked?"

"I haven't forgotten." Devon's voice was tight. "Caprington will be ready for you when you return."

"Good. And how is my son?"

"Xavier is fine. He misses you."

"Tell him I will see him soon." The emotion twisted inside him, coiling like a snake ready to strike.

Devon's brow furrowed. "Are you well, sir?"

"I'm fine," Havok snapped. "He's fighting for control again. I must go."

The vision blurred, the scene slipping away like water through her fingers. Ava staggered, blinking back into the dim light of her room. Her heart raced as she clung to the bathroom doorframe for balance.

Havok's words echoed in her mind. *Ava won't cry for her mother forever.* Had he truly thought about the day her mother died? The realization stung like a fresh wound.

And then there was the other revelation. Xavier—Havok's son? Her chest tightened as her mind raced. Could it be true? She wanted to dismiss it, to deny it outright, but Havok's twisted machinations made anything possible.

Time crashed down on her. She had been in Caprington for four months, her life consumed by rage and destruction. She had let Havok's emotions become her own, losing herself in his shadow.

Ava clenched her fists. *No more.* She couldn't keep drowning in his hatred. She was stronger than this—stronger than him. She had to be.

CHAPTER TWENTY-NINE

NEWFOUND SURPRISE

The morning sun bathed the little village in a warm, golden glow. A gentle breeze carried the fragrant scent of lavender mixed with a hint of turned earth and wildflowers. The brightness of the day was jarring, a stark contrast to the oppressive darkness she had been drowning in for the past month. The heat of the sun felt foreign on her skin, almost too inviting, as if the world mocked her inner turmoil.

"Hey," a voice called from behind, breaking through her thoughts.

She turned around to find Xavier standing there. His casual smirk didn't quite match the awkward energy between them. "Hey."

"Mind if we venture out into the city?"

Ava hesitated, unsure how to respond. "Sure."

"Let's go in my car."

She raised an eyebrow but followed him to where his sleek, ostentatious sports car gleamed under the sunlight. He slid on his sunglasses, clearly attempting to exude a relaxed confidence, but it didn't quite land. It lacked the effortless allure that Gabriel's presence commanded. She slid into the passenger seat, the leather cool against her skin, and buckled up as he started the engine with a low purr.

The drive into the city was quiet, the landscape shifting from the quaint charm of the village to the imposing elegance of tall, glass-covered buildings. Modern structures gleamed alongside older ones, creating a patchwork of history and innovation. Ava stared out the window, her thoughts fragmented as they weaved through the bustling streets.

"Chinese sound good?" he asked.

"Sure." She wasn't particularly hungry. The idea of food seemed mundane, but she knew she needed to eat.

He pulled up to an upscale Chinese restaurant where a valet attendant opened Ava's door. She stepped out onto the polished stone of the sidewalk. The chic face of the restaurant made her feel underdressed in her simple clothes, and she hugged herself as they entered.

"Little much for lunch, don't you think?"

He shrugged. "It's good food."

Inside, the space was sleek and minimalist, with warm wood tones and golden accents. The hum of conversation and clinking silverware filled the air. Ava followed Xavier to their table, her shoulders stiff as she felt the curious eyes. She wasn't sure if it was paranoia or reality, but she couldn't shake the feeling of being watched.

"Relax," Xavier said. "No one knows what happened last month."

She let out a slow breath. "How do you feel about all of this?"

"What? You or the massacres?"

"The massacres."

He leaned back in his chair, his sunglasses pushed onto his head, exposing tired eyes. "I don't know. I've been doing this for so long that it doesn't faze me anymore. Which probably makes me sound like a complete ass."

"It doesn't," Ava said, her tone softer. "It just sounds like you're tired. Maybe it's becoming too much."

The waitress placed two glasses of water on the table. Xavier ordered without consulting Ava, which annoyed her, but she bit back her irritation and managed a faint smile.

"I gotta say." He leaned forward a little. "I've really enjoyed getting to know you."

Ava's stomach twisted. She didn't want this conversation. "When is our next massacre?"

He hesitated, his jaw tightening. "For you, not for a while. Call it probation if you will."

"Oh."

"Havok wants you to recruit until he can trust you again."

"What?"

He sighed. "Yeah. Havok doesn't want you to annihilate entire cities. Not until you can follow orders. So, you'll be joining Gabriel, Donovan, Zeke, and Mallory. They're out on assignment now, but when they return, you'll join them."

She didn't know what to think. Were they actually putting her with Gabriel? Was it a test, or did they really believe that she supposedly hated Gabriel? "When do they return?"

"Tomorrow."

"What do I do until then?"

"Practice. Have fun."

"Is there a library or bookstore around?" Ava asked.

"Castle library not big enough?" He chuckled. "Yeah, we have several. The city has everything you could imagine. It's not just castles and mountain towns."

The food arrived, an array of dishes that seemed excessive for two people. Ava's stomach growled despite herself as the fragrant aroma of spices and cooked meat wafted toward her.

"This is crispy orange chicken," Xavier explained, serving her small portions of each dish with an almost childlike enthusiasm. "Egg Foo Young, Zhaijangmian, and of course, pot stickers. Try everything."

Ava took tentative bites, the flavors dancing across her palate—sweet, tangy, savory, and rich. For a moment, the simple pleasure of eating eased the heaviness in her chest.

"Why do you hang out with me and no one else?" she asked suddenly, her curiosity genuine.

"Because I like you."

Ava fidgeted in her seat. "Doesn't that cause problems for you?"

"Probably. But I don't care." He said it so simply, as though it were the easiest thing in the world.

Ava thought about his words, about the strange camaraderie that had formed between them despite everything. She wanted to believe he was sincere, but the memory of Havok's vision lingered in the back of her mind.

Was Xavier really Havok's son? Or was this another of Havok's manipulations? She pushed the thought aside, focusing on the moment, the food, and the tiny sense of normalcy.

Once Xavier retrieved his car from the valet, they drove through the bustling city streets toward a large, two-story building. Ava's heart fluttered at the sight of it. The building had an old-world charm, its brick façade adorned with ivy creeping up the sides. Despite the modern signage indicating it was a bookstore, its grand arched windows and ornate stone carvings hinted at a past life as a library.

Stepping inside, Ava's breath caught. The air smelled of aged paper and polished wood, with a faint hint of lavender from a nearby candle display. Rows upon rows of bookshelves stretched toward the high ceiling, their dark mahogany frames gleaming under the warm, golden light of antique chandeliers. It felt like stepping into another world—one untouched by the chaos of her life.

For the first time in weeks, she felt a glimmer of something resembling excitement. It was a welcome reprieve from everything. She slinked along, trailing her fingers along the spines of the books, savoring the soft, textured feel beneath her fingertips.

"This place is incredible," she murmured.

Xavier trailed behind her, his hands shoved in his pockets as he observed her with mild curiosity. Ava still couldn't quite reconcile the man walking patiently through a bookstore with the one who had tormented her and her friends not long ago. Had he really changed, or had he always been this way beneath the dangerous façade?

"What is it about books that you love?" he asked.

Ava paused, pulling a worn hardcover from the shelf and examining its faded gold lettering. She considered his question for a moment. "No matter what's happening in my life, I can always turn to a book and lose myself in it. It's comforting, knowing I'm not alone in what I'm feeling. Someone, somewhere, has felt the same."

Xavier leaned against the edge of the shelf, tilting his head as he studied her. "Maybe I should start reading."

"Why do you say that?"

He shrugged, a faint smirk playing on his lips. "Escaping reality sounds like fun."

"You don't seem very happy."

He glanced away, his smirk fading. "We weren't really raised to live happy lives, if you haven't noticed. We kill first and figure out the rest later."

She frowned. "What's something you've always wanted to do? Something just for yourself?"

He blinked at her, as if the question had caught him off guard. "I don't know."

"Well, think about it," she urged, her tone gentler now. She gestured toward her growing stack of books. "In the meantime, how do we pay for these?"

Xavier chuckled, raising an eyebrow. "Are you planning on becoming a hermit?"

"No," she said defensively, though her smile betrayed her amusement. "I can read fast."

"We don't pay." He tilted his head toward the counter where a clerk sat. "But they'll mark it off their inventory. No stealing allowed, technically."

"Oh. Right."

After dropping the heap of books into the trunk of Xavier's car, they spent the rest of the afternoon wandering the city. The streets bustled with life—bright shop windows displaying everything from handmade trinkets to high-end fashion. Street vendors lined the sidewalks, their stalls bursting with fresh produce, colorful scarves, and intricate jewelry. The air carried the mingling scents of roasted coffee, spiced pastries, and something savory wafting from a nearby café.

It almost reminded her of home—the carefree joy of her old life, before everything had gone dark. For a fleeting moment, she let herself forget who they were, what they had done, and the roles they had to play. Here, among the shops and laughter, she wasn't Ava the Water Enchanter. She was just Ava.

Night blanketed the city as Xavier and Ava cruised through the glowing streets, the car's interior bathed in the soft blue and white hues of neon lights reflecting off the windshield. The skyline shimmered, the buildings standing like illuminated beacons against the inky sky. It was strikingly beautiful—a sharp contrast to the turmoil Ava had been mired in for weeks.

"One thing comes to mind that I've always wanted to do," Xavier said.

"What's that?" she asked as he turned into the driveway of an opulent hotel. The valet approached, opening her door with a practiced bow.

She hesitated, looking at Xavier. "I don't think—"

"It's okay. I promise it's not what you think," he said with a mischievous smirk.

Reluctantly, Ava stepped out and followed him inside. The lobby was breathtaking, a decadent display of wealth and refinement. Crystal chandeliers cast prismatic light across the space, velvet drapes framed towering windows, and polished marble floors gleamed like glass underfoot. It reminded Ava of the hotel from the first night of her journey to Caprington—luxury masking the chaos that lurked beneath.

As they walked to the front desk, a bachelorette party burst into laughter nearby, their carefree joy cutting through the tension Ava carried. It was jarring—a reminder that normalcy still existed in Caprington. People lived their lives here, oblivious to the undercurrent of darkness that fueled the Cimmerians' existence.

The receptionist greeted Xavier with a professional smile, handing over a key card after a brief exchange. Xavier wasted no time, grabbing Ava's hand and leading her to the elevator.

"What are we doing?" she asked.

"Something reckless." He grinned, pressing the button for the top floor. "And if we get caught, we'll be grounded."

She raised an eyebrow. "Grounded?"

"Yeah. It's our version of punishment. Jail time, forced labor—cleaning the castle, scrubbing the village streets. The works."

"That doesn't sound so bad," she muttered, though the thought of being confined again made her stomach churn.

The elevator dinged, and they stepped out onto the rooftop. Ava's breath hitched. The space was stunning—an open-air terrace with a sleek infinity pool that In one corner sat a small bar with soft ambient lighting, where a handful of patrons watched a sports game on TV.

"I've always wanted to skinny dip," Xavier announced casually.

Ava gawked at him. "You picked a public place for this?"

"Yeah." He grinned. "You up for it?"

"People will definitely see." She eyed the patrons at the bar.

"There's like four people up here, and none of them care. They're glued to the TV."

"I'm not drunk enough for this."

Xavier rolled his eyes, tilting his head in mock exasperation. "Fine. I've got something else in mind."

"Okay," she said warily, following him back to the car.

As they left the city and began climbing into the mountains, the lights of Caprington faded into the distance. The road wound, the car hugging the curves as Xavier drove with ease.

The view stole Ava's breath. Snow-capped peaks glowed under the moonlight, and far off, she could make out the glittering cascade of a waterfall. It brought back memories she'd rather forget—the day she'd almost drowned trying to stop the rushing water so the Elders could pass safely.

She shivered, pushing the thought aside. "Where are we going?" she asked.

"It's a surprise."

Ava leaned back in her seat, trying to let herself relax. The silence between them wasn't awkward, but she couldn't shake her amazement at how much her perception of Xavier had shifted. This was the man who had haunted her nightmares and struck her down without hesitation—yet now, he was taking her on what felt like a casual road trip.

"Have you ever done this before?" she asked.

"Done what?"

"Let go of everything. Rebelled. Just lived."

"Not really. Not like this."

She glanced at his profile, noting the tension in his jaw and the way his hands gripped the steering wheel, as though holding onto more than just control of the car. He was a contradiction—dangerous, yet vulnerable in ways she hadn't expected.

The road bent again, revealing a stunning vista of the mountains and the glowing waterfall in the distance. Ava turned her gaze to the scenery, letting its beauty soothe her restless thoughts. For a brief moment, she forgot about Havok, the massacres, and the darkness that had consumed her. High above the city, she could breathe again.

Her gaze drifted back to Xavier. Moonlight flickered across his face, highlighting the man who had once tormented her and her friends, who had reveled in her suffering. And yet, here he was—almost normal. Was this a new side of him, or another game? She clenched her fists, unsure if hating him less made her despise him more.

The car rolled to a stop, gravel crunching beneath the tires. Xavier stepped out first, the crisp mountain air rushing in as Ava hesitated. The sharp scent of pine and damp earth mingled with the faint metallic tang of frost. The world there felt raw, untamed, brimming with quiet energy that thrummed beneath the stillness of the night.

"Come on." He nodded toward a narrow dirt trail that disappeared into the dense forest ahead.

Wrapping her arms around herself, Ava followed, her breath forming small white clouds in the chill air. The towering trees loomed above, their skeletal branches weaving together to form a canopy that blocked out the stars. Shadows clung to the edges of the path, their depths seeming to shift with each step. The only sound was the crunch of their boots on the frozen ground, a steady rhythm against the silence.

"Do you know where you're going?" she asked.

Xavier glanced over his shoulder, a faint smirk curling his lips. "Oh yeah. I know this path like the back of my hand."

The trail grew steeper, and Ava's legs burned with effort as they climbed. Gasping for breath in the frigid air, she pushed onward. The trees thinned, the forest giving way to an open expanse.

Ahead, a massive rock jutted out over the abyss, its surface flat and sheer, like the edge of the world itself. It teetered over the drop, daring gravity to claim it. Ava froze at the sight, her stomach twisting. Memories of cliffs and turbulent water surged unbidden, and she took a shaky step back, her gaze darting away from the void.

Xavier turned to her, holding out his hand. "I promise it's safe."

Her heart pounded against her ribs. "I think I'd rather not plummet to my death, thanks."

He chuckled, the sound oddly comforting. "I won't let that happen. Trust me."

Her instincts screamed at her to stay back, to turn and run, but against her better judgment, she reached out. Her hand was damp and trembling as it slid into his cool, steady grip. Step by step, he led her closer to the edge, her body fighting every inch of the way.

"Afraid of heights?" he asked, a teasing note in his voice.

"Isn't it obvious?"

"I won't let anything happen to you."

When they reached the edge, Xavier released her hand and gestured outward. Ava hesitated, her stomach lurching as she forced herself to look.

Her breath caught.

The view was staggering. Far below, the lights of the city glimmered like scattered stars, reflecting on the ink-black water that stretched endlessly beyond the cliffs. The village nestled in the valley below was a delicate cluster of golden light, dwarfed by the towering peaks that framed it. The abyss beneath them yawned wide and unforgiving, yet the beauty of it all was undeniable, overwhelming.

For a moment, Ava's fear receded, replaced by something else—an ache that was both awe and longing, as though the view was too vast, too infinite for her to hold on to.

"What's down there?" She trembled.

"Water." Xavier pointed to the faint shimmer in the distance. "It connects to the fjord below."

"How high are we?"

"About two thousand feet."

A shiver ran down her spine, a mixture of awe and dread. "What are we doing here?"

"I wanted to show you this. And ... I wanted to cliff dive."

Her heart stilled. "What?" She backed away.

"I've always wanted to, but I've been too afraid." He laughed nervously, the sound tinged with self-deprecation. "Of course, everyone mocks me for it."

"How does anyone survive that fall?"

"The water's cursed." He shrugged. "It breaks the fall."

"That's the worst explanation I've ever heard."

He grinned, reaching into the air as if throwing something. Suddenly, a glowing orb appeared, casting a soft golden light as it floated downward. Ava watched as it illuminated the jagged cliffs and gnarled branches, finally touching the water below. The orb rippled, its glow spreading across the surface in a way that was both mesmerizing and unsettling.

She stiffened. The sight was familiar, too familiar. Was that the same magic luring her to the frozen lake when she fell into a coma?

Her fists clenched at her sides. She leveled her breathing, forcing herself to remain calm. She needed to leave. Now.

"Are you okay? You're tense." Xavier touched her arm. "We don't have to do this if you're scared. Trust me, I get it."

"I ... I'm fine." She pulled her arm away. "Why do you want to jump so badly?"

He turned back to the cliff, his gaze distant. "Because I want to feel free. Just for a moment. Like it's my choice. Something I decided."

That caught her off guard. "You're not free now?"

His shoulders tensed, and he sighed. "I can't talk about this with you."

"Why not?" she pressed, moving closer.

"You ask too many questions," he snapped, though there was no real anger in his voice.

"You can talk to me."

But he shook his head.

The tension between them settled, and Ava studied him in the dim light. For the first time, she saw something beyond the cruel façade he wore—something broken and yearning. It struck a chord within her, and she hated she could understand him.

"Are you going to jump or not?" She crossed her arms.

"Only if you do it with me."

Her stomach lurched. "Why me?"

"I don't know. I feel like I can be myself around you. And I want to share this with someone who gets it."

Her heart hammered in her chest as she weighed his words. The thought of jumping off a cliff terrified her, but a strange part of her craved the freedom he spoke of. Maybe, just for a moment, she could let go.

"Fine," she whispered, swallowing her fear. "I'll do it."

Xavier smiled—a genuine, almost boyish grin—and held out his hand. "Let's do this."

Her body trembled as she took his hand, her pulse pounding in her ears. Together, they stepped to the edge, the blackness below yawning like a predator waiting to devour them.

"Don't look down," he said. "That makes it worse."

"Too late for that."

"Ready?" He tightened his grip.

"Not even a little."

Xavier took a deep breath and leapt, yanking Ava with him into the void. The wind hit her face like a freight train, roaring in her ears and whipping her hair around her face. Her stomach plummeted, but then came the weightlessness—a sensation so pure and freeing it stole her breath. For the first time in weeks, months even, she felt unshackled. The darkness within her—the guilt, the rage, the endless ache of loss—fell away, leaving only the rush of the moment.

Ava let out a laugh, carried away in the rushing air.

The water emerged below, glinting in the moonlight. Bracing for impact, she hit the surface with the grace of a practiced diver, slicing through cleanly. Cool water enveloped her, a perfect, silent embrace. The impact sent ripples outward, but the water was gentle, as though it understood what she needed.

For a moment, she stayed below, her lungs burning a little, savoring the pressure of the depths and the absolute stillness. She opened her eyes, the muted, dark blue world around her eerily calm. Slowly, she surfaced, gulping fresh air and pushing wet hair from her face.

Xavier was already treading water nearby, droplets streaming down his laughing face. His hair clung to his forehead, and his exhilaration was infectious.

"We did it!" he shouted, his voice echoing off the surrounding cliffs. "That was exhilarating! How do you feel?"

Ava couldn't help the grin spreading across her face. Her adrenaline surged, making her limbs feel light and her chest buzz with energy. "Amazing." She turned to him. "How do *you* feel?"

"Incredible." His grin widened, boyish and genuine. "That was exactly what I needed."

"Better than skinny dipping?"

He laughed, a sound that was surprisingly warm. "Yes. Much better. Thank you."

"For what?"

"For braving that fall with me." His tone softened, and for a moment, his wild energy gave way to something more subdued.

"You're welcome," she said, surprised to realize she meant it.

Xavier tilted his head, treading water more lazily now. "What about you? What's something you've always wanted to do? Something you're afraid to face?"

The question hit her harder than expected. What hadn't she feared lately? Death hovered over her—a shadow that refused to lift. And there was something deeper, something sharper: the fear that no matter what she did, it wouldn't be enough. She would never be enough. Her answer slipped out before she could stop it. "Being vulnerable to someone."

Xavier blinked. "Why does that scare you?"

She treaded water, turning her gaze to the black expanse of the fjord. "Because I'm afraid of what they'll see. I've made peace with who I am, or at least I thought I had. But letting someone in? Letting them see the mess I've become? It's … terrifying."

"I doubt you're as messed up as I am, but I get it."

"What makes you so screwed up?" She knew much of his dark past but wanted to hear his truth.

Xavier hesitated, the playfulness fading from his expression. His gaze shifted to the cliffs, and the tension in his shoulders tightened. "Another day," he whispered. "We should head back to the castle."

Ava nodded, her curiosity tugging at her, but she didn't push. They climbed out of the water, their soaked clothes clinging to them and dripping onto the rocky ground. The night air was sharp and cold, biting against her skin. She warmed herself with her ability, but Xavier didn't seem to mind the chill, his damp hair sticking to his neck as they walked back to the car.

As they settled into the quiet drive back, Ava's thoughts churned. Xavier's actions didn't align with the cruel, malicious man she'd known. He'd been vile, threatening, and remorseless. But this man—this version of him—seemed almost human. Kind, even. It made her stomach twist with discomfort.

Could this be the real Xavier? Or was it a test? Did he know she was feigning memory loss, playing her own game of deception? She studied his profile as he drove, the faint glow of the dashboard lighting his features.

No matter what, forgiveness wasn't something she could grant him so easily. Not after everything he'd done. And yet, a small part of her, one she wasn't ready to acknowledge, wondered if maybe—just maybe—there was more to him than she'd ever allowed herself to see.

CHAPTER THIRTY

SAFE AND SOUND

The morning sun streamed through Ava's window, painting golden patterns across the stone floor. The memories of her day with Xavier played on a loop—his vulnerable moments, the glimmers of humanity she hadn't expected. Was it authentic, or was he simply a pawn in Havok's manipulative game? She didn't know, and the uncertainty gnawed at her. She almost felt for him, and she was no better than any of the other Cimmerians.

Now, she was to join Gabriel for recruiting. A punishment, they called it. Ava's chest tightened. Was she meant to feel regret for being barred from massacres? The very thought made her stomach churn. She swallowed hard, brushing a strand of hair from her face with trembling fingers.

A soft knock on the door shattered her reverie, and her heart leapt, a traitorous flutter she tried to suppress. She froze for a moment before striding to the door and pulling it open.

Gabriel stood there, his presence as steady as it was jarring. His expression was impassive, his dark brows drawn in a neutral line. For an agonizing moment, he said nothing, his silence more deafening than any words. His blue eyes scanned her quickly, cool and detached, before settling somewhere over her shoulder as if she were nothing more than another soldier.

"Havok's orders," he clipped. "You're coming with us."

Her breath caught, and her pulse raced in her ears. She wanted to collapse into his arms, to apologize for what she'd done and beg for some flicker of the connection they once had. But his tone, his posture, the utter lack of recognition in his gaze—it all kept her rooted to the spot. She nodded, her movements mechanical. The warmth she had once seen in him was gone. Was it a mask, or was it her fault?

They walked in silence through the winding corridors of the castle. A stifling tension hung between them, heavy with unspoken words, she couldn't bring herself to voice. Outside, the crisp morning air bit at her skin.

The others were waiting, Donovan, Zeke, and Mallory.

Donovan sneered the moment his eyes landed on her. "Seriously? This should be good."

Gabriel raised his hands in mock surrender. "Not my decision."

"She's only going to screw up again," Donovan said.

"Not under my watch."

Donovan barked out a laugh. "Didn't she try to drown your ass? She's gonna get us all killed."

Ava stiffened, shame washing over her like ice water. She turned her gaze away. "I won't. I learned my lesson."

"Let's hope you have." Gabriel held out his hand.

Her heart faltered as she placed her hand in his. For the briefest moment, she thought she felt his thumb brush against her knuckle, a gesture so fleeting she didn't know if it was real. The sharp snap of teleportation enveloped them.

The first village stood silent, its cobbled streets slick with the remnants of an overnight rain. The thatched-roof houses seemed to lean toward one another as if to guard their inhabitants. Ava stayed close to Gabriel, her steps faltering as her shame pressed harder with each passing moment. She couldn't feel anything from him. But she was scared—terrified—of turning off her emotions even for a few minutes.

"Okay, we need to find these people." He rattled off a few names, and the group split up.

Ava followed Gabriel, her silence mirroring his. She dreaded what they might be forced to do if the deserters didn't comply. When they found the first two, pale-faced and trembling, Ava held her breath as Gabriel's calm but firm commands persuaded them to surrender. He teleported them back to the castle, leaving Ava alone with her thoughts.

Each time he vanished, her chest tightened, and when he reappeared, the ache grew. The rhythm of his departures and returns felt like a cruel reminder of how far they'd drifted from the bond they once shared.

By the time they reached the second village, the sky had turned a breathtaking palette of orange and purple, dusk settling over the quiet streets. They stopped at an inn in the town's center to rest for the night. The inn smelled of herbs and wood polish, but the subdued whispers of the patrons sent a chill through Ava. The villagers lowered their heads, their gazes avoiding the group. Fear clung to the air like smoke.

Gabriel approached the front desk, his tone businesslike as he requested five rooms. The keys clinked against the counter as he handed them out.

"We start at seven." He handed Ava her key without looking at her, then turned and disappeared down the hallway.

She stood in the dim lobby, the key cold and heavy in her hand. Her heart twisted as she watched him go, his rigid shoulders and steady gait a stark contrast to the whirlwind of emotions churning within her. She clenched the key tighter, the metal biting into her palm. For all their shared history and unspoken connection, it felt like they were strangers now, and she didn't know if they could ever find their way back to each other.

As she climbed the stairs to her room, her thoughts circled around the day's silence between her and Gabriel. She had imagined their reunion so many times, but never like that—so cold, so distant. Maybe she could find the words, the courage, to reach him.

Her room was small—a bed, a bathroom, and a window that framed the moonlit village below. She walked inside, closing the door behind her, and she set the key on the nightstand.

Moonlight streamed through the window, casting gentle, silvery patterns on the floor. Ava paced, her bare feet brushing against the cool stone. Each step mirrored the chaos in her heart, the rhythm disjointed and uneven. The faint scent of lavender drifted in from the village below, teasing her senses with its soothing promise, but even that familiar fragrance couldn't calm her racing mind.

Pausing by the window, she stared out at the moon. Wispy clouds crept across its surface, shadows darkening the pale glow. Ava felt the same shadows creeping into her thoughts, threatening to consume her again. She closed her eyes, her shoulders sagging with regret.

"Ava?"

Her eyes flew open, her heart leaping at the sound of his voice, and she spun around.

He was there, standing in front of her, and she couldn't breathe. Gabriel's eyes were a storm—dark and consuming—pulling her under like a riptide she didn't want to fight.

The soft moonlight illuminated him as he stood in the doorway, his eyes burning with intensity. Relief and longing surged within her, crashing over her like a tidal wave.

"Gabriel…" she whispered.

In two swift strides, he was there, pulling her into his arms. His warmth surrounded her, and she inhaled the familiar scent of juniper—a salvation, a reminder of something real and unbroken in a world that had shattered around her.

She gripped his shirt, her entire body trembling as the dam she'd built inside her ruptured. Long buried emotions threatened to consume her, but his hold on her tightened. His hand cradled the back of her head as though he feared she might slip through his fingers.

"I couldn't stay away," he murmured into her hair. "Not anymore."

A sob caught in her throat as she whispered, "I'm so sorry, Gabriel. Forgive me. I don't want to take anything for granted. I don't even know who I am anymore. I turned it all off—everything. I didn't care who I hurt, what I destroyed. I didn't care about anyone—not even you."

He pulled back to meet her eyes, his hands cupping her face. "You cared. You just buried it so deep you couldn't feel it. But I knew, Ava. I knew you'd come back to yourself."

"I killed so many innocent people. I hurt you. I don't know how to make any of it right."

"You don't have to make it right," he said firmly. "You just have to keep moving forward. You're not Havok, Ava. You're not the things he forced you to do."

"I'm so sorry I hurt you. I keep hurting you."

"Ava, stop. There's nothing to forgive."

The tears she had tried so desperately to hold back spilled over, trailing hot paths down her cheeks. "No. How can you forgive me? After everything—"

"Because I love you," he said simply. "Because I see you, Ava. Not the things Havok made you do. Not the darkness you're afraid of. I see you."

The raw sincerity in his voice unraveled what little remained of her defenses. With a broken sob, she buried her face against his chest. Her cries wracked her body, and still he held her.

"I don't deserve you," she murmured once the tears subsided.

"You deserve more than I could ever give you," he countered. "But I'm not going anywhere. No matter what."

She pulled back, her swollen eyes searching his face. "Gabriel…"

"I know. I know, Ava."

He leaned in, his lips brushing hers in the barest whisper of a kiss. The warmth of his breath lingered against her skin, and his touch, so gentle, sent a shiver cascading down her spine.

Her back met the wall, and he was on her in an instant, his hands framing her face, his lips capturing hers with an urgency that stole her breath. It wasn't gentle—it was fire, wild and burning. A hunger she'd never felt before crashed into her, and she held onto him as though he were the only solid thing in the world.

He kissed her like he was trying to memorize every inch of her, to carve the moment into his bones. His hands slid down, fingers grazing the curve of her waist, pulling her closer until there was nothing between them but air that crackled like lightning. Her chest rose and fell against his, their breaths coming fast and uneven, a rhythm that matched the pounding of her heart.

"Ava," he whispered, her name breaking like glass in his throat. "I missed you."

She opened her eyes—barely—only to find him looking at her like she was something sacred, something precious he didn't dare believe was real. The weight of it shattered her. She gripped the back of his neck, pulling him back to her, their lips meeting again, harder this time. The collision sparked down to her fingertips.

They stumbled backward until her knees hit the edge of the bed, and suddenly they were falling, the world spinning around them until there was nothing left but *this*. His shirt was gone, discarded without thought, and her hands skimmed the smooth expanse of his shoulders, the curve of his back. He was heat and strength and softness, a contradiction in every way, and it made her dizzy.

Her breath hitched when his hands found the buttons of her shirt, slipping them free one by one with excruciating slowness. Gabriel paused, his gaze dragging over her like a caress.

"Beautiful," he murmured, so soft she almost didn't hear him.

A flush crept up her neck, but she didn't look away. She couldn't. She was a moth, and he was her flame, the pull of him irresistible.

Then his lips were on her again—her jaw, her throat, the hollow at her collarbone—each kiss unraveling her, thread by thread. She clutched at him, her fingers pressing into his skin like she could anchor herself there, like she could stop the world from falling apart beneath her. But the world was already gone, and there was only Gabriel—his hands, his mouth, his warmth sinking into her bones and chasing away the darkness.

They found each other in the spaces between breaths, in the silence that buzzed with electricity. Layers fell away—clothes, fears, the weight of the past—and all that remained was the truth of who they were.

When they moved together, it was as if the universe finally aligned, every broken piece sliding into place. His name slipped from her lips in a whisper, a plea, a prayer. And he answered her, his touch reverent, his voice raw as he whispered her name in return. Ava shattered, the storm inside her calmed, and the world tilt until there was nothing but light.

When it was over, and their bodies stilled, Gabriel gathered her close. They lay tangled together, skin against skin, heart against heart, breaths mingling.

Ava pressed her face to his chest, listening to the steady rhythm of his heartbeat. The sound grounded her in a way she hadn't known she needed.

Gabriel's hand traced lazy circles along her back. "I'll always find you," he whispered. "Even in the dark."

"I love you."

Bathed in moonlight streaming through the window, Ava believed him at that moment. The doubts, the pain, the guilt—all of it faded, replaced by the quiet strength of his love and the fragile but growing belief that she could find her way back to herself.

She pressed a hand to his cheek, her thumb brushing against the stubble on his jaw, and smiled—a small, genuine smile that hadn't graced her lips in far too long.

Gabriel mirrored it, his eyes shining with something she hadn't dared hope to see. Understanding and unwavering faith in her.

For the first time in what felt like forever, Ava felt whole.

The faint blush of dawn crept through the thin curtains, painting the small room in muted shades of gold and gray. Ava stirred, her body heavy with a strange mix of exhaustion and relief.

She blinked, her eyes adjusting to the soft morning light, and her gaze landed on Gabriel. He sat on the edge of the bed, his back to her, shoulders tense. His hand moved through his hair, a motion she recognized as one of deep thought.

Her chest tightened, a mixture of tenderness and unease flooding through her. "Gabriel?"

He turned to her, offering a faint smile. It didn't reach his eyes, but the care in his gaze was undeniable. "I couldn't sleep."

He shifted, resting back against the headboard, and opened his arms for her. She moved to him, letting him gather her close.

"There's something I need to tell you," he said.

A bowling ball dropped into her stomach. "What is it?" Trembling, she turned to look at his face.

His fingers brushed against hers. "While you were … gone," he said carefully, "I've been trying to figure out how to break the link between you and Havok."

"You have?"

"I couldn't just stand by and watch him control you. The nights I wasn't recruiting, I was in the library, searching for answers. And I found some."

Her pulse quickened, hope and fear tangling inside her. "What did you find?"

He hesitated, his eyes dark with a mix of frustration and determination. "The link—it's not just a connection. It's a prison. A binding spell created through ancient necromantic rituals. It ties your life force to his, intertwining your powers, emotions, even your memories."

"That's why I've been seeing his memories. Why I've felt his rage so strongly."

"Yes." His grip on her hand tightened. "But it's worse than that. Those memories aren't random. Havok planted them deliberately. They're chosen to manipulate you, to feed your anger, to keep you tethered to him."

A shiver ran down her spine, and she pulled the blanket closer. The violation of it all hit her like a wave, leaving her raw and exposed. "So, turning off my emotions … it just gave him control? Access to my mind? Did he see everything—everything about me, about us?"

Gabriel shook his head, his gaze firm. "No. If he had, he would've acted differently. He would never have allowed you to leave the castle with me, for one."

"But his voice … I heard it. He told me what to do, and I did it. And then he punished me for it."

"I think that the punishment wasn't just for your actions. It was a way to break deeper into your mind. To force you to let him in fully. But," he added quickly, "there's hope."

"Hope?"

"The link binds him as well. If you can resist his emotions, keep your own identity strong, you might be able to turn it against him. To weaken his control. To fight back."

"You think I could get inside his head?"

"It's possible. It won't be easy, Ava. And it would be dangerous. If you're able to control him, he may fight back and realize what's going on. And I don't know what he'd do. He won't kill you."

"But he'd torture or kill someone else."

He nodded. "I also found references to an ancient order of Enchanters who specialized in breaking curses like this. Their descendants might still exist. Maggie believes Aaron or Gustav might know more, but finding the descendants won't be easy."

His dedication overwhelmed her then. He'd been doing all this—for her. Even after everything she'd done to him. A surge of emotion swelled in her chest, bringing tears to her eyes. "You've been doing this all on your own?"

"Of course. Ava, you know I would do anything for you. And you are not alone. I need you to know that."

The words hit her with more force than she expected. She lowered her gaze, her chest aching with gratitude and guilt. "I don't deserve you."

Gabriel tilted her chin up, his gaze locking with hers. "Don't start that."

Her tears spilled over, hot and silent, as she leaned into him, her head resting against his shoulder. His scent—juniper and something uniquely Gabriel—wrapped around her, soothing and familiar.

"I've missed this," she murmured.

"Me too." He pressed a kiss to her hair. "One day, Ava. One day, we'll have this every morning."

She tilted her face toward his, their foreheads touching. "I don't want this to end."

"It won't," he whispered, his lips brushing hers in a kiss.

For now, in the quiet dawn, the world and its dangers faded away, leaving only the two of them—holding on to a fragile hope that felt just within reach.

CHAPTER THIRTY-ONE
REUNION

Guilt clung to Ava as her hand hovered over Klaus's doorknob. Her stomach clenched as a painful knot of fear constricted her breath.

Would anyone want to see her? Would they welcome her back? Both the Cimmerians and her friends had cast her out—except for Melissa and Gabriel. But Gabriel wasn't there now; he was out searching for the descendants of the ancient Enchanters, risking everything to save her. The thought brought a pang of guilt and loneliness. Could she even hope for forgiveness from the others after everything she'd done?

Her chest tightened as she turned the knob and pushed the door open. The room was quiet, the faint sound of her footsteps on the wooden floor magnified as she descended the hidden stairs. The heavy scent of wax and old books filled her nose. When she reached the bottom, the voices she'd heard speaking in urgent whispers went silent.

She entered, and the room fell silent. Their gazes hit her—some wary, some guarded, others tired. For a moment, she felt like an outsider again, a stranger in the place she had once called home.

Ava swallowed hard. "Um, I'm sorry. I didn't mean to interrupt you. I came to—"

"No, you're fine." Melissa got up and hugged her. "It's good to see you."

"Welcome back." Nicole offered a tentative smile.

"I know I've been a terrible friend. I can't expect you to forgive me, but I need you to know how sorry I am."

The group softened, their wary expressions melting into something more vulnerable. One by one, they approached her, offering hugs and reassurances.

Melissa rested a hand on her shoulder. "Don't worry about it. We know how hard it's been. Being linked to Havok can't be a picnic. Those weren't your thoughts. His rage wasn't your rage."

"Besides," Thomas added, smirking, "now I can officially say I've been shot. Add it to the résumé." A ripple of laughter lightened the tension.

With a determined glint in his eyes, Link stepped forward. "We've been working on something. A way to even the odds in this war—and maybe help you break your curse."

Ava's brow furrowed. "What do you mean?"

"We've been talking to some of the villagers, but it hasn't been as successful as we hoped." Melissa said.

Link exchanged a glance with Melissa before pulling a thick, ancient-looking book from a hidden alcove in the wall. Its cracked leather cover and faded gold lettering hinted at the power it held. "We're going to summon spirits."

The words hung in the air like a thunderclap.

Ava stumbled back, her heart pounding. "No. Absolutely not. Do you remember what happened the last time?"

"Ava, hear him out," Melissa said. "This isn't like before."

"How is it not?" Ava snapped. "We're talking about summoning entities that could possess us, manipulate us—kill us. You can't control them!"

"We can," Link said. "I've been studying this for months after Gabriel learned it was necromantic. Gabriel found this Spellcaster's book in the library's forbidden vaults. It's detailed, Ava. It explains how to summon spirits and how to protect ourselves."

"You think an old book is going to save us from the kind of darkness we're inviting in? That's insanity."

Link approached, clutching the book like a shield. "Ava, I know it's dangerous. But we don't have any other options. You've seen what Havok can do, and you know what we're up against. We need this."

She opened her mouth to argue, but Melissa stopped her. "Link's not wrong. We've thought this through. And it's not just about the war—it's about helping you too. If there's even a chance we can find answers about the curse, isn't it worth trying?"

Ava bit her lip, her heart hammering. The room felt smaller, the air heavier, as if the walls themselves were closing in. Her gaze flicked to the others. A solemn expression replaced Thomas's usual easygoing demeanor, his arms clasped across his chest. Gillian chewed her bottom lip, avoiding Ava's eyes. Even Nicole stood with her hands clasped in front of her, her knuckles white.

"This is insane," Ava whispered. "You're asking me to trust something we can't control. What if it goes wrong? What if one of you gets hurt—or worse?"

"We know the risks," Link said. "That's why we've been preparing. The book details protections—amulets, wards, even a binding circle to keep the spirits contained. We'll be careful."

"Careful?" Ava's panic spilled out in a wave. "You think 'careful' is enough when summoning something that could destroy us? I've been through this, Link. You haven't."

His face tightened. "I know you're scared. But sitting here doing nothing isn't an option. We're losing ground, Ava. We've been here for five months, and we are no closer to having an army. Every day, Havok's grip tightens. We have to fight back."

"How?"

"I can control it," he said. "I've been practicing."

"Practicing? How? With what?"

Link hesitated, glancing at Melissa before answering. "I've been summoning minor spirits. Harmless ones. Just to learn. And it worked."

Her stomach churned. "You've already been doing this? Without telling me?"

"We didn't want to worry you," Melissa said. "We needed to be sure it was even possible before bringing you into it."

"You think that makes it better?" Ava snapped, the anger bubbling to the surface. "I'm the one linked to Havok. I'm the one who's been inside his head. Don't you think I should've had a say in this?"

"Ava," Melissa said. "We're trying to help you. All of this is for you."

She shook her head. "No! I can't let all of you risk your lives for me. Gabriel's already risking his."

"You don't get to decide what we do," she said. "We need you to trust us."

Ava's gaze flicked between them, her chest heaving. Trust. The word was a knife twisting in her gut. She wanted to trust them—wanted to believe they could find a way out of this nightmare. But the memories of her last encounter with spirits were too raw, too vivid.

"What exactly is the plan?" she asked finally.

Link's shoulders eased. "We'll use the binding circle. The six Elementals will anchor the circle while I call the spirits. The rest will stand guard outside. We'll use amaranth to protect ourselves from possession, and if things go wrong, we'll have countermeasures in place."

"And what are you hoping to gain from this?" Ava crossed her arms over her chest.

"An army," Link said. "And answers. Maybe the spirits can tell us something we don't know—about Havok, about your curse, about how to end all of this."

A hush settled over the room again.

Ava stared at the floor, her thoughts a whirlwind of fear, anger, and reluctant hope. She didn't like it. Not one bit. But she could see the determination in their eyes, the desperate need to do something—anything—to turn the tide.

"When?" she asked.

"Tonight," Link said. "At midnight."

Ava's stomach dropped. Tonight. So soon. She swallowed hard, her throat tight. "Fine. But if anything goes wrong, I'm stopping it. I don't care what the plan is."

"Understood," Link said.

Melissa touched her arm again. "We've got this, Ava. We're in this together."

Ava nodded, though her heart still raced. Together. The word felt fragile, like glass on the verge of shattering. But for now, it was all she had.

CHAPTER THIRTY-TWO

LOVE LIES BLEEDING

Despite the cool air brushing Ava's skin, the room was sweltering. Too many people, too much tension. Her palms were slick with sweat, and the knot in her stomach tightened with every passing second. She clenched and unclenched her fists, trying to steady her trembling hands. The soft candlelight only added to the heaviness of the moment, the shadows dancing on the walls like silent specters.

She glanced at the circle Klaus had drawn in the center of the room. Bundles of candles that burned with an unnatural intensity surrounded the meticulous lines, etched with precision. Link handed out amaranths—a necklace of deep red flowers strung together with delicate care. The petals hung like droplets of blood, vivid and startling.

"It's called Love Lies Bleeding," Link said. "Wear it under your shirt. It has to touch your skin to protect you."

Ava's fingers brushed against the rough string as she slipped the garland over her head, its cool weight settling against her chest. The name's irony didn't elude her. Love Lies Bleeding. It felt painfully appropriate. Her throat tightened as her thoughts spiraled—visions of her past mistakes, of Havok's control, of the lives lost because of her.

She flinched when Link squeezed her hand. "It'll be okay." How could anyone promise safety against spirits that defied nature itself?

The group took their places around the circle, their movements stiff and hesitant. Ava hesitated at first, her feet rooted to the floor. She forced herself forward, slipping between Thomas and Jeremy. Their hands reached for hers. Her pulse pounded in her ears as Link chanted in Latin, the words ancient and unfamiliar, yet they seemed to hum with power.

Ava closed her eyes, focusing on Colden. She pictured his warm smile, his kind eyes, the way he'd always been there for her before everything fell apart. The image of him was so vivid that for a moment, she could almost feel his presence.

A sharp intake of breath from Melissa made Ava's eyes snap open. The yellow candlelight had turned an eerie shade of blue, the flames licking higher as shadows began to shift and ripple within the circle. A heavy, charged air hung in the space.

Ava's heart raced, her throat tightening as figures emerged from the flames. Wisps of smoke twisted and solidified into human shapes, their forms ghostly and translucent.

One by one, the spirits stepped out of the circle, their faces becoming clearer with each passing second. Colden's warm smile sent a jolt through Ava's chest. Tears blurred her vision as Savina appeared beside him, followed by Thomas's father, Sean, Aidan, Ronan, Nathan, and the faces of the New Orleans coven. A pang of guilt and sorrow hit her at the sight of them—their deaths were on her hands.

"Colden?" she whispered.

"Hello, Ava," he said.

Her body trembled with the urge to run to him, to wrap him in a hug, but he was only a shadow of the man she remembered. Tears flowed down her cheeks. "I miss you. I'm so sorry for what happened. I—"

"No apologies," he said. "It's good to see you."

Nearby, Thomas looked at his father's spirit. "Dad?"

"It's good to see you too, son," Mr. Arrington said, his gaze softening as he looked at Thomas.

Ava's tears fell harder as Savina's hand brushed her shoulder, her spectral touch sending a shiver through her. "We've been watching you all." Quiet pride filled her voice. "You've all done so much."

"What?" Thomas said bitterly. "We've been doing terrible things."

Savina shook her head. "But only to defeat Havok. And that's why we're here. To help you finish this."

"We need to break the curse on Ava," Link said.

A voice cut through the room, sharp and familiar. "I can help with that."

Ava's head whipped around, her breath catching in her throat. A figure stepped out from the group of spirits—a woman with long red hair and piercing eyes. Her heart stilled as recognition washed over her.

"Mom?" The word came out as a whisper, barely audible.

The woman nodded, her gaze soft but unwavering. "Hello, Ava. I know I did a terrible thing—an unforgivable thing. I was young and foolish, and I thought I was doing what was best. But I love you, Ava. I've always loved you."

Tears burned in Ava's eyes, and her body felt frozen in place.

"That's why I'm offering my soul in place of yours," her mother continued. "When you kill Havok, let me be the one to go. Not you."

The room fell silent. The air was thick from her words. Ava's mind raced, her emotions a chaotic whirlwind. Anger, sorrow, disbelief—they all crashed into her at once. Her lips trembled as she tried to form a response, but no words came.

"Promise me you'll take care of yourself. Take care of Connor. Tell him I love him."

Ava's knees buckled, and she clutched Jeremy's hand for support. Tears streamed down her face. "Why now? Why offer this now?"

Her mother's gaze softened with regret. "Because I never thought it would come to this. I thought we could stop Havok before it got this far. I was wrong. But this is my chance to make it right."

Ava nodded, her throat too tight to speak.

"We will help you win this," Colden said. "Call us when the time comes, and we'll fight with you."

"How long can you stay when we call you?" Melissa asked.

"Long enough," Savina said. "But we'll need a strong tether to this world."

Link cleared his throat. "I'll prepare everything. We'll make it work."

"I'll be ready," Luci said. "I'll do what needs to be done. I won't let you face him alone."

The ambiguity left Ava uneasy. There were too many unknowns, too much left to prepare.

As the spirits faded, Colden met Ava's gaze. "This isn't goodbye," he said softly. "We'll see each other again."

She nodded, her heart aching. Silence fell over the room once more as the last of the spirits vanished, leaving Ava and her friends standing in the dim light of the candles. Her mother's offer hung heavy in the air, a bittersweet hope that they might finally have a way to end this.

But it wasn't without a cost.

The rain fell in a misty drizzle, soft but relentless, veiling the landscape in a silvery haze. Water beaded on Ava's skin and trickled down her neck, soaking through her jacket until the fabric clung to her. Each step on the sodden ground squelched, her boots sinking slightly into the mossy terrain. The briny tang of the nearby fjord mingled with the earthy scent of rain-soaked pine, but it did little to ease the knots in her stomach.

She paced in front of Caprington's towering gates, her arms wrapped around herself. The torches along the walls flickered, their light barely penetrating the dense, wet gloom. Midnight had come and gone, and still Gabriel hadn't returned.

She needed him. Needed to talk to him. Her mind churned with fragmented images of the spirits: Colden's familiar smile, Savina's calming presence, and her mother's piercing gaze, both a comfort and a wound. The revelation that her mother had pledged her soul to Havok to save Ava lingered like a sharp thorn in her chest, impossible to remove.

The chill seeped into her bones, but it wasn't just the cold that made her shiver. *Where is he? What if something happened?* The thought twisted through her mind, relentless and sharp. Her breath hitched as she tilted her face toward the rain, letting it mask the tears she didn't have the strength to wipe away. Each droplet was cold and biting, mingling with the salty tang of her sorrow.

The sharp snap of a branch echoed in the stillness. Ava froze, her heart stuttering in her chest. She squinted into the mist, her pulse racing as her eyes darted over the shadowed tree line.

A figure emerged, his form materializing through the veil of rain like a phantom. Her breath caught. It was him. Gabriel.

Relief surged through her, leaving her lightheaded and unsteady. He moved with quiet purpose, his dark coat heavy with rain and his hair plastered to his forehead. Even in the dim light, she could see the exhaustion etched into his face, the countless burdens carried in the tension on his shoulders.

She bolted toward him. He halted, his head snapping up. His gaze locked onto hers, and for a moment, he didn't move, as though he were trying to convince himself she was real. Then, in a blink, he was gone, the faint shimmer of displaced air the only sign of his teleportation.

He stood before her, hand on her shoulder, his dark eyes searching hers. "Ava, what are you doing out here?"

"I need to talk to you. And I was worried about you."

His brow furrowed as he reached for her hand. "Come with me."

The words barely registered before the world around her shifted. The rain disappeared, replaced by the sound of waves and the crisp ocean air. His teleportation hum faded, leaving them on a rocky outcrop overlooking the fjord.

Ava blinked, disoriented. The moon broke through the clouds, its pale light shimmering across the water and illuminating the jagged cliffs that surrounded them. Before her, a dark, endless sea stretched into infinity, its surface shimmering with starlight. The air was sharp and clean, carrying the faintest whisper of pine from the forests above the cliffs.

"What is it?" he asked.

Ava wrapped her arms around herself and struggled to find the words. The warmth of his presence clashed with the cold fear that had settled deep in her heart. "We called the spirits tonight. Colden and Savina said to call them when the time was right. That they would conjure an army somehow to help us."

"Good. What else happened? I know there's more."

She clenched her teeth. "My mom showed up. Said she would take my place when we killed Havok." She couldn't stop the tears. "But she abandoned me. She's the one who did this to me. What if she doesn't show up? What if I can't stop Havok? I don't want to die, but I don't see another way out."

He frowned. "We'll find another way."

She shook her head, the damp air biting at her tear-streaked face. "I don't know, Gabriel. Everyone's risking everything—just for me. And it's not fair. I'm the one who can end this. I'm the one who should be risking everything."

His jaw tightened. "You're talking about sacrificing yourself."

She tilted her head, her chin rising in challenge. "What's one life compared to thousands, Gabriel?"

"You promised me."

"You don't understand—"

"No! You wanna try to be a martyr, fine. But don't stand there and act like you have no one to think about. What about your dad? What about me, Ava?"

The words punched her. She stumbled back a step, her boots slipping on the moss-slick stone. Hot tears streamed down her face. "I don't have a choice, Gabriel! Don't you get it? You've been poring over books for months. Link's been studying necromancy. I even turned off my emotions to diminish the link. We've tried everything, and we're no closer to breaking this curse."

He froze, his breathing uneven as her words settled between them. The sharp scent of salt filled the air, mingling with the tension so thick it was almost suffocating.

His expression softened, the fire in his eyes replaced by something more vulnerable, almost broken. "You think I don't know how hopeless it feels?" he asked. "But you don't get to give up. Not on yourself. Not on us. We'll figure this out. I don't care how long it takes."

Ava's breath hitched, and her shoulders sagged. The fight drained out of her, replaced by an aching sorrow. "I'm scared, Gabriel. I don't want to die. But how many people have to die just so we can figure out how to save me? If it's the only way to save everyone, what other choice do I have?"

Her knees buckled, and she crumpled to the ground, her palms pressing into the cold, wet stone as sobs wracked her body.

Gabriel was there in an instant, kneeling beside her and pulling her into his arms. She clung to him, her fists gripping the fabric of his coat like he was the only thing anchoring her to the earth. "You're not dying," he said fiercely. "Do you hear me? I'm not losing you."

His words broke through her despair, and she buried her face against his chest, letting his warmth and steady presence soothe the storm inside her.

"I'm so tired of fighting. Of feeling like I'm losing myself to him every time I shut down. It's like he's always there, waiting for me to slip."

Gabriel's jaw clenched, his eyes fixed on hers. He paused, the silence stretching, and a twist of unease tightened in her stomach. Finally, he exhaled, his shoulders sagging. "Then don't slip. Push back."

"What?"

He gripped the back of his neck. "If Havok thinks he can control you … use it against him. Probe his mind. Figure out what he's planning."

She blinked, startled by the suggestion. "You want me to *willingly* step into his mind? Gabriel, you can't be serious."

His lips pressed into a thin line, and for a moment, it seemed like he might take it back. But he nodded. "I know it's dangerous. I know how much it's already cost you. But … you've been seeing his memories, haven't you? That connection is there whether you want it or not. Maybe—just maybe—you can turn it into something we can use."

She shuddered at the thought. Her hands curled into fists at her sides. "Gabriel, if I go too far … if I let him in—"

"That's why you won't. You're stronger than him, Ava. You've always been stronger. But we can't keep waiting for answers to fall into our laps. If anyone can navigate that link without losing themselves, it's you."

Her chest tightened, a war raging inside her. His suggestion terrified her, but there was truth in his words—a sliver of hope in a situation that Havok's control had always dictated. "I don't even know where to start."

"Think of a memory you want to see. Not one he wants you to see. Remember who you are and hold onto that. Havok can't take that from you. Not unless you let him."

A long silence stretched between them. Finally, she swallowed hard. "Will you stay? While I do it?"

"You don't even have to ask."

For the first time, she let herself believe—for a fleeting moment—that they might find a way forward. Together.

Ava sat cross-legged on the floor, her hands trembling as she rested them on her knees. Gabriel sat beside her, close enough that their arms almost brushed.

"I'll give you an hour," Klaus said. "It's getting close to morning, and you'll both need to be gone by then." His words lingered in the air like a warning. He shut the door, leaving them alone in the room.

Ava stared at the quivering flames, her stomach twisting in nervous anticipation.

"Do you know what memory you chose?" Gabriel asked.

"I want to see the moment she promised my soul to him."

"I'm right here beside you."

Closing her eyes, she inhaled deeply. The scents of wax and smoke faded as she focused inward. The candlelight dimmed behind her eyelids, and the room fell away until it was only her, her thoughts, and the darkness.

A faint, cold thrumming of her connection to Havok pulsed in the back of her mind, making her shudder. Reaching out felt like plunging her hands into freezing water, the sensation prickling and numbing as she pushed deeper.

Shadows pressed against her consciousness, fragmented memories clawing at her like sharp talons. She gritted her teeth, steadying herself. Gabriel's breathing steadied her.

Then she found it.

The cabin.

Her vision snapped into clarity, and the room dissolved. Ava wasn't herself anymore. She was Havok.

The dull, warm glow of the firelight illuminated the coarse grain of the floorboards and the worn edges of the furniture. Havok paced, every movement a calculated show of control. The weight of Colden's body was a strange, irritating sensation—like wearing clothes that didn't quite fit. But it was useful tonight. Lucinda would believe the charade, at least at first.

The door creaked open, and Havok didn't need to turn to feel her fear. It hung in the air like a tangible presence, sour and electric, a mixture of terror and determination.

"Lucinda," Havok said, his voice warm, familiar—an imitation of Colden's that he knew would catch her off guard. He fought the urge to sneer as she faltered, her steps hesitant.

"Colden," she whispered.

He turned, studying her. She clutched her cloak, her knuckles white, and the faint glint of steel peeked out beneath the folds. The dagger.

The sight amused him. "Are you all right? You look … different."

Her gaze faltered, guilt flashing in her eyes. He could practically hear her thoughts, her pathetic resolve crumbling.

When the dagger finally rose, he let his mask slip, his lips curling into a cold smile. "You hesitated," he said, his voice slipping into his true self—a hiss that filled the room like smoke.

Lucinda froze, her wide eyes locked on him.

He could feel her trembling, see the dagger shake in her grasp. "Did you really think I wouldn't notice?" he taunted, his words dripping with venom. "Pathetic."

Her breath hitched as she stumbled back. "I—I was trying to—"

"To save him?" Havok cut her off, relishing her panic. "Don't lie to me. Colden isn't here right now."

The game was his now.

Stepping closer, he let his gaze fall to her stomach. He'd noticed her protective movements, the way her hand lingered there when she thought no one was looking. His grin widened.

"Afraid of losing her?"

Her gasp was a melody he savored. The dagger slipped from her hand and clattered to the floor. "Leave them alone," she choked out.

Havok tilted his head, watching her with calculated interest. "And why should I do that? Your child means nothing to me."

Her eyes burned with desperation, her hands clenching into fists. "You're wrong. She will mean everything. A Seer saw her future—a Water Enchanter stronger than any who came before her. She'll be part of a coven of Elementals destined to change the balance of this world."

Havok's curiosity piqued. A coven of Elementals? He stepped closer. "Control them," he murmured, his mind already racing. The thought of harnessing such power was intoxicating. "A coven loyal to me. Your daughter will make a fine start. Swear her soul to me, Lucinda. Bind her life to me. I'll even let you live long enough to see her grow. Refuse, and I'll ensure neither of you see another sunrise."

Tears welled in Lucinda's eyes as her knees buckled. "But binding her life to yours—"

"I know what it will do. You can save her now or you both die."

"I swear," she choked out. "I swear her soul to you."

"Excellent."

The moment Gamel's spell sank into her, a sickening green glow illuminating the room, Ava felt herself pulled back. The cabin dissolved into shadows, and she gasped, her eyes flying open as she returned to herself.

Gabriel's hands steadied her shoulders. "Ava? What did you see?"

Her breath came in shallow bursts. A rising tide of nausea threatened to send her sprawling, her chest heaving with each shuddering breath. Sweat beaded along her forehead. "She was going to kill him," she whispered. "She knew Havok was inside Colden. She promised my soul to him. And she … she didn't tell anyone. She had years to tell me. Tell Savina. Tell someone. She could've helped me."

Gabriel held her against him.

The fire of her resolve burned brighter.

Lying in bed, Ava watched the morning rain slide down the windowpanes in thin, silvery streams. The glass distorted the outside world into an indistinct blur of grays and greens. Each drop caught the faint light, shimmering before joining the rest in a race to the windowsill. The muted patter of rain against the glass filled the silence, a steady rhythm that should have been calming but wasn't.

Her fingers tightened around the edge of the pillow. Havok's voice had been quieter lately, but his presence still lingered at the back of her mind, a cold shadow she couldn't shake. He had sent her on missions that had pushed her to the brink—massacres, tasks soaked in blood. But why? Wouldn't her death have broken the connection? Unless…

The thought made her stomach twist. Unless the link wasn't what Klaus believed it to be.

Ava drew in a shaky breath, her chest tightening as her pulse quickened. The memory of her last dive into Havok's mind resurfaced, icy and raw. She had promised herself she wouldn't do it again unless she had no other choice. But the questions gnawed at her, their claws scraping at the edges of her sanity.

Closing her eyes, Ava pressed her forehead into the pillow, the faint scent of lavender from the fabric softener doing little to soothe her nerves. Her fingers dug into the pillow's soft fabric as she focused, letting herself sink into the cold, consuming connection to Havok.

This time, the connection felt colder, heavier, like stepping into a storm. Shadows swirled around her as she latched onto Havok's consciousness, drawn toward his thoughts like a moth to a flame.

And then she was there.

The memory unfolded, vivid and immediate. She was Havok.

He stood in his vast chamber, its towering glass walls revealing the stormy skies beyond. Rain lashed against the panes, the sound muffled but insistent.

The door opened, and Xavier strode in, his usual confidence tempered with caution. "Ava's doing well with the recruiting. Should I move her back to the massacres? Moscow is coming up, and—"

He swatted at the air dismissively, like swatting a fly. "That won't be necessary."

Gamel materialized from the shadows, his robes brushing the ground as he stepped into the light.

Xavier stiffened, his usual composure faltering. Fear radiated off him in waves, a silent scream masked behind a stoic face.

"The Elementals are becoming more compliant," Gamel rasped. "One more massacre should weaken them enough for the ritual."

"What ritual?" Xavier asked, his mask of confidence slipping further.

Havok turned and locked his dark eyes onto Gamel before flicking to Xavier with cold amusement. "You will have to excuse my son. He does not yet know of our plans."

Gamel nodded, his bony hands clasped in front of him, the glow of green runes pulsating along his fingertips.

"Plans?" Xavier barely masked his worry.

Havok's smile widened, a cruel curve that sent a chill down Ava's spine. "Once the Elementals have been broken, I will link them to myself, one by one, through Ava. She is the key," Havok said. "The bridge. Her link to me is already forged. Through her, I will extend that connection to the others. Once they are all linked, their powers will be mine. Gamel will sever the bonds, and they will become nothing more than empty shells."

"And then?" Xavier pressed, though Ava could feel his dread.

"Then she dies," Havok said simply, turning back toward the glass wall. His reflection stared back at him, a dark specter against the rain-streaked panes. "She is expendable. They all are. Their power is all that matters."

The color drained from Xavier's face.

"I know you have a ... fondness for Ava, but sacrifices must be made, my son. This is bigger than you or her. This is about power. Control. And when the time comes, you and I will rule."

The memory vanished, throwing Ava back into her own body with a gasp. She bolted upright, her chest heaving as her mind reeled from what she had seen.

Her skin was clammy with sweat, her muscles trembling. Her fingers gripped the edge of the mattress.

She wasn't just a pawn. She was the bridge. The massacres weren't just about destruction—they were about breaking the Elementals' spirits, weakening their resistance and power so Havok could bind them through her.

And when he was done, when their power was his, he would kill them all.

The revelation crushed her chest. She had to warn the others. But how could she tell them that Havok's plans centered on her, that she was the key to their downfall?

The rain outside grew heavier, the sound rising to a relentless drumbeat, mirroring the frantic rhythm of her thoughts.

CHAPTER THIRTY-THREE
AURORA BOREALIS

Ava and the other Elementals walked alongside Xavier, Link, Nicole, Eve, and Anais. The so-called Onyx Order. Ava's every step seemed to echo louder than it should, as if the castle itself was holding its breath. Like it knew what would happen to them after Moscow.

A week had passed since Ava learned of Havok's plan. She had broken her silence to the group that morning, recounting everything she had seen in Havok's mind: the massacres as part of a calculated ritual, his plans to strip their powers, and the horrifying realization of her role as the bridge connecting him to the others. Frustration, fear, defeat, sadness had overcome each of them. They had debated and argued, but Moscow still loomed—a deadly inevitability they couldn't escape.

Ava promised herself she wouldn't get lost in the emotionless void again. She would turn off her emotions for the massacre, deal with the consequences later. But the thought terrified her; the last time she had turned herself off, she hadn't recognized the person she had become. The icy detachment, the monstrous efficiency—it wasn't her.

It couldn't be her again.

As they traveled through the tunnels to Moscow, the damp air pressed against her skin like a suffocating blanket. The first time she had been in Russia, Gabriel had teleported her there. She had been so wary of him then, unsure of who or what he was. Now, that uncertainty was reserved for herself.

Snow didn't blanket Moscow as she had imagined when they emerged. The crisp night air smelled of asphalt and smoke, the kindling of destruction already lingering on the breeze. The sky above was clear, dotted with a sea of stars that seemed indifferent to the horrors unfolding below. Ava's breath misted in the chill, translucent clouds dissolving as quickly as they formed.

"Let's get this over with," Xavier muttered.

She glanced at him. His shoulders were tense, and his jaw was tight. He looked exhausted, the strain of something unseen tugging at his every movement. She wondered if he had ever learned how to turn off his emotions or if, like her, he carried the unbearable weight of it all.

The massacre began with the deafening roar of explosions. Flames erupted into the night like angry suns. The orange glow painted the city in violent strokes. Screams tore through the air, piercing and desperate, blending with the cacophony of chaos.

Ava moved, her mind a blank void as her body obeyed the orders Havok had etched into her very soul. The aftermath rendered Moscow a wasteland. It was a graveyard, a testament to the brutality they had unleashed.

Her hands shook as she surveyed the smoldering ruins. Another massacre. Another chapter in the horror story

Havok was writing with their lives. Ava promised herself it would be the last. No more blood. No more innocent lives. They had to stop Havok before the ritual began.

But Xavier. He haunted her thoughts. He was the key to turning the tide, the link to convincing others. And yet, every time she looked at him, doubt gnawed at her resolve. Could she trust him? Could he be trusted?

As they made their way back through the tunnels, the silence was heavy, broken only by the shuffling of their boots against the concrete. Ava's eyes darted to Xavier. He stared at the ground, his lips pressed into a thin line.

"Are you okay?" she whispered.

"I'm fine," he snapped.

Ava reached out, her fingers brushing his arm. "You don't have to pretend with me."

Xavier stopped, his dark eyes narrowing as he looked at her. For a moment, his face contorted with something unspoken—frustration, guilt, pain. "We should go." He turned and left her standing alone in the corridor.

He had been quieter than usual, his sharp retorts and forced bravado replaced by something heavier. Guilt, maybe. Or doubt. She couldn't tell, but the cracks were there, and if she was going to convince him to help them, she had to act now.

As they approached the main hall, the rest of the group dispersed, heading to their quarters without a word. Ava stayed behind, waiting for the right moment.

"Xavier," she said.

He glanced up, his jaw tightening at the sight of her. "What do you want?"

"Please talk to me. I know something's wrong."

"Leave it alone." He turned away, but Ava caught his arm.

He hesitated, his muscles tensing beneath her touch. For a moment, she thought he might open up, but then his mask slipped back into place. "You shouldn't concern yourself with me." He pulled his arm free. "Focus on surviving."

"Why do you keep doing this? Pushing me away, pretending everything's fine when it's not?"

He raised his hand and grazed her cheek. His eyes searched hers, and he teetered on the edge of breaking. "I can't," he said. "I can't do this, Ava."

"What are you so afraid of?"

His hand dropped, his shoulders trembling as he took a step back. "Because I love you." The words fell from his lips like a confession he couldn't take back. "I've loved you since the moment I met you, and it's killing me, okay? Knowing what's going to happen. Knowing I can't stop it."

Ava hesitated, her heart aching at his despair. She wanted to say something—to reach out and pull him back—but the look in his eyes stopped her. It was the look of someone who had already decided they were beyond saving. "What's going to happen?"

"I don't deserve you. And I can't—" He shook his head, his fists clenching at his sides. "I can't betray him."

"Tell me."

He stepped back, his eyes dark and guarded. "I can't." He stared at her for a long moment, his lips pressing into a thin line. He turned on his heel and walked away, his footsteps echoing in the empty corridor.

Ava exhaled shakily, leaning against the wall as the tension drained from her body. He was close to breaking. She could feel it. But until then, she would have to keep pretending.

Pretending she didn't know about Havok's plans, and pretending her heart wasn't somewhere else—with Gabriel.

The tavern hummed with celebration, the air thick with the bitter tang of spilled ale and the harsh smoke from a nearby hearth. Laughter and cheers erupted in bursts. The room felt stifling, each breath harder to take as the walls seemed to close in on her.

Her stomach churned. The memories played like a relentless reel in her mind—children's cries silenced in an instant, buildings engulfed in flames, and the iron-rich smell of blood saturating the air. No amount of ale could wash away the visions. No amount of noise could drown out the screams.

Her pulse raced as her vision blurred. The room spun. Heat rose from her chest, and the sharp edge of panic clawed at her throat. She shoved her chair back, its legs screeching against the wooden floor, and bolted toward the door.

The cold night air hit her like a slap, but it wasn't enough. With a desperate, ragged intake of breath, she stumbled forward, her lungs burning. Sobbing, she knelt in the mud, her hands on her stomach.

I can't do this anymore. I can't keep killing. I can't keep pretending.

A sudden snap of a branch shattered the silence. She flinched, her head jerking up as panic prickled her skin. A shadow emerged from the dark, and her heart clenched in her chest.

"It's me," Gabriel said softly, stepping into the weak light of a nearby lantern. His soaked hair clung to his forehead, and his crystal-blue eyes brimmed with concern.

Relief coursed through her like a wave.

Kneeling beside her, he pulled her into his arms. "Come on."

The familiar pull of teleportation yanked her from the damp street. The world blurred, spinning with a hum of displaced energy, and when it stilled, Ava gasped.

They stood on a frozen lake, the surface glimmering like glass beneath their feet. Towering snow-capped mountains surrounded them, their jagged peaks silhouetted against the dark sky. Above, the Northern Lights danced like lovers in waves of green and blue, their ethereal glow casting a soft light over the pristine landscape.

"It's beautiful," Ava whispered, her breath fogging in the frigid air. "How did you get away from Eve?"

Gabriel chuckled, his lips brushing her ear. "Told her I needed the bathroom. Figured I'd take a detour."

She leaned back against his chest. The steady rise and fall of his breathing calmed the storm raging inside her. "I tried to get Xavier to talk, but he wouldn't. He thinks it's too late for him, and maybe it is. But for us? For the others? How do we stop this? How do we stop him?"

Gabriel turned her to face him. He planted his hands on her shoulders. His intense gaze met hers, crystal blue eyes filled with determination and a flicker of helplessness he rarely showed. "We'll figure it out," he said firmly. "I don't know how yet, but we will. Just hold on, Ava. Please."

"Why can't we stay here? Why can't we run away?"

His thumb brushed a stray tear from her cheek, and he tipped her chin up, forcing her to meet his gaze. "Because we can't leave them. Not until this is over. But when it is, we'll leave. Together. We'll go anywhere you want."

Ava surged forward, her lips crashing into his in a kiss that was as much desperation as it was love.

He wrapped his arms around her, pulling her flush against him. The icy air around them seemed to vanish as their kiss deepened, his lips warm and commanding against hers. The taste of him on her lips, the scent of him in the air, fueled her hunger for him even more.

Her hands glided up his chest, fingertips brushing against the rapid rhythm of his heart. He groaned, threading his fingers through her hair and tilting her head to deepen the kiss. Her touch drifted to the hem of his shirt, slipping beneath to meet the heat of his skin. He shivered under her fingers, his lips parting from hers to trace a slow, burning path along her jawline and down to her neck.

"Gabriel…" she breathed.

He stilled for a moment, resting his forehead against hers. His ragged breathing hitched in his chest. "You drive me crazy, you know that?"

Ava's lips curved into a faint smile. "Good."

He gave a soft laugh, then sighed. "We have to go back."

She frowned, her heart sinking. "I know."

Gabriel pressed a lingering kiss to her forehead, his arms tightening around her one last time. "I'll come to you tonight. Just hold on until then."

She nodded, trying to memorize the feel of his warmth, the steadiness of his presence, before something ripped it away again.

He took her hand and teleported them back.

Chaos erupted around them.

The sudden burst of noise and light shattered the fragile peace they'd carried back with them. They broke apart, their connection severed by the turmoil engulfing the village. Fires roared, their amber tongues licking at the night sky, casting an eerie glow over the cobblestone streets. The pungent stench of smoke filled the air, burning her throat and making her eyes water. Explosions ripped through the night, sending debris raining down. Shouts and screams mingled with the relentless crack of gunfire and the hum of magic.

Ava's heart raced, her breaths coming in short, panicked gasps. Cimmerians scrambled like Ephemerals caught in their massacres, fear stark on their faces. Bolts of magic streaked through the sky, brilliant bursts of red and gold, each one punctuating the chaos with a deadly flare.

She froze, her body trembling. "What's happening?"

"I don't know—"

A sharp, deafening crack pierced the air.

Ava's world narrowed to Gabriel as he staggered, his hand flying to his chest. Blood seeped through his fingers, dark and vivid against his pale skin. His knees buckled, and he crumpled to the ground.

Everything moved in slow motion.

"Gabriel!" Ava screamed. She lunged, her hands summoning water.

But she never reached him.

A searing pain ripped through her body. It felt like fire coursing through her veins, each nerve alight with agony. Her muscles seized, locking her in place. With a violent tilt, the world spun, her vision fading as her strength ebbed. Her body collapsed into unseen arms.

Her head lolled to the side, her heavy-lidded eyes struggling to focus. Through the blur of pain, she saw Gabriel lying motionless on the ground, his lips forming unheard words. His eyes fluttered and then closed.

"Gabriel…" she whispered, the word barely escaped her lips before darkness consumed her.

CHAPTER THIRTY-FOUR

HUNTED

Ava woke paralyzed, a cold weight pressing her against the uneven ground. Her body refused to move, as if invisible hands had pinned her down. Panic clawed at her throat, her breath quickening as she tried and failed to twitch her fingers. The sound of frantic footsteps and muffled voices reached her ears, pulling her attention to the chaos unfolding around her.

Her heart raced as her gaze darted across the ruined space. The sacred site was a graveyard of grandeur, its stone walls covered in moss and cracks, ancient carvings glowing in the lantern light. Fragments of shattered statues lay scattered across the ground, their once-majestic forms broken and bleeding into the dirt.

Bodies lay crumpled in bloodied heaps, their groans of pain and sharp screams cutting through the damp air. Ava's stomach churned as she took in the grim scene, her chest tightening until her eyes landed on Gabriel.

He lay sprawled on the ground, motionless. His chest stirred, each breath shallow and labored. The sight sent a fresh wave of panic crashing through her. *No. Not him. He can't be gone.*

She craned her neck, to get a better look. Beyond him, she recognized other familiar faces—Anais, her arms and legs bound, slumped against a crumbling wall. Thomas was beside her, his face pale but alert.

"Oh God, Gabriel," she whispered, but the chaos drowned it out.

"They keep piling up!" a man screamed. "We have to retreat."

"Not until they're all dead," another voice barked.

"They'll wipe us out before we even make a dent!"

Ava tried to call out, but her voice faltered as footsteps approached. Two figures hovered over her—a man and a woman. The man's features were soft, uncertain, while the woman's sharp hazel eyes cut into Ava like a blade. She leaned in to inspect her.

"It's wearing off," the woman said tersely. "Give her another dose."

"No, wait!" Ava pleaded. "Please, I have to heal him. He's dying!" Her words came in a rush. "You can do whatever you want to me after, but please. Let me heal him."

The woman snorted. "Do you think we're idiots?"

"I can heal your injured, too. Please!

The man hesitated, his hand still holding the needle poised above her arm. He glanced at the woman. "What if she's telling the truth?"

"Don't be stupid, Adam" the woman snapped. "Why would a Cimmerian want to help us?"

"I'm not a Cimmerian," Ava said quickly, warm tears rolling down her cheeks. "It's a ruse. My father is an Ephemeral. We're trying to take Havok down from the inside. Please—if you don't believe me, just let me heal him. That's all I'm asking."

The woman's eyes narrowed, but after a tense moment, she motioned for Adam to switch syringes.

He replaced the vial with one of a different color. "This will give you your movement back. But if you try anything—"

"I won't," Ava said.

The needle pricked her skin, and a cold rush spread through her veins. The tingling warmth that followed was almost unbearable, but as her fingers twitched, she focused on one thing: Gabriel.

Ignoring the guns still trained on her, she scrambled to her knees and crawled to his side. His skin was ashen; his chest struggled to rise. Tears blurred her vision as she summoned water. "Stay with me." The liquid shimmered, weaving itself into his skin, mending torn flesh and sealing jagged cuts. Ava smoothed his damp hair back, her fingers shaking as she rested her ear against his chest. "Please, Gabriel. Come back to me."

A faint heartbeat. Relief hit her like a wave, and she cried into his shirt. She kissed his cheek, lingering for a moment before turning to the others. She couldn't stay with him—not yet.

The captors watched in stunned silence as Ava turned to the next injured person. One by one, she mended broken bones, sealed gaping wounds, and restored shallow breaths. Each act drained her energy, but she pressed on, refusing to stop until every groan of pain quieted.

"She's ... actually doing it," the woman said, her voice softer now, tinged with something that almost sounded like awe.

"We can use her, El," Adam said.

By the time Ava returned to Gabriel, her limbs quivered with exhaustion. She sank to the ground and pulled his head into her lap, her fingers tracing the contours of his face. He was warmer, his breaths deeper, but his eyes remained closed. The ache in her chest deepened. "Why hasn't he woken up?"

"The serum," Adam said grimly. "It's designed to suppress your kind completely. It'll take time."

Ava's heart sank. "But I healed him. The serum shouldn't still be affecting him."

"Healing fixes the body," El clipped. "But this is magic suppression. It doesn't just fade."

"It doesn't kill?" she asked, hopefully.

"No. We use it to weaken so we can kill your kind." She furrowed her eyebrows. "You really care about him."

"I love him." She caressed his face.

"You aren't like the other Cimmerians," Adam said.

"Because I'm not one," Ava said again. "My name is Ava Hannigan and I'm a Water Enchanter."

A woman stood up from the crowd of the wounded, weariness etched into her features. A braid contained her dark, silver-streaked hair. She made her way toward Ava. "You're Lucinda's daughter."

Gripping Gabriel's shirt, she nodded, not knowing what the confession would bring. "Yes."

"I knew your mother. I'm Zara. We've sided with Hunters trying to take down Havok."

"You're Enchanters?" Thomas asked.

"Some of us. Some are Hunters."

Zara. The name tugged at something buried deep within Ava's mind, a thread she couldn't quite grasp—until it hit her. *Zara left her crying over Luci.* Devon had told Havok that. Zara had killed her mother.

Ava's chest constricted, her breath hitching as the connection slammed into her. She didn't know what to say, how to process the face in front of her with the name that carried so much weight.

A sudden rustle drew her attention. Anais stirred, her bound limbs shifting against the cold ground. She blinked, her eyes narrowing when they landed on Ava. "What the hell is going on? What's wrong with him?" She jerked her chin at Gabriel. "Why are you—"

"Quiet," Thomas muttered, his tone sharp.

"So, it's true," Zara said. "The Elementals joined Havok willingly."

Ava exhaled slowly. "We did join, but only to try to infiltrate his ranks so we can defeat him. We've been pretending, letting them believe our memories were erased."

"You've been lying this whole time?" Anais yelled. "What about Gabriel? He's with Eve, not you. What's going on?"

"We faked our allegiance to Havok because we had no choice," Ava said firmly.

Anais opened her mouth to retort, but El raised a hand, silencing her. "So why haven't you killed Havok yet?"

"Because we can't," Thomas said. "Not yet."

Adam narrowed his eyes. "What are you waiting for?"

Ava tightened her grip on Gabriel's shirt, her knuckles white against the fabric. The words stuck in her throat, choking her. She glanced at Anais, whose eyes burned with accusation, and at El, whose gun trembled as if awaiting an excuse. She shuddered. "I'm linked to Havok's soul."

Silence followed her words.

Anais's eyes widened, her expression shifting from disbelief to something Ava couldn't quite name—pity? Horror?

Thomas swore under his breath.

El stared at Ava as though seeing her for the first time.

"That's why you lost it," Anais whispered. "You're ... you're tied to him?"

Ava nodded, shame pooling in her chest. "If I die, he dies."

A flicker of something dark crossed El's face. Her hand darted toward Adam's pocket and snatched his gun.

"Stop!" Adam lunged for her, but she was already raising the weapon, her gaze locked on Ava.

Ava cowered, her heart leaping into her throat as she braced for the shot.

A burst of light erupted between them. Fire crackled along Thomas's outstretched hands, the air humming with residual energy as he intercepted the attack.

The gun discharged with a sharp, deafening crack, the bullet ricocheting into the sky.

El stumbled back, her face pale but defiant, her grip tightening on the weapon.

Adam seized her arm, twisting it until the gun clattered to the ground.

She struggled against him, her breath coming in frantic gasps. "Let me go!" she hissed, her voice trembling with rage, but Adam's grip held firm.

"What the hell are you doing?" Adam shouted.

"She's the key! If she dies, he dies. Don't you get it?"

"And then what?" Adam growled. "You think the rest of the Cimmerians won't hunt us down for revenge? She just healed everyone! Use your head."

El struggled for a moment, then her shoulders sagged. "He's too powerful," she muttered. "We'll never beat him."

"So, if what you're saying is true, the Elementals want to defeat Havok?" Zara said. "Is it just you six?"

"No, there are other Enchanters faking," Ava said.

"This is unbelievable!" Anais yelled.

"But there are thousands of Cimmerians. None of them would switch sides. They were born this way." Ava looked at Anais. "Or had their memories wiped."

"Why are you looking at me?"

"Havok erased your memories. Your father's an Elder, locked in a cell in Caprington."

Anais froze. "You're lying."

"Haven't you ever wondered why you don't remember anything about your childhood?" Ava pressed. "Havok took you because he didn't want you to rebel."

Anais faltered, her confidence cracking. "No ... no, that's not—he wouldn't—"

"He would," El said quietly. "And he did."

Ava brushed a hand over Gabriel's forehead. "We've all lost people to Havok. He's taken everything from us. But if we work together, we can stop him."

El's fingers curled into fists. "You're asking us to trust *you*."

"I'm asking you to fight for something better," Ava said. "For everyone he's taken from us."

Ava held her breath, her eyes locked on El's. For a moment, no one moved.

"What are you going to do with her when you return?" El asked, nodding toward Anais.

"If she doesn't side with us, we'll have to manipulate her mind," Ava said flatly, though the words tasted bitter on her tongue.

Anais scoffed, her glare piercing. "You're just going to erase me? Change who I am to suit your agenda?"

"If we have to," Ava said. "You know too much. We can't risk you running to Havok."

Anais's defiance wavered as doubt flashed in her eyes. "You really think you can win?"

"It's worth trying. Isn't that better than living under Havok's shadow forever?"

"And how do we know this isn't just a suicide mission?"

"Because we're on the inside," Ava said. "Havok thinks we're loyal. We've let him believe that while we work to bring him down."

El crossed her arms and narrowed her eyes. "Then what's the plan? A real plan, not vague promises."

"We weaken his forces," Ava said. "We rally more people—Enchanters, Hunters. Anyone willing to fight."

El's eyes softened, though her posture remained tense. "If we do this, it has to be a coordinated effort. No rash moves, no surprises."

Ava nodded. "Agreed. Let's make a plan."

CHAPTER THIRTY-FIVE

A LIGHT IN THE DARKNESS

El approached Ava as the tension in the room ebbed. "You both need to rest," she said. "Come with me."

Ava glanced down at Gabriel, still unconscious but breathing steadily, and nodded. "Thank you."

El led her through the ruined hallways of the sacred site, away from the main gathering. Lantern light flickered against the walls, casting elongated shadows over the faded carvings of symbols and ancient rites. The damp scent of moss and stone filled the air, mingling with the faint metallic tang of blood that lingered from the battle.

"This way." El stepped over a crumbled section of floor and around a fallen pillar. She stopped at a narrow archway, hidden by vines that had grown unchecked over the years. "It's not much, but it's private."

Ava ducked under the low arch and walked inside. The room was small and humble, its walls adorned with faint remnants of carvings that might have once told stories of the Enchanters who had built this place. A soft patch of moss had grown in one corner, offering a makeshift bed.

The faint trickle of water echoed from a cracked basin on the far wall, its steady rhythm soothing in the stillness.

El turned to leave, but paused in the doorway. "You've done more than enough for us," she said. "Get some rest. We'll figure out the next steps in the morning."

Drained, Ava could only manage a small nod. "Thank you, El."

El gave a curt nod and disappeared back into the ruins.

Thomas appeared a moment later to help Ava move Gabriel to the mossy corner. Together, they lowered him, Gabriel's weight heavier than she expected as her arms trembled with effort.

Thomas gave her a brief, reassuring squeeze on the shoulder and left.

Ava sank onto the ground beside Gabriel. She brushed a hand across his forehead. Her thoughts churned as she watched him, wanting him to wake.

A victory over Havok was possible, but her curse persisted. The unknown bore down on her, threatening to crush what little hope she clung to.

"Please wake up," she whispered. "Please don't leave me. I need you."

"Grasshopper."

Her heart stopped. Her head snapped down, her eyes locking onto his. His lids fluttered open, revealing the endless blue depths she thought she might never see again. They were a light in the darkness, a promise that not all was lost.

"Gabriel," she breathed, a sob tearing from her chest. She flung herself forward, wrapping her arms around him. She kissed his forehead, his cheeks, his jaw—all of him.

He shot up, his arms pulling her close. "Are you okay?"

She laughed through her tears, the sound trembling on the edge of hysteria. "You just woke up from almost dying, and you're worried about me?"

He leaned back enough to cup her face with both hands. His gaze searched hers. "Yes."

"I'm fine. Are you okay?"

"I'm groggy, but I'm fine." He offered her the faintest smile. "What happened?"

Ava climbed into Gabriel's lap, straddling his thighs with her knees. "Later." She pressed her lips to his. The kiss was desperate, raw, an outlet for all the fear and relief tangled in her chest. She poured everything into it—every moment she thought she'd lost him, every second she wished she could have saved him. Her lips trembled against his, her fingers fisting in his shirt as though he might disappear if she let go.

His hands slid into her hair, his fingers tangling in the strands with a possessive reverence. His lips, soft as velvet, moved against hers, then with a growing urgency that mirrored her desperate need.

When they broke apart, her chest heaved, her forehead pressing against his as she fought to catch her breath. "You scared me," she whispered. "I thought I'd lost you. I can't—I couldn't do this without you."

"I'm here," he said. "I'm not going anywhere, Ava. Not without you."

Her fingers trembled as they splayed across his chest, feeling the steady rhythm of his heartbeat beneath her palm. "I'm so scared, Gabriel," she said, the words tumbling out in a fragile whisper. "Of losing you. Of what's coming. Of who I might become."

He held her face in his hands, his touch both strong and tender. "We're going to find a way."

She leaned into him, her lips brushing his in a kiss that was softer this time, slower. The urgency melted into something deeper, something that spoke of solace and love. His lips trailed from hers to her jaw, then lower to the hollow of her neck, leaving a trail of fire on her skin.

"I need you," she whispered. "I want you."

"You've always had me."

He shifted beneath her, one arm encircling her waist as he flipped her onto her back. The cool moss pressed against her shoulder blades as he hovered above her, his gaze locking onto hers. Moonlight streamed through the canopy, casting his features in stark relief—the sharp line of his jaw, the dark intensity of his eyes.

Her fingers fumbled with the buttons of his shirt, her frustration mounting until she tore the fabric apart, sending the buttons scattering across the moss.

Gabriel let out a low, husky laugh that sent a shiver through her. "Impatient, are we?" he teased.

"You're one to talk," she shot back, but her words were stolen as he kissed her neck, trailing fire along her skin.

His confident hands explored her body, making her heart race. His deliberate, unhurried touch left her trembling with each pass of his fingers across her skin. Her shirt and bra fell away under his deft movements, his palms grazing her bare skin with a heat that sent waves of desire coursing through her.

His lips found hers again, claiming her in a way that weakened her knees. The kiss was slow, almost tormentingly so, each stroke of his tongue against hers a promise that left her gasping for more. Her fingers gripped his shoulders as she pressed herself against him, desperate for the closeness, for him.

His hands moved to her hips, his fingers hooking beneath the last barriers between them. With one fluid motion, he removed them, his touch trailing down her thighs. Ava's pulse hammered as his mouth followed the path his hands had taken, leaving a blazing trail of kisses along her heated skin. She moaned as his teeth grazed her, just enough to make her arch toward him in a silent plea for more.

His body pressed against hers, every inch of him solid and warm as they moved together in a rhythm that felt achingly perfect, their breaths mingling as they lost themselves in each other.

She could die in that moment, and it would have been enough. She could drown in his heat, in his all-consuming passion, in the unspoken depth of his love. Each shallow, broken gasp she managed felt stolen, her chest rising and falling as the overwhelming pleasure of his touch unraveled her completely. She was floating, soaring higher and higher, her body alight and pulling him with her into the abyss of their shared desire.

A guttural gasp escaped him. The sight of him—his head tipping back, his eyes squeezing shut as if he could barely hold himself together—sent a fresh wave of heat cascading through her. His fingers dug into the moss beneath her as she felt him tremble.

As they lay tangled together afterward, Ava rested her head on Gabriel's chest. His fingers drew soothing circles on her back, and for the first time in days, maybe weeks, she felt a spark of hope—a fragile but fierce determination to fight for a future with him.

She closed her eyes, letting the moment sink in. She wanted more of this—more moments of quiet, of safety, of love. Gabriel's touch reminded her of everything she still had to fight for. The thought of losing him, of losing herself to the curse, was unbearable.

Her fingers brushed over his chest, her movements tentative but deliberate. *I don't want to die.* The realization hit her with the force of a tidal wave. For so long, she'd convinced herself that accepting her fate was the only option, that sacrificing herself was the noble path. But lying here with Gabriel, feeling his warmth and the strength of his arms around her, she realized how much she wanted to live.

He shifted, his hand moving to cradle her face. His gaze met hers, deep and searching. "What is it?"

Ava blinked back the sting of tears. "I want to fight. I want to survive, Gabriel. I don't want this to be the end."

A small, tender smile curved his lips. "Then we'll fight. We'll get through this. And when it's over, we'll have a life, Ava. Together. Whatever you want. Wherever you want."

"Don't let go."

Gabriel pressed a kiss to her temple, his arms tightening around her. "Never," he whispered.

CHAPTER THIRTY-SIX

THE STORM

The morning air was crisp, the faint scent of dew clinging to the earth as the first rays of sunlight stretched over the camp. Most of the group was busy preparing for the day ahead—sharpening weapons, packing supplies, murmuring in hushed voices. Ava's gaze swept over them before settling on Zara.

The older woman stood alone near the edge of the forest, her back to the camp, one hand resting on the hilt of her dagger as she stared into the trees. There was a stillness about her, a quiet intensity that made Ava hesitate. Her heart pounded in her chest.

Ava considered turning away, pretending the revelation didn't matter. But hearing her name in Havok's memory refused to let her go. *Zara left her crying over Luci.* She'd killed Ava's mom, leaving Ava sobbing.

Ava swallowed hard and approached. Her steps faltered as she drew closer, her emotions roiling beneath her skin. Anger, sadness, confusion—they twisted together, leaving her unsure of what to say.

"Zara."

The woman turned, her hazel eyes sharp and assessing. She said nothing, waiting, her hand falling away from her weapon.

Ava took a deep breath. "I saw something. In Havok's mind." Her fingers curled into fists at her sides. "It was you. You killed my mother."

Zara didn't flinch. Her gaze remained steady. "I did."

The blunt admission stunned Ava. She had expected denial, excuses, anything but this confirmation.

"Why?" The word came out sharper than she intended. "Why did you do it?"

Zara's jaw tightened, her gaze shifting away for a moment before locking back on Ava. "Because I had to."

"That's not good enough!" Anger bubbled to the surface. "She was my mother. She didn't deserve to die."

"No. She didn't." Her voice was steady, but there was a faint glint of something—regret? Pain? "But Havok ordered it. And when Havok gives an order, you follow it, or you die."

Tears pricked her eyes. "You could've said no. You could've fought back."

"And what then?" Zara's voice hardened, the edge of bitterness creeping in. "You think I wanted to kill her? That I didn't hate every second of it? I was under Havok's control, just like everyone else. Saying no wasn't an option. It's never been an option."

Ava stared at her, the fight draining from her limbs. The truth in Zara's words was suffocating, and the weight of her own memories—the things Havok had made her do—pressed down on her. She shook her head, her voice a broken whisper. "I don't know if I can forgive you."

"I'm not asking you to. But if you want to defeat Havok, then you have to understand what we've all been through. Your mother … she was strong. She fought for what she believed in. And I…" Zara's voice faltered, and for the first time, a crack appeared in her stoic demeanor. "I took that from her. From you. That's something I'll carry with me for the rest of my life."

She wanted to scream, to lash out, to make Zara feel even a fraction of the pain she carried. But the anger was tangled with sadness, a deep ache that refused to settle. "I don't know what to do with this. I don't know if I should hate you or pity you."

"Feel whatever you need to feel. But don't let it consume you. Havok's done enough of that to both of us."

Ava looked away, her chest heaving. "She deserved better."

"She did. And so do you."

Ava's breath hitched at the admission. She walked away, her chest aching more, yet her resolve even stronger. Havok had taken too much from her, from all of them. And she would make sure he paid.

Gabriel, Ava, and Thomas stood at the center of the room, their presence commanding the attention of the gathered Enchanters and Hunters. The tension in the air was like a storm ready to break.

Gabriel's sharp gaze scanned the crowd, his posture rigid. His eyes stopped on Anais, and his expression darkened. "Are we sure we should talk about this in front of her?" he asked, his tone cool and measured.

"I told her about Gustav," Ava said. "She doesn't believe me though."

Anais folded her arms, leaning against the wall. "You really expect me to believe you? After everything, you think I'll just switch sides?"

"You should," Gabriel said cooly. "Ava's telling the truth. Havok doesn't care about you—none of them do."

Anais scoffed. "And you do? You abandoned us. Left us for dead. You've got no right to judge."

"I left because I realized there's more to life than being a puppet," Gabriel shot back. "You can make that choice, too."

"What choice? You think Havok won't hunt me down? That I can just walk away from everything I've ever known?"

"You've already fought against him without realizing it," Ava said. "That strength? It's yours. Not his. And it's not too late to use it."

Anais hesitated, her defenses slipping for a moment. "If we take down Havok and I left, then what? What's left of me?"

"Whatever you want," Ava said. "You'd have us. And Gustav."

Anais flinched. "If he wanted me, why didn't he come for me?"

"He tried," Gabriel said. "He's still trying."

Anais lowered her head as if weighed down by the revelation. The cracks in her armor were visible now.

Thomas crossed his arms. "Look, I grew up with a Cimmerian father. Ava's mom was a Cimmerian. I didn't even know about my father's true nature until recently. The things he said about Ephemerals—they made me hate them, too, for a while. And it didn't help when Ava fell in love with one. But here's the thing: he wasn't a bad person. Actually, he was pretty damn cool.

"You're always going to have enemies, Anais. But killing an entire race or forcing them to become something they're not? That's not the answer. Life's fragile—precious—and Havok tosses it aside like it's nothing. All this death, all this destruction … it's not worth it."

Anais let out a sharp breath, her arms wrapping tighter around herself as if shielding against something she couldn't fully face. "I've always wanted more."

"And you can have more," Thomas said. "You deserve more."

Ava watched as Anais's gaze darted between them, the internal battle etched into her features. For the first time, there was a spark of something in Anais's eyes—doubt, hope, or perhaps both.

Someone cleared their throat, and Ava turned.

Ava turned around to see El, Adam, Zara, and the others standing.

"What's the plan?" El asked. "How do you plan to take him down?"

Gabriel stepped forward, his voice steady as he outlined the strategy: build an army, coordinate a surprise attack, and work together to dismantle Havok's reign.

El and Adam exchanged a skeptical look.

"You're asking a lot of trust," El said.

"And we're giving it too," Ava said. "We don't have much time. Will you help us?"

El hesitated but nodded. "We'll gather as many as we can. Where should we go?"

Gabriel met her gaze. "I'll teleport you to a safe location. Only I'll know where it is, so Havok can't track you. The Cimmerians won't let this go unanswered."

El nodded again. "Understood. And Ava…" She paused, her expression softening. "I hope you're right about this."

Gabriel teleported El, Adam, and the others. When he returned, he slipped his arm around Ava's waist. "We need to talk before we go back. Caprington's not going to be the same when we return. Not after this."

Ava nodded, a familiar tightness coiled in her chest. "The ritual. Do you think the attack delayed it? Or sped it up?"

"That's exactly what I'm worried about," Gabriel said. "If Havok thinks the Hunters are a bigger threat now, he might want to act fast. He won't risk losing the chance to link with the other Elementals."

Thomas pushed off the wall, his brow furrowed. "Do we even know how close he is to starting the ritual?"

"We know it has to be soon," Ava said.

"Thomas, I need you to warn Klaus and Link," Gabriel said. "If Havok speeds up his timeline, they need to be ready to move. We can't afford to be caught off guard."

He nodded. "I'll send a message after we're done here."

Gabriel turned to Anais. "Talk to Gustav. He needs to rally more support now, not later. If Havok accelerates his plans, we'll need every ally we can get."

Anais straightened, her sharp gaze locking onto his. "And what do I tell him? That the plan's falling apart?"

"No," Gabriel said coldly. "You tell him the truth—that we're adapting. Havok's playing a long game, but we're going to outmaneuver him."

Anais hesitated, then conceded with a nod. "Fine. But don't expect miracles."

"The key is making Havok think we're still loyal," Gabriel continued, his focus shifting back to Ava. "If he suspects otherwise, we're done. We go back and act like the mission was a success—no cracks, no hesitations."

"And what if he doesn't buy it?" Ava asked.

"Then we improvise. But we don't show our cards until the last moment."

Thomas frowned. "What about the ritual? What if it's already started?"

Gabriel's expression darkened. "It won't. Not without Ava. Havok's too calculated to take that risk."

"And if we can't stop it?" Her voice was barely above a whisper.

Gabriel turned to her, his blue eyes steady, unyielding. "We will. No matter what it takes, we'll find a way."

"What if I can't play my part?"

"You can. And you will. You've come too far to doubt yourself now."

He glanced around at the group. "We can't hesitate when the moment comes. Thomas, Anais—you know what you need to do. Ava, you stay close to me. We'll figure out when the ritual is as soon as we're back. No distractions, no second-guessing."

Ava took a deep breath, her fear solidifying into determination. "We'll end this," she said, her voice resolute. "One way or another."

Smoke hung heavy in the air, curling in lazy tendrils that blurred the edges of the ruined village. The morning light struggled to break through the haze, casting an eerie gray pall over the crumbling remains of Caprington. Burned roofs jutted upward like broken ribs, their jagged silhouettes framing the soft, ashen sky. Piles of rubble spilled onto the streets, a grim testament to the destruction that had swept through the village.

Villagers crept through the wreckage, their faces pale and hollow with exhaustion. Some sifted through the debris with trembling hands, while others stood motionless, as if their grief had rooted them to the ground. The pungent stench of smoke hit Ava like a slap, mingling with the faint, metallic tang of blood. Her throat tightened as memories surged—her own home reduced to ashes, the lives lost in flames, the overwhelming helplessness.

She forced herself to keep moving, but her gaze snagged on the bodies. They lay scattered and broken, their forms barely recognizable beneath layers of soot and blood. Were they Hunters, Enchanters, or Cimmerians? Did it even matter? They were all casualties of a war that had gone on far too long.

The scene felt too familiar—an echo of Lighthollow, where the same devastation had unfolded. The same senseless death. Her chest ached with a mix of rage and guilt, a growing pressure that threatened to suffocate her. *We have to end this.*

"Ava!"

The shout cut through her spiraling thoughts, sharp and startling. She turned toward the voice, and her breath hitched as Xavier sprinted toward them, his face etched with relief and worry.

Gabriel dropped her hand.

Xavier stopped short, his breathing heavy. Relief flashed in his eyes, but he masked it quickly, straightening his posture. His gaze lingered on Ava, searching her face for signs of injury or distress. "You're okay. We were so worried. We sent out a crew to find you. The Hunters—"

"They're dead," Ava interrupted.

"All of them?"

"Yes," Thomas said. "Burned the bodies."

Xavier nodded, but his expression didn't soften. "It's just the four of you? No one else?"

"No," Gabriel said. "Who else is missing?"

"The prisoners." Xavier's jaw clenched. "The Hunters got into the castle and released them. Some might still be buried in the rubble, but…" He trailed off, running a hand through his hair.

The shocking news left Ava reeling, her stomach twisting in agony. The prisoners. They hadn't crossed her mind during the chaos. The Hunters had never mentioned them—hadn't even hinted at their escape. A flicker of doubt ignited, spreading like wildfire through her thoughts. *Had they been freed? Or had we been played?*

"We'll deal with it," Xavier continued, his tone sharpening, a forced confidence masking the uncertainty in his eyes. "Havok wants to see everyone in the Great Hall tonight at seven."

a cold wave of dread crashed over her. Havok. The very name constricted her chest. Facing him now—after everything she'd learned, after the fragile alliances they'd forged—felt like walking into a trap. Her pulse quickened, her breaths shallow. She swallowed hard, forcing herself to nod.

The group began their trek toward the castle, their boots crunching against loose stone and ash-streaked rubble. A smell of burning wood and smoke intensified, coating her skin and clothes. Only the occasional cough or low murmur from villagers sifting through the remnants of their lives punctuated the heavy silence.

Every broken building, every pile of debris, was a reminder of their failure to stop it sooner. The jagged ruins stretched around them like an open wound, raw and unhealed. Ava's gaze lingered on a collapsed roof, the scorched beams resembling skeletons clawing at the sky. Her chest tightened further. *Havok did this. And he'll do worse if we don't stop him.*

Gabriel's fingers brushed hers. "Breathe," he murmured.

Though she gave a slight nod, the tempest within her raged on. Havok's presence pressed against her mind, suffocating and relentless.

The ritual. It hovered like a menacing storm cloud. Did Havok already suspect their plans? Had he learned of their alliances? Her nails dug into her palms as panic bubbled beneath the surface.

The sound of the gates creaking open raised the hairs on Ava's arms. The castle loomed before them, cold and imposing, its shadow swallowing the faint light of dawn. Ava's steps faltered, the gravity of what awaited them threatening to crush her.

"We'll figure this out." Gabriel's gaze met hers with unwavering determination.

She wanted to believe him. She had to.

Because there was no turning back now.

CHAPTER THIRTY-SEVEN

CLEMENCY

The shower did little to soothe Ava's frayed nerves. Hot water poured over her, washing away the dirt and grime, but did nothing to cleanse the dread curling in her chest. In less than eight hours, the ritual would begin. She couldn't run—Havok would find her. He always did. The steam from the shower clung to her skin as she stepped out, her heart pounding like a war drum.

She threw on her clothes, opened the bathroom door, and froze.

Gabriel was sitting on the edge of her bed, his head in his hands. The sight of him—usually so composed and strong—undone like this sent a pang of sorrow through her chest.

"Gabriel?"

When he looked up, her heart clenched. His eyes glistened with unshed tears, their piercing blue dulled with worry.

"I don't know what to do," he said. "I don't know how to stop the ritual. Unless…" He broke off, his fists clenching. "Unless I take you away from here—far away."

She crossed the room and placed herself between his legs, pulling him to her. He buried his head against her chest, and she kissed the top of his head, her fingers threading through his hair.

"I'm sorry," he whispered. "I'm supposed to be strong."

"You are strong, Gabriel." She knelt in front of him, tilting her face up to meet his gaze. "But you can't always be the one saving me. I have to figure this out. And we don't even know for sure if Havok is doing the ritual tonight."

His eyes bore into hers, raw and full of despair. "I can't lose you."

Her heart fractured at the pain in his voice. Time was slipping away, and with it, her hope of finding an escape. "What if we start the battle tonight?"

"We aren't ready." He shook his head. "The Hunters and Enchanters—"

"They can finish what they started. Link can call the Spirits."

His jaw tightened. "Can we still trust the Hunters and Enchanters? They took the prisoners, Ava, and I don't even know where they took them."

"Then go back to El and Adam. Find out the truth. In the meantime, I'll find Link and the others. Ready or not, we have to act."

He pulled her up from her knees and into his lap, his arms wrapping around her as if she might vanish. His lips found hers in a kiss that was urgent, tender, fervent. "I love you."

"I love you."

A sharp knock shattered the moment.

They both froze.

Another knock followed, louder this time.

Gabriel swore under his breath and slipped into the bathroom, the door clicking shut behind him.

Ava took a steadying breath and opened the door.

Her stomach dropped. "Xavier."

He brushed past her without waiting for an invitation, his movements restless and tense. He strode to the window, peering out as if expecting an ambush, then paced toward the wardrobe, his hands on his hips.

Her heart pounded as she closed the door, trying to maintain her composure. "Are you okay?"

He swallowed hard, his Adam's apple bobbing. "We need to talk. Somewhere private. Before tonight." His eyes flicked around the room like he was searching for something—or trying to avoid looking at her. The tension rolling off him made Ava's pulse quicken, and for a moment, she debated whether to press him now or wait. "Okay," she said finally. "I'll meet you outside in a minute."

Xavier nodded and left the room.

The door closed with a soft thud, and Ava exhaled a shaky breath.

Gabriel emerged from the bathroom. "I don't like this."

"He's nervous," Ava said, though her own nerves were frayed.

"I don't want to leave you alone with him."

"I know. I'll be fine. You have to see El and Adam. I'll talk to Link when I get back."

"You'd better come back safe." He cupped her face and kissed her with a fierceness that made her knees weak.

She clung to him for a moment. "I will."

"Be careful."

With a final glance, she turned and left.

The sky hung heavy with thick, gray clouds, casting a muted light over the village below. Smoke lingered in the air, the acrid scent mingling with the damp earth. The villagers moved in silence, their faces pale and weary as they cleared debris from the streets. Broken carts and shattered glass littered the cobblestones, stark reminders of the chaos from the night before.

From the tower, Ava watched them, her heart heavy with guilt and dread. The castle loomed in the distance, its dark silhouette sharp against the ashen sky. The air was damp, clinging to her skin and filling her lungs with the weight of everything they'd done—and everything they had yet to face.

Xavier stood a few steps away, his hands resting on the stone ledge as he surveyed the scene. His profile was sharp, his jaw tight as though he was waging some internal battle. The usual confidence he carried had dimmed, leaving behind a tension that made the air between them feel brittle.

"This is ridiculous," he said. "It wasn't supposed to be like this."

"Isn't it always like this? War doesn't care who gets hurt."

"There's something I need to tell you, Ava. Before we go back." He finally turned to her, his dark eyes burning with an emotion she couldn't quite place. "Your memories," he mumbled. "They weren't just altered. Klaus and Havok took them. Everything you were. Everything you loved. They erased it all."

Ava's heart skipped a beat. "I know they altered my memories. That's not news."

He shook his head, letting out a sharp sigh. "No, Ava. You don't understand. It's not just alterations. Havok made you think you were one of us—made you think the Elders stole your life. But that's not true. They didn't take anything from you. Havok did."

She gasped. Why was he telling her this? What angle was he playing? She had to tread carefully. "Why are you telling me this now?"

His jaw worked as if struggling to find the words. "Because I'm tired of lying. Because you deserve to know the truth. And because ... I can't keep pretending I don't care."

Her stomach twisted, and she stumbled back, his hands falling to his sides. "Tell me the truth," she said quickly, needing to steer the conversation away from his confession. "Everything. Start from the beginning."

"Your mom was a Cimmerian, but you weren't born one. You grew up with the Elders, believing we were the enemy. And, yeah, we've been at war for centuries, but who's really right in any of this? When we met, my job was to bring you and the Elementals here. It took a while, but we succeeded. We kidnapped members of your coven to lure the Elders into a fight on our turf.

"Havok doesn't want just any soldiers. He wants you. Elementals are stronger than any of us. Hunters can't even kill you."

"What?"

"They have a poison—potent enough to weaken Enchanters in minutes. But Elementals? You're immune. It only immobilizes you. That's why Havok values you so much. He's trying to rebuild his army, and you're his greatest asset."

That explained so much—why the Hunters' attacks on her had failed, why Havok had been so relentless in pursuing the Elementals.

"I hate what I've done to you," he said.

"Why did we hurt each other?"

"You were acting in self-defense. I was doing my job. Trying to prove myself to Havok."

She took a step closer. "You didn't have to do any of it. If you love me, like you claim, why didn't you stop?"

He ran a hand over his tired face. "I do love you. And I don't expect you to ever feel the same. But I couldn't stop. Not with Havok watching. Not with…"

"What aren't you telling me?"

His gaze darkened. "Havok is my father."

Her breath caught. The vision she'd had—it was true. "I thought you said Ephemerals killed your parents."

"They did. Havok found me as a baby and raised me. He loves me like his own. He's taken care of me. He's not the monster you think he is, Ava."

"Maybe not to you," she countered.

Xavier's gaze softened as he leaned against the stone wall. "Havok was … everything to me when I was a kid. He raised me, taught me, made me feel like I mattered in a world that didn't seem to care much. When the Elders took him down— when I thought they'd killed him—I was devastated. It was like the ground was ripped out from under me." He paused, the tension in his jaw betraying the emotions simmering just beneath the surface. "I threw myself into training after that, pushing harder, getting stronger, like maybe I could honor him somehow. Devon Maunsell stepped in around then—he was kind of a leader in his way—and that's when I learned the truth."

He glanced at Ava, his dark eyes searching hers. "Havok wasn't dead. He was alive, trapped inside Colden's body. And he still found ways to reach me. Letters, little notes … reminders that he was still there, watching, guiding. It gave me purpose, knowing he hadn't truly gone. But it also … changed things. I had to learn to see the man I thought was invincible as someone who could lose, someone who could bleed." His voice softened further, a hint of vulnerability creeping in. "And someone I couldn't always save."

Ava's stomach twisted as she listened to Xavier's words, each revelation hitting her like a stone dropped into a bottomless well. Havok, the monster she feared, had been someone Xavier loved. Someone who had guided him, raised him, and even in the shadows of death, found a way to stay present in his life. The letters, the training, the devotion—it painted a picture she hadn't been prepared to see.

How could Xavier see him that way? As more than the cruel, calculating force that had tormented her and countless others? It wasn't just loyalty—it was love. A bond forged in trust and history, twisted by lies and manipulation. Her chest tightened, a strange cocktail of pity and frustration swirling inside her. How could Havok weave himself so deeply into someone's life while leaving ruin in everyone else's?

She glanced at Xavier, catching the vulnerability in his eyes. For all his strength and bravado, this wasn't just a story to him. It was his truth. And yet, Ava couldn't shake the unease curling through her. "But he's been waging war for centuries against Ephemerals. Why?"

"I'm not supposed to talk about it. Hardly anyone knows the full story."

"Tell me," Ava pressed. "If I'm going to continue killing Ephemerals, I deserve to know why."

"Havok wasn't always the man you know now. He once loved someone—Lenorah. She was his world. They were happy, had a child. He wanted no part of the war his family waged against the Ephemerals."

"What happened?"

"His family happened. They hired Hunters to kill Lenorah and his daughter. They wanted to force him back into their war. It worked. He lost everything, and it broke him. That's when he became the man you see today."

Ava's stomach churned, bile rising in her throat. The visions she'd seen flashed through her mind—the woman's gentle smile, the child's innocent laughter, both ripped away in an instant. And now, to learn that Havok's own family had orchestrated their deaths? It made her chest ache with an uncomfortable mix of sorrow and anger. "And he's been killing Ephemerals ever since?"

"Yes. But it's not just about revenge anymore. He's waging his family's war, but it's become his war now. He let revenge and darkness consume him until there was nothing left. He erases minds, forces people to bind themselves to him, and makes them train endlessly. Everything he does is about control. And you…" He pressed his fingers to his temple. "There's a reason why you're seeing Havok's memories, Ava."

Her heart skipped a beat. Was he about to confirm what she already knew? The link? The ritual? She forced herself to stay calm, to act surprised. "What do you mean?"

Guilt and despair were etched on his face. "You're linked to Havok, Ava. Your mother promised your soul to him."

"What?" she acted surprised.

"Lucinda tried to kill Havok when he was still weak. His soul was just beginning to take root inside Colden. Lucinda knew what he was becoming. He forced her bind you to Havok."

"What happened to her?" she asked. No one ever told her why Havok had her mother killed.

"Havok kept her alive to control her. To control you. She was leverage—proof of what could happen to anyone who defied him. She tried to escape with you and your father. To run ... to hide you from Havok. He found out and had her killed."

Ava turned away, pressing a hand to her chest, as if she could hold the ache inside. All those years, she'd carried anger, resentment toward a woman she believed had abandoned her. And all along, her mother had tried to stop it—had tried to save her. She took a deep breath, not wanting to break down in front of Xavier.

"There's more," he said. "From the moment Havok found out about your coven—all of you Elementals—he's been obsessed. He doesn't want you in his army. The massacres? They've been distractions, ways to weaken you, to make you compliant."

Ava's breath hitched. Even knowing the truth, hearing it said aloud made her feel as if the walls were closing in.

"He's planning on using you as a bridge. Through you, he'll link to the other Elementals. But doing that..." He paused. "It will kill you. I begged him to spare you." He ran a hand through his hair and paced in front of her like a caged animal. "I tried to delay the ritual, to find a way to stop it. But after the Hunters' attack, he's more determined than ever. I don't know what else to do. He won't listen to me."

For a moment, Ava felt a pang of pity for him despite everything. "The ritual," she whispered, her pulse quickening. "Is it happening tonight?"

With a slump of his shoulders, he stopped pacing. Regret filled his eyes. "Yes."

She froze, struggling to breathe. His confession hit her like a speeding train. Her mind raced, calculating their dwindling options.

"I have to go." She bolted toward the stairs and sprinted down them.

"Ava! Wait—"

But she couldn't.

Ava rushed through the darkened streets, her heart pounding in sync with her racing thoughts. The scent of rain lingered in the air, mingling with the faint metallic odor of the city. She didn't stop until she stormed into Klaus's quarters.

"The ritual is happening tonight," she blurted out.

Gabriel, Klaus, and Link turned toward her. Brows furrowing.

Gabriel rushed up to her.

"Are you certain?" Klaus asked.

"Xavier told me everything. He tried to delay it, but it's happening. We need to alert everyone."

Klaus straightened. "I'll handle it. You all need to prepare."

"We don't have time. The others need to know now." She clenched her fists. "This could be the last chance we have."

Link exchanged a look with Gabriel. "Klaus and I will take care of everything. Take her to the cave."

"The cave?" Ava asked. "What? What's going on."

"El and Adam rescued everyone," Gabriel said. "They're at the cave."

She gasped. "Aaron? Gustav?"

He nodded. "And more. They're waiting for us."

Tears pricked her eyes, a mix of relief and urgency swirling in her chest.

CHAPTER THIRTY-EIGHT
REUNITED

The cool, damp air inside the cave wrapped around Ava like a chill embrace, carrying the earthy scent of moss and timeworn stone. The candlelight cast a waltz of shadows on the rugged walls, each movement adding to the cave's mystique. Her breath caught in her throat, her pulse quickening as she took in the familiar scene. It was the very cave where she and Gabriel had shared their first kiss, a moment that once filled her with warmth and security.

When her eyes adjusted, a small gasp escaped her lips. Sitting around a modest fire were the faces she had thought she might never see again: Gustav, Aaron, Natalia, Moira, Joss, and Konstantin.

Ava stumbled, her composure nearly broken by the sight of them alive. One by one, they rose to their feet, their gaunt faces lighting up with recognition and relief. Tears blurred her vision as each embraced her. Natalia's arms were thinner than Ava remembered, her strength faltering as she held on. Joss whispered her name like a prayer, her violet eyes glistening.

Gabriel stood by Ava's side, letting the reunion unfold. "I'll be right back."

She spun, catching his arm. "Where are you going?"

"To get a couple more people." His tone was steady, but he couldn't hide the exhaustion on his face.

Her grip tightened. "It's too risky. You're still weak."

"I promise I'll be back."

She let go, and he disappeared.

Moira's hand slipped into Ava's. "He'll come back." The group settled back around the fire, and Ava sank to the ground between Natalia and Joss. Lines of weariness and hunger etched on their faces.

"I've missed you so much." Joss leaned against Ava. Her voice was thin, her usual fire dimmed.

Ava nodded, her throat too tight for words. She turned to Natalia, whose hollow cheeks and dull eyes made Ava's chest ache. "They took your powers, didn't they?"

Natalia gave a weary nod. "You look like shit," she said with a weak smirk.

"Have you looked in a mirror lately?"

Natalia's lips twitched. "Touché. Glad to see you're still you."

Ava dropped her gaze, her smile fading. "I wasn't for a time. What happened?"

"Maggie and Kira freed us," Aaron said. His voice was deeper, rougher than she remembered. His graying hair and lined face told the story of their suffering as much as his words. "They have been working with Zara and other Enchanters. When Hunters attacked, they used the chaos to release us. The guard was gone, and we took a chance. Escaped through one of the old tunnels."

"Maggie and Kira?" Ava asked. "Where are they?"

"They stayed," Aaron said. "To keep up the ruse."

"We didn't know what you all were planning," Natalia said. "When you willingly joined the Cimmerians ... I couldn't believe it."

"I'm so sorry," Ava said. "For everything. I've done terrible things. And Gabriel—he still loves me, even after all I've done."

Natalia reached for Ava's hand, her grip firm despite her frailty. "Whatever happens here stays here, Ava. It's not who you are. Once this is over, you leave it behind. Gabe knows that. He loves you because you see him for who he is, and he sees you the same way. Don't doubt it."

Ava's eyes brimmed with tears, but she nodded. She hadn't realized how much she needed to hear those words.

Gabriel returned with Thomas and Eric.

Joss sprang to her feet and threw her arms around Eric.

With tears in his eyes, Thomas pulled Moira into a tight embrace.

Gabriel gasped for breath. "I have one more person to get," he said and disappeared once more.

Anxiety twisted in Ava's stomach as she watched him. He looked utterly exhausted, his eyes heavy with fatigue. He needed to rest.

Thomas and Moira held each other like they'd been adrift at sea and had finally found a safe harbor.

Joss clung to Eric, her tears soaking his shirt.

For a moment, Ava allowed herself to bask in their joy, even as her nerves coiled tighter.

When Gabriel reappeared, he wasn't alone. All eyes turned to the slender figure at his side.

Anais.

"What is she doing here?" Joss demanded as she pulled back from Eric.

Aaron and Gustav both rose, their faces wary.

Anais stood frozen, her wide eyes darting around the group until they landed on Gustav. Something shifted in her expression—uncertainty giving way to longing.

Gustav's voice cracked as he spoke. "Anais?"

Her lips trembled. "Father?"

Ava's breath caught. The raw vulnerability in Anais's voice was something she had never heard before.

Anais took a tentative step forward, her gaze locked on Gustav like she was studying everything about him. "My memories are ... I-I remember you. It's ... true. They took me from you."

Gustav's face crumpled, tears glistening in his eyes. "Yes. And I will never forgive myself for not bringing you back."

Anais's chin quivered. "I wouldn't have come back. But I want to now."

"You are home, my child." Gustav opened his arms.

Anais crossed the space between them and fell into his embrace. Her sobs filled the cave, raw and unrestrained, as he held her, his own tears streaming down his face.

Gabriel stepped beside Ava, wrapping his arms around her like a protective shield. His body trembled, and she winced at the sight of his exhaustion, every unsteady breath warm against her neck. She tightened her hold; her worry deepening as she gazed into his pale, weary face.

Holding his hand, Ava led him to the wall and urged him to sit. As soon as he settled, he drew her into his lap.

"Gabriel, you're exhausted. It's written all over your face."

"Whatever the Hunters put in their serum—it's still in my system."

Fear spiked in her veins. "Are you going to be okay?"

He pressed a soft kiss to her forehead. "Aaron can enhance my strength."

She pulled back enough to meet his eyes, confusion knitting her brows. "What?"

"Look, we've been doing a lot in the background and couldn't tell you because of your link to Havok."

Her stomach twisted at the mention of the link. "Like what?"

"Aaron, Gustav, all of them—they've got their powers back. A few of us have been sneaking them food and helping them regain their strength." His gaze softened as he brushed a strand of hair away from her face. "We didn't want Havok finding out through you."

"They know how to break the curse?"

His frown deepened. "We can't break it. But the ritual isn't happening. We're going to stop it before it begins. We'll call the Spirits."

Her breath hitched as the full weight of Gabriel's actions to protect her came crashing down. Tears stung her eyes, and she searched his face, overwhelmed by the sheer magnitude of his love and sacrifice. The enormity of it all left her speechless.

"I was so scared earlier," he continued. "When Xavier said the prisoners were released, I had no idea what had happened to them or where they were. I thought—" He swallowed hard. "After you left your room, Klaus found me. He told me how Maggie and Kira released the prisoners."

Ava's fingers curled into his shirt, her pulse hammering in her ears. "You did all of this—for me?"

Gabriel's gaze softened, his hands cradling her face. "You think I wouldn't move heaven and earth for you? I'm not losing you, Ava. Not to Havok. Not to anyone."

His words sent a shiver through her, equal parts fear and hope. The firelight reflected in his blue eyes, a glimmer of determination cutting through his exhaustion. She snuggled close, finding comfort in his warmth that calmed her anxiety.

"We'll stop him," he said. "One way or another, we'll end this."

"Together."

The damp chill of the cave faded away, replaced by the heat of their resolve. Whatever happened next, they would face it side by side.

Gustav approached Ava and Gabriel. "Thank you. Thank you for bringing my daughter back to me."

Ava got to her feet, and he pulled her into a warm, fatherly embrace. His arms wrapped around her, and Ava felt the depth of his gratitude. She nodded, unable to speak past the lump in her throat.

Anais stood beside her father, her fingers lacing his. She glanced up at him, a faint smile tugging at her lips despite the tears that clung to her lashes. "When I first saw him there, inside the castle, something pulled at me," she whispered. "He was familiar, but I couldn't place why. I thought I had never met him before." Her voice wavered as she looked back at Gustav. "But he has my eyes. And the same ridiculous nose." She gave a nervous laugh and wiped her cheeks.

But when her gaze shifted to Ava and then to each of the others around the fire, her expression hardened. Her voice carried a new strength, one that resonated with the quiet courage of someone choosing their own path for the first time. "I am Anais Kovalevsky," she said, her tone steady, her chin lifted. "And I am no longer a Cimmerian."

The cave fell silent, her declaration hanging in the air like a spark waiting to ignite. Then, one by one, the group met her gaze, their own resolve reflecting at her.

A tiny spark of hope flickered in Ava's heart.

CHAPTER THIRTY-NINE

FAILURE

Only ninety minutes left. Every second wasted felt like a thread unraveling the fragile plan they had pieced together.

Ava and Gabriel lay tangled together on the bed, his warmth a fragile shield against the storm brewing outside. His lips pressed against hers with fervor, his hands moving over her as if trying to memorize every inch of her. His touch was tender, yet urgent, like he was trying to hold on to her even as time threatened to pull them apart.

She met his eyes, those deep, endless eyes that had always been her anchor. Reaching up, she cupped his cheek, her thumb brushing against his stubbled jaw. "I love you so much. You're everything to me, Gabriel."

His forehead rested against hers, his breath warm against her lips. "I love you with all my heart, Ava. When this is over, we'll have each other. Forever."

His words sent a pang through her chest, a mixture of hope and fear tightening her throat. She wanted to believe him. She needed to believe him. But so many things could go wrong in the battle.

As his lips traveled to her neck, her collarbone, her shoulder, chills swept over her skin. Her fingers tightened around his arms, her body responding to his touch. When his lips found hers again, she wrapped her arms around his neck, pulling him closer, needing to feel him—to remember him.

Then everything shifted.

The air grew heavy, and her lungs burned as if she'd inhaled fire. The room dissolved, replaced by an overwhelming wave of intense heat that enveloped her like a suffocating cloak. Smoke billowed, stinging her eyes and throat. The roar of flames was deafening, a constant backdrop to the cries of the dying. And yet, she wasn't herself.

She was Havok.

He stood tall in the center of chaos, his dark robes whipping around him in the hot, ash-laden wind. Flames devoured the village, casting flickering shadows across cobblestone streets painted with blood. The air was thick with the metallic tang of it, mingling with the smoke in a nauseating blend. His soldiers moved like shadows, swords flashing as they cut down fleeing villagers. The smell of burning flesh rose, a horrific scent that clung to everything.

A man staggered through the chaos, clutching his side as blood seeped through his fingers. Without hesitation, Havok raised his hand and lifted the man into the air, his legs kicking in a frantic, useless attempt to escape. The man's hands clawed at his throat, where an unseen grip tightened. Havok's lips curled into a cruel smile, a dark satisfaction blooming in his chest as the man's face turned blue, his veins bulging.

The body dropped to the ground with a sickening thud, lifeless.

A scream shattered the air—a sound of raw, unfiltered agony. Havok turned, his gaze landing on a woman bound to a stake, flames coiling around her body. The fire danced, its hungry tongues consuming her clothes, her skin, until it drowned her piercing cries.

"Mommy! Daddy!"

A child's voice sliced through the noise, fragile and desperate. Havok's gaze snapped to a small blonde boy running toward the burning figures of his parents, his tiny legs moving with a determination that shouldn't have belonged to someone so young.

For the first time, something inside Havok faltered. He reached out and scooped the boy into his arms, cradling him against his chest.

The world went black. The sounds of fire and screaming faded into nothingness, leaving Havok standing in a void, the boy trembled in his arms. Slowly, the darkness lifted, and Havok stared into the child's eyes. Wide, unblinking, filled with a mix of terror and defiance.

Power pulsed from the boy—a raw, untamed magic that resonated against Havok's own. He tilted his head, studying the child as a strange emotion sparked within him. It wasn't pity. It wasn't guilt.

It was possession.

This one, Havok thought, his grip tightening around the boy. *I won't kill him. He'll be mine. My weapon. My son.*

"Ava? Ava!"

Gabriel's voice dragged her back to reality. As the vision disappeared, she gasped for air and trembled.

His hands framed her face, his eyes wide with worry. "What is it? What did you see?"

"Havok ... he killed Xavier's parents. His entire village. And he raised Xavier as his own, telling him it was the Ephemerals who did it."

Gabriel stiffened and cursed. "Xavier's whole life has been a lie."

Ava nodded, her hands clutching Gabriel's arms as her mind raced. "I have to tell him. He needs to know the truth."

"Ava, are you sure? We don't know how he'll react."

She met his gaze. "If there's a chance I can get through to him, I have to try."

He pressed a kiss to her forehead. "Then go. But be careful, Grasshopper. And come back to me."

She nodded and slipped out of the room. The vision remained in her thoughts. But beneath the fear and uncertainty, determination burned bright.

Xavier needed to know the truth.

And Havok's lies had to end.

CHAPTER FORTY

MAN ON FIRE

When Ava reached his door, her heart pounded in her chest, each beat echoing in her ears. She turned the knob and let herself in, the click of the latch louder than it should have been in the oppressive silence. Pressing her back against the door, she took a steadying breath. The single lamp beside his bed barely illuminated Xavier as he stood by the window, gazing out into the night.

He turned at the sound of her entrance, his expression shifting from surprise to guarded concern. "Ava. What are you doing here?" He moved closer.

Her throat tightened. The words she needed to say seemed to choke her. "I have to tell you something."

"What is it? Is everything okay?"

She hesitated, gripping the doorknob behind her as if it might ground her. "I remember everything."

His breath caught. "What do you mean?"

"I remember you kidnapping Ephemerals and turning them into Enchanters. Taking Peter from me. Burning my house. Torturing me when I was in a coma. All of it." Her words came out in a rush.

All the blood drained from his face. "What? How is that possible?"

"Klaus never took our memories away. We've been faking it the whole time."

Xavier staggered back a step, his lips parting as if to argue, but no words came. Shock etched deep lines across his face, and his dark eyes widened. "You've been living like us this whole time?" he finally said. "And you knew the truth all along? Why would you do that?"

"Because we had to," Ava said. "Ever since we got here, we've been planning to kill Havok and the Cimmerians."

His eyes bulged, and she thought he might lash out. But he stood there, the muscles in his jaw twitching as he processed her words. "Everything you ever said or did was a lie?" She could see the conflict on his face—a mix of betrayal, anger, and pain.

"No." She stepped toward him. "Not everything. I've gotten to know you, Xavier. You're not the monster I thought you were. None of you are. You've shown me another side of you—a side that can be better."

His jaw clenched, and for a moment, the cold, hateful expression she had known for years resurfaced. But it melted into something softer, something broken. "You've been pretending all this time, plotting to destroy everything," he said. "Why are you telling me this now?"

"Because I want you to make a choice. You don't have to follow him, Xavier. You don't have to keep living like this."

"I can't betray him. He's my father."

"He's not your father," she snapped, her frustration boiling over. "He killed your parents, Xavier. He slaughtered your entire village and lied to you."

His eyes widened. "No," he whispered, shaking his head. "You're lying."

"I saw it. I saw it in one of his memories. He destroyed your family and raised you as his own. He manipulated you, erased your memories."

He turned away, his shoulders shaking as he struggled to breathe. "Why are you telling me this?" he asked hoarsely. "Why now?"

"Because you deserve to know the truth. And because I need you to fight with me. We can end this, Xavier. Together."

He turned back to her, and the anguish in his eyes nearly broke her resolve. "I can't. Even if everything you're saying is true, I can't kill him."

"You don't have to. But help me. Help us."

"You don't understand. You can't kill him either."

Her heart skipped a beat. "Why not?"

"Because it will kill you! If Havok dies, you die."

"I know. But he's planning the ritual, and if he goes through with it, I'm going to die."

Xavier let out a growl and punched the wall. "Dammit! I thought if you joined us—if you accepted the Cimmerian way—he wouldn't need the ritual. I thought I could protect you." He looked away, shame flickering across his face. "I didn't know what else to do. I can't lose you, Ava. Not like this."

Her anger flared, but it was mixed with something deeper—a sadness she couldn't shake. "I've made my choice, Xavier. This war has to end, no matter the cost."

"And what if that cost is your life? I can't stand by and let you do this."

"You don't get to decide that for me. I'm not asking you to kill him but fight for what you *believe*. Fight for what you *want*. It's your life. You make the decisions and decide your fate. Fight with me so you can live free."

He shook his head, his eyes glistening. "I don't deserve those things. I won't betray him, Ava. Even if he's not my real father, he's the only family I've ever had."

Ava's heart twisted. She wanted to scream, to shake him until he understood, but she knew it wouldn't change anything. "Then will you stop me?"

He met her gaze. "No," he said after a long pause. "I won't stop you. But I won't help you, either."

She nodded slowly as tears pricked her eyes. "Goodbye, Xavier."

"Goodbye, Ava," he whispered.

She turned and walked out, crushed by his rejection.

CHAPTER FORTY-ONE

ILLUSORY LIGHT

Thirty minutes.

Ravens circled above the castle, their dark wings cutting through the heavy clouds. One dipped low, its croaking cry reverberating in the night's stillness. Ava shivered, her eyes tracking the bird as it vanished into the shadows. The omen was not lost on her; it was for her—a symbol of death, her death. She had made her peace with it. She would sacrifice herself to kill Havok.

"Ava?"

The sound of Gabriel's voice pulled her from her thoughts. She turned to see him standing there, his expression a mix of determination and heartbreak.

"Are you ready?" he asked.

No. She swallowed hard, forcing the word out. "Yeah."

He embraced her. His grip was tight, almost desperate, as if holding her close could stop time. "Me too," he murmured against her hair and pressed a kiss to her temple.

He pulled back, his hands framing her face. His thumbs brushed her cheeks as his eyes searched hers, filled with emotions too complex to name. His kiss was deep and all-consuming.

Ava melted into him, clutching his shirt, trying to memorize the feel of him—the taste, the scent, the way he held her as if he'd never let go. She didn't want this to be their last. She wanted more—more time, more life, more of him.

When he finally pulled away, his breath was unsteady, and the pain in his eyes was unbearable. He swept her hair aside, his fingers trembling.

Ava looked away, unable to hold his gaze without breaking.

He sighed and took her hand in his, their fingers interlocking as though the connection could tether them to something solid.

Together, they walked to Klaus's room, their footsteps echoing.

Inside, the tension was palpable. A small group of allies stood in the room, their faces a mask of determined fear.

"The Hunters and Enchanters are stationed near the village." Klaus cut through the silence. "They're waiting for the signal—a bomb. That will mark the charge. Our allies inside the castle are positioned strategically. Their orders are clear: take down Havok's guards and clear the way for the Elementals." He looked at Ava. "You have to get to Havok as quickly as possible. We'll handle everything else."

Ava nodded, her throat too tight to speak. "I'm ready."

Melissa took Ava's hands, her grip fierce, her eyes shimmering with unshed tears. "We'll make it. We're not losing you." She pulled Ava into a tight hug.

The others—Lance, Jeremy, Thomas, Gillian—all embraced her, their shared fear and love binding them together.

When they pulled apart, Link began the ritual. The ancient Latin incantation reverberated through the air, the cadence of his voice a haunting echo in the dim cave. The fire in the center roared higher, twisting and shifting as if alive, until the first hints of ghostly forms emerged from the smoke.

Ava's breath caught as familiar figures appeared—Colden, Savina, Sean, Aidan, Ronan, Nathan. Their ethereal shapes shimmered, their eyes alight with purpose and resolve. But as the fire's light illuminated each spirit, her gaze darted desperately through the crowd. Her mother was nowhere to be seen.

Her chest tightened, the sharp sting of betrayal cutting deeper than ever. She clenched her fists at her sides. She had dared to hope, even knowing better. And once again, her mother had failed her.

"She's not here," Ava whispered.

More spirits continued to materialize, their translucent forms filling the space until the air hummed with energy. Link's voice shifted into a second incantation, sealing the veil to prevent malicious entities from slipping through. The room grew crowded with spectral allies, and Ava's heart felt hollow.

Her palms were clammy as she released Thomas and Jeremy's hands. Her mother's absence wasn't just a personal betrayal—it was a death sentence.

Gabriel gathered her in his arms, and she sank against him.

Colden floated closer, his ghostly form flickering like a flame caught in the wind. "Ava, magic is rarely absolute. The bloodline may bind this ritual, but there are cracks in even the strongest spells. We won't abandon you."

"We can't take her place, but we can fight the magic, weaken Havok's control," Savina said. "It might not stop the ritual entirely, but it could buy time—enough for Gabriel, the others, and the spirits to act."

Ava wanted to believe them, but their words felt like a fragile thread against the storm raging inside her. The ache in her chest refused to be soothed. *This is it*, she thought bitterly. *I'm going to die.*

Gabriel cursed under his breath and tightened his hold on her.

"I love you," she whispered. "You've been everything to me since the day I met you. You were the one thing that made sense in all this chaos. You always reminded me what really mattered."

He shook his head. "Don't you dare say your goodbyes, Ava."

Her trembling fingers pulled a folded note from her pocket. She held it out to him. "Give this to my dad. Please."

"I'm not giving it to him. You are."

"Gabe..." Tears blurred her vision. "We both know—"

"Stop." His voice was raw, and a tear escaped down his cheek. "Don't say it. Don't you dare."

Ava inhaled deeply, trying to commit everything to memory—the juniper scent of him, the way his arms held her like a shield, the way his lips trembled when he kissed her. She buried her face in his chest, listening to the steady rhythm of his heartbeat.

"I love you with all my heart," he whispered.

Her chest tightened, and she choked back the tears that lodged in her throat. She had to be strong. Brave. It didn't matter that her heart weighed a thousand pounds.

They held each other for what felt like an eternity, the silence heavy with unspoken fears. When Gabriel kissed her again, she clung to him, wishing she could freeze time and stay in this moment forever.

"Are we ready?" Link asked.

Ava stepped back, her hand still clasped in Gabriel's. She nodded. "Yes. It's time."

CHAPTER FORTY-TWO

THE RITUAL

The Great Hall brimmed with Cimmerians, their murmurs rising like the hum of an agitated hive. Havok stood behind his chair, his knuckles gleaming white as he clenched the back. Scanning the crowd, his black eyes landed on Ava. His gaze sent a shiver crawling down her spine, and she could feel him probing at the edges of her mind. She clenched her mental defenses tighter, refusing to let him in.

She wasn't sorry the Hunters had attacked—not even a little—but she knew Havok would make someone pay.

By his side stood Maggie, Sorcha, Peter, Katarina, Kira, and Eric, their faces a mix of stoic loyalty and subtle unease. Xavier moved to the front, his posture rigid, though his steps betrayed hesitation. His eyes found Ava's, tinged with apology.

When the crowd finally quieted, Havok eased his grip on the chair, though his expression remained grim. "It appears," he began, "there are traitors among us."

A collective gasp swept through the hall, followed by a flurry of whispers.

Ava held still, her breathing shallow. *Did Xavier tell him?* A lump formed in her throat, but she swallowed it down. She couldn't show anything—especially not fear. Havok wouldn't kill her, not yet. But he could kill someone else. Her stomach churned. *What if it's Gabriel?*

"Silence!" Havok's voice cracked like a whip, and the room fell into stunned quiet. "These traitors," he continued, "tipped off the Hunters, allowing them to attack us. They also released the prisoners."

The blood drained from Ava's face. *Oh no. Maggie. Kira.* She kept her face impassive, her hands at her sides. Her emotions threatened to betray her, but she pressed them down with every ounce of willpower. If she gave herself away now, the plan would unravel. Havok would kill them all.

"I am forced," he said, "to demonstrate, once again, what happens to those who betray their coven." He raised his hand, and a knife flew through the air, landing neatly in his grasp.

He moved behind Maggie, his steps slow and deliberate. The hall felt like it was holding its breath. Ava's heart thudded loudly in her ears as the blade glinted in the dim light. With one swift motion, he dragged the knife across Maggie's throat.

Ava flinched as blood spilled in a crimson arc, pooling at Maggie's feet as she collapsed to the ground. Gasps and muffled cries rippled through the crowd. Some turned away, but no one dared move.

Ava clenched her teeth and stared straight ahead, refusing to let the nausea in her stomach take over. *Don't react. Don't react.*

Sorcha handed Havok a towel, and he wiped the blade as though cleaning a tool after a mundane chore.

"Now," Havok continued, "I know she didn't act alone. Whoever helped her would do well to step forward now for a quick and painless death. Otherwise…" His dark eyes scanned the room, lingering on Ava. "I will make your death slow and excruciating."

Kira stepped forward, her movements graceful despite the impending doom. Ava's chest tightened, and she bit the inside of her cheek to keep from screaming. *Why, Kira? Why are you giving yourself up?*

Kira turned to the crowd, her chin held high. Her brown eyes showed no fear, only a quiet strength. Ava wanted to close her eyes, to block out what was coming, but she forced herself to watch. When the blade slid across Kira's throat, Ava's knees nearly buckled. The sound of her body hitting the floor echoed like a gunshot.

The room spun. The copper scent of blood and the suffocating stench of fear filled the hall. Ava's stomach churned and sweat beaded on her brow. *Hold it together. Don't faint. Don't cry. He'll see it.*

Gabriel's hand brushed hers, steadying her as she swayed. "Breathe," he whispered, so softly only she could hear.

"Clean this up," Havok ordered, gesturing to two disciples. They hoisted Maggie's and Kira's bodies over their shoulders, blood dripping with every step. The sight made Ava gag, and the metallic tang in the air clung to her senses like a stain.

"Elementals." Havok cut through the heavy silence. "Come forward."

Ava straightened, brushing her fingers against Gabriel's in a fleeting gesture of comfort. Her legs felt like lead as she walked toward the front. She forced her breathing to steady, but her heart hammered against her ribs.

Havok's smile was thin and cold as he moved closer to her. "The time has come. For you all to make the greatest sacrifice." His gaze locked on Ava, and she felt the full weight of his power pressing against her defenses. "You and I are very similar. I'm privileged to be linked to you. It's a connection like no other Enchanter has ever experienced. But I must say…" He leaned in, whispering, "you make it very difficult to read your emotions."

Ava feigned confusion, tilting her head. "Linked? What do you mean?"

His thin smile widened, his eyes glinted with amusement. "We just are. It's quite beautiful, really. But for the first time, I actually felt something from you last night. Pain. Deep, gut-wrenching pain."

She fought to keep her expression neutral. "The Hunters attacked us. We lost soldiers."

"Indeed, we did." His gaze lingered on her for a moment longer, as if savoring her discomfort.

Havok flicked his wrist. Gamel appeared and snatched her hand. The world seemed to slow.

Then the explosion came, rocking the castle to its foundation. Dust and debris rained down, and the hall erupted in chaos. Screams and shouts filled the air as another bomb detonated, the shockwave rattling the walls.

The war had begun.

CHAPTER FORTY-THREE

BLOOD AND GLORY

Another deafening explosion reverberated through the ancient castle, shaking its towering walls until they groaned under the immense force. Chunks of stone cascaded down, crashing to the ground with thunderous roars. Thick clouds of dust billowed out, stinging Ava's eyes with gritty particles and filling her nostrils with the scent of smoke and earth. The panicked screams of people pierced her ears, mingling with the sharp clash of weapons and the relentless rumble of crumbling walls.

Cimmerians scattered like ants, their shouts of confusion ricocheting off the high ceilings of the Great Hall.

In an instant, Gamel and Havok vanished into thin air.

Ava's fists clenched, and a swell of anger propelled her forward.

"Hunters!" someone shouted.

Another explosion boomed, shaking the castle once more. Ava stumbled, her ears ringing and muffling the surrounding chaos as her vision swam.

Focus. You can't stop now.

A scream tore through the hall as a group of Cimmerians barreled toward her, their weapons raised, and faces contorted with fury. Ava planted her feet, adrenaline surging through her veins. She thrust her hands forward, water erupting into a vicious torrent. The liquid twisted and shimmered, forming razor-sharp edges that sliced through her attackers. Heads rolled, and bodies crumpled to the ground, the water pooling beneath them like a dark, glistening tide.

"Traitor!" A guttural scream cut through the chaos.

A man lunged at her, swinging a blade aimed for her throat. Ava ducked, the blade whooshing past her ear. She spun, using the momentum to send a jet of water into his chest. The force slammed him against the crumbling wall, and he slumped to the floor.

Nearby, flames leapt from the walls, engulfing curtains and debris, while jagged boulders hurled by Melissa smashed into clusters of Cimmerians. Each impact shook the ground, sending shockwaves through the hall. Thomas's fireballs streaked through the air like miniature suns, igniting anything they touched in bursts of searing orange and red.

Out of the corner of her eye, Ava caught a flash of movement—spirits rushing toward the Cimmerians. The spectral forms plunged into their bodies. Anguished cries followed as the Enchanters collapsed to their knees. Possessed, the Cimmerians turned on their own, striking with newfound ferocity. When their hosts died, the spirits moved to the next body, their relentless assault continuing.

Electric orbs flashed, lighting the dim hall with bursts of blinding white. Tornadoes roared through the space, their winds carrying screams and debris like whispers of destruction. Ice daggers flew in deadly arcs, finding their marks in Cimmerian hearts. Fire climbed the walls like living creatures, devouring anything in its path, while boulders crashed through the castle's ancient stone, leaving craters in their wake.

Ava moved through the crumbling hallway, the sound of distant explosions and screams reverberating through the stone walls. She turned a corner and froze.

Donovan stood in her path, his lips curling into a sneer. "I've been waiting for this. You're going to pay for betraying us."

Water swirled around her hands in shimmering coils. "We'll see."

The temperature in the corridor spiked, the air rippling with heatwaves.

Ava's water hissed and evaporated, leaving her hands empty.

Donovan lunged, his fist arcing toward her. She ducked; the blow missed her face, and she retaliated with a blast of water from her palms. It hit him square in the chest, knocking him back a few steps, but he recovered.

"Nice try." He thrust his hands forward, and a wave of blistering heat surged toward her.

She countered with a stream of water, the two elements colliding in a cloud of steam that obscured her vision.

Donovan charged through the mist, his body a blur of heat. He slammed into her, and they both hit the ground hard. The air exploded from her lungs as he pinned her down.

She twisted beneath him, driving her knee into his stomach and flipping him off her. Scrambling to her feet, she beckoned the water; a roaring wave that crashed into Donovan with the force of the ocean. He hit the wall with a sickening thud, but his heat manipulation evaporated the water almost instantly.

"You're persistent," Ava muttered, her chest heaving.

"You're dead." Donovan lunged again.

This time, Ava didn't hesitate. She sidestepped his attack and raised her hand, water coiling into a razor-sharp whip. With a sharp flick of her wrist, the whip struck, slicing deep into Donovan's neck. His eyes widened in shock as he stumbled. Blood gushed from the injury.

He collapsed to the ground.

A sudden blow from the side sent Ava sprawling. The impact jarred her ribs, and her head smacked against the cold, hard stone. Stars burst across her vision, and the metallic taste of blood filled her mouth.

"You killed him!" Eve shrieked. She straddled Ava, slamming a fist into her jaw.

Sharp, blinding pain erupted across her face. Ava gritted her teeth and raised her arms, blocking the next strike just in time. She summoned water, thrusting it upward into Eve's chest. The blast knocked Eve backward, sending her skidding across the floor.

Eve snarled and lunged forward again, her dagger gleaming in the firelight.

Ava scrambled to her feet, her ribs screaming in protest as she sidestepped the attack and swept Eve's legs out from under her.

Eve landed hard, a grunt escaping her lips. She sprang to her feet with predatory grace.

They clashed again, grappling and striking in a violent dance. Each blow sent ripples of pain through Ava's battered body, her muscles screaming for relief. Eve slashed with the dagger, the blade nicking Ava's arm. Blood dripped down her forearm, blending with the sweat coating her skin.

"You'll die here, just like the rest of your pathetic coven!" Eve spat.

Ava dodged a swing and punched Eve hard in the ribs sending her stumbling back. Eve drove her shoulder into Ava's stomach and slammed her into the wall. The air rushed out of Ava's lungs, and she crumpled to her knees, gasping.

The world around Ava blurred, a crushing haze swallowing the battlefield. The voices of her allies, the rattle of weapons, and the crackle of elemental powers faded into an eerie hum. Shadows coiled at the edges of her vision, taking the shape of ghostly figures that whispered words she couldn't understand. A chill ran down her spine as her breath came in shallow gasps.

"What's wrong, Ava?" Eve taunted. "Losing your grip?"

Ava's legs wavered beneath her, her balance unsteady as the dreamlike fog deepened. Eve's silhouette twisted into something else entirely—Gabriel stood before her, his blue eyes cold and unforgiving.

"You'll never be enough," the illusion hissed, his voice laced with disdain. "You'll fail them all."

Ava shook her head, trying to clear the vision. "No, this isn't real. You're not real."

But her denial was met with a cold laugh, Eve's mocking tone intertwining with the illusion's words. A sharp, burning pain lanced through her side. She gasped, her hand flying to the cut, warm blood spilling over her fingers.

The dagger gleamed in Eve's hand, her eyes wild with triumph. "Does that feel real enough for you?"

Staggering back, Ava clutched her wound. The pain broke through the fog. The haze flickered, and she forced herself to concentrate, calling the water.

Shadows crept up Eve's legs, coiling and locking her in place. Her eyes widened in panic. "What—what is this?" she choked, struggling against the shadowy tendrils.

Ava's gaze snapped to Xavier, standing in the distance, his hand outstretched and his expression strained but resolute. The shadows tightened, rendering Eve immobile.

In a flash, Gabriel appeared, teleporting behind Eve. His blade gleamed as he drove it through her chest with deadly precision. With a strangled gasp, Eve collapsed, lifeless.

Gasping for air, Ava doubled over, clutching her side. Holding her steady, Gabriel examined her wound.

She summoned water to her hands, pressing it against the wound. The cool liquid knitted the torn flesh together, the pain receding into a dull ache.

"Are you okay?" Her eyes darted to Gabriel's blood-soaked shirt. Her heart lurched at the sight of the deep crimson staining his neck and chest, the metallic scent of blood sharp in the air.

His skin was pale, his breathing uneven as he gave her a weak nod. "It's just a scratch."

"It's not just a scratch," she snapped, her hands trembling as she gently tilted his chin to examine the gash on his neck. Blood continued to seep, trickling in a sinister red line down to his collarbone. "Hold still."

She pressed her palm over the wound. Heat blossomed beneath her touch, her power surging to life and pouring into him like a rushing tide. The bleeding slowed, and the jagged edges sealed.

Gabriel exhaled, his tense shoulders relaxing. "Thanks. Come on."

When she finally looked up, her gaze met Xavier's. He nodded once and turned to face an approaching enemy. Ava's heart twisted as she watched him fight. *He's with us. He's fighting with us.*

Relief and hope surged through her, fragile but burning brighter with every passing second.

CHAPTER FORTY-FOUR

FIRE AND HONOR

Shots echoed like thunderclaps, ricocheting off the stone walls of the Great Hall. Ava ducked, her breath hitching. Hunters armed with serum-loaded guns stormed the castle, their shouts mingling with the cries of combatants. Natalia, Moira, Joss, and Aaron led the charge, their powers tearing through the chaos. Somewhere outside, Ava assumed Gustav and the Russians were holding the perimeter, but inside, the battle was pure bedlam.

Flames devoured tables and chairs, the heat rolling in waves that made the air shimmer. The once-elegant drapes blazed like funeral pyres, collapsing into the water Ava had flooded across the floor. Shards of glass from shattered windows crunched underfoot, mingling with splinters and the jagged edges of broken stone.

A woman lunged at her, eyes wild with fury. Ava sidestepped, seized the woman's head, and wrenched it. The snap echoed in her ears as she fell to the floor. Water trickled down Ava's arms, forming into a sharp-edged knife in her hands. She slashed through the next wave of enemies, each stroke calculated, each motion efficient.

Out of nowhere, someone slammed into her, driving her to the ground. Her shoulder scraped against the rough stone floor, and the impact knocked the air from her lungs. Pain seared through her as something sharp slashed across her back, hot and agonizing, sending fiery bursts of pain radiating outward. Ava gasped, and a crushing weight pinned her in place.

Her head snapped back as her attacker yanked her ponytail, the sharp tug making her vision blur. His breath, rancid and humid, brushed against her ear, sending a shiver of disgust down her spine. "I will go down in history for killing an Elemental," he growled, pressing the cold, wet blade against her throat.

Panic swelled through her veins, but her powers didn't respond. Her heart sank with the realization. *Benjamin. The power negator.* He was smothering her magic, leaving her vulnerable.

Desperation fueled her strength. She gritted her teeth, her mind racing. With a sharp jerk, she slammed her head backward, her skull connecting with his chin. The impact sent a jolt through her body, rattling her teeth, but it was enough. He groaned and loosened his grip, allowing her to twist free.

Her back screamed in protest as she scrambled to her knees, gasping for breath. She turned to face him, her vision swimming.

Benjamin glared at her, blood dripping from his lips. His sneer twisted into something darker, more dangerous.

A loud crack reverberated above them, splitting the air like a whip. Her eyes darted upward, and dread seized her chest. The massive chandelier, its intricate crystals glinting in the light, swayed violently. The chain groaned, its hold weakened as gravity fought to claim it.

"Ava!" she heard Gabriel's sharp cry slice through the air.

Time slowed as the chandelier's base snapped free from its moorings. The enormous structure crashed, showering the area with deadly, falling crystal shards.

Ava barely had time to react. She threw herself flat against the ground, her arms shielding her head as the chandelier crashed with a deafening roar. The impact shook the floor beneath her, and the vibrations rattled through her bones. A searing pain lanced through her as jagged shards of crystal sliced into her side and shoulders.

Shattering glass and splintering metal cut short Benjamin's scream. The grotesque crunch of his body made Ava wince, but relief mingled with her horror.

Dust and debris clouded the air. Coughs wracked her body, and each breath was a painful effort as she clutched her side. Warm blood seeped through her fingers, the sting of the cuts sharp and persistent.

Summoning her strength, she reached out with her free hand and concentrated. Water rose from the debris and pooled around her wounds. She gasped as the icy relief spread through her, her injuries slowly knitting together.

For a moment, the world was still. Ava lay there, her chest heaving as she took in the carnage. Shattered crystal glittered like fallen stars around her, mingling with the dark pool of blood spreading beneath the chandelier.

The castle walls groaned under the relentless assault, each explosion shaking the floor beneath Ava's feet. She wiped the sweat from her brow, and her gaze darted across the chaotic battlefield. She had to find Havok. He couldn't escape.

"No! Moira!" Thomas's desperate scream froze Ava in her tracks.

She spun toward the sound, her eyes locking on the glowing streak of energy hurtling toward Moira's back. The world slowed as Ava processed the danger, every instinct screaming for her to intervene—but she was too far, too late.

Moira turned, her eyes widening in terror as the deadly light closed in.

"No!" Thomas roared again, his body a blur as he threw himself into the path of the energy.

The glowing energy enveloped Thomas, his body arching as his muscles seized. The crackling sound of the energy searing through him drowned out every other noise, leaving only its shrill hum, and the agonized contortion of Thomas's face.

"Thomas!" Moira's scream shattered the silence as his motionless body fell with a ghastly thud.

Ava's breath caught in her throat, her chest tightening like a vise. She stumbled toward him, her knees weak, but stopped short as Moira collapsed beside his body, cradling his head in her trembling hands.

"No, no, no," Moira sobbed, her tears carving streaks through the dust and blood on her face. "Please, Thomas. Wake up. Please."

The chaos around Ava blurred into a distant hum. Thomas's blue eyes stared unseeing at the ceiling, his face locked in an expression of anguish and determination. It was the face of a man who had given everything for the people he loved.

Her pulse thundered in her ears. He was gone. Thomas—the unshakable, infuriatingly cocky flame who had always been there to light the way—was gone.

No. This can't be real. Get up. Please get up. Her heart screamed for her to run to him, but her feet stayed rooted. Her chest constricted as Moira released an anguished scream.

Lance's roar shattered the moment, his hands glowing with raw power as he obliterated the enemy who had killed Thomas. But the victory felt hollow.

The groaning of the east wall reached a fever pitch, a low, resonant rumble. Cracks raced like lightning bolts along the stone, chunks of debris raining down as the structure began to give way.

Natalia appeared beside Moira. "Come on," she urged gently. "We'll take him with us if we can, but we have to go now!"

Ava froze, her eyes fixed on the wall as it buckled inward, the colossal mass teetering like a predator stalking its prey. Time seemed to slow, the noise of battle fading to a distant hum. All she could hear was the frantic pounding of her heart, each beat louder than the last.

She should move. She had to move.

But her body refused to listen. Her legs felt like lead, her mind screaming at her to run, but all she could do was stand there, staring as the wall began to collapse, its shadow stretching toward her.

It was going to crush her.

The realization hit like ice water, sharp and paralyzing. Her breath hitched. She'd come so far, fought so hard—and now this?

Her eyes darted toward the battle raging around her, the chaos a blur. The faces of her friends flashed in her mind—

Gabriel, Natalia, Moira. Thomas, dead on the ground. Grief and fear tangled in her chest, rendering her powerless as the wall gave a final, deafening groan.

Ava closed her eyes. She braced herself for the impact, the crushing weight, the end.

CHAPTER FORTY-FIVE

SALVATION

The world tilted.

One moment, Ava stood in the shadow of the collapsing wall, her breath caught in her throat. The next, a powerful force yanked her backward, making the ground disappear beneath her feet. Her eyes flew open, dust stinging as her surroundings blurred into motion.

A deafening crash filled her ears, the impact shaking the ground and sending a shockwave of air that knocked the breath from her lungs. Choking on the dust, she blinked, trying to make sense of what had happened.

Strong arms steadied her, and she looked up into Xavier's eyes. "Come on!" he shouted as he pulled her onward.

Behind them, Lance, Melissa, Jeremy, and Gillian followed, their faces streaked with grime and determination, their breaths labored but steady. Each of them carried the scars of the battle so far—bloodied knuckles, tattered clothing, and haunted eyes—but none faltered.

"I can still get you to Havok's chamber," Xavier yelled over the din of explosions and screams. "I'll get you past the bodyguards. After that, you're on your own."

Ava nodded, her throat too tight to respond. "Thank you," she managed.

The castle breathed with the sounds of war—shouts, the metallic clash of weapons, and the raw energy of unleashed powers colliding. The walls shuddered as explosions outside sent shockwaves through the structure, dislodging chunks of stone and raining dust from the ceiling.

The night outside roared with chaos, a kaleidoscope of destruction. Flashes of light erupted as powers collided—fire, wind, water, and electricity tearing through the darkness like vengeful gods.

The Elementals fought like a seamless unit, each wielding their powers with deadly efficiency.

Melissa raised both hands. Massive boulders erupted from the stone floor, hurtling through the air with bone-crushing force. The sound of stone colliding with flesh was sickening. "Get to Havok!" she shouted as she stomped the ground, sending a jolt that knocked several Cimmerians off their feet.

To her left, Jeremy spun in place, his movements fluid as the wind responded to his every command. A tornado swirled around him, carrying debris and enemies alike in a vortex of destruction. "Keep moving!" He sent a gust barreling down the hallway, slamming a group of advancing Cimmerians into the far wall. A sickeningly loud crunch of bones filled the air.

Lance stood at the center of their formation, his golden aura pulsing with power as he absorbed incoming energy attacks. A blast of fire streaked toward him, but he caught it, his hands glowing brighter as he redirected the attack back at their enemies. The explosion sent bodies flying, screams piercing the air. "I'm running low!" he warned, beads of sweat dripping from his brow. "I need a second to recharge!"

Gillian darted forward, her movements sharp and precise. Her fists glowed silver as she struck a towering Cimmerian in the chest, and he collapsed instantly, clutching his head and groaning in agony. She turned to her next target, leaping onto the back of another attacker, her arms locking around his neck as she whispered venomous words, her power seeping into his mind. He dropped his weapon, dazed, and collapsed at her feet.

Ava's water knife glistened under the lights, carving through enemies with brutal precision. She moved with calculated grace, her blade slicing throats and limbs. Each strike met with a spray of blood that mingled with the pools forming on the stone floor. Her breath came in ragged gasps, but she pressed on, her heart hammering against her ribs. *There's no end to them. We'll never reach Havok in time.*

"Go!" Xavier barked, shoving them toward a side door as more Cimmerians advanced toward them. They slipped through into a narrow and dark hallway. Dust fell from the ceiling, coating their hair and shoulders as the walls groaned with the force of distant explosions.

Xavier led them to a stairwell, only to be ambushed by another wave of Cimmerians. The air grew colder as they ascended, each step a battle against exhaustion and fear. Ava's muscles screamed in protest, but she pushed forward, her focus unrelenting.

When they reached the double doors outside Havok's chamber, a line of guards awaited them, their stances rigid, their expressions calm and resolute. Ava's heart sank. It was too quiet here, too deliberate. This was no random skirmish—Havok had prepared for them.

"Sorcha," Xavier growled. His dark eyes locked onto the woman at the center of the group, her pale face a mask of smug confidence.

She smirked, arms crossed over her chest. "Xavier. You've chosen the wrong side. How predictable."

Melissa stepped forward, her hands clenched into fists. "We can do this the hard way or the easy way."

Zeke chuckled. "Good luck getting through us."

Melissa hurled a massive boulder toward them. The earth-shattering impact shook the ground—but the rock splintered into harmless fragments as it hit an invisible shield. The shards scattered, clattering to the stone floor.

Ava's stomach twisted. Of course, Havok would have a protection shield in place.

Xavier lunged for Sorcha, the two grappling with raw fury.

Zeke raised his hands, and a black, swirling orb formed between his palms. Its edges shimmered with a malevolent energy that seemed to bend the air. With a flick of his wrist, he launched the orb toward them.

"Move!" Ava dove to the side. She barely registered the sharp sting of stone scraping her palms as she landed beside Xavier and Melissa. The orb struck the ground, and the floor buckled beneath it, creating a black hole that pulled everything around it with a deafening roar.

The pull was immediate, terrifying. Wind howled like a banshee, sucking dust, debris, and loose objects into its ravenous depths. Ava gripped the stair railing with white-knuckled desperation, her heart pounding as the ground beneath her began to crumble.

"Melissa! Do something!" Ava screamed.

Melissa's eyes blazed. She slammed her palms into the floor, and the earth responded, a deep rumble echoing through the air. The floor trembled as cracks spiderwebbed outward, swallowing some of them into the void below. The shield protecting the guards swayed, lines of light spattering across its surface.

Gillian darted toward Katarina and Peter, her jaw set. "They're in a trance!" she yelled. "I can't break through!"

"Try harder!" Melissa shouted, her focus never wavering as she sent another boulder crashing into the failing shield.

Gillian grasped Katarina's shoulder, her silver-glowing hands shaking as she pushed her power toward her. Katarina's hand glowed with a radioactive light, sending pain shooting through Gillian, but she gritted her teeth, refusing to let go. A strangled cry escaped Katarina's lips, and her eyes finally cleared.

The shield collapsed with a resounding crack, and the barrier disintegrated into a fine mist.

Ava turned her attention back to Sorcha just in time to see the woman smirk. Sorcha lifted Xavier into the air with an effortless flick of her wrist. His body dangled like a puppet on a string, limp and unresponsive.

"No!" Ava's scream tore from her throat, but her legs felt rooted in place.

"Sweet dreams," Sorcha taunted. With a cold smile, she released him.

The world slowed. Xavier's body tumbled through the air, his arms slack, his dark eyes staring into nothingness.

"Xavier!" A desperate, raw plea escaped Ava's lips. She threw her hand forward, willing her power to reach him, to save him. But her water slapped against the black hole's edge.

The void devoured him in an instant, swallowing him whole.

Ava stared, frozen in place, her mind struggling to comprehend what she'd witnessed. *Xavier ... no. This wasn't supposed to happen.*

Her knees hit the ground, his sacrifice crashing down on her like a tidal wave. Tears burned in her eyes, but she didn't let them fall. The world around her faded into a dull hum, the chaos of battle dimming into a muted roar.

"Ava!" Melissa's voice pierced through her haze, jolting her back to reality.

The fight wasn't over.

Ava's head snapped up, her grief morphing into a cold, burning fury. She pushed herself to her feet, locking her gaze Sorcha, who had turned to face Melissa.

Ava launched herself forward. Water erupted from her hands, slicing through the air in sharp, deadly arcs. It collided with Sorcha's conjured defenses, sending sparks and steam flying.

Meanwhile, Lance and Jeremy rushed forward to engage Zeke, who conjured another swirling black orb. Jeremy's tornado winds fought against its pull, holding it at bay while Lance absorbed a blast of energy meant for Gillian. The two struggled to maintain their footing as the ground trembled beneath them.

Melissa slammed her fists into the floor again, sending a seismic shockwave that cracked the walls and buckled the stone beneath the guards. "Go, Ava! We've got this!"

"Break the trance on Peter!" Ava shouted back.

A sudden explosion rocked the hallway as Zeke hurled another orb. This time, the resulting black hole collapsed the ceiling, sending debris crashing down and forcing the Elementals to scatter. Dust and rubble filled the air, choking Ava as she stumbled forward.

When the dust settled, Ava found herself separated from the others. Gillian, Melissa, Jeremy, and Lance were on the far side of the rubble, fighting desperately to hold back the remaining guards.

Ava turned and sprinted toward the staircase leading to Havok's chamber. Every step was heavy with grief and fury, but she pushed the emotions down, forcing herself to focus. Havok's defeat was the only way to end this.

CHAPTER FORTY-SIX

THE GREAT UNKNOWN

The battlements groaned under the destruction as Ava burst through the heavy door, her heart hammering against her ribs. Through the thick storm clouds above the shattered castle, the moon's pale light struggled to pierce the night sky. The thick, salty air enveloped her as the crashing waves below reverberated like a war drum.

Havok stood at the edge of the battlements, his black cloak billowing in the wind, his cruel smile twisting like a scar across his pale face. The sky behind him churned in ominous spirals, the weather mirroring the darkness that radiated from him. "You're the one who's going to kill me," he said.

"I am." His calm voice dripped with amusement. His black eyes locked onto hers, unyielding and cold. "What makes you think you can?"

Ava didn't waste words. Her muscles tensed as she gathered water from the air, droplets swirling into orbs in her palms. She lunged, but an invisible force slammed into her chest like a battering ram.

She flew backward, her body colliding with the stone wall with a sickening crack. Pain flared in her ribs, but she gritted her teeth and pushed herself to her feet.

Havok staggered, clutching his chest, his face flickering with surprise.

"What's the matter?" Ava rasped, spitting blood onto the stone. "Hurts, doesn't it?"

Havok's glare darkened. "So, you've figured it out. The link." He took a step forward. "That's why you won't win. Every strike you land on me only brings you closer to death."

"I don't need to survive." With a flick of her wrist, she conjured a watery whip that lashed across Havok's chest. It struck him like a tidal wave, sending him to his knees. The pain ricocheted back into her, a white-hot agony searing through her. She stumbled but stayed upright.

Havok clutched his chest, gasping. "You're a fool like your mother. She wasn't brave. She was desperate. Weak. She gave you to me, Ava. She gave you because she couldn't save you herself."

Ava hurled the water at him with the force of a cannon.

Havok deflected it, splintering the stone floor beneath their feet. He laughed, a hollow, mocking sound. "Did you think you were special? You're another pawn. Another sacrifice."

Ava's fury boiled over. She slammed her hands into the ground, and water erupted from the stone cracks, swirling into a vortex around them. The wind howled, and the storm clouds above opened, rain pelting down in icy sheets. The air turned electric, charged with the ferocity of her power.

"You should want the same as me," he said. "You all should."

"This isn't my war, Corbin. It's a war your parents created. They hired Hunters to kill your family. You let the darkness consume you. I felt it too. But unlike you, I found a way out."

Havok's smile vanished. He hurled a boulder at her, and she barely dodged the rock grazing her shoulder. Pain stabbed through her arm. She moved toward him, weaving through the debris as she hurled water projectiles at him. Each one hit with brutal precision, and each strike sent the same pain coursing through her own body.

Havok staggered back, his breathing labored. "Do you think this changes anything? Kill me, and another will rise."

"No," Ava said firmly. "Because we're making sure every single one of you dies with you—and your revenge."

"Xavier—"

"Is dead."

Havok's expression faltered. His face grew pale, his eyes narrowing with grief and rage. "And you're ready to die along with all of this?"

"Yes."

"What a foolish girl."

"No," she whispered, water streaming from her hands. "That was my mother."

Summoning all her strength, she reached for the ocean below. The roar of the waves grew deafening as a massive column of water surged upward, towering like a living giant. The spray soaked her face, mixing with her sweat and blood. She guided the water, her arms trembling under the weight of its power.

Havok's expression shifted—fear flickering beneath his rage. He braced himself, his hands glowing with the dark energy of his telekinesis. The air crackled between them as their powers clashed, the battlements crumbling under the force.

"You don't have the strength," Havok taunted, though his voice wavered. "You'll destroy yourself before you destroy me."

Ava's muscles screamed in protest, but she didn't falter. "That's the plan."

The tidal wave loomed closer, a shadow of doom cast over the ramparts. Havok raised his arms to stop it.

A cold sensation swept through her. Her body stiffened, and she felt herself slipping away.

As a violent spasm racked her body, she no longer had control of her movements. Panic surged through her as her grip on the water faltered. She tried to move, but it was as if her limbs were shackled, her mind yanked into a foreign current of power.

It's me, Ava. A voice echoed in her mind, soft yet resolute. *Let me in.*

Her breath hitched. *Mom?*

I'm here. I'm ready.

I thought—

Link kept it open for me. Let me in, Ava.

Ava's resistance melted, and her mother's presence enveloped her like a warm embrace. The struggle for control faded, replaced by a sense of unity. Her hands moved of their own accord, guiding the tidal wave with a precision and power that wasn't all hers.

She turned to Havok, hatred blazing in her chest, but her lips curved into a smile that wasn't her own.

I love you, Ava. Please never forget that. Her mother's voice carried a finality that pierced through Ava's heart.

Havok's eyes widened as the water crashed down, swallowing them both in a relentless torrent. The impact shattered her, leaving her breathless and disoriented, the world spinning around her. The cold embrace of the water dragged her down.

The churning water tossed Havok around as his body convulsed, his eyes rolling back in his head. The air around Ava seemed to lighten, the darkness lifting. For the first time in years, she felt ... free.

It was as though a shadow had been peeled away from her soul, the oppressive connection severed. The knot of hatred and fear that had burrowed inside her unraveled, leaving a strange lightness in its place.

She could breathe.

Havok floated upside down, his lifeless body a pale silhouette in the swirling depths. Relief washed over her, mingling with the ache in her chest. At least she'd have peace knowing her death meant something. That it saved thousands of people.

Her father's smile flashed in her mind, followed by Gabriel's. The thought of them brought a bittersweet ache to her chest, a fleeting moment of peace in the chaos.

The ocean's pull carried her downward, but she felt no fear. No anger. No darkness. It was over.

Another wave struck her. The force drove her downward, spinning her in the current. Her lungs screamed for air as the icy water pressed in, unrelenting. Pain exploded in her skull as her head slammed into a jagged rock.

Stars burst behind her eyelids, and darkness claimed her.

CHAPTER FORTY-SEVEN

ONE LAST GOODBYE

Wake up.

The words floated in the void, distant and muddled, like echoes in a dream. Ava couldn't place them, couldn't fully understand. Was she dead? Her body felt heavy, numb, like she was adrift in an endless sea. There was no pain, only stillness, a vast emptiness that stretched on forever.

Wake up, Ava. Please. A desperate tone trembled with emotion. It pulled at something deep inside her, stirring the embers of consciousness. She wanted to reach for him, to hold onto that familiar warmth, but her limbs wouldn't respond. Was this death? Was she with Colden and Savina now? The thought sent a pang of sorrow through her. She hadn't had the chance to say goodbye to Gabriel, to her father, to her friends.

Please open your eyes.

The voice was closer now, more urgent, cutting through the fog. Ava's senses flickered to life, fragile and unsure. A faint scent teased her nose—juniper. Gabriel. It wrapped around her like a lifeline, pulling her from the abyss. She clung to it, following the warmth it promised.

Her eyelids fluttered open, the world around her blurring into focus. A faint orange glow danced in the distance, casting shadows that swayed and flickered. She realized she was lying down, her head resting against something solid and warm. Gabriel. He held her, his body a shield against the chill that clung to her soaked skin.

She blinked, the effort monumental. Her throat burned, raw and dry, as if she'd swallowed fire and saltwater. "Gabriel..."

His body jerked in surprise, and he pulled back to look at her, his eyes wide with disbelief. "Ava? You're alive."

She managed a faint smile, her lips trembling. "I think so."

He crushed her against him, his arms trembling as they held her tight. His body shook, and she felt the damp warmth of his tears against her cheek. "Don't cry," she rasped, her throat scraping like sandpaper. "I'm here."

Gabriel pulled back enough to cradle her face in his hands. His lips found hers in a chaotic, desperate kiss, messy and full of emotion. It was everything—relief, fear, love—all wrapped into one.

Ava's heart swelled as she kissed him back, her hands finding their way to his face, holding him like she might lose him again.

"I thought I lost you," he murmured against her lips, his breath warm against her damp skin. "I couldn't—" His words broke off, and he pressed his forehead to hers, his eyes squeezed shut.

"You didn't lose me," she whispered. "I'm here, Gabriel. I'm here."

He helped her to her feet, his arm steadying her. Her legs wobbled, unsteady as a newborn foal, but she managed to stand. Ava glanced at the horizon, her chest tightening with awe. She was alive. Somehow, against all odds, she had survived. Her mother had saved her, sacrificing herself to give Ava another chance. The daylight felt warmer, brighter, more precious than ever.

She turned to Gabriel. "I thought I was gone."

He cupped her face. "You're not. You're here, and I'm not letting go of you. Not now. Not ever."

Ava leaned into him. Her heart ached with gratitude—for her mother, for Gabriel, for the second chance she hadn't dared to hope for. She would live. She would fight. And she would hold onto the people she loved no matter what lay ahead.

Ava scanned the ruins of the castle and the devastation that stretched into the woods, the village, and even the sea. The once-proud battlements were reduced to jagged remnants. Seeing the exhausted and grieving Enchanters and Hunters huddled together, their faces etched with pain, broke her heart.

She exchanged a look with Melissa, who broke down, her sobs echoing through the quiet aftermath. Jeremy and Gillian flanked her, wrapping their arms around her for comfort. Ava's breath caught. *Where was Lance?*

Melissa's tear-streaked face turned pale, and her eyes widened. "No!" she cried.

Ava turned, her stomach lurching. Through the haze, she saw Link and Nicole emerging from the shadows, supporting an unconscious Lance between them. His head lolled forward, blood smearing his temple, but as they neared, his eyes fluttered open. Relief flooded Ava as she exhaled.

"Lance!" Melissa rushed to his side. She dropped to her knees, cupping his face. She peppered him with kisses. "Are you okay? Please, talk to me!"

Lance groaned and managed a weak nod, his lips quirking into the barest hint of a smile.

Around them, others embraced or leaned against one another for support. Natalia and Moira clung to each other, while Eric and Joss held each other. Peter, Katarina, and Konstantin gathered in a circle. Aaron approached them, blood caked across his face, his gait uneven. Grime smeared every survivor; their clothes were torn, and tears streaked their faces.

Anais and Klaus stood among a few Cimmerians who had turned against Havok, their faces solemn.

"Is everyone okay?" Jeremy asked, his topaz eyes full of concern.

"For the most part," Link said.

The air grew colder, and an eerie stillness descended. Spirits materialized, their forms shimmering in the settling dust. Savina. Colden. Gustav. Thomas. Sean. Xavier. Maggie. Kira. Dozens of others surrounded them, their faces serene yet mournful.

Ava's chest tightened as her eyes darted between the spirits. Her mother's absence cut deep, a fresh wound amid the chaos. She had saved Ava with her soul, but now she was truly gone.

"It is time for us to return," Savina said.

Colden placed a hand over his heart. "We are proud of all of you. The nightmare is over. Live your lives to the fullest. Love deeply. Make mistakes. You are free."

Tears slipped down Ava's cheeks as she whispered, "Thank you. I love you all."

"Thank you, Ava," Xavier said. "For believing I could be better."

"You're free now," Ava said. "In the way you deserve."

He smiled, a flicker of the Xavier she had glimpsed during his final moments. "I'll be seeing you," he said and faded into the ether.

Thomas appeared next, his grin sheepish but warm. Ava's chin quivered. "Thomas ... you weren't supposed to die."

Gillian sniffled. "None of us were."

"Don't cry," he said. "Just tell my mom I love her." Thomas's expression softened as he turned to Moira. "Just when I find the perfect woman, I die." His attempt at humor cracked.

Moira sobbed, her hands trembling as she reached out to him. "I'll never forget you, Thomas. I'll always love you."

Thomas leaned closer, his spectral hand hovering above her face. "I love you, Moira. Always."

And with that, he vanished, leaving them staring at the empty space where he had been.

CHAPTER FORTY-EIGHT

THE NEW WORLD

The silence was haunting. Only the occasional rustle of the wind disturbed the stillness, carrying with it the faint cawing of ravens in the distance. Above them, vultures circled, their shadows cutting through the pale morning light as if marking their grim intent. Ava shuddered as the reality of their task crushed her chest.

Searching for days through the rubble was an act of both duty and heartbreak. The castle's once-mighty walls lay in ruins, reduced to jagged heaps of stone and splintered wood. Dust still hung in the air, mingling with the scent of charred earth and blood. Ava's hands trembled as she lifted a broken wooden beam, revealing what she feared the most.

Every time they uncovered a body, her stomach twisted, her breath catching. Gabriel stood nearby, silent and steadfast. As soon as they found someone, he would gather the body in his arms and teleport them to their families. Ava didn't know how he kept going, how he bore so much loss. But he did. His jaw was tight, his blue eyes hard and unyielding, masking the storm she knew was raging inside him.

She knelt to lift another panel of wood, her heart sinking as Xavier's body came into view. His face was pale, his expression strangely serene, as though he'd finally found the peace he'd been searching for. The dark stains of blood on his shirt were a stark reminder of the violence that had taken him.

"He was just a kid," Ava murmured. Tears blurred her vision as she brushed debris from his face. "He didn't deserve this."

El strode over, her lips curled in disdain. "Ugh, let the vultures have him."

"No. He deserves a proper burial."

Gillian's face contorted into confusion. "What? After everything he did?"

"He was someone's son," Ava said. "Taken from his family. Forced into this life. His mind was erased—his choices stolen from him. He deserved better than Havok."

For a moment, there was only silence.

Finally, Gillian gave a reluctant nod. "Okay. We'll bury him with the Elders."

The day dragged on as they moved from site to site, their hearts heavy with grief. They buried Xavier, Maggie, and Kira with the Elders, the sacred burial ground miraculously untouched by the destruction. The wind whispered through the trees as they lowered each body into the earth.

Their last stop was the Enchanter cemetery, where they buried their fallen. The ground was uneven, littered with remnants of battle, but they worked, digging graves and offering quiet prayers for the dead.

By the time they finished, Ava had blistered and raw hands, but she didn't care. Each shovelful of earth felt like a small act of penance, a way to honor those who had fought and died for their freedom.

As they stood in the fading light, Adam and El approached. El's hair was matted, and a jagged gash ran down the side of her face, the dried blood a harsh contrast against her pale skin.

"Thank you for helping us with this war," El said.

Ava nodded. "You're welcome. But we should thank you for trusting us." Her gaze flickered to El's wound. "Would you like me to heal that for you?"

El shook her head, a faint smirk tugging at her lips. "No. I'm okay with the consequences of war. Adds character."

The words tugged at Ava's memory, a bittersweet echo of Gustav's voice. She swallowed hard, forcing a small smile. "Where will you go now?"

"Home," El said simply.

Adam stepped forward, his eyes filled with determination. "We'll keep the tunnels intact as we rebuild Caprington. It will be our home again, a place of strength and renewal. We hope you'll visit us someday."

Ava hesitated. The thought of returning to Caprington stirred a complex mix of emotions. The pain of what had happened there would never fully fade, but, in time, the scars would give way to something new. "Perhaps."

Adam and El exchanged a nod before retreating, their silhouettes disappearing into the shadows.

Ava exhaled, her shoulders sagging.

Gabriel appeared beside her, his hand warm and steady on her back. "Are you ready to go?"

She turned to him, her eyes glistening with unshed tears. "Not yet," she whispered, her gaze drifting to the graves. "But I will be."

As the sun dipped below the horizon, casting the world in hues of gold and crimson, Ava stood rooted to the spot, her heart heavy but resolute. They had survived. They had won. And now, they had to live.

CHAPTER FORTY-NINE

FATHERS

The summer sun blazed down on them, warming Ava's skin. She closed her eyes, soaking in the sunlight, the heat sinking into her bones and chasing away the lingering chill of the tunnels. The humid air clung to her like a second skin, sticky and suffocating but familiar. The scents of lilies, roses, and wisteria drifted on the breeze, sweet and heady, weaving through the earthy smell of freshly turned soil. Ava inhaled deeply, savoring it.

Everything was green—vibrant, overwhelmingly alive. The world stretched before her, a canvas of lush vegetation, wild and untamed. The sky above was a soft, powdery blue, scattered with a few lazy clouds, as if even nature had taken a moment to exhale.

She was home.

With each step toward Blackhart Manor, Ava's heart pounded harder, its beat reverberating in her chest like a drum. Emotions swirled within her building to a crescendo. Relief, joy, and sorrow all fought for dominance. When the Gothic mansion came into view, she nearly crumbled.

Tears welled in her eyes, her vision blurring as she took in the familiar silhouette.

It stood undamaged. The beautiful Victorian structure, with its sharp steeples and mansard roofs of gray stone, loomed as a testament to resilience. Sunlight glinted off the diamond-shaped panes of the arched windows, casting intricate patterns of light onto the ground. The twin turrets peeked out from the structure's edges, their round tops visible. The glass ceiling of the conservatory sparkled, catching Ava's eye, along with the raven statues perched like watchful sentinels.

But the garden—the majestic, meticulously cared-for garden—drew her focus. The vibrant blooms and sculpted hedges seemed to droop in mourning, their once-vivid colors dulled. Kira and Savina had tended to this space, pouring life into it. Ava's heart sank at the thought of it wilting without them.

She reached the conservatory doors and swung them open. The air inside was warm and rich with the scent of herbs and flowers. It hadn't changed. The sense of familiarity was comforting, but it brought with it a pang of sadness. Savina, Colden, and the others who once filled this space with life and laughter would never return.

Moira pushed past her. "Cara!"

Ava turned and sprinted through the halls. "Dad!" she shouted, her voice echoing off the stone walls.

Her feet carried her to the base of the grand staircase, where Cara appeared, tears streaming down her face as she collided with Moira in a tight embrace. Behind them, Ava saw Mrs. Arrington and her father descending the stairs. Her breath hitched at the sight of him—his gangly frame, his freckled arms, his neatly combed gray hair streaked with remnants of reddish-brown. He wore an old baseball jersey, one she'd seen countless times before. She had missed him, all of him.

Tears spilled down her cheeks as she ran to him, throwing her arms around his neck and burying her face in his chest. His woody scent surrounded her.

"Ava," he whispered, pressing a kiss to the top of her head. He wrapped his arms around her, strong and safe. "I missed you so much."

She couldn't speak. The lump in her throat was too thick, her emotions too raw. She held onto him, relishing the feeling of being home, of being held by the one person who had always been her anchor.

"It's so good to have you home."

But the moment shattered as Mrs. Arrington's voice rang out. "Thomas?"

Ava turned, her heart sinking at the sight of Lance, Gabriel, and Link carrying Thomas's body, wrapped in a cloth. Mrs. Arrington let out a heart-wrenching cry and collapsed, her knees giving way. Jeremy caught her, holding her as sobs wracked her small frame.

"I'm so sorry, Mrs. Arrington." Lance lowered Thomas's body to the ground.

Ava tore her gaze away, unable to watch the pain etched on Mrs. Arrington's face. Around her, parents reunited with their children. Mr. and Mrs. Rollins clung to Melissa, their tears mingling as they held her. Jeremy, Gillian, Lance, Link, and Nicole found solace in their families' arms. Even Mr. McNabb had come for Peter, embracing him with a relief so palpable it hung in the air.

But Ava's heart broke anew as she caught sight of Cara crumpling into Moira's arms, her body shaking with sobs as Moira told her of Nathan's death. Ava wiped her tears, knowing Nathan's young son would grow up without a father. The loss was staggering, suffocating, but there was one thought that provided solace: no more fathers would die in a war against the Cimmerians. It was over.

CHAPTER FIFTY
HOMEWARD BOUND

A re you ready to go home?" her father asked.

The words were music to Ava's ears, like the first melody after years of silence. The mental and emotional exhaustion weighed on her like a wool coat soaked with rain, heavy and unrelenting. She nodded. "Yes." She glanced back at the Manor, its silhouette framed by the setting sun. "I'll see it tomorrow."

Her father leaned toward Gabriel and whispered something in his ear. A moment later, Gabriel's warm hand wrapped around hers, and the world shifted. The faint scent of juniper clung to him as they teleported, the air around them crackling with magic.

When her feet hit solid ground, Ava blinked, taking in the sight before her. A pristine white two-story house stood against the backdrop of a cobalt-blue sky. Its black shutters framed the windows, and white columns flanked a dark blue door that gleamed in the sunlight.

"Where are we?" she asked.

Her father gave her a sly smile and rubbed the back of his neck. "I built this while you were away."

"What?"

"Well, I didn't like the apartment, and I missed our house."

She blinked back the sting of tears. "Dad, it's beautiful."

He chuckled, his voice tinged with pride. "I know you'll probably want to live somewhere else eventually—you're an adult now—but this is home. Always. If you want it to be."

Ava stepped closer to him and wrapped her arms around his neck. "Thank you, Dad. I don't plan on going anywhere for a while."

As they entered, the fresh scent of new wood and paint greeted her, clean and welcoming. The walls were painted in warm hues of light chocolate, dark red, and cream, blending together like a comforting embrace. She noticed the furniture—some brand-new, some familiar pieces from their old apartment—placed to create a cozy atmosphere.

When they reached her room, Ava froze. A queen-sized bed sat against the wall, its dark purple comforter accented with soft gray tones. The light gray walls were soothing, a stark contrast to the chaos they'd left behind. The entire room radiated peace and safety, and she couldn't stop the tears that welled in her eyes.

She turned to her father. "Thanks, Dad. I love you."

"I love you too, Ava." He pressed a kiss to her forehead. "I'm so glad you're home. Get some rest." He smiled at her before retreating.

Gabriel stood near the door, his lips curving into a hesitant smile. "I feel like I'm imposing."

She shook her head. "No. But I'm sure you want to get home and tend to things there."

His brow furrowed, a passionate fire in his eyes, as he sauntered closer. "The only place I want to be right now is with you. I've spent too much time away from you. Pretending I didn't know you was torture. But you were in my thoughts every single day, keeping me strong."

Ava's breath caught. "I was?"

He sighed, a mix of exasperation and affection in his tone. "I wish you'd stop sounding surprised every time I tell you these things. It's the truth, Ava."

"Sorry. It's just ... you're so strong. You let nothing get to you. It surprises me that you've chosen me."

Gabriel's expression softened as he cupped her face in his hands. "You've said that before. I need you to believe me. I love you, Ava. You are the strong one. How many people do you know who would sacrifice their life to save millions?"

"You."

He smirked. "Touché. But that's why we work so well together. That's why I love you. You fight. You don't give up. You're stubborn as hell, but you have reasons. You're an incredible woman, Ava, and I'm lucky you've chosen me."

"Did you ever hate me? Even when I ... tortured you?"

His eyes darkened with emotion as he held her gaze. "Never. Not once. I knew it was you, not some brainwashed version of you. I was hurt—because I didn't understand. But hate you? No."

Her tears spilled over. "I'm so sorry."

He tilted her chin up, brushing a tear away with his thumb. "No more apologies. Leave it in the past. We're here now. Together." He kissed her gently, the touch of his lips a promise.

Ava reached behind them, turning off the lights as moonlight poured into the room, bathing them in silver.

They climbed onto the bed, and she nestled into Gabriel's chest, inhaling his familiar scent. "This is perfect."

"Yes, it is," he murmured, his lips brushing her hair.

But her peace shattered when she heard a voice—low and cold. "Well, isn't this lovely?"

Her blood turned to ice. She jerked upright as Gabriel moved, shielding her. Her heart slammed against her ribs. It couldn't be.

"Havok," she gasped. He stood in the shadows, his black eyes gleaming with malice.

Gabriel stiffened. "You're dead."

Havok smiled, raising his hand.

Ava's throat closed, the invisible grip tightening around her neck. She clawed at her throat, gasping for air as the room spun. *This can't be real.*

"Ava! Ava!" Gabriel's voice pierced the fog, and the pressure was gone.

She woke with a gasp, clutching the sheets, her chest heaving.

Gabriel was beside her, pulling her close. "It was a dream." He kissed her forehead. "He's gone, Ava. This is real. I'm here."

She trembled in his embrace, her breaths uneven. "It felt so real."

"I know." He stroked her back. "But he can't hurt you anymore."

Her breathing steadied.

"Feel like taking a trip to the library?" he asked.

She gave a small laugh through her tears. "You know I'd never say no to that."

CHAPTER FIFTY-ONE

FAREWELL

They gathered in the cemetery under the relentless heat of the high summer sun. Ava wore a black dress that bound her, the fabric soaking in the sunlight and amplifying the warmth. She cooled herself with her ability, letting it flow around her skin.

The scent of freshly turned earth mingled with the faint aroma of the lilies and roses placed on the graves. The gentle hum of cicadas filled the background, a cruel reminder that life outside this solemn space continued unabated.

Thomas and Gustav were being laid to rest, side by side, and Ava's heart clenched at the sight of the polished coffins being lowered into the ground. She couldn't believe she was saying goodbye to Thomas—the first boy she had ever cared for. He hadn't been the perfect boyfriend, but he had become a steadfast friend, someone who had grown and changed in ways she admired. He had found love, real and raw, and had died saving Moira, the woman who had brought out the best in him.

It wasn't fair.

Hot tears welled in her eyes, blurring her vision as she scanned the sea of faces. Among the mourners, there was a memorial for the others—Savina, Maggie, Kira, and countless more. Their names etched in stone were a stark reminder of the price they had paid.

The funerals passed in a blur of sorrow, a haze of tears and whispered condolences. Ava clung to Gabriel's hand. He hadn't let go of her once, and she knew he never would. His warmth traveled up her arm, a small solace in the sea of grief.

As the ceremony concluded and the group dispersed, Ava led Gabriel down a small path off to the side. The gravel crunched beneath their feet, and the canopy of trees above offered some relief from the oppressive sun. They came to a stop at a simple grave, its gray marble tombstone shaded by the branches of an old oak.

Her mother's name was etched into the stone, the letters stark against the polished surface. Ava's breath hitched, and the words blurred as her tears welled up again. Her throat tightened as memories flooded her—the brief, bittersweet moments they had shared before the end. Gabriel had once told her about visiting his uncle's grave to say his peace, and now it was her turn.

Her fingers brushed over the engraved name, cool and solid under her touch. Despite the pain and betrayal her mother had caused, Ava had found it in herself to forgive. Her mother had made the ultimate sacrifice, saving Ava's life when it mattered most. That act, however fleeting, had mended what little bond they had left.

"Thank you, Mom," she whispered. She wasn't sure if her mother could hear her but saying it out loud lifted a weight off her heart. Maybe the words were more for herself than anyone else. "You gave me my life back."

Gabriel kissed the back of her hand, his lips warm and steady against her skin. He didn't say anything—he didn't need to. His presence was enough.

Her father approached, placing a comforting hand on her shoulder. His fingers trembled, and when Ava looked up, she saw the tears shining in his eyes. It always broke her heart to see her father cry, a reminder of his quiet strength and enduring love.

"She did a brave thing. But you were even braver." He shook his head, his shoulders sagging. "I can't believe ... you could've died."

Ava placed her hand over his, squeezing. "We all could've. But I'm grateful for what she did."

Her father nodded, his lips pressed into a thin line as he fought back his tears. The three of them stood in silence, the grave before them a tribute to the sacrifices made and the love that remained. The sun filtered through the branches above, casting shifting patterns of light and shadow on the ground. Somewhere in the distance, a bird sang, its melody clear and hopeful.

For the first time in a long time, Ava felt peace.

Later that evening, Blackhart Manor was alive with a bittersweet energy as the coven gathered for a farewell and memorial party. The manor's old walls, which had seen countless moments of joy, heartbreak, and unity, now bore witness to one of their most poignant gatherings. Despite the sadness that lingered, the warmth of being surrounded by friends and family was undeniable. It was what they all needed to start healing.

Ava entered the parlor, her steps slowing as memories flooded back. The room hadn't changed—it still carried that faint, comforting scent of aged wood and books, mingling with the earthy aroma of the roses and wisteria blooming outside the windows. She remembered standing in this very room with the Elementals not so long ago, nerves twisting in her stomach. That night, Colden and Savina had told them about Devon Maunsell's escape. That night, they had received their empathy necklaces and taken their first steps into the Aureole. It felt like a lifetime ago.

Aaron stood near the fireplace, his posture dignified despite the toll the war had taken on him. His russet hair, now streaked with gray, caught the flickering firelight, and the lines on his face seemed deeper, etched by grief and exhaustion. Yet, his brown eyes held a wistful warmth as he addressed them.

"Savina and I created empathy necklaces for each of us," Aaron began. "So, we could always feel each other's emotions and know when one of us was in danger. Although we lost our original necklaces, she kept spares." He lifted the lid of a large wooden box, revealing rows of velvet pouches. "I invite you all to take one and keep our tradition alive."

Ava's chest tightened as comfort washed over her. The room was silent except for the soft rustle of movement as everyone approached the box. For once, she didn't hesitate. Taking one of the pouches, she opened it to reveal the familiar pewter pentacle pendant. The intricate Celtic scrollwork gleamed, each curve cradling tiny garnet stones, and the larger garnet at the star's center caught the light like a drop of blood.

She removed the necklace from its backing, the cool metal brushing against her fingertips as she clasped it around her neck. The familiar hum bloomed within her, a gentle ripple of connection spreading outward. Ava closed her eyes, letting herself feel the emotions of those around her—grief, relief, exhaustion, determination. There were some presences she would never feel again, but she cherished the ones that remained.

Clutching the pendant, she focused on one connection in particular. She froze as the wave hit her, the sudden rush of emotions so vivid and overwhelming that it left her breathless. It wasn't just a feeling; it was *him*—a whirlwind of immense love, compassion, and happiness that crashed into her like a tidal wave and wrapped around her like a warm, unyielding embrace. Her knees nearly buckled under the intensity of it, the depth of his emotions pouring through the connection as though they were her own. A smile tugged at her lips, soft and unbidden, as she clung to the warmth of it, her heart swelling in ways she hadn't thought possible. It was intense, raw, and utterly undeniable.

"Now maybe you'll believe me when I tell you how much you mean to me," Gabriel whispered in her ear.

Ava turned, her smile growing. "Not going to live that one down, am I?"

He shrugged, the corner of his mouth quirking up. "Guess you'll have to find out."

Nearby, Anais hesitated before stepping forward to take a box. She cradled it, as if unsure whether she deserved it. "I vaguely remember this. My father had one, didn't he?"

Aaron nodded. "We all did."

Anais fastened the necklace around her neck, her movements careful, almost reverent. Ava felt the flicker of her emotions—fear, hesitation, and a fragile relief. It seemed like Anais felt like she was home.

The group moved to the conservatory, where the warm glow of candles illuminated the room. A spread of food covered the long table, and the mingling aromas of roasted meats, fresh bread, and spiced vegetables made Ava's stomach grumble. She and Gabriel filled their plates, savoring a rare moment of normalcy as they sat down with the others in the dining hall.

Around the table, weary faces gathered, shadowed by grief but lit by a fierce determination. Ava glanced at each of them, her heart swelling with pride and sadness. They had survived the battles and losses that battered and scarred them. And they remained undefeated.

"Man, I don't remember the last time I ate so much." Lance leaned back in his chair and stretched his legs under the table.

"Oh my God, I know," Eric chimed in.

Jeremy grinned, his topaz eyes sparkling. "Do you remember that hot dog eating contest you and Thomas did back in eighth grade?"

Gillian groaned. "Ugh, that was so disgusting."

Lance laughed, his grin wide and genuine. "We ate so many hot dogs. I still can't eat them to this day."

"He was so proud of that stupid trophy," Ava added, shaking her head fondly.

"How many did he eat?" Moira asked, her eyes wide.

"Like twenty-five." Ava said.

"He won a lot of trophies," Mrs. Arrington said. "He was one of the best quarterbacks in the state."

Moira's expression softened. "I can't imagine him being a football player."

"He lived and breathed football," Melissa said. "So does this one." She jerked her thumb at Lance.

"There's nothing wrong with that," Lance protested.

"I miss cheering," Gillian admitted.

"You were a cheerleader?" Moira asked.

"Yeah."

"Wow. There's so much about you all that I don't know," Moira said.

"You and me both," Anais added from her spot near Natalia. "I'm learning, though. Let me guess." She met Ava's eyes. "You were homecoming queen?"

Ava burst out laughing, the sound rich and unexpected. The others joined in, and for a moment, their shared grief lifted.

"Ava is no princess," Melissa teased. "Gillian's our homecoming sweetheart."

"Except I never won," Gillian said. "That always went to Nicole."

All eyes turned to Nicole, who blushed and smiled. "That was a lifetime ago."

"Yeah, it was," Link said, his tone reflective.

Anais bit her lip. "Guess I have a lot to learn."

"You will." Natalia patted Anais's hand. "They were quite annoying little brats when I first met them, but they've grown on me." She offered a warm smile at Ava.

"What now?" Nicole asked.

"Sleep." Link leaned back against the wall with a tired grin.

Ava smirked, catching Gabriel's eye. "I don't know. Maybe travel. Help rebuild the cities." Her tone softened as she turned to Nicole. "What about you?"

"Boston."

"Still on the college kick, eh?" Link teased, raising an eyebrow. "Does that mean we're gonna have to go back to high school and actually graduate?"

Nicole rolled her eyes and gave an exaggerated sigh. "We can just get our GEDs."

"Maybe *you* can." Link's playful smirk earned a snort from Nicole.

The laughter faded, leaving behind a solemn quiet. They all knew what the silence meant—they were delaying the inevitable. Saying goodbye. But not forever.

Peter, Katarina, and Anais were the first to stand. One by one, the others followed, each movement heavy. Ava's chest tightened as the goodbyes began.

Anais approached Ava, her lip quivering. Then, with a sudden burst of emotion, she wrapped Ava in a tight hug. "Thank you," she whispered. "I really owe my life to you."

Ava squeezed her back. "It's not necessary. I'm glad I could show you the truth."

When they pulled apart, Katarina stepped forward, her expression full of admiration. She gave Ava a quick, firm hug. "You are truly the bravest woman I know. I promise we'll visit."

Then Ava met Peter's weary brown eyes, and for a moment, a thousand unspoken words passed between them. She'd loved him once—deeply—but it felt like a lifetime ago. Now, the bittersweet pangs of nostalgia mingled with gratitude.

"Russia, huh?" she said.

Peter nodded. "Yeah. Makes sense."

"I'll miss you both," she said.

Peter pulled her into a hug. "I have you to thank for my life. You brought me into a world I never thought was possible, and you helped me become a stronger, better person."

"You taught me a few things too." She smiled. "I wish you both happiness."

"Take care, Ava."

"You too, Peter."

When they left the Manor, Ava felt a slight pang in her chest, but relief tempered it. Peter deserved happiness, and she knew he'd find it.

As the laughter died down, Ava caught Gabriel's eye across the room. He winked at her, and her heart fluttered. No matter what else the future held, she knew one thing with absolute certainty—she loved Gabriel, and she planned to spend the rest of her life with him.

When the time came to leave, they gathered in a tight group hug, holding onto each other as if the strength of their bond could ward off the sorrow of goodbye. They shed tears, made promises, and left, knowing they would always have each other, no matter where life took them.

"How are you holding up?" her father asked, stepping beside her as the others departed.

"I'm good. Considering." She hesitated, her fingers brushing against the pendant around her neck. "I have a hard time with emotions now. I spent so much time blocking them."

Her father squeezed her hand. "You're here now. That's what matters."

She nodded, her thoughts drifting. The hum of emotions from the empathy necklace reminded her of all they had lost—and all they had saved. The absence of some presences was like an ache in her chest, a hollow echo, but she wore the necklace with pride, a testament to the connections they had forged.

"I didn't know if I'd ever see you again," her father said.

Ava swallowed hard, her throat tightening. "I know. I wish I could've sent messages or something."

"You're here now," he repeated, his tone full of quiet reverence. "I'm so proud of you, Ava. You've become such a mature, confident, beautiful young woman."

"Thanks, Dad."

"I take it you want to date him?" He nodded toward Gabriel, a teasing smile softening his features.

Ava rolled her eyes, though a smile tugged at her lips. "He's great."

Her father nodded in approval. "You deserve the best, and I think you may have found him."

Gabriel approached then, his blue eyes warm as he greeted her father. "Good evening, Mr. Hannigan." He extended his hand.

Her father shook it, his gaze appraising. "I hear you want to date my daughter."

"Dad, stop!" Ava groaned, heat rushing to her face.

"Yes, sir, I do," Gabriel replied with a respectful smile.

Her father leaned in. "Treat her well. Give her everything she needs and deserves. Love her for who she is. And don't you dare hurt her, or—"

"Dad!"

Gabriel's smile grew. "I have no intention of hurting her. I plan to love her forever. She's my soulmate."

Ava's heart skipped a beat. He said it with such ease, as though it were the simplest truth in the world.

Her father studied him for a long moment before nodding. "You're a good man, Gabriel." Then he turned to Ava. "Ready to go home?"

"Yeah. I'm ready."

Ava smiled as she watched her dad sleeping soundly in his recliner, the rhythmic rise and fall of his chest offering a rare moment of peace. The glow from the dim lamp illuminated the lines of exhaustion etched into his face, but he looked content, at rest. She draped a blanket over him, tucking it around his shoulders.

Turning, she reached out her hand toward Gabriel, who waited nearby. He laced his fingers through hers, their touch warm and reassuring, and followed her into her room. Gabriel closed the door behind them with a soft click, the sound muffled by the thick carpet beneath their feet.

He slipped his arms around her waist, pulling her close. She leaned back into him, her heart fluttering at the familiar strength of his embrace. The steady beat of his heart against her back grounded her for a moment. Then she twisted in his grasp, her hands finding their way around his neck. Their eyes met, and in an instant, she pulled him down for a kiss.

His lips were warm and firm, molding perfectly against hers. But this time, it was more than a kiss. As he deepened it, her breath hitched, and the connection through their necklaces roared to life. She felt it all—his love, fierce and unyielding, wrapping around her like a shield; his desire sparking against her skin; and the way every fiber of his being responded to her touch, her kiss, as though she were his gravity. It was raw, consuming, and overwhelming. It wasn't just a kiss—it was a window into his soul, and it left her breathless.

He lifted her, his hands firm yet gentle, and she wrapped her legs around his waist. The world around them faded as he carried her to the bed.

Hovering above her, Gabriel's lips pressed to hers again, his kiss igniting a fire that burned through her entire body. Heat pooled in her chest as his tongue traced hers, and she let out a soft, trembling sigh. The room felt electric, charged with the energy that only he could bring.

When his lips traveled to her neck, she moaned. His hands slid under her shirt, and a pleasurable chill shot through her at the feel of his calloused palms against her skin.

"We shouldn't do this here," she whispered as his lips grazed her stomach. "He could hear us."

Gabriel looked up, a mischievous grin lighting his face. "We haven't started making noise yet." His eyes sparkled with a teasing glint.

She punched his arm, eliciting a deep chuckle from him.

His laugh was warm and infectious, vibrating against her skin as he rested his chin on her chest. "Where did you have in mind?"

"I don't know," she murmured.

With a playful smirk, he flipped her, so she was lying on top of him. She pressed kisses along his neck, the soft scent of him—juniper and a hint of pine—filling her senses. "If you keep doing that, I can't concentrate on where to go."

She smiled against his skin, her lips trailing soft kisses along the curve of his collarbone. Her hand slipped beneath his shirt, her fingertips gliding over the warm, sculpted muscles of his stomach. The slight hitch in his breath made her heart race. She pressed her lips to his chest, then lower, lingering on the ridges of his abs, her touch deliberate and teasing.

A deep groan escaped him, his body tensing under her touch, every muscle coiled with anticipation. But as her lips continued their slow, tantalizing exploration, he exhaled, his arms tightening around her as he surrendered to the sensation. Then he relaxed. "Now we can be as loud as we want."

She lifted her head in confusion. "It's dark in here. Where are we?"

He reached behind him and flicked a switch. Soft blue and green string lights illuminated the room, casting a gentle glow on the walls. "My room."

Ava glanced around, taking in the massive bed and the scattered rose petals that covered it. "Preparing for something?"

"Hey," he said with a wink, "a guy's gotta do what he can for romance."

"This is your house?" she asked, straddling him as she sat up to take in the details.

"And Eric's," he replied, his tone light.

"What color are the walls? Dark blue?"

"Yes." He grinned, his hands resting on her hips. "Are we really going to talk about my room?"

"For now," she teased.

He shifted, flipping them so she was beneath him once more. Their laughter faded into soft breaths as he kissed her. His hand slid along her thigh, igniting a trail of heat as his mouth moved to her neck. Her shirt fell open, and his lips followed the curve of her collarbone.

"You're wearing too many clothes," he muttered against her lips, his voice low and rough with impatience. His fingers hooked into the waistband of her pants, tugging them down with a deliberate urgency that sent a shiver racing up her spine.

Her breath hitched as the cool air met her skin, quickly replaced by the heat of his touch as his hands slid along her hips, guiding her even closer. His lips found hers again, insistent and unrelenting, while his movements spoke of a hunger barely kept in check.

When she pulled his shirt over his head, her hands stilled for a moment, her gaze tracing the hard lines of his chest as the soft light highlighted every defined muscle. The way his chest rose and fell, his breaths heavy with anticipation, sent a warmth spiraling through her. Her fingers brushed over his skin, savoring the contrast between the strength of his body and the vulnerability in his crystal-blue eyes as they locked with hers. Her breath hitched again, her heart pounding in her chest.

"You're all I've ever needed." He took her hand and guided it to his chest, pressing her palm over his heart. The rapid, steady thud pulsed against her skin, mirroring the frantic beat of her own. "It's been doing that since I first met you."

"I've never been happier. And now, we have forever."

His lips captured hers again, the kiss deep and consuming, drawing her into a world where nothing else mattered. His hands moved over her body, peeling away the remaining layers between them until there was nothing left to hide. The warmth of his skin against hers was intoxicating, his touch igniting sparks that coursed through her with every caress.

As their bodies pressed together, their movements grew unhurried, a rhythm of shared trust and unspoken promises. The world outside faded completely, leaving only them—wrapped in warmth, light, and a love that felt infinite.

Ava felt it in her bones—a rare stillness, a calm she never thought she would experience. They had fought. They had bled. They had lost. But they had won.

And now, as Gabriel's arms enveloped her and the promise of a new beginning settled around them, Ava allowed herself to hope, to dream, and to live.

It was over. The war, the pain, the loss. All of it.

And as she fell asleep to the rhythm of his heartbeat, she knew it was the start of everything. Together, they had forever. And forever was enough.

ACKNOWLEDGEMENTS

First of all, I would like to thank all of my readers and fans. Your incredible support does not go unnoticed. I couldn't do this without you.

To all the musicians I have ever listened to and who continuously inspire me.

To Jennifer for all the countless hours of advice, and many years of friendship.

To Paige. Do you know how awesome you are? I am so happy we found each other, and that you are always there when I need you. To Chani for all of your editorial advice and support. To my awesome betas and street team. You rock! To Sarah, who is an amazing cheerleader and supporter. To Angie and Rachel. To Nicole for letting me vent and for being my friend.

To my mom and Rob; my dad; Patrick, Morgan, and Alison. Thank you for believing in me and my dream. I love you all.

PLAYLIST

Great Northern – Houses
Halestorm – Break In
The Birthday Massacre – Cover My Eyes
Lacuna Coil – Nothing Stands In Our Way
Kodaline – All I Want
Plumb – Don't Deserve You
Gabrielle Aplin – Salvation
Delain – Electricity
Kerli – Chemical
Of Monsters And Men – I Of The Storm
The Airborne Toxic Event – Half of Something Else
Marcy Playground – All The Lights Went Out
Hans Zimmer – Time
Ben Harper – Amen Omen
Audiomachine – The Truth
Fall Out Boy – My Songs Know What You Did In The Dark
Sarah McLachlan – Possession (Acoustic)
Evanescence – Sick
Snow Patrol – Set The Fire To The Third Bar
Great Northern – Driveway
Sarah Blasko – Illusory Light
Breaking Benjamin – Failure
Halestorm – I'm Not An Angel

ABOUT THE AUTHOR

Carrigan is the author of several young adult novels that make you cry and whisk you to faraway places. Though born in Cullman, Alabama, she grew up in Birmingham and moved to Atlanta at 18. She earned her BA in English and her Master of Arts in Professional Writing at Kennesaw State University. For as long as she can remember, she was always making up stories and characters inside her head, sometimes using her dolls to act out the scenes.

When she's not writing (which is rare), she's spending time with her family and friends, listening to music, playing with her furbabies, Ella and Ozzie, and cheering on her Atlanta Braves.

You can visit her online at www.carriganrichards.com.

www.ingramcontent.com/pod-product-compliance
Lightning Source LLC
Chambersburg PA
CBHW011137310726
48972CB00009B/2752